The Genesis Tree

So thankful
for your friendship, Kara!
Blessings,
Heather

The Tethered World Chronicles

Book one—The Tethered World
Book two—The Flaming Sword
Book three—The Genesis Tree

The Genesis Tree

Book Three of
The Tethered World Chronicles

Heather L.L. FitzGerald

The Genesis Tree
Published by Mountain Brook Ink
White Salmon, WA U.S.A.

The website addresses recommended throughout this book are offered as a resource. These websites are not intended in any way to be or imply an endorsement on the part of Mountain Brook Ink, nor do we vouch for their content.

This story is a work of fiction. All characters and events are the product of the author's imagination. Any resemblance to any person, living or dead, is coincidental.

Scripture quotations are taken from the King James Version of the Bible. Public domain.

ISBN 9781943959-29-7
© 2017 Heather L. L. FitzGerald

The Team: Miralee Ferrell, Jenny Gibbs, Nikki Wright, Cindy Jackson

Cover Design: Indie Cover Design, Lynnette Bonner, Designer

Mountain Brook Ink is an inspirational publisher offering fiction you can believe in.

Map illustration by William Love@sevenoversix.com

Printed in the U.S.A. 2017

Dedication

For Billy...my soulmate, best friend, and the love of my life. Thank you for your unwavering belief in the gifts that God has given me. These stories would never have blossomed from my fertile imagination without your support. I love you.

Also for McKenzie, Garrett, Delaney, and Olivia. You are my inspiration and joy. You were children when I began this writing journey but have grown into amazing adults as the publishing goal loomed into view. I hope these adventures were worth the wait and will be a special gift to share with your own families one day.

*"Then I heard every creature in heaven and on earth and **under the earth**...saying: To him who sits on the throne and to the Lamb be praise and honor and glory and power, for ever and ever!"* Revelation 5: 13

*This book is a work of fiction from a Christian worldview. The ideas are strictly from the author's imagination, portraying what might be possible in places that Scripture is silent.

** A cast of characters' list with descriptions is located at the back of the book for your convenience.

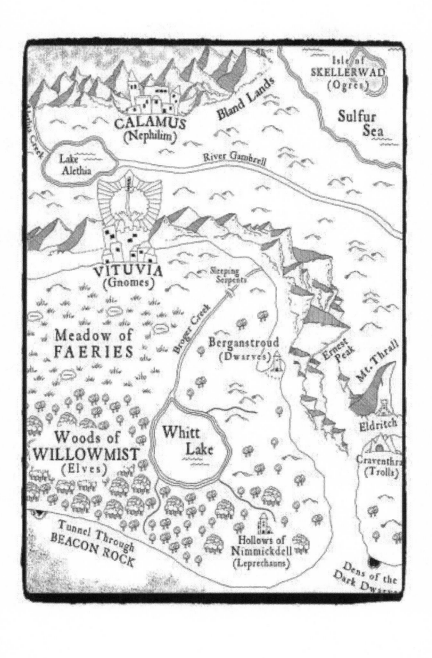

CHAPTER ONE

"KATU CHANNEL 2 NEWS. WE'D LIKE to ask you a few questions." A female voice called to us through the front door after a rapid-fire knock.

My eleven-year-old sister, Sophie, catapulted from the couch. "I'll get it!"

"Hang on." I heaved myself out of the beanbag chair—my favorite place to curl up with a good book—and hobbled to the door. With my foot in a walking cast, everything I did took twice as long. "Let me see if it's for real."

Sophie stepped aside, hand on the knob. "What do they want with us?"

I squinted through the bubble of glass without answering my inquisitive little sister. A distorted camera lens stared back from the shoulder of a guy with a bushy goatee and oversized, black-rimmed glasses. He stood behind a lady whose face looked misshapen through the peephole. "Looks legit."

Sophie twisted the knob on one of the deadbolts. Although we had three installed for our sleepwalking brother, Brock, we only used one when he was gone. My sister pulled the door open dramatically, which is pretty much how she does anything.

A redheaded woman wearing a pale blue dress and too much makeup blinked at Sophie, then at me. I recognized her from television.

"Hello!" She gave us a syrupy smile from behind her microphone. "I'm Michelle Gaelyn with KATU Channel 2 News. Is this the residence of Sasquatch specialist Amy Larcen?" The hipster cameraman pointed his lens at us. A red light blinked, indicating he was recording.

Sophie glanced at me. Our mother—and said Sasquatch specialist—wasn't home. I guessed my sister was uncertain about how to answer.

I stepped closer to Sophie. "She's unavailable at the moment."

The woman blinked again. "We wanted her to weigh in on your neighbor's claim to be in possession of the body of a dead Bigfoot." She jerked a thumb behind her, indicating the house across the street. "His press conference begins shortly. Said he welcomes skeptics, reporters and questions. What a crazy coincidence that the man who swears he has a Yeti lives across the street from a Yeti expert."

I faked a laugh to cover a gasp of indignation. Our diabolical neighbor had called a press conference to show off the body of a Bigfoot? Though I was well aware of the corpse, I had no idea the creep planned to play show-and-tell with it. Such publicity would be dangerous.

The reporter stuck her microphone in my face.

"Yes. Crazy." My heart hammered a distress call. "Um, I'll let my mother know you came by."

"Has she inspected the body?" The redhead placed a navy stilettoed heel into the doorway. "Surely your neighbor, Joseph Marshall, has shown your mother his trophy catch. Normally we would dismiss such hype as yet another hoax, but Mr. Marshall emailed some very convincing photos."

I stiffened. Though this woman could have no idea of the bad blood between us and our neighbor, she was quickly gravitating toward my disagreeable side by mentioning him by name. His *fake* name, in reality.

"Actually, this is the first I've heard. And I'm certain she would've mentioned something if she knew." I shrugged. "Also, you might want to do a little fact checking about the man himself. Joseph Marshall *isn't* his real name, so who knows what he plans to display to the media today. I'd be careful, if I were you."

The reporter took a step back, bumping into the cameraman. "Really?" She pressed her lips together and smoothed her skirt with her free hand. "Well. I—I thank you for your time. And the...tip."

"You're welcome." I couldn't help but smirk at her reaction.

Sophie stuck her hand in the air and waved. "We'll tell Mom you came by when she gets home."

"*Sophie.*" I yanked her behind me.

"Oops."

"Here's my card." The woman shoved her business card at

me. "Please have your mother call if she has anything to add, after the broadcast. I'm flabbergasted that your neighbor has kept this to himself. She has an excellent reputation."

I closed the door and leaned against it, eyeing my sister. "Breaking news...Joseph *Delaney* isn't going to mind his own business and stay out of our lives."

"Mom's gonna flip out when she hears this." Sophie shook her head and ambled back into the living room.

A door creaked upstairs. My brother Brady towered from the top step, his blond hair wet, a piece of toilet paper stuck to his jaw where he'd evidently cut himself shaving. "Mom's going to flip out about what?"

Before I could answer, Sophie squealed. "Oh my goodness! A van from Animal Planet just pulled up to the curb."

I lurched over to the couch, followed by my brother. The three of us perched on our knees, peeking through the blinds at the boxy vehicle enveloped in the bright, catchy logo of the Animal Planet channel. They'd parked on our side of the street.

"What's going on?" Brady nudged me.

"Apparently Mr. Delaney—aka Mr. Marshall—plans to capitalize on that Yeti his wife Abigail killed helping dad escape from their basement. He's holding a press conference or something."

"Seriously?"

Sophie bounced on the cushion beside me. "Yep! Channel 2 News just knocked on the door 'cause they wanted to ask Mom a few questions."

Brady groaned. "Mom *is* gonna flip. This is not the kind of exposure she needs."

The driver of the van got out and walked across our grass to the back of his vehicle. He opened the rear doors, which blocked our view of his movements. Another man slid out of the passenger seat, then disappeared on the other side.

A pickup truck from KOIN 6 News pulled up behind the Animal Planet guys, in front of the house next door.

I raised an eyebrow at Brady. "He's got quite the audience. Since when do major news stations take Bigfoot findings seriously? They've stonewalled Mom for years."

"That reporter said Mr. Marsh—Delaney—sent very convincing pictures." Sophie hopped off the couch. "I'm gonna go outside and watch."

"I don't know..." Before I could finish my thought, she was out the door.

"Good luck keeping Sophie in the house when there's a circus out front." Brady chuckled and stood, offering me a hand. "Besides, aren't you the least bit curious? We should probably keep an eye on things."

I clutched his forearm and pulled up with most of the weight on my good leg, and Brady helped me hobble to the door. It occurred to me, with a stab of surprise, that his shoulder was now level with my chin. Though younger by seventeen months, and about my height at the beginning of summer, he had shot past me by several inches. It startled me to imagine my other brother, Brock, being this tall. He was Brady's identical twin, and I had barely seen him throughout our family's very peculiar summer.

Sophie stood in the middle of our driveway, gaping at the reporters and camera crews milling across the street. Brady and I stood behind her.

"I'm gonna text Mom." What would she say to this craziness? I pulled my phone from my back pocket and noted the time. Nearly four in the afternoon. Though she'd probably be home any minute, I went ahead and divulged the news. When the wrath of Mom arrived, this circus would come to a screeching halt.

Other people gathered on their front porches or in their yards, peering at the commotion. Our next-door neighbor's kids, RJ and Bethany, dashed across the lawn and set about mauling the Animal Planet van, pointing at the different species depicted on the sides and peeking through the windows.

The irony of the situation made me shake my head. Mr. Marshall, whom we now knew to be Mr. Delaney, had been the world's nosiest neighbor for the five or six years he had lived across the street. He seemed to be spending his retirement watching us from his front porch, or from the front window of his home, blurred by a haze of cigar smoke. We used to joke that he'd moved here merely to gawk at our homeschooled family, like we were some sort of novelty or lab specimen.

The unfortunate truth of it, we had recently discovered, was worse than our silliest speculations. He knew secrets about my family...secrets I had only learned at the beginning of summer. The man had been watching us. Watching and waiting.

Now all eyes and cameras were on him. What did he hope to accomplish?

I had a sinking feeling he was trying to revive something that recently had died—and it wasn't Bigfoot. It was his sick agenda that my family had managed to sabotage a month or so back. It looked as if Mr. Delaney wanted to resurrect his foul and nefarious plans right in our faces.

My hand instinctively sought the little book charm hanging around my neck, a gift from my dad. Although I often messed with it absentmindedly, stress drove me to zip it back and forth along the silver chain like it might catch fire. And at this moment, I was smoking mad at what I was witnessing across the street.

The front door of our neighbor's house opened. Reporters and onlookers turned to watch. A cloud of smoke preceded Mr. Delaney's stout body like unintended special effects. He tipped his newsboy hat and stuck his thick thumbs in his suspenders, waddling toward the garage door. The crowd shifted to his driveway and would have blocked our view, if not for his property's steep incline.

The man grinned, cigar clenched in his teeth at the side of his mouth. "Glad you all could make it today. I promise it'll be worth your time. You'll have an opportunity to take a brief look and snap some photos. Then I'll answer a few questions."

Even through the veil of smoke, I saw his beady eyes peer at me and my siblings, as if daring us to speak up and threatening us if we dared.

He removed something from his pocket with a flourish. The mechanical humming of the garage door commenced, and it lifted like a slow-motion curtain revealing a stage. Bright lights set up inside the garage beamed onto the large silhouette of something lying on a table beneath a blue plastic tarp. Mr. Delaney walked to one end, grasped the cover, and pulled it away with a *swoosh*.

CHAPTER TWO

FROM THE MURMURS AND GASPS OF the onlookers, they sounded impressed. Bodies and equipment crowded into the garage, cameras flashing and recording. Curious neighbors rushed to join the frenzied crowd. One little kid buried his head against his mother and she pulled him away, looking horrified as well.

I didn't need to see the creature for myself. My father had recently been guarded by that brown, hairy ape-man while he was a prisoner of Mr. Delaney, and I was glad the thing was dead. I'd met more than my share of Yetis over the course of summer, and I liked the dead ones best—with a couple of exceptions.

I also knew they preferred a different moniker. Legends? Definitely. But their folklore went back further than nicknames like Bigfoot and Sasquatch from our local Pacific Northwest lore. Back to darker tales in superstitious and unenlightened times. These hulking, hairy monsters were really *Trolls*.

Mr. Delaney strolled the fringes of the crowd looking like the cat who swallowed the canary. He even had the nerve to glance at Brady, Sophie, and me and tip his hat.

My anger flared at his cockiness. I felt Brady tense beside me. Before we could get too riled up, I spotted our minivan, weaving through the crowded street toward the house. Mom nosed the Honda Odyssey into our driveway and stopped, the back bumper extending into the street. The driver's door flew open, and she bounded out in yoga pants and a ponytail, looking more soccer mom than Bigfoot expert. She left the door flung wide.

"Please tell me this is a sick joke." Her voice held a tremor that seemed to come from sparks of anger firing in her eyes.

Brady shook his head. "He's obviously a sick man but this ain't no joke."

"Mom, what are you doing?" Nicole, my seven-year-old sister, was yelling from inside the van. The side door slid open and she hopped out, looking from us to the crowd across the street. "What's going on?"

Mom flexed her jaw and took a deep breath. "I'm not sure, honey. Please stay with me."

"Mom, Mom, Mom!" Nate, my baby brother, flailed his legs in his car seat, strapped and trapped.

"I'll get him." I leaned inside the van. "Hey, little man, are you ready to get out of this seat?"

"Yesss." He clapped his dimpled toddler hands. "Want to get out."

I unlatched his buckles, and he wriggled onto the floorboard. He had a new pair of tennis shoes that lit up when he walked. He stomped his feet and giggled at the lights.

"Those are the coolest shoes ever." I snatched him up and carried him to where the others stood. He leaned his head on my shoulder, which shoved his curly black hair in my face. We had adopted Nate from Ethiopia when he was a baby, and I envied his thick, corkscrew curls and smooth, dark skin.

"The nerve of that man." Mom shook her head.

"Channel 2 News came by." Sophie grabbed Mom's sleeve. "They wanted to talk to you about the Bigfoot body."

"Oh really?" Mom raised an eyebrow at Sophie. "So they dismiss my research for years, but one shout from Smokey the Bear over here, and they come running. Ugh."

Nicole stood on her tiptoes peering across the street. "What are they looking at?"

"Sweetie, why don't you take Nate into the house and get him a snack. There are some bananas that need to get eaten." Mom took Nate from my arms and plunked him on the ground next to Nicole.

"But what are they doing?" Nicole didn't move. "Hey, RJ! What's going on?"

RJ and Bethany turned and waved at my sister.

"Nicole, I'm not going to say it again." Mom's tone left no room for arguing.

Nicole slouched away, and Nate toddled along beside her.

Mr. Delaney's voice rose over the commotion. "All right, all right. Step back. As you can see, this here Sasquatch met his maker from the end of my shotgun." Mr. Delaney lifted his hat and scratched his head. "That overgrown monkey picked the wrong house to wander into."

A smattering of laughter peppered the crowd.

"What a liar." Brady crossed his arms. "But there's no way to prove it."

Mr. Delaney raised his hands to quiet everyone. "Before I take questions, let me show you one other little surprise."

He disappeared into the garage. The crowded driveway made it difficult to see. When he came back into view, he lifted his arm and revealed something boxy covered with a black cloth. "In this cage is another legendary creature. Though much smaller than Bigfoot here, it's still a creature of folklore that most people pass off as the figment of overactive, super-stitious imaginations."

"Mom!" Sophie turned anxious eyes on her. "What do you think he has in there?"

"Shh." Mom held up a finger but didn't peel her gaze from Delaney.

"I figured if I sweetened the pot, so to speak, I'd have your attention." Mr. Delaney took a long draw on his cigar and puffed a cloud of smog at the crowd. "Because what I want you to know is that there's more where these came from."

"More what?" someone shouted.

"More Yetis. More real, live folklore, my friend." He held up the shrouded cage with one hand and removed the black cloth with the other. The crowd blocked my view of the contents. A collective gasp morphed into awkward laughter.

"I can't stand it. Let's go inside." Mom stomped toward the house.

My siblings and I looked at Mom, then back across the street. Go inside? How could she go inside? I didn't move.

"Oh—the groceries." She strode to the Odyssey and shut the driver's and passenger's doors, then popped the hatch-back. "Are you guys going to stand there or come help?"

I could hear questions shooting off across the street. It sounded as if Mr. Delaney was trying to regain the upper hand, but I couldn't concentrate over the crinkling sound of plastic grocery bags. I trudged to the back of the minivan, where lumpy sacks slouched their Fred Meyer grocery store logos. Brady tossed me a disappointed glance, and I followed him into the house, several bags in each hand. Sophie brought up the rear. We placed the sacks on the kitchen counter and started putting groceries away. Tension permeated Mom like too much perfume. No one spoke.

A knock on the door made me drop a can of organic corn.

Sophie shoved a jar of peanut butter into the pantry and started toward the door.

"No you don't." Mom stopped Sophie with an upraised hand and marched out of the kitchen, leaving my sister deflated.

I heard the front door open and a voice say, "Michelle Gaelyn, KATU Channel 2 News. Can I ask you a few questions about Joseph Marshall and the Bigfoot body he has on display?"

No one moved inside the kitchen.

"I have no comment," Mom said.

"No comment? You're a Sasquatch expert, and there's a very convincing body across the street. Doesn't that intrigue you?"

With a finger to my lips, I crept to the foyer and the others followed.

"Mr. Marshall hasn't bothered to include me in his escapade. I'm afraid that leaves me without comment." Mom stepped back and tried to swing the door shut.

The reporter thrust her microphone across the threshold. "What about his claim to present a live Sasquatch to the world at his upcoming press conference?"

Mom lifted her chin. "I'm afraid I don't know what you're referring to. Now if you'll excuse me."

Michelle Gaelyn pressed a persistent, manicured hand between them. "I personally requested that Mr. Marshall invite you to the press conference next week. If he wants his claims to be taken seriously, he should include you in his presentation."

Mom cocked her head. "Well, you should've checked with me first."

"Mrs. Larcen, he plans to bring a live Bigfoot for the world to see. You're a Bigfoot expert. I can't imagine why you'd want to miss something like this. Plus, he claims he'll bring a gnome and a leprechaun for the press conference." The woman chuckled. "Of course, he claimed to have an elf in his little cage today but it was empty. He said it must've escaped. Still, that Yeti looked authentic. It was convincing enough to make us want more. I really hoped to get your reaction to run with the spot on the six o'clock news."

While the woman spoke, I watched my mother's body language surrender. She heaved a sigh. "I'll say something."

"Terrific!" The reporter turned to her cameraman. "Roll camera."

The goateed dude stepped back, and I watched the camera light blink to life.

Sophie looped her arm through mine and stretched toward my ear. "This is cool."

The reporter stood poised like a contestant in a beauty pageant. "I'm here with world-renowned Sasquatch expert Amy Larcen, bringing you the breaking story that has coincidentally unfolded right across the street from her home. Amy, your neighbor, Joseph Marshall, has produced a very credible-looking Bigfoot body today. Have you had a chance to inspect it?"

"I have not. As you well know, I've only learned about the body this afternoon, but I plan to pay my neighbor a little visit. Soon." Mom's voice held thinly veiled sarcasm.

"I see." The reporter flipped her ginger hair behind her shoulder. "And do you have any comment about the press conference that Joseph Marshall scheduled for next week in Pioneer Square? He's promised to bring creatures straight from the pages of folklore, including a living, breathing Sasquatch. What do you make of such claims?"

"I make them out to be full of hot air, to be honest. But I suppose time will reveal the truth."

"Will we be able to count on you to participate in the press conference? I know your feedback would be valuable."

"Oh, yes. Wild, uh, Yetis couldn't keep me away."

Michelle laughed. "Excellent. The world looks forward to hearing from you, as well as seeing if Mr. Marshall can deliver what he's promised." She turned to face the camera. "Stay tuned, folks. KATU will have all the latest information on the upcoming press conference. And remember, you were first to hear from Sasquatch expert Amy Larcen here, on KATU Channel 2 News."

The camera light winked off, and Michelle extended her hand to my mom. "Thanks for taking the time to visit today. Here's my card. Please call if there's anything new that would be relevant."

"You bet." Mom nodded and shut the door. She turned and leaned against it, catching sight of us. "Well, never a dull moment around here."

"Can we watch the news tonight?" Sophie skidded up to Mom and grabbed her hand. "You're gonna be famous. Wait 'til Dad hears about this."

Mom smirked. "Yeah, that ought to be interesting. Dad will probably want to share the gift of sign language with Mr.

Delaney." She raised her fist. "Right in his cigar-smoking kisser."

CHAPTER THREE

"THERE'S MOM!" SOPHIE STABBED HER FINGER excitedly at the TV.

"Move." I swatted her hand from in front of my face.

Seven pair of Larcen eyes were glued to the flat screen TV, platefuls of chicken Caesar salad balancing on our laps—with the exception of Nate. He sat in his highchair, playing with slices of grilled chicken and cheese.

"Mommy!" Nate waved at Mom's image on the screen.

Dad aimed the remote at the television and cranked the volume.

"...*I suppose time will reveal the truth*," the recorded Mom stated, disdain oozing from the television pixels.

I glanced at Mom to see her reaction. Her hand was sprawled across her face but she peeked between her fingers. "Ugh. I look so unprofessional in my yoga pants."

"Why are you on TV?" Nicole sat in the beanbag chair and poked her fork from Mom to the TV. "Does this have something to do with your work? Hey, that's Mr. Marshall."

"*Shh.*" Dad increased the sound to ear-splitting.

Images of the dead Yeti were spliced into the segment. Matted, nut-brown fur filled the screen. A brief, partially blurred shot of the fatal, blood-caked wound was replayed several times. The camera panned to Mr. Delaney, standing near the leathery, gorilla-like face. He puffed habitually on his stubby cigar while promising a live exhibition in Portland at the Square. The parting shot was a final glimpse of Bigfoot.

How had he managed to preserve the body of the beast? It had been five weeks since Mr. Delaney's wife shot the thing. I wondered what *she* thought of her husband's bold escapades. Was she watching the news from wherever she now lived? Despite our neighbor's bold claims to the contrary, *she* had killed that creature to free my dad—and herself—from Mr. Delaney's tyrannical schemes. Her husband had left the Yeti guarding my father in their house. In the meantime, the man went away to plot with other Trolls about total world dominance. And no, that's not an exaggeration.

Quiet-spoken Abigail Marshall had blasted the furry giant with a shotgun and put an end to my dad's imprisonment, which helped put an end to Mr. Delaney's plans.

Or so we thought.

When the ordeal was over—an ordeal that left me with a broken ankle and Brady with a few dead Trolls under his belt—we were powerless to punish Mr. Delaney for his involvement. And he knew it. Pandora's box could not be shared with local law enforcement. Even if we risked exposing our family's connection to a land full of legends, who would believe a word without proof? Such proof meant placing many creatures, and our friends, in danger. It was a risk we wouldn't dare take.

But Mr. Delaney planned to offer the world the evidence it craved. And, in the process, endanger our family and folklore-friends by parading to the media what *we* had so carefully guarded—for untold generations.

And the media was lapping it up.

A live shot of Michelle Gaelyn, in the KATU studio, came on the screen. "After we readied this spot for this broadcast, one of our editors made a fascinating discovery."

A video rectangle popped up next to the reporter. Slow-motion footage played in the inserted screen. "Watch carefully, folks, as Mr. Marshall lifts the cover off the cage."

A painfully slow version of Mr. Delaney's earlier antics began. He reached a burly hand to the black cloth and ever so slowly pulled it free.

"There! See that?" The reporter's voice was giddy. "Watch again in case you missed it."

A few frames of film replayed several times. Finally, the shot froze with the cover halfway off the cage. A colorful blob could be spotted inside. By the magic of computers, a red circle appeared around the shape. Though it was blurry, something was obviously there in one frame and gone the next.

"Mr. Marshall claimed to have an elf—an *elf*—in this cage." Michelle Gaelyn's eyes blinked excitedly, defying her otherwise polished demeanor. "Once he removed the cover and found nothing inside, he claimed the elf was either invisible or had escaped. Of course, the onlookers scoffed at him. But I have to admit," the video replayed and froze with the splotch visible in the frame, "something is definitely in this cage. And then it's *not.*"

The camera cut back to the reporter. "An elf? A cat in costume? Who knows. As a journalist, I'm definitely curious to see what Mr. Marshall and Mrs. Larcen will present to us this next week in Pioneer Square. As a native Portlander, I'm fascinated by the local folklore. This is a story that I'll be following. And I look forward to bringing it to our audience. Back to you, Sean and Melissa."

The screen filled with the two news anchors—one raised his eyebrows while the other nodded skeptically. "An elf? Bigfoot?" Sean said with a grin. "You've certainly got us curious."

The screen went dark. Dad smacked the remote onto the coffee table. His greying temples pulsed with the flex of his jaw.

Nicole squirmed onto her knees and popped up in front of the television. "Mom, why were you and Mr. Marshall on TV? Does he have a pet Bigfoot? Did it die?" She tossed out the questions casually, as only the daughter of a Sasquatch expert could.

"Baby." Mom puffed out her cheeks and released a slow breath. "It's complicated. But, yeah, I guess you could say his pet Bigfoot died. And remember, his name is really Mr. Delaney."

"But they called him Mr. Marshall on the news." Nicole crossed her arms.

"Yeah," Mom waved dismissively, "guess it doesn't really matter."

Dad stood and paced between the television and coffee table. He looked like a caged animal ready to pounce. I glanced at Brady and Sophie, sharing looks of concern. Since his kidnapping, our carefree, creative father had become a pressure-packed firecracker with a short fuse.

Between my mother's occupation of Sasquatch-ology and my dad's unusual entrepreneurial foray—owning a local cosmetology school—we were graced with a set of easygoing, nonconformist parents. And although I shied away from divulging their quirky professions to, well, anyone, I did appreciate their carefree ways.

But all that had changed this summer. As I watched my father stride back and forth, filling the room with tension I could all but stuff in my pocket, I longed for the way things used to be.

Sort of.

I missed our peaceful household, true. But in exchange for this great upheaval of life-as-I-knew-it, a bolder side of my personality had emerged. It was a satisfying discovery. But one that came at great personal cost.

This brave, new Sadie had inherited a key with the potential to start World War III—one part of the recent makeover I wished I could forgo. Instead, the unique key, disguised as a ring, encircled my right ring finger, looking like an innocuous piece of jewelry. I stared down at its familiar gold swirls, remembering how it had been my Great Aunt Jules' wedding ring. But this summer I had become her successor and the latest in a long line of key keepers whose task was to hide this powerful little key in plain sight.

With a frustrated grunt, I covered the ring with my other hand. There were times, like now, when I wanted to forget I even had it.

Dad stopped pacing and threw up his hands. "No matter how I approach it, we're basically stranded at sea. We have no choice but to swim along with this charade and hope to make it to shore."

"I like charades."

"Liam," Mom tilted her head, "let's talk about this after I get the little ones to bed."

Nicole sprawled dramatically in the beanbag. "I'm not tired. I wanna play charades."

Dad grinned and scooped her up. "Tell ya what. If you get ready for bed quickly, we can play a round of charades before you go to sleep."

"Yes!" She pumped a fist in the air, then wriggled out of his arms and scurried up the stairs.

Mom slid Nate's tray away from his bibbed belly and plucked him up. "We'll be back in a jiffy."

"Come on, kids, let's clean up." Dad unlatched the messy tray and headed to the kitchen. The rest of us hopped up and worked to clear the living room of the dinner debris. My dad's willingness to interrupt our latest crisis to play pretend with Nicole was another interesting twist in the family dynamics, thanks to our precarious summer. When you nearly lose your life, or the life of someone you love, your priorities do some seismic shifting.

In the kitchen, we worked in silence. I guessed the others were contemplating the "breaking news" as well. Like Dad, I couldn't see a way around our involvement with the loathsome neighbor and his meddling plans.

Besides, what better way to keep an eye on the trouble-maker than for Mom to march into the media mayhem and pull off a believable performance of her own?

Brady stood at the kitchen sink and scrubbed the stainless-steel salad bowl with vengeful strokes. He couldn't believe his parents were agreeing to go along with what Mr. Delaney was forcing on them. But was there an alternative?

Brady couldn't think of one. *Besides sabotage,* he said to himself. *Yes.* "Sabotage," he whispered. He liked the way the word slipped out with a snarl. That would be his personal mission. If Mr. Delaney planned to parade carefully guarded secrets before the eyes of the world, Brady would do what he could to bring the man down before he got off the ground.

A lot could happen in a week, give or take. Brady had learned that fact earlier this summer when his parents were kidnapped by Trolls and taken to the Tethered World—a vast land tucked below the earth's surface and teeming with creatures that had once roamed the Garden of Eden. He vowed to do all he could to prevent Mr. Delaney from jeopardizing his family's privacy—not to mention the lives of those he loved, both above and below ground.

He was a Guardian of the Sword, after all. Well, guardian in training. After round two of dangerous underground insurgencies, he had come home for a brief reprieve. He would resume his training at the end of September, bringing a semester's worth of sophomore curriculum back to the Land of Legend—the heart of the Tethered World, inhabited by the Gnomes, Dwarves, and Trolls. The end of September was only a week away.

A lot could happen in a week.

CHAPTER FOUR

"OH, GREAT. JUST GREAT." I GAPED at a digitally enhanced photo taken precisely when Mr. Delaney lifted the cloth from the cage. A photographer had managed to snap the timely shot of a frightened Elf hugging his slender legs, cowering in the corner of the kennel. His deer-in-the-headlights-gaze and distinctly pointed ears stared up at me from above the fold of the *Columbian.*

"What is it?" Sophie took a bite of toast and leaned across the table. Her eyes popped. "That *is* an Elf!" She tore off another hunk of bread with her teeth and chewed with disgust. "Sadie, we have to rescue the poor thing."

I held my hand in front of her crumb-covered face. "Finish eating first." Standing up, I snatched the newspaper from the table and headed to the living room to show Mom.

"*Then* we can go rescue the Elf?" Sophie called to me.

"Not sure it's that simple, Soph." I turned back to see her stuffing the other half of the piece of toast into her mouth. "Remember what Dad told us last night. We have to watch and wait for opportunities. You can't just pound on his door and demand the Elf's freedom."

My sister shook her fist. "I'd like to try," which sounded like "I vike to fry" with her mouthful of bread.

In the living room, Mom sat in her favorite chair, which angled toward the front window looking out on Mr. Delaney's property. A cup of coffee was in her hand, and her laptop was open on the table beside her. I tossed the paper on her lap.

"I guess it's official. That's a pretty clear photo, thanks to the photographer's angle and shutter speed."

Mom set down her cup and picked up the paper, scrutinizing the picture and the article. Then she looked at me and sighed. "I've had a phone call from another news station and three emails from syndicates through my blog. Things could get out of hand if we're not on top of our game. Even then, how do we stop the social media tsunami from wiping us out? In a matter of days we could lose all that we've fought for this summer and all that our ancestors have worked to protect for thousands of years."

I sighed and plopped on the couch. "Sounds like we have to plan for worst case scenario."

"I'm afraid so." She pointed at our neighbor's house. "And he's up to no good. I can tell."

"What do you mean?" I glanced out the window behind the couch and caught a glimpse of Delaney's house through the blinds.

"He's gone in and out all morning."

"But he's been busy like that every day since we returned." I raised an eyebrow at her. "How is today any different?"

She shrugged. "Maybe it's not. But now we know he has an agenda. Which makes me suspect everything he does twice as much as I already did."

"You want me to snoop around and figure out what he's up to?" I couldn't believe those words had come out of my mouth. I barely recognized myself anymore.

"No, not yet anyway. Dad decided to buy a pair of binoculars on his way home from work."

"Reverse spying. I like that. But he keeps his blinds shut tight these days. I don't think he's watching us like he used to."

"Now what?" Mom stood and peered through the wooden slats of the blinds, gaping them open with her fingers. I did the same. Mr. Delaney's front door opened. He sauntered into his yard, a hammer in one hand, a sign attached to a wooden stake in the other, and a cigar between his teeth. The stout man walked across his weed-infested lawn to the mailbox. He stepped off the curb and turned his back to us, swinging the hammer as he drove the stake into the ground. He stepped into the street, continuing to block the view, apparently admiring his handiwork. Then he turned and faced our house, tipping his hat. Mom and I jerked away from the blinds, though we could still see him through the slats.

The man smacked his potbelly and puffed like a chimney. He was laughing as he waddled back inside his house, and I read the sign—No interviews without appointment. Call 360-555-7134.

Brady stuffed a forkful of spaghetti into his mouth, savoring the tangy spice of his mom's homemade sauce. A stray noodle dangled past his chin. He leaned over to Nate and noisily sucked the rogue noodle into oblivion.

"Brady..." His mom rolled her eyes.

His little brother giggled and plucked a single noodle from the tray on his highchair with marinara-glazed fingers. After several tries, he dangled one orange noodle like a worm, his eyes twinkling mischievously.

"That's right." Brady imitated Nate with a noodle from his own plate. "You've got it!"

"Just what he needs." Sadie smirked. "More messy, bad habits."

The two boys slurped their noodles in unison. Brady felt a tinge of pride at the new skill he'd passed on to his baby brother. Brock had never been enthusiastic about goofing around with food, preferring to avail himself of napkins to stay mess-free.

"Ugh." Nicole wrinkled her nose. "Boys can be so disgusting."

Sophie jabbed a meatball with open hostility. "Dad, we have to rescue the Elf from Mr. Delaney."

"Patience." Dad held up a warning finger. "If we react impulsively, Pandora's box may explode all over the Pacific Northwest. It won't be pretty."

"Probably won't look any worse than Brady's spaghetti-splattered face." Sadie shoved a napkin at him.

"But the Elf could *die*." Sophie looked like she might burst into tears.

Brady wiped his chin. "I think Dad's right. Timing is everything. But," he smacked the crumpled napkin onto the table, "that doesn't mean I haven't been watching the creepy old man since we got back."

"And?" Sophie leaned across the table.

"Sophie, elbows down." Mom pointed.

"*And* I know behind his privacy fence there's a greenhouse. And a shed." Brady lowered his voice. "And we all know how lazy the man is. He let his wife do the mowing when she lived there."

"So, now he's suddenly interested in growing things?" Sadie raised an eyebrow. "Yeah right."

"We don't know how long that greenhouse has been there, or what's in it. It was probably Abigail's refuge from her husband's tyranny. And half the houses in the neighborhood have a shed." Mom wiped Nate's face with her napkin. "What's your point, Brady?"

"Just that, you know, it wouldn't be too hard to sneak over to his yard and poke around." Brady shrugged. "It's not like breaking into his house or something."

"It's still trespassing." Mom leveled her gaze on Brady.

"But Mom," Sophie said, "maybe the Elf is in the shed. It would be easy to let him go."

Dad gave an impatient sounding grunt. "Joseph has a shot gun. Abigail used it to blast that Yeti to kingdom come. I don't need him aiming that thing at one of you."

Mom looked relieved. "Thanks, hon. I agree we need to put a stop to his schemes, but we don't want to rush in and do something we'll regret."

"Exactly." Dad gave a single nod and glanced at Brady. "So let's sneak over there together. Set your alarm for two a.m."

CHAPTER FIVE

THE TROLL STOPPED PACING IN CIRCLES and pressed his leathery lips together. He gave the char-skinned Gargoyle a brooding glare.

The enormous bat-like creature smirked, his jaundiced eyes gleaming with amusement. "What? You don't like my terms?"

"Not in the least. I refuse to agree to them." The Troll's booming voice was amplified in the cave. He noticed the Gargoyle wincing at the noise, causing his one bulbous eye to protrude even more. This gave the Troll a measure of satisfaction.

"No need to yell, my friend." The Gargoyle sounded imperious. "Besides, it's not as if my terms are negotiable." The hulking, black figure shrugged. "Take it or leave it."

The Troll leaned in to the Gargoyle's personal space. "Listen, Malagruel, if you think—"

"*Prince* Malagruel," the Gargoyle cut in. He clamped his hands on the Troll's shoulders, then brushed and patted them in a patronizing manner.

"As I was saying." The Troll flicked the Gargoyle's hands from his shoulders and stepped back. "There's no way in Mount Thrall that I'll partner with you once this revolt is finished. I came here to offer you a position working *for* me, not next to me. You've been holed up and ostracized for centuries. I thought you might see this as an opportunity to forge a strong alliance with the most progressive force the Tethered World has seen. Looks like you aren't smart enough to understand all those big, helpful words."

"But I'm the one with the capacity to get what you want. In return, there's something I want." The Gargoyle grinned condescendingly, a yellowed fang slipping across his lower lip. "I want shared authority. It's as simple as that."

The Troll shook his head and stuffed his hands into the pockets of his drawstring trousers. "Forget it. It was a mistake to come here. I thought the news of what Joseph Delaney is up to, topside, might make you see the need for this course of action. But I was wrong." He took long strides toward the narrow entrance of the cave, shaking his head.

Malagruel sneered. "Oh, I see the need."

The bulky frame of the Troll stopped but didn't turn around.

"I see that you need me and my services more than you're willing to admit."

The Troll continued to move away, clearly finished with the conversation.

"If you don't agree with my terms," the Gargoyle called after him, "I'll inform Chief Nekronok that one of his eleven sons has mutiny on his mind." He chortled like a mad man. "Now *that* will be an entertaining conversation."

I winced at the dazzling sunlight that blazed through my bedroom window, leaving no doubt that I had overslept. My brain had been quite unwilling to shut off the night before. It rarely did. Something about the prone position coaxes all manner of wacky scenarios from my imagination, along with a burning need to see each idea out to its unlikely end. Add to that my strong conviction that my sleuthing skills are of Nancy Drew caliber—something I'm convinced of only after eleven p.m.— and my brainwaves and heart rate are on a continuous loop of crazy ideas infusing my body with adrenaline.

I lay still. A lack-of-sleep headache pounded behind my eyes, making me want to burrow under the blankets and, well, sleep it off. But if I didn't get up pronto, Mom would send one of my siblings to wake me—a form of torture that rivaled riding roller coasters, an activity I despise with a passion bordering on a phobia.

I lugged my fat cast from beneath the covers and sat on the edge of the bed. Four days to go in the awkward, lumpy thing, and then Uncle Brent would set my foot free, like a butterfly emerging from its cocoon.

My uncle was a pharmacist and had an odd collection of medical devices, one of which was the tiny electric saw used for removing plaster casts. My broken ankle was set by Doc

Keswick—a Dwarf who practices in Berganstroud, the land of the Dwarves in the Tethered World. The cast was old school, white plaster of Paris that looked like I shoved my foot into a homemade papier-mâché piggy bank. But it did the job. To avoid questions from our family doctor, along the lines of, "What doctor in modern America is still using plaster casts?" my parents decided to let Uncle Brent remove it. He knew all about the Tethered World and our adventures there, so no explanations would be necessary.

Technically, my uncle should have participated in our family's underground exploits. But at some point in life he had refused to have anything to do with the place, which helped shed light on why he and Mom aren't especially close. That revelation had left me reeling. I didn't like my forced-by-birth-right involvement with the Tethered World. The notion of someday walking away had held tempting possibilities.

But after everything that happened on my last visit, there would be no more thoughts of leaving. I no longer wanted mutiny, or even what I dubbed normalcy. Nope. When you're in the trenches of war with others, when friends literally save your life, when you've stared evil in the eyeballs and know what it wants to do to those you love—it's a done deal. You're committed. For life. No room for speculation.

End of story.

Add to those intense and personal reasons one tall, dark, and handsome superman who, quite literally, had swept me off my feet, and I had almost converted from loathing to liking—the Tethered World, that is.

I definitely *liked* superman, although I had only recently been willing to admit it. It was the kind of like that came from sharing deep, life-altering circumstances and not merely from a surface attraction. But let's be honest, it didn't hurt that he had frosty blue eyes set off by deep olive skin and long, black braids. And it didn't hurt that he happened to have a set of glossy, feathered wings attached to his back, either. And did I mention that he told me I'm beautiful?

No, he's not an angel, although I've referred to him as my own personal guardian. And he's not really a superman, even though I've called him a real, live superhero.

His name is Xander, and he's a Nephilim warrior who snatched me out of the air as I hurtled toward certain death. He also helped rescue my parents when they were being tortured. And he's made his affections for me quite clear, even though I keep insisting there's no way on earth—or under the earth—to make it work. Still, it's been a monumental task to push my blossoming feelings aside.

Smiling as I thought of Xander, I wiggled my purple-polished toes that peeked out of my cast. They looked like five purple polka dots hovering a few inches off the carpet, jostling for blood flow and longing for freedom. With a sigh, I got dressed and headed downstairs, anxious to hear about the midnight exploits of my brother and father.

Sophie looked up from the kitchen floor where she sat with Nate on a beach towel. Cheerios, apple slices, and two juice boxes littered the space between them.

"We're having a picnic." She lifted her cranberry-grape juice in greeting.

"Picnic!" Nate clapped. "Sadie wanna picnic?"

How could I resist? "Of course. But only if you'll share." I plopped down beside him, my back against the sliding glass door.

He handed me a single Cheerio, carefully placing it on my outstretched palm. "I will share."

"Thank you!" I popped it into my mouth, trying not to think about the mushed food that coated his fingers and had settled into the creases of his palm.

Brady shuffled into the kitchen, bleary eyed and sporting a severe case of bed head.

"You look awful." Sophie wrinkled her nose.

He scowled but said nothing, retrieving a bowl and spoon from the cupboard.

"Rough night?" I asked around a mouthful of apple. "What did you and Dad find at Mr. Ridiculous's house?"

Brady shrugged and poured a mound of cornflakes into his bowl. "Nothing much."

Good grief. I'm a girl. Gimme some details. Since he obviously needed time to get his body and brain coordinated, I nibbled my apple and tried to be patient. I waited for him to get a few mouthfuls into his bottomless beast of a stomach.

"Not that I was expecting you to find the cast of *Monsters Inc.* in his backyard," I tried again, "but could you elaborate maybe a teensy bit?"

Brady wiped a dribble of milk from his chin and shrugged again. "I mean, the things he had back there wouldn't look suspicious in anyone else's yard. But considering the source, it's hard not to wonder what he's up to."

"What *things*?" Sophie looked from Brady to me with an exasperated stare.

"A shed. The door wasn't shut all the way, so we could see his lawnmower and stuff. And a greenhouse." Brady paused to shovel a mound of wilting flakes into his mouth. "Looked pretty new, if you ask me. Not that I paid much attention to his backyard in the past, but I would've noticed that strange plastic building from the street that runs behind his house. I used to ride my bike over there all the time."

"What's so strange about a greenhouse?" I balanced a Cheerio on my nose and Nate giggled.

Brady tipped his bowl back and slurped the milk. Nate snatched the cereal. I glanced at Sophie and then at my wrist, pretending to check my watch.

"I guess it's weird because he didn't use to have one. Why the sudden interest?" He shoved his bowl away and swiped a napkin from the center of the table, wiping his mouth. "I mean, he's all busy with Bigfoot and Elves or whatever, right? But he suddenly wants to grow flowers?"

"Is that what he has in there?" Sophie asked.

"Nah—at least I don't think so. A bunch of tiny pots with little sprouts. Some bigger pots with bigger sprouts. Maybe they haven't bloomed yet, but it's not like I tried to figure out the species or something. We took a quick look and left."

I hopped up and stuck a piece of bread in the toaster. Hunger had gotten the best of me. "So...nothing suspicious."

Brady brought his bowl to the sink and ran the water like he wanted the bowl to drown.

"Sounds like you missed out on sleep for nothing." I leaned a hip against the counter, waiting on my toast. "Guess we have to put up with your grouchiness for no good reason at all."

"Whatever." He raked his fingers through his hair. "There were actually a couple of things that looked out of place. More out of place than the greenhouse."

Sophie stopped halfway across the kitchen carrying a box of wet wipes. She seemed to be watching Brady with bated breath.

"Saving the best for last, I see." I raised an eyebrow. "Do tell."

"There was this huge rectangular thing under a giant tarp." He gestured with his arms for emphasis, outlining the shape. "It had wheels. As we got closer I could tell it was a horse trailer."

"He doesn't have a horse." Sophie squinted suspiciously.

"Horse says neigh!" Nate chimed in.

"Dad lifted the end of the tarp and—well, I half expected some beast to be trapped inside and scare the spit out of us with a snarl. Another Yeti, maybe. Or even the body of the dead one." He shook his head. "Nothing."

"That's a letdown." I waved him away and worked on buttering my toast. "Thanks for stringing us along."

"Not entirely." Brady crossed his arms. "We could see where someone had souped up the inside. Instead of being empty, there were cages of all different sizes. One of them was definitely big enough for Bigfoot."

The kitchen was quiet, except for the gurgling noise of Nate sucking on an empty juice box.

I sighed. "Sounds like he has plans for a variety of residents."

"No!" Sophie blinked back tears. "He can't kidnap our friends and stuff them into those cages. We can't let him. We *have* to do something."

Brady gave a slow nod. "We will. Somehow."

I touched his arm. "What else? You said there were a couple of strange things."

"Yeah…" Brady took the time to plop his bowl onto the top rack of the dishwasher. "It may be nothing at all. Or it may only be a cellar or a storm shelter."

"Storm shelter? We might need an ark for the rain, but who has a storm shelter around here?"

Brady grimaced. "I'm only trying to tell you what it looked like. It was a square hole in the middle of the grass, about three feet by three feet, made of thick concrete. It stuck up out of the ground by several inches." He spread his arms to show the size. "It was sealed off with a heavy steel lid, bolted into the cement. And the lid was padlocked."

"That is weird," I said around a mouthful of toast.

"So it's like a trapdoor?" Sophie the sleuth had reported for duty.

"Yep." Brady leaned back against the counter. "But with a lock like that, he's hiding something."

CHAPTER SIX

THE WEEK WHIZZED BY IN A flurry of preparations for what we dubbed "the showdown at Pioneer Square." We learned that Mr. Delaney had set up a website dedicated to his side of the duel. Although Mom had yet to find the stomach to speak to the man that she planned to challenge, there was no doubt that he *knew* his revelations would be disputed—by the skeptics as well as my mother.

The website showed photos of the dead Yeti from several angles. The body lay on a bed of dry ice for preservation. One of the captions claimed that the creature had been embalmed. Another tab, dubbed "folklore," showed two photos of the horrified Elf, little limbs pulled up protectively as he huddled in the corner, with a promise of "more photos to come."

Sophie had stomped around the house in a foul mood every day since the chaos began. She was mad at Mr. Delaney for his capture of the little Elf and mad at the rest of us for not planning a brazen rescue. My parents kept her on a tight rein, afraid she'd try something stupid. They continued to assure her that caution was the best plan in the volatile situation. Rash actions might endanger more creatures and even the family.

We were now two days away from the showdown. Mom planned to phone Mr. Delaney and discuss his itinerary, though it was doubtful he would reveal anything. And she wouldn't be able to change his mind. The man obviously enjoyed his new celebrity status. Along with TV coverage, he had been featured in the *Columbian* and *Oregonian* newspapers. Vehicles came and went across the street, giving him more visitors in a week than he'd had since he moved in. The last time I saw the man outside, he was wearing dark sunglasses.

Mom said she wouldn't lie about the Bigfoot body and claim

it was a fake, but she had no problem exposing "Mr. Marshall" to be a fraud. She spent her days digging up what she could about our neighbor's shady past, courtesy of Internet search engines, to discredit him in front of the world.

In the midst of the tiresome preparations, speculations, and decisions about possible confrontations, I had been diligently counting the days until my ankle would be freed from bondage.

And today was the day.

No more bathing with my foot hanging off the edge of the tub to keep it dry. No more hobbling on the cast or using crutches when it ached. No more single-shoe days.

I silently cheered as Brady opened the minivan's sliding door to help me out. We had arrived at Uncle Brent's for the great unveiling. At long last my brother finally possessed his driver's permit and chauffeured everyone he could, anywhere they wanted to go.

Settled on a recliner at my uncle's house, I watched my five-year-old cousin Felicity somersault into the kitchen. Uncle Brent hopped over her compact body, not missing a beat. The kid rarely walked anywhere. Instead, she flipped, rolled, or ran on all fours. She needed to be in gymnastics. Or the zoo.

Uncle B landed a noisy kiss on my cheek. "Is my leetle specimen ready for de experiment?" He hunched over and rubbed his hands together, mad-scientist style.

"Ha ha." I gave him a deadpan gaze. "If you so much as shave a hair off of my undoubtedly hairy ankle with that saw, I will contact my lawyer. Do you have malpractice insurance, doctor?"

He laughed and turned to my mother. "Hey, sis." He placed his hands on her shoulders. "Are you hanging in there? You look tired."

Mom drooped as if the question only added to her burden. "Of course, I'm tired. This stupid showdown at Pioneer Square is barreling toward us."

"Aw, come 'ere." My uncle folded Mom into his arms, and she relaxed against him.

Although he had distanced himself from the Tethered World—which had caused a rift in their relationship—things had improved since our return. Mom had let him into her confidence, and he openly questioned us about what we'd gone through and stopped by to check on things. I smiled at the two of them embracing. It helped to know someone else in the family had our backs.

That job description used to fit our Aunt Jules, but we didn't have the benefit of her steadying presence right now. She had accompanied us on our last trip below and enjoyed a miraculous but painful reunion with her husband, our Uncle Daniel. They'd remained behind for health reasons.

The two had been separated since their honeymoon more than four decades ago. He had been considered Missing in Action at the close of the Vietnam War. Mysterious circumstances surrounded his disappearance, but he was eventually presumed dead by everyone except Aunt Jules. These circumstances included one William Joseph Delaney—aka the infamous Joseph Marshall—who also happened to be my Uncle Daniel's cousin.

Yeah, it's a convoluted tale that would make a good book—though it would have to be classified as fiction because no one would believe it. Frankly, I'd been living through it, up close and personal, and I barely believed it myself.

All that to say, our circle of confidence was tight. Family-sized. What Mr. Delaney proposed to do would destroy the fragile bubble we had created and continued to guard.

"Let's do this." Uncle Brent came over to where I sat and wrinkled his nose. "Man, that's one ugly cast. I forgot how these plaster things make you look like a mummy."

I gave him a look and smoothed the towel beneath my leg on the recliner's footrest. "Gee, thanks."

"Don't mention it." He plugged the cord into the outlet beside me and revved the saw to an annoying whine. Uncle Brent held the tool at arm's length and spewed forth an evil laugh. "It's *aliiive!*"

I raised my eyebrows and looked at Mom. "I'm not sure this is such a great idea."

"Aw, relax." He knelt beside my foot. "I'll try to only make superficial cuts into your skin."

Mom busied herself at the sink, filling a bowl with warm, soapy water. She toted it over with a washcloth and towel, kneeling on the opposite side from where Uncle Brent worked. Thankfully it was a simple procedure—a cut along both sides, followed by a tool that pried the cast open like a giant pistachio shell.

"This is the fun part." Uncle Brent grimaced at the inside of the cast and held it away from himself. "You learn how much skin you shed beneath these cocoons. It's pretty disgusting."

Ugh! Based on what I saw, "disgusting" sounded like flattery. My poor ankle looked shrunken and deformed. Matted brown hair formed a protective layer on flaking, crusty skin. My gag reflex threatened to take over.

"All right, let Nurse Amy have a look." Mom used to be a nurse, and she inspected my ankle with a keen eye, turning it gently from side to side. My uncle collected the debris and slipped outside, probably to put the nasty chunks of plaster in the garbage. He returned empty-handed. Mom worked like a pro, giving my foot a sponge bath. I couldn't help but look at the morbid thing. It appeared to belong to someone else. An old lady, perhaps.

"Will I be able to walk normally, right off the bat?" I asked whoever had an answer.

"More or less." Mom squeezed warm water from the cloth and let it run down my shin. "It'll feel weird. Very stiff. I'll show you some physical therapy exercises to do each day."

Uncle B tossed something floppy onto my lap. "Wear this if you're going to walk a lot. It'll help."

A stretchy ankle brace lay across my legs. I picked it up. "Beats a cast any day."

Wild squeals announced my little cousins' arrival. Brady lumbered into the den on all fours. Felicity and her little sister Ava straddled his back. Both wore cowboy hats and holsters. My brother plowed through the dangling leaves of a potted plant. Uncle Brent cultivated a wide variety for their medicinal properties—both inside the house and out. They were so many, it was getting out of hand.

"Wrong way, Strawberry." Felicity yanked Brady's shirt like a pair of reins. "I wanna go upstairs."

"Strawberry?" Uncle Brent snickered. "That's not a very manly name."

"Uh, excuse me? It's the name of a horse from *The Chronicles of Narnia*," I volunteered.

Brady redirected himself without comment. It hurt my knees just to watch him.

Uncle Brent shrugged. "I guess if it's good enough for C. S. Lewis..."

Mom wrapped my foot in a dry towel, and I couldn't help a sigh of satisfaction. I felt whole.

"Where's Val?" Mom straightened and picked up the bowl of dirty water. "I thought she was off today."

My uncle averted his gaze. "I told you, she's pretty freaked out about our family's connection to the Tethered World. She'll come around, but we need to give her space. She's still upset about my keeping it a secret all these years."

Poor Aunt Valerie. She had no idea about our crazy situation when she agreed to keep Nate and Nicole for a while on our last visit below. She thought we were taking a little spur-of-the-moment vacation. A getaway with the older kids. Instead, her babysitting responsibility lasted for a couple of weeks without any contact from us. Uncle B eventually had to fess up. She didn't take the news well and threatened to call the authorities if we didn't return by the end of the week. We made it back with one day to spare.

Still, every last one of us had been placed on her naughty list, and she always managed to have an errand to run when we showed up.

"Can't say I blame her for being upset, Brent." Mom crossed her arms and leaned against the kitchen counter. "It's taken me years to work through my feelings about your leaving me on my own with the Tethered World."

"I know, I know." Uncle B held up his hands in surrender. "I haven't handled things well with either of you, I admit. But I'm truly trying to do the right thing now. I hope you believe that."

"I do." Mom's voice softened. "And I have another favor to ask."

I slipped on my flip-flops and stood, for the first time in weeks, on my own two feet, sans cast. Thanks to the serious conversation, no one celebrated with me, which was fine. Standing felt awkward.

"Would you mind keeping Nate and Nicole when we head to Portland for the press conference? Brady and Sadie will be with me. And there's no keeping Sophie home either, I'm sure."

My ankle felt like it belonged to someone else. I paced between the recliner and coffee table, making an effort not to lift my leg higher than normal. Without the heavy cast, it seemed to float up of its own accord.

"Uh, let me check with Val," Uncle Brent said. "I was planning to come down and watch. Lend moral support and all."

"Oh! That would be appreciated." Mom looked pleased. "Very much so."

"I don't think she'll mind, since it's only for a few hours. And the girls love to play with Nate and Nicole." Uncle Brent finally noticed my unsteady stride. "Hey! Look at you."

Both he and Mom eyed my efforts. Walking was getting easier and feeling more natural. Hopefully it showed.

"Thanks, Brent." Mom pecked his cheek. "We'd better get going. I've got a lot of planning and praying to do."

My uncle gave Mom a quizzical look. "Are you going to claim his Bigfoot is fake, or just that the old man is a diabolical fool?"

Mom sighed as if all the uncertainty in the universe boiled down to that one weighty question. She slowly shook her head. "No, I won't lie. I'll confirm that he does have a Bigfoot. But I hope to convince the world that Delaney himself is a fake—a fake who's crazy. And crazy translates to dangerous."

CHAPTER SEVEN

THINGS DIDN'T GO AS PLANNED. AT least not according to Brady's plans that he had hoped to accomplish before the dreaded showdown. One day left, and he still hadn't found a way to sabotage Mr. Delaney's impending bombshell.

Of course, it might have something to do with the rent-a-cop Mr. Delaney had hired. The dude sat out front in a sedan sporting the intimidating logo "Bad-Guy Busters! Who ya gonna call?" Brady was pretty sure there was a copyright on that slogan.

The donut-eating man in uniform—whose middle also resembled a donut, prompting Brady to dub him Slim-Jim—sat with his window down, substantial elbow hanging out, head gently bobbing to music. Brady set his alarm throughout the night, hoping to catch Slim-Jim dozing on the job. The man either slept all day or was related to nocturnal animals like possums and skunks, because whenever Brady checked, the guard was wide awake. He often changed positions, sitting on the hood of his car or leaning against the door, but night after night, Brady failed to find an opportunity to safely wreak havoc.

The activity level during the daytime hours increased as well, and Mr. Delaney's house seemed to never be vacant.

Tonight was his last chance. At 3:30 a.m. Brady woke for his second try of the night. He'd been careful to vary the setting of his alarm, hoping there might be a magical hour when Slim-Jim couldn't resist nodding off. But so far, to no avail.

Even though he didn't expect a different result now, he had to at least check. Of course, after a week's worth of stilted sleep he felt miserable dragging himself out of bed. The first evening he'd gotten dressed, ready to prowl, but that quickly became a hassle.

Brady yanked a pair of sweatpants over his boxers and shuffled down the hall. He rubbed his eyes and approached the curtains, bracing himself for the glare of the street light. He blinked until his eyes adjusted.

Same car. Same place. Same elbow poking from the window. Everything he expected to see. But wait...

He squinted his eyes to focus, certain he was seeing things. Slim-Jim's head angled in a peculiar way. Brady blinked, his adrenaline buzzing at a low hum. While he watched, the security guard's head lolled sideways to his shoulder, knocking the man's uniform hat from its perch. The hat landed upside down on the pavement, but the man didn't move.

Brady practically levitated to his room. He dove into a hoodie and sneakers, then snatched a lock-pick set from his nightstand, courtesy of Amazon. Making his way downstairs, careful to avoid the creaks and groans of the familiar path, he tiptoed through the den and let himself into the garage. Between the three clunky sets of deadbolts on the front door and their Corgis, Ollie and Mindy-loo, roaming the backyard, the garage seemed the safest option. It had a door that opened into the side yard.

Brady snatched an LED flashlight from a cluttered shelf, pulled the sweatshirt's hood over his blond hair, and stepped into the slivery moonlight. From the corner of his house, he strained to catch a glimpse of the snoozing guard while using the family cars as a protective barrier. He dashed to the front end of his dad's Civic and peeked over the top like a human-sized prairie dog, popping up and crouching down repeatedly.

Slim-Jim hadn't budged.

Since Mr. Delaney had a history of watching the Larcen house at all hours, Brady concentrated on the front window, looking for any sign of a shadow or silhouette.

Nothing.

With a nervous gulp and shaky legs, he maneuvered across the street. His gaze darted from the guard, whose snores sounded like a croaking bullfrog, to the front window and door. Brady halfway expected to see his scumbag neighbor waddle outside to intercept the deed.

Once Brady slipped past the Bad-Guy Busters car, he ducked behind the hedge of rhododendrons that ran alongside Delaney's driveway. His heart had revved to a fierce tempo, and he paused to catch his breath at the side of the house.

Some Guardian of the Sword I'll make, he thought. *I can't even trespass without hyperventilating.*

Brady repeated the series of movements that he and his father had rehearsed the week before. From the gate, he dashed to the back corner of the house. From the corner, he bent low and ran to the far side of the tarp-covered horse trailer, skipping the shed and greenhouse this time around. He felt better with the trailer between himself and Mr. Delaney's windows, although Brady felt certain his imagination was set on "overreact and hallucinate" by now.

Squatting with his back against the tarp, he willed his pulse to slow and his breathing to even out. Since his worst teenage offense thus far had been toilet papering a neighbor's yard, he had no idea what to do next. He only knew he needed to find a way inside the scumbag's house so he could free any captive creatures—likely in the basement—and pull the plug on whatever device was keeping the dead Yeti from decomposing.

And if he found a live Yeti, as Mr. Delaney had promised? He had no idea. It wouldn't be likely that he'd be sneaking out unnoticed if he was, indeed, able to sneak in. If all the captives were free, then Mr. Delaney's plans would be ruined. Or postponed, at least. That hopeful outcome offset the risks.

Brady breathed out a prayer, wondering if it was acceptable to pray for successful illegal activity. Then he flattened himself to the ground. Since the horse trailer had wheels, he could squirm beneath it and hide, scoping out the house in relative safety.

He'd no sooner finished his army crawl than a silence-shattering thump startled him, causing him to ram his head into the metal trailer above. He smothered his yelp into the grass and instinctively shot a hand to the throbbing spot at the back of his head. Despite the noise his own head had made, he knew no one had heard it. The sound of hammering blows continued in rapid-fire rounds of five pounding bursts with a slight pause between. Once over the initial shock and jab of pain, Brady peered around the trailer wheels, trying to determine where the racket was coming from.

His gaze fell on the latched and locked metal lid that lay flush in the grass. The cellar, or whatever it was, rattled beneath the repeated blows of someone below. Maybe Mr. Delaney was trapped inside his own hole. Brady wondered whether he should aid the enemy or let him suffer.

The back-porch light flickered to life. Brady sucked in another breath of surprise and squirmed to the middle of the trailer and away from the puddle of light cast by the floodlight. He saw the sliding glass door open. After a brief fumble with the curtains, Mr. Delaney huffed from the house in striped pajamas, his comb-over waving in wild gyrations above his head. What most stood out to Brady was that the man wasn't covered in a shroud of cigar smoke. Brady couldn't recall ever seeing the old geezer without a smoldering nub clenched between his teeth.

"I'm comin', I'm comin'!" Mr. Delaney's voice barked over the metallic blows erupting from his yard. He held out his hands as if he could muffle the noise by doing so. "Quit making such a racket."

Whoever or whatever was trapped inside didn't stop pounding. Brady's head seemed to throb in rhythm to the beat. He wriggled in the opposite direction from the hatch door, maintaining his view but desperate to escape notice.

Brady heard Mr. Delaney blurt a stilted chain of curses between huffs of breath. The man shuffled to a stop in front of the clanking cover and stomped on the lid. The mystery person inside finally stopped their incessant hammering. From his hiding place, Brady could only see Mr. Delaney from the shins down. The man's burly hands appeared, fumbling to slip a key into the padlock.

A flash of dread washed over Brady. What if it was Mrs. Delaney who was trapped in there, being punished for helping his dad? But a quick replay of the powerful beating on the metal door made Brady nix the idea.

But who? Or what?

Grumbling a final expletive, as if it were the magic word, Mr. Delaney turned the key and released the lock. He tossed the padlock to the side and slid a substantial bolt from its latch. But before Delaney could take hold of the metal handle, the lid flew open, smacking his hand and sending him reeling backward.

In one fluid motion, the furry bulk of a Troll rose from the hole in the ground.

CHAPTER EIGHT

I SHOVED MY HALF-EATEN WAFFLE away, nauseated by the tale Brady was sharing. Mr. Delaney had a Troll for a houseguest at this very moment?

"Let me get this straight." Mom's fork clattered to her plate, fingers curling into fists. "There's a tunnel in that man's backyard that's connected to the Tethered World? A *tunnel?*"

Brady nodded. "That's what it looked like. And it wasn't only a Troll that came out. He dragged two lumpy sacks behind him. One of them wiggled and squirmed like crazy when he dropped it on the ground. The Troll said he had a Gnome."

"What?" Sophie pushed her chair back and stood up, her nostrils flaring. "Dad, we have to do something."

Dad had been unusually quiet while Brady spoke. He had that I'm-choosing-my-words-carefully look. "Sit, Sophie." He pointed his finger at her in a downward motion, then looked at Brady. "What you did was idiotic. Going over there and snooping around all alone. Very dangerous. Just..." He turned away with a grimace of disgust, his teeth on edge.

"I agree, hon, but what's done is done. We need to know what else he saw. It's going to affect everything happening in Portland today." She gave Brady a stern look. "Not to say you're off the hook, mister, but we'll save the lecture for later. Go on."

A wounded look flashed across my brother's face. Poor guy. He was only trying to help.

He gulped. "So, um, yeah. Something was wiggling in the sack. It must've had a gag because I could hear it grunting, but it didn't speak. The Troll said he brought Delaney a 're-pugnant Gnome' as he had requested." He air-quoted the label as he explained.

"I'll show him repugnant." Sophie pumped a fist like a boxer. "And I'm not even sure what it means."

Brady gulped down his milk, leaving a white mustache across his fuzzy lip. "Then a Leprechaun came out after the Troll. Cranky, like every other Leprechaun we've met, complaining that he couldn't keep up with the Troll."

"So one Troll, one Gnome, one Leprechaun." Mom ticked off the list on her fingers. "Anything else? We know he already has an Elf inside, if he hasn't killed it yet."

Sophie gasped and smothered her mouth with her hand.

Brady shook his head. "Nothing else came through. They stood there talking for a minute. I could only see Delaney and the Troll from about the ankles down. But I could see the Leprechaun all the way up to his chest. I was praying he wouldn't crouch down for some reason and see me."

"Would've served you right," grumbled Dad.

"What did they say?" I shoved my napkin over to Brady, unable to take him seriously with his milky lipstick smudge.

My brother wiped his mouth. "Mr. D said, 'Sargon'—I guess that's the dude's name—'why are *you* here? I thought Nekronok was coming.' And before the Troll answered, Delaney said, 'And what's the big idea, banging loud enough to wake the dead? You want my neighbors calling the cops? I wasn't expecting you here until dawn in the first place.'" Brady coaxed my plate toward him with his finger. "You don't want this?"

"No. But finish your story." I drummed my fingers on my placemat.

"Yeah, so the Troll says," Brady dropped his voice to a menacing whisper, "'You will refer to my father as *Chief* Nekronok. Got it? His Worshipful Master shouldn't be traveling into the dangers of an unknown land. Once we have the Topsiders' attention and they know we mean business, he'll make a proper appearance.'"

"Nekronok is a chicken, sending his son to do his job." Sophie glowered at us like it was entirely our fault.

"Enough." Mom held a silencing hand in Sophie's direction. "Another word and you can join Nate and Nicole in the other room watching *Veggie Tales.*"

Brady fidgeted with the placemat in front of him. "Mr. Delaney didn't argue. He asked the Troll if he brought proper attire for the press conference. Sargon said he did. The stupid Leprechaun kept nosing around the tires and kicking at the other sack. I squished myself into the shadows and hoped he wouldn't notice me."

"Then what?" Dad did not sound happy.

"Then..." Brady shrugged. "The Troll picked up the sacks and followed Mr. D toward the house. They left the hole in the ground wide open, too. The Leprechaun sniffed around the yard like a dog. I half expected him to start marking his territory. At the back door the Troll grunted, 'Fig. Get over here,' and the little runt followed them inside. I waited a long time, in case something else crawled out of the hole. Eventually I got sleepy and figured I'd better get home before I fell asleep under the trailer."

Dad glowered at my brother, shaking his head. "Do you know how many ways that little escapade could've gone wrong? We could've easily woken up to find you missing this morning. That was a reckless idea, Brady. Thank God, you're back to tell about it, but I'm disappointed in your lack of judgement. I'm not sure if you're ready to go back to Vituvia and resume your training to be a guardian."

The devastated expression on Brady's face broke my heart. I had to say something. "But Dad, isn't learning good judgment part of the training he'll receive? We're all figuring this out as we go, but I think we've come a long way in a short time. Especially Brady."

My brother's glance was appreciative. Dad sighed and slouched back into the dinette chair. He appeared to loosen his hostile grip on the situation.

Dad looked from me to Brady. "I'm sorry, Brady. Every event over the past week seems to add tinder to a keg overflowing with gunpowder. And my own particular keg has a short fuse. I don't agree with what you did. It was stupid, to put it bluntly. But you're courageous for trying, and the information is certainly helpful. And yes, your sister is right—you've proven yourself in the face of adversity exceptionally well. Further training in Vituvia will only improve on your God-given gifts." Dad held out his hand. "My apologies."

Brady stared at the offering, his face serious. Something in my brother's eyes told me that this apology and gesture between him and Dad meant more than what it appeared on the surface. Like moving a tassel on a graduation hat from right to left, Brady clasped Dad's hand and graduated into manhood.

Mom never could bring herself to speak to Mr. Delaney about

the conference in person. After our discussion, Dad offered to take her over or speak to Delaney on her behalf, but she refused. She did, however, phone him, speaking in clipped tones and inquiring what his agenda would be. I stood at the counter doing my ankle exercises while listening to her half of the conversation.

The man was tight-lipped. I could hear most of his short but condescending answers through the receiver. He obviously knew my mom despised what he was doing. No doubt he liked having the upper hand, which meant he would keep his cards close. No surprises there.

In regard to the press conference, her only request was to be introduced first—a favor she asked of Michelle Gaelyn, the reporter, rather than Mr. Delaney. The reporter had become the press conference PR person, for lack of a better term, arranging the set-up in Pioneer Square. Mom said the woman naively assumed that she and "Mr. Marshall" were now bosom buddies, working together for their shared love of all things Bigfoot.

Mom didn't care what the reporter thought, as long as my mom could take the stage first. She'd spent the week digging into Joseph Delaney's past, dredging up every negative thing she could find. He had been suspended from school for fighting. He had disappeared for years and had changed his name. Mom hoped that enough suspicion could be cast to cause the media to dismiss any claims about folklore and the Tethered World as questionable. Maybe they'd even suspect the walking-talking Bigfoot to be a realistic costume if they doubted everything else.

"Ready, little brother?" I stood in the doorway of the boys' bathroom, waiting on Brady to finish his man-grooming.

"Yep!" Brady raked a blob of hair putty through his dirty-blond locks, making the front curve up and over in an accidentally-on-purpose style. "Whaddya think?"

"I think Mom is the one who's going to be on TV, not you." I grinned at our reflections in the mirror.

The fact that there would be cameras everywhere hadn't escaped me either. I'd taken the time to curl my hair in twisty, loose spirals and had put on my favorite hippie-style tank—the one with the crocheted straps and flowing fabric. I would've liked to wear my wedged heels, but with my newly freed ankle still aching and wobbly, I had to settle for strappy sandals. I decided not to wear the brace but bring it in case my ankle complained.

Brady's brown eyes smiled at mine. "Lookin' good, sis."

"Thanks."

"Uncle B is here!" Sophie, the family watchdog, called up to us from downstairs. She'd been an overly excited preteen girl all day, and I'd had about enough. Brave and clever as she was—unnaturally so—she was still eleven years old, which automatically made her annoying fifty percent of the time. Maybe more.

I went to my bedroom and snatched my purse from the dresser before heading downstairs. Brady was already with Uncle Brent doing the guy-handshake thing which ended in a slap-on-the-back sort of hug.

"Aunt Val picked up Nate and Nicole earlier," Sophie informed our uncle.

"Just the way we planned it." Uncle Brent gave her a thumbs up.

I turned at the sound of my parents' door creaking open. Mom and Dad appeared at the top of the stairs looking tense but sophisticated. Mom wore wide-leg black trousers, heels, and a steel-grey blouse. The cuffs on Dad's pinstriped dress shirt were folded up, his top button undone, sans tie. They looked like two polished professionals in the business world rather than a Bigfoot blogger and artistic cosmetologist.

"Wow. You two look like you're going to a funeral." Uncle Brent grinned in his goofy, teasing way. "Remember to smile for the cameras, sis."

"Shut up, Brent. I'm in no mood."

Yikes! Mom never told people to shut up. I chuckled at the look on Sophie's face. She was obviously struck by Mom's moodiness.

Uncle Brent raked a hand through his wavy blond mop. "Sorry. You know I'm not so good in tense situations."

"We know." Dad shot him a warning look.

"I'll drive." Brent dangled his keys. "You two can chill or talk shop or whatever you need to do. Traffic on I-5 is always a bear, so let me maneuver it."

"Fine with me." Mom retrieved her briefcase from the foyer table.

Dad slid his arm around her shoulders. "Got everything you need, babe?"

Mom took a deep breath. "Everything but my nerve."

And she pressed her head against his shoulder and burst

into tears.

CHAPTER NINE

BRADY AND I SAT IN THE third-row seat of Uncle Brent's Suburban, exchanging anxious looks. Although Mom had collected her emotions, dried her tears, and fixed her makeup, an awkward, fearful silence clung to our family like a parasite. Even Sophie, who rode in the middle seat beside Mom, had curbed her usual yammering.

Through the window, I watched the deep blue of the Columbia River spill into view as we crossed the bridge between Vancouver, Washington, and Portland, Oregon. The river had been a constant in my life, the blood in the veins of my childhood. Like the nearby mountains, it made me feel part of something bigger. In its chilly depths, I had learned how to swim, and from its westerly course I had learned my directions. I could find north, south, east, or west based on my relation to the river. The lives of those around it puddled together, mingling on its banks. Our river, like our coffee, was a common denominator, not a divider.

"And the traffic problems begin." Uncle Brent braked as we approached the rear end of a semi-truck.

"At least we left plenty early." Mom dug something out of her purse. "Gum?" She brandished a fresh pack of wintergreen Trident between herself and Sophie. My sister tossed me a piece, and I chewed it with all the nervous energy of a beaver in construction mode.

I leaned into Brady, welcoming the normalcy of chit-chat. "Were you able to catch Mr. Delaney leaving the house with his, uh, entourage of creatures?"

Brady shook his head and rolled his eyes. "I, uh, I fell asleep."

I nudged him with my elbow. "Too many late-night shenanigans, huh?"

He grinned.

"That's okay, I was busy taking my frustrations out by re-arranging my bedroom." I nodded, satisfied. "You'll have to check it out. Looks good."

Sophie swiveled around in her seat to see us. "Do you think we'll get to sit on stage with Mom? You know, like how the president's family gets to sit behind him when he speaks?"

"I definitely hope not." My cheeks flared, imagining it.

"Don't be silly, honey." Mom chuckled. "This is not some formal event. We'll be lucky to have a dozen people there, giving us the time of day."

"But!" Dad held up a finger. "If Joseph presents those creatures to the cameras as he plans, things are going to blow up in a hurry. Social media won't stop buzzing."

"Which is why I *must* be permitted to speak first. To set the tone." Mom leaned her head against the back of the seat. "Lord, we need You to do this for us. *Please.*"

Dad navigated from the passenger seat, checking the clogged arteries of traffic on his GPS to find the easiest route downtown. Portland perched on the banks of the Willamette River, which gave it the nickname of Bridgetown. Drivers had their choice of steel structures to cross to get into the heart of the city.

"I'd take the Fremont Bridge and circle around the backside to the square." Dad gestured at his phone. "A few more miles but a lot less traffic."

Brent navigated the congestion, and we finally hit the Fremont. Crossing the Willamette meant we were close to show time. My heart suddenly ballooned, inflating nervously with each beat. I concentrated on what was outside the window rather than the explosion of emotions inside the car. Everyone seemed to shut down or tense up all at once, and the Suburban felt too small to contain the stress that radiated from the six of us.

Snaking through the hipster-dom that is Portland, we passed microbreweries and coffee roasters, eateries and boutiques, and my favorite place to spend an afternoon: Powell's Books. I looked longingly at the brick edifice as we inched past. I'd give anything to be exploring its multi-leveled nooks and crannies instead of facing a firing squad of reporters and playing nice with our repugnant neighbor.

"The traffic is ridiculous for this time of day." Uncle Brent tapped the steering wheel impatiently. The light had turned green, but there were so many cars in front of us, we couldn't pull into the intersection without blocking it.

"Maybe you should let me out close to the square, before you park." Mom fished a compact from her purse and inspected her hair and makeup. "I really don't want to rush to get situated."

"You betcha, sis."

We inched along for several more blocks. Finally, Nordstrom department store loomed into view. Nordstrom faced Pioneer Square along Broadway.

"What on earth?" Dad stretched his neck, trying to see around the car ahead. "I—I think all of this traffic is for the press conference, babe." He twisted around to face Mom. "The square is cram-packed."

"Nuh-uh." Mom peered out the window. Brady and I couldn't see much from the third seat, but we tried.

Uncle Brent whistled long and low. "Looks like you're gonna get your fifteen minutes in the spotlight today. Why don't you hop out here? You can walk faster than I'm driving."

"Okay." Mom's voice sounded faint. "Make sure you guys push to the front of the crowd. I need to be able to see your faces."

"We will." Dad squeezed her knee. "Love you."

"You too." Mom opened the car door and got out. "Pray for me."

"You've got this!" Sophie cheered before the door slammed.

The Suburban made a right turn, and I spotted Mom striding purposefully through the crowd. Wait, did I see picket signs? What could people possibly be picketing?

Once we found a parking space and walked to the square, I got to see the crazy commotion for myself. In true Northwest fashion, a diverse group of people gathered in "Portland's living room"—the locals' nickname for Pioneer Courthouse Square. Besides the usual downtown foot traffic of shoppers, people watchers, Starbucks patrons, and commuters catching the light-rail train, a mass of bodies milled about. Near the old courthouse, which faced the square opposite from Nordstrom, a platform had been erected.

"Whoa!" Brady whistled through his teeth while we surveyed the crowd. We stood beside a life-sized bronze of a man holding an umbrella, and I sidled into the shade it offered.

The brick square was a city block in size but had an upper and lower level. We stood above the crowd, at the top of an enormous semi-circle of wide stairs that doubled as seats. On any given day, people sat on the steps and listened to music or sipped their coffee. Standing at the top gave us a good view of the swarm of people below. A flat brick basin stretched from the bottom of the stairs all the way to the adjoining streets.

On the stage, tech geeks were busy setting up a podium with a mic and a few folding chairs. I spied several news vans parked along the street, including KATU's and the brightly festooned Animal Planet vehicle.

Although the majority of the crowd looked like curious citizens, clusters of the fringe factor were making their appearance. A large group right below us looked like they had come straight from the latest Comic-Con. I nudged Brady and pointed. There were at least four Bigfoot costumes along with two Chewbaccas. Several people sported faery wings—some with antennae—and it appeared that most of the creature groups from *The Lord of the Rings* were well represented. The majority were busily snapping selfies and looked to be there for the fun of it.

Some of the crowd were holding signs, and I saw now that they weren't actually picketing. Many of the neon-colored poster boards were sporting the slogan We Believe! I also saw a few that had the initials PETOS. Beneath the large letters it read "People for the Ethical Treatment of Sasquatch."

"Where's Mom?" Sophie squinted in the direction of the stage. "It's so crowded I can't find her."

"We'll make our way over there in a sec." Dad placed a hand on her shoulder. "I'm speechless, you guys. This is not what I expected."

Uncle Brent laughed. "Amy is officially doing her part to keep Portland weird, as they say."

"Hey look!" I pointed past the costumed crowd. "They're selling things at those tables."

"Can we check it out?" Sophie asked.

Dad shrugged. "Might as well head down. Gotta make our way to the front and find Mom."

We picked our way through the crowded stairs, brushing past a man with elf ears, a long, belted vest, and pointy shoes. *If you only knew how far off the mark you are, buddy.*

Three tables lined the walk that faced the courthouse. Bigfoot paraphernalia covered the first two displaying keychains, T-shirts, and other odds and ends. Sophie stopped and giggled at a shirt that read "I saw Bigfoot at Pioneer Square!"

A grizzled looking mountain man sat behind the third table with a hand-scrawled sign that read Book Signing taped to the front. Glancing at the titles, I learned he'd been kidnapped by Bigfoot *and* aliens. Separately. He had two different books.

"These are true stories, folks," he called. "Let me share them with you."

I heard Brady snickering behind me. "We could tell him a few stories of our own," he said. "And ours *would* be true."

A blaring horn pierced the crowd noise and made me jump. Its awful screech continued, making everyone turn to the sound. Mr. Delaney maneuvered his Dodge Ram truck through the crowd, his arm hanging out the window. The truck pulled a horse trailer, covered in a tarp.

I bit my lip, wishing I had X-ray vision. Lightheartedness evacuated the premises.

"Comin' through!" Delaney yelled at anyone within earshot.

I glared, but he didn't seem to notice our family in the crowd. At the intersection ahead a police officer stopped traffic in both directions. How had Mr. Delaney managed to get the cooperation of the local authorities?

He made a wide left turn and pulled behind the platform, stopping when the back of his trailer was even with the middle of the stage. People bunched against the stage and craned their necks at the trailer. We followed my dad and Uncle Brent into the mass of curiosity. Ignoring a few protests, we worked our way to the front.

I finally spied Mom, sitting on the edge of the stage next to Michelle Gaelyn. They appeared to be having a serious disagreement. Mom frowned and gestured emphatically while the reporter looked as if she was trying to explain something whenever she could get a word in.

Sophie glanced over at me. "Mom's not happy."

"Nope." I chewed the inside of my cheek and hoped Mom would chill out before the cameras rolled. She needed to appear confident, not stressed.

Brady checked his watch. "Starts in ten minutes."

My heart bounced around in my chest at his announcement. I felt so nervous for my mom. For my family. For the creatures and family below ground who surely would suffer if things went haywire. Taking deep breaths, I tried to focus on anything else to calm myself down. Why hadn't we stopped by Starbucks? At least a chai tea would keep me somewhat distracted. I looked past the stage, above the top of the trailer, and tried to ignore the excitement buzzing around us. My gaze traveled across the nearest buildings, then wandered to the old stone courthouse.

The ornate structure was nearing its one hundred and fiftieth birthday. Although it was once the commanding presence of downtown Portland, it was now dwarfed by the tall buildings surrounding it. Still, it had a regal quality, like the White House on a smaller scale. It had a similar dome on top, sandwiched between twin peaks.

I blinked, then stared wide-eyed, trying to comprehend what I saw. "Brady..." My voice cracked. Without taking my eyes off the courthouse I tugged his sleeve. "*Brady.*"

"What?" He sounded annoyed.

"Do you see what I see?" I pointed at the courthouse.

"What's wrong?" From the corner of my eye I could see him looking from the courthouse to me.

"There, on top of those two peaked rooftops."

"Yeah, what about it?"

"I...um, I don't ever recall seeing Gargoyles up there."

CHAPTER TEN

My body quaked. To steady myself I latched onto Brady. My eyes didn't leave the stone statues perched on the rooftops. How had it come to this? How could my life above ground and my secret connection below collide into chaos in a matter of days? Between Bigfoot making his television debut and Gargoyles watching it happen, my world was splintering apart. I wanted to puke.

"This can't be good," Brady whispered in my ear. "I think I recognize the one on the left. He looks like that creep Ophidian—Malagruel's worm that abducted me."

My gaze ping-ponged between the two statues. "What do we do?"

"I don't know. That stone is only a disguise. One of us needs to be watching them at all times."

Feedback from the microphone made me wince, and I covered my ears. "Okay. You keep an eye on the stage for now, and I'll watch the evil twins."

Someone tapped the mic, testing it. "How ya doing, Portland?" The voice of Michelle Gaelyn commanded the attention of the crowd.

Cheers and applause clamored throughout the square. I couldn't help but steal a quick glance at the set-up. Mr. Delaney sat behind the reporter on the left side of the stage. Some guy in a safari costume sat beside him. Mom had been seated opposite, beside a man in a black suit. He looked CIA. Or maybe FBI. One of those official, alphabetical combinations. Had he been wearing a pair of dark glasses, I might have expected an alien invasion to be imminent. But he appeared as uncomfortable and out of place as I guessed my mom felt.

"I thought *I* was watching the stage." Brady nudged me.

"Yeah, sorry." I turned my attention back to the Gargoyles.

Still there.

"Who's ready to see Bigfoot?" Michelle Gaelyn asked. The crowd whistled and cheered. The sound of digital cameras whirred and clicked around me.

"I can't see." Sophie sounded desperate.

"Stand by me." Uncle Brent waved her over.

"Sadie, what are you looking at?" Dad's voice brought me round. "Why are you staring at the courthouse?"

"Oh, you know—I don't like crowds." I shrugged. Should I tell him? Mom would freak out if she saw all of us freaking out. I decided to wait for her sake. "But I like architecture." He gave me a wary look but didn't press, and I returned my gaze to the figures perched on the courthouse. It would be hard to watch two unmoving statues with everything else going on.

"Let me get the formalities out of the way," the reporter went on. "Then we can get to the real reason you've come today. To finally get a glimpse of that elusive figure of Pacific Northwest folklore. Hey, I see some fun Bigfoot signs toward the back—" The Comic-Con groupies drowned her out for a moment. "That's right! That's right!" Michelle Gaelyn yelled over the din. I didn't think she sounded very professional. "Let me tell you something, friends. I had an amazing opportunity earlier today. Mr. Marshall introduced me to Sargon, the Sasquatch you're about to meet."

I spun toward the stage. Mr. Marshall—er, Delaney—did *what*? Oh, he really was laying it on thick to get everyone eating out of his hand. Mom blinked several times, a clue that she was surprised by the revelation as well.

The crowd hushed at the news. The reporter chuckled in a lighthearted way. "Yes! And let me tell you, I am now a bona fide Bigfoot believer. You guys are going to be *a-mazed* when Sargon takes the stage." She leaned into the microphone and dropped her voice. "You can watch my exclusive interview on KATU news tonight."

I rolled my eyes, then glanced at the Gargoyles. They hadn't moved. *Boring!* I leaned over to Brady and said, "There's too much going on to stare at the courthouse."

"It's okay." Brady gave a one-shoulder shrug. "We'll take a peek every so often. It's not like we can do anything from here anyway."

Michelle put on her professional face and attempted to rein in her giddiness. "Let me introduce our panel, and then we'll move on to bigger and, uh, hairier matters." The reporter turned to my mom. "To my left, we have Amy Larcen. Amy has a longstanding reputation in the field of cryptozoology, the study of mythical creatures. She's a Bigfoot expert who has spent many years tracking the elusive legend and also has a popular blog dealing with those same mythical creatures. You may know her as the Faery Blogmother if you follow her online."

Mom waved her hand and looked as tense as I've ever seen her.

"Next to Amy we have Seth Ferrell, a professor of botany and plant pathology at Oregon State University. He's also a consultant with the FDA."

Aha! I knew he looked alphabetical. Brady and I exchanged perplexed glances. Why was *he* here?

The reporter went on. "From the Oregon Museum of Science and Industry, we'll hear from Calvin Bon Trager." The man in the cheesy safari outfit lifted off his seat slightly and tipped his leather hat.

"And, finally, the man who has some pretty amazing connections to some pretty fantastic creatures—give a warm welcome to Mr. Joseph Marshall!" Michelle stepped back from the microphone, clapping her hands along with the onlookers.

I gaped to see him step forward, waving. Mom looked like she wanted to throttle the reporter. Our neighbor would get to speak first.

Mr. Delaney lumbered up to the podium dressed in the same ill-fitting navy suit and newsboy cap he had worn when we learned of his traitorous actions in the Tethered World. For once, the man didn't have a cigar stub clamped beneath his mustache.

He took his time adjusting the mic, as if he wanted to bask in his new-found admiration. His eyes fell on me and lingered long enough to make me uncomfortable.

"Thank you all. Thank you." He nodded and waved, bushy eyebrows bobbing up and down like hyperactive caterpillars. "Glad to see your enthusiasm for the cause. If you're this gung-ho now, wait until I bring out all my little friends."

Mr. Delaney gripped both sides of the podium and took a steadying breath. "I know you've got some big expectations. And I promise to deliver on those. But I'm afraid the excitement of what you're about to witness may very well push other equally important matters out of the way. So, won't you please indulge an old man? I'll start small and save the best for last."

"Spare us the dramatics," Dad whispered beside me.

"I thought Mom was gonna speak first." Sophie stepped in front of me. "Hey, I can see better here."

"She thought so as well, judging by the look on her face." I tugged on Sophie's ponytail. "You're getting too tall. I can barely see over your head anymore."

"Allow me to give you a brief history." Mr. Delaney lifted his hat enough to run a hand beneath it. "If you've ever wondered why there are rumors all over the world of creatures like Bigfoot, Leprechauns, and the like—going back thousands of years, mind you—it's because they do, indeed, exist."

"Prove it!" yelled someone from the audience.

I glanced up at our chiseled onlookers roosting on the courthouse. They hadn't budged.

The old man held up a calloused hand. "I plan to, but I don't want to put the cart before the horse, so hear me out. Today I'll prove that these creatures have been living closer than you think, showing up for the occasional visit. But I'll save the long version for another day. For now, let me tell you that the land these creatures inhabit contains something else of interest to the world at large. Something that explorers have longed to find. A valuable item with the potential to lengthen life."

He turned toward the man dressed in safari gear. "Mr. Bon Trager, would you please bring me the potted plant beneath my chair?"

The khaki-clad dude complied. I hadn't noticed the little sprout underneath Delaney's seat.

"Dad!" Brady pointed at the stage. "That's one of those plants we saw in his greenhouse."

"Sure is."

Mr. Delaney held the plant up. "This simple little sprout is rooted from a cutting of a tree the likes of which few have ever seen. It only grows in the land I'm going to tell you about, inhabited by these strange creatures."

Sophie turned and looked from me to Brady. "Do you think it's...?"

I nodded, stricken with another urge to lose my lunch. He could only be referring to the Tree of Life, grown from the seed of a fruit from the original tree in the Garden of Eden. It flourished in the Garden Dome of the palace of Vituvia, where Brock lived. But how did our slimy neighbor get his hands on a cutting from that tree? The Gnomes kept the tree—along with the Flaming Sword of Cherubythe that protected both the tree and the Tethered World—guarded like a bank vault. It must be fake, meant to bolster the angle he wanted to play.

"Mr. Ferrell here," Mr. Delaney pointed at the man beside Mom, "is testing samples from the bark, the sap, and the leaves of the sproutlings. We don't have complete results in yet, but he'll testify that the preliminary findings look promising. Powerful elements of the tree have the potential to revolutionize the drug and cosmetic industry. There's enough—"

"Who cares! We came to see Bigfoot," a heckler interrupted. Jeers of agreement swelled in the square.

"All right, all right." Mr. Delaney held up his hands in surrender. The crowd quieted to a rumble. "I hear ya. Tell you what—let me go ahead and introduce the main attraction. When you see that this is serious business, that it's authentic, I'm sure you'll be more inclined to listen to what else I have to share."

The man's slimy gaze fell on me once again, and I had a sickening feeling that I would dislike what was coming even more than I expected. Mr. Delaney grabbed the wide lapels of his suit coat and stood straight. "Portland, and the world at large, I give you Sargon of Craventhrall."

CHAPTER ELEVEN

THE BACK DOOR OF THE TRAILER opened and a caramel-colored Troll ducked his head and stepped out. Straightening to his near seven-foot height, he surveyed the crowd with a detached curiosity then stepped up onto the platform. He wore black drawstring pants and a charcoal vest heavily decorated with military bars, stars, and emblems. I questioned their authenticity. The strange insignia that I'd seen branded onto Trolls' shoulders and engraved on the floor of their sanctuary sat squarely over his heart.

The crowd reacted with a jumble of gasps and murmurs, spiked by a few panicked screams. I instinctively covered the ring on my hand, as if the Troll might know my secret. Sargon strode confidently across the stage. He looked comfortable, like he spoke in front of masses of humans every day. His bulky, linebacker body dwarfed the podium and Mr. Delaney. It looked as if Professor FDA and safari dude might pass out or have an embarrassing accident. Mom glared molten lava in the Troll's direction, but he ignored her. From the back of the stage, Michelle Gaelyn's wide grin looked like it might permanently damage her face.

Mr. Delaney beamed up at the brute like a proud papa. Of course, this Troll's dad was actually Chief Nekronok or "His Worshipful Master"—*gag*—as he preferred to be addressed. The beast had eleven sons, and I'd thus far met two. One, named Rooke, was as evil as his father. The other...well, Chebar was a dear friend who secretly worked from the inside of his father's diabolical dynasty to protect the interests of the good people and creatures in the Tethered World. If not for Chebar, our excursions below would have ended in tragedy.

Sargon studied the crowd beneath his heavy brow, roaming the upturned faces. His gaze flitted past me then jerked back with a gloating sneer. He smacked his leathery lips like he anticipated sampling me and a few others for an appetizer. I steeled myself to glare back unflinchingly, though a fearful tremor raced through my body. Cameras clicked and captured the occasion for all of social media to see.

"Greetings, Topsiders." His voice was deep but less snarly than his father's.

Voices in the crowd cried out in shock and disbelief. These people did *not* expect to meet a talking, intelligent animal. I took in the expressions around me; they reflected a mixture of horror and excitement.

The people were mesmerized.

Their reactions clearly amused the Troll. He grinned slyly, revealing yellowed fangs, and leaned down into the mic. "It would seem that I'm not quite what you expected."

Nervous laughter peppered the crowd. Someone shouted, "That's a great costume!"

His thick neck swiveled slowly, back and forth. "Not a costume, my friend. Though I do see some rather poor imitations among you today." He gestured in the direction of the "I believe" crowd. "But I understand your hesitation. I believe you Topsiders have an expression, 'Seeing is believing,' correct? It seems that believing is not quite so simple when it comes to something that's been rumored to be a legend for hundreds of years."

"Prove it!" another heckler yelled. Others chorused their agreement.

Sargon's face clouded. I couldn't read whether he felt impatient or if he failed to understand how he could prove himself. Mr. Delaney stepped up beside him and tilted the microphone sideways to speak.

"Hang on, now, folks. I know this is beyond your expectations. Maybe you came here to see a beast in a cage, not expecting to meet an intelligent being. It ain't easy to wrap your mind around it." He pointed to a couple of guys near the stage. "You two, why don't you come up here and get a closer look."

Two hipsters in plaid shirts and well-groomed beards took the stage. Sargon stepped back, stretched out his massive arms, and tolerated being poked and inspected as the two circled him. They reached trembling fingers to touch the skin on the Troll's hands, stroke his fur, and generally gawk like a couple of kids given the opportunity to meet a captured wild animal. Sargon towered nearly two feet taller than the men, and his lengthy fingers could've encircled their necks with ease.

One of the guys stepped to the microphone and stuttered, "He's definitely legit." He shook his head with a bewildered expression, and the two hopped off the stage.

Sargon returned to the podium. "I'm sure you have more questions. The purpose of today, however, is to mark the first occasion when my kind have officially contacted your people. This is only the beginning of what we hope to be a new and cooperative relationship. My father, Chief Nekronok of Craventhrall, is eager to forge an alliance of trust with you, our new friends. We have much to offer you. In turn, you may have some things of benefit to us. We look forward to a favorable and healthy relationship."

"How many of you Yetis are there?" a voice interjected. "Where are you guys hiding?"

A look of annoyance clouded Sargon's ape-like face. He probably had expected to be revered like royalty rather than having to explain and prove himself.

Welcome to the world of skeptics, creep.

"I'm told we are on a limited schedule. These questions will be answered in time." He grasped the podium with both hands and suddenly gave me a hard stare. I took an instinctive step back, stepping on Brady's shoe. "In fact, allow me to introduce you to someone who has visited the land where I come from and has agreed to be a liaison between your people and my own."

No, no, no, no!

"Sadie Larcen is a young woman who will make a great ambassador on behalf of Craventhrall." He gestured to me. "Sadie, please say hello so your fellow Topsiders can put a face to your name."

The stage began to tilt and swirl. Panic ricocheted through my chest. I pressed a hand to my forehead and breathed deeply, hoping to prevent myself from passing out on camera. Mom caught my eye, her face a reflection of every shred of dread that electrified my body. With another steadying breath, I stepped forward, but Dad put his hand on my arm.

"No, Sadie—you don't have to go up there." Dad looked at Sargon on the stage and yelled, "You can't force her to do this. None of us are going to cooperate with you."

Sargon gave a low, amused chuckle. "Pardon the momentary disagreement, friends." He addressed me in a syrupy voice. "Sadie, I know it's been difficult for you to come around to our point of view, much like our skeptical friends gathered here. Let me ease your mind by delivering a message to you from your brother Brock, who visited Craventhrall recently. He sends his love and plans to stay with us for some time."

There was no missing Sargon's implied threat. The Trolls had my autistic brother in their clutches to ensure my cooperation. I was definitely going to puke. But first I had to get myself together and play nice for Brock's sake.

My dad still held my arm. I shook him off and said into his ear, "Let me try to keep the peace for the moment, Dad. We'll figure it out." I'm sure I sounded much more confident than I felt. With unsteady movements, I pushed through the few people who stood in front of me and, not seeing any nearby steps, climbed onto the stage. Mom had lost her professional demeanor and leaned over, elbows on knees, with her fingers pressed to her temples. A tear trickled beside her nose.

Sargon stepped back and gestured to the podium like Mr. Manners. I glared with every ounce of spite I could muster and went to the mic. The sea of faces and cameras paralyzed me. They were star-struck by what they were witnessing, which wasn't helping our cause. How could I feign cooperation enough to appease the Trolls so they wouldn't hurt my brother? How had everything unraveled to such depths of despair *again*?

I steadied myself by looking at my family. Their eyes were round and anxious, heads subtly nodding. My shaking hand encircled the mic and tipped it closer. "Hello." I swallowed hard, and my nervous gulp was picked up by the microphone for all to hear. My face grew warm, giving the cameras something to catch as well. "I'm Amy Larcen's daughter, Sadie. It, uh, it's true. I've been to Craventhrall. I've met many Tro— Yetis." I didn't want to reveal their real name yet. "There's quite a big world to explore and explain. I'm not sure why, but they want me to be some sort of ambassador between our world and theirs. I don't completely understand what they want me to do, but *for now* I will do it."

I stepped back, not wanting to give the impression that I'd take questions from the audience. My gaze flitted over to the courthouse, and I froze. A large, winged Gargoyle had just touched down on the top of the center dome.

CHAPTER TWELVE

BRADY FOLLOWED HIS SISTER'S STARTLED GAZE to the other side of the street. Between Sadie's forced speech and the news about Brock, he didn't think he could get any more riled up. But the sight of the oversized Gargoyle perched on the dome, one hand steadied on the flagpole, revved his pulse into overdrive. The big thug hadn't bothered to take on the appearance of stone. And while Brady watched, the other two imps morphed from grey statues into chalky black demons.

Sadie was suddenly beside him. He heard Mr. Delaney droning on about a Leprechaun but tuned out the ridiculous man. His focus narrowed to the only three things that mattered. The Trolls had Brock. Three Gargoyles lurked nearby. Tiny Trees of Life were growing across the street from his house. Mr. Delaney could continue with his PR charade, but Brady needed to know what was *really* going on.

"What do you think we should do?" Sadie practically shouted into his ear as the crowd's excitement swelled.

"I don't know," he shouted back. Brady fought a torrent of thoughts that clamored for his attention. None of them made sense. All were tainted with anger and, if he was being honest, a temptation to commit murder.

The crowd fell into a hush when Mr. Delaney retrieved a cage from the trailer. Brady lowered his voice. "This is bad. Things are getting too far out of control with this stupid press conference."

Dad reached a hand to Sadie's shoulder. "You handled that beautifully, honey."

Brady could see tears puddling along his sister's lashes.

"What do we do about Brock?" she asked.

"We'll get to the bottom of it as soon as this ridiculous stunt is over." Dad hooked his thumb toward the stage, where a spiteful Leprechaun rattled the bars of his cage.

And then disappeared.

Brady grimaced at the slack-jawed amazement on people's faces as many of them gasped. Then the crowd became animated again. Brady heard some complaining that the Leprechaun must be a fake or an illusion, while others demanded that Mr. Delaney "do that trick again."

Uncle Brent scooted close and put an arm around Sadie's shoulders. He raised his voice over the clamor so that even Brady could hear. "That was tough. You handled it well."

Sadie blinked, and a tear cascaded down her cheek. "Are you going to get involved now, or are you happy to just let me handle it, since I'm doing it so well?" Her voice was loud and bitter.

Zing! Brady thought. *Good one, sis.* His uncle flinched, and Brady realized he didn't feel the least bit sorry for the guy.

"Guess I deserved that." Uncle Brent stuffed his hands in his front pockets and glanced away. The crowd grew quiet again as they watched Delaney return the cage to the trailer. The Leprechaun had not reappeared for them. "Trust me, girl, I'm all in. This is going to be a group effort."

"It's been one all summer long." Brady heard the sarcasm and hurt in Sadie's voice. Uncle B must have too—he stepped back to where Sophie stood gasping as Mr. Delaney returned to the podium with another cage.

Part of Brady's brain knew he should care which of his small friends from folklore were being held captive, but his brother's own captivity filled the bulk of his thoughts. The rest of his grey matter was focused on the three Gargoyles that watched the events from the top of the courthouse. He stepped closer to Sadie and nudged her with his elbow, gesturing with his eyes to the dome.

"I think the big one might be Malagruel," Sadie said into his ear. "Looks like him from here, but I didn't see if his tail was missing."

"Yeah, might be." Brady tensed when he saw the two smaller Gargoyles backing away from the peak. "I think they're on the move."

"We should follow them. At least the one that you think is Ophidian. He can't fly, right?"

"No. I think that's why they call him a worm." Brady grabbed Sadie's wrist, pulling her behind him. Two strides later he stopped abruptly, and she plowed into his back. "Look, he's scaling down the wall. How is that possible? Come on!"

Brady led his sister through the transfixed spectators. They had nearly reached the sidewalk when Brady heard his father's voice.

"Hey! Where are you two headed?" Dad grabbed Sadie's other hand and anchored them in place, scowling as he glanced from Sadie to Brady. "Mom should be up soon. You need to stay with us."

Brady considered telling his dad about the Gargoyles, but what if he didn't let them investigate due to the danger? If that happened it would be infinite torture for Brady to lose track of the Gargoyles, not to mention a possible hazard to the citizens of Portland. It was his duty to quietly check on things with Sadie's help. If there was a problem, they could come back and alert his parents. Why cause a scene right before his mom had to face this crowd?

Brady tried to arrange his features into a confident, trustworthy expression. "We'll be back in a few. There's something we really need to look into. Trust me."

Dad studied their faces. "Okay." He nodded. "After everything you overcame this summer, I do—I trust you." He looked back to the stage. "But you'd better show up soon. Mom needs to see all of us supporting her."

"Yes, sir." Brady nodded.

Dad retreated and the two dodged traffic, heading around to the north side of the courthouse.

"Shoot!" Brady pulled up short. "Stopping to explain things to Dad meant we lost sight of that worm. Wonder which way he went."

"Well, it's broad daylight. He's not exactly going to blend in." Sadie pointed to the backside of the courthouse. "Let's keep our eye on the shadows close to the building and follow it all the way around. Maybe we'll spot him."

They fell into a slow trot, keeping their eye on the contours of the building and shrubbery. After two right hand turns, they approached the opposite corner from where they began, with the crowded square situated across the street. They slowed beneath the shade of a large tree to take one last look.

"*Psst.*"

Brady's eyes scoured the blades of grass as he wondered where the sound originated. It sounded like the hissing of a giant snake, and he held no affection for anything with a forked tongue after this summer's escapades.

"Did you hear something?" Sadie craned her neck to either side.

"Larcens! Up here," a voice called from above.

Brady squinted into the branches of the tree. Halfway up, one limb quivered beneath the weight of...someone. The shadows and sunlight played a game of illusion. Brady stumble-stepped back, trying to get a better view. More movement from one limb to the next meant whoever lurked up there was moving closer.

"Can you see me?" the voice asked.

Then, suddenly, Brady could. The shadows finally revealed what was easily hidden in the darkness. A charcoal figure came into view, leaning its angular face in their direction.

The Gargoyle had found *them*. Except it wasn't Ophidian, the one Brady and Sadie had been seeking. Ophidian had a snub-nosed, snake-shaped head that you couldn't mistake, even from a distance. He resembled a man-sized gecko, slit nostrils and all. This Gargoyle looked much more like a human. With the exception of five nodular bumps that made up the brute's brow bone, he could've been a young man one would pass on the street—if people on the streets wore leathery black unitards, which was entirely possible in Portland. Except his black unitard was actually his skin. The char-black hide all but disappeared into the shadows. Like Ophidian, his golden eyes were reflective in a nocturnal animal kind of way.

Brady placed a protective arm in front of his sister. No way would he let this thug lay a finger on her.

"Listen to me." The Gargoyle hopped to a lower branch. "You want to help your brother, right? Meet me at Powell's Books in a half an hour. Pearl Room, mathematics section."

"Yeah, right. Like we're going to trust you." This creature might have been less creepy than Ophidian, but he was still on the enemy's side. "Want to give me your Starbucks order so I can swing by and pick it up on the way?"

The Gargoyle gave Brady an intense look which caused the nodules on his head to shift around peculiarly. "I understand your reluctance. There's absolutely nothing I can say to make up for how either of you were treated in our world. The only assurance I can offer is that we aren't *all* devoid of a conscience. At least I'm not. If you'll hear me out, I might convince you of this. Powell's books. Pearl Room. Thirty minutes."

Before Brady could sputter a "forget it," the creature dropped out of the tree. The instant he touched the ground, he morphed into the scenery. Like a chameleon, his skin rippled effortlessly from black to tree-bark brown to grassy green. If Brady hadn't known to watch the shimmering impressions that skimmed across the lawn, refracted briefly on the side-walk, and melded into the crowd, he never would've guessed anything was there.

Brady remembered how Sadie had described the Gargoyles' shapeshifting abilities on her last journey to the Tethered World. Malagruel, who proclaimed himself the prince of these beasts, had taken on the form of their father, pretending to nurse Sadie back to health. It had been a convincing and con-fusing act as he tried to persuade Sadie to switch her allegiance.

But this was Brady's first experience with shapeshifting. He gaped after the Gargoyle, then turned to Sadie. "That was kind of cool."

"Whatever." Sadie pulled her gaze from the crowd and gave Brady a panicked look. "What should we do? I don't trust him."

Brady took a deep breath, wishing the right answer could tap him on the shoulder so he would know for sure. "He seemed sincere. I know he might be lying, but we have to start somewhere to save Brock. I mean, Powell's is a very public place. It's not like he wants us to meet him in a deserted alley or something."

Sadie seemed to consider this while she studied him. Then she cocked her head. "Well, I wouldn't do it by myself. But there are two of us, so I think we can take him if we have to." She glanced toward the podium, where she could hear her mother speaking—and getting booed. "Do we tell Dad?"

Brady inhaled through his teeth, considering his dad's re-action to a secret meeting with a Gargoyle. He'd hate it. He'd probably think it was a trap. And he might be right. But if this was a chance to rescue Brock, Brady *had* to try.

"Uh...I don't think so. Let's plan on asking for forgiveness rather than permission."

CHAPTER THIRTEEN

I FELT HORRIBLE FOR MOM. THE onlookers wanted none of what she was trying to sell, like she was some annoying telemarketer. They quite preferred anything Mr. Delaney could dangle before them, like a bunch of greedy kids clamoring for Santa Claus.

Brady and I stopped by for a courtesy appearance. Though I argued about it at first, I decided to go along with keeping our plans under the radar. Things were falling apart for Mom, which meant our escapades wouldn't be welcomed, let alone seriously considered. And how could we pass by a possible opportunity to save Brock? It felt worth the risk and possible repercussions.

We had little time to spare and several blocks to walk in half an hour. But to keep our parental units from freaking out, we went back to find Dad, Uncle B, and Sophie still standing near the front of the stage. We watched as Mom floundered with her notes. In the brief silence, someone shouted, "Bring back Bigfoot!" Others picked up the mantra and made a chant out of it, drowning out anything she hoped to say. Mom bit her lip and her chest heaved—a sign that meant her emotions were right under the surface and ready to leak out of her eyes at any moment.

With a jolt, I noticed Sophie slipping around the backside of the stage where the trailer was parked. "Dad!" I pounded on his arm in a panic, then pointed. "Sophie is going to the horse trailer."

With a groan, Dad dashed between bodies and looped around the stage. A security guard stood nearby, but he faced the podium, watching the proceedings rather than focusing on the cargo behind him. No doubt Sophie saw this as the perfect opportunity to release the captives from the Tethered World.

Brady elbowed me. "We've gotta go." He stepped over to Uncle Brent. "Hey, since this is nearly over, Sadie and I are going to head over to Powell's. If you could pick us up there, that'd be great." He pulled me into the all-encompassing crowd before Uncle Brent could protest.

I turned and hollered over the unhappy grumblings directed at my mother, "Text me and tell me which door you want to pick us up at."

We jostled through the bystanders whose numbers appeared to have grown as the buzz traveled over the airwaves and the social media highway. People pressed in and made it difficult for us to find our way out. We ascended the steps by Starbucks and, like a lab rat trained to follow the scent of cheese, I felt myself salivate over the smell of coffee that wafted from inside. Too bad that Gargoyle didn't give us his order so we could stop by.

We thrashed our way through a steady stream of people who all seemed to be heading in the opposite direction. It reminded me of elementary field trips to the fish hatchery, watching salmon fight their way upstream to spawn. I found a new appreciation for the feisty fish.

My ankle decided to remind me that I shouldn't be trying to swim upstream or power walk through Portland. A twinge of pain shot through the side of my foot with each step, and I wondered if salmon registered pain as they smacked the water and rocks to forge ahead to their breeding grounds. I had a sudden urge for smoked salmon, which seemed kind of cruel in the middle of my commiserating with them.

Our destination loomed into view. The red-and-white-striped marquee proclaiming *Powell's Books, Used & New Books* triggered a second lab rat-wants-cheese moment. This was one of my favorite places to spend an afternoon, a store my parents had visited as children, and where I imagined my future novels sitting in stunning array on the local authors table. Any Gargoyle that wanted to lurk around its hallowed shelves couldn't be all bad.

"What section did he say?" Brady opened the front door and let me pass. "This place gets me completely turned around. Too many stairways and color coded names—it's like some living, breathing organism."

"He said the Pearl Room." I took the lead, heading for a set of stairs. The mingling scent of old building and new books rejuvenated my sagging attitude. "I know where it is."

"Of course you do. And what kind of color is pearl? It's not even a color, it's a piece of jewelry."

I ignored him, concentrating on climbing the stairs with attention to my aching ankle. Though I loved the familiar creak and groan of the well-worn wood beneath my feet, I stopped after a few steps and rotated my ankle. "Let's take the elevator instead. The Pearl Room is on the third floor, and my ankle is complaining."

We detoured to the elevators. Brady jabbed the Up button multiple times. The easy conversations and milling noise of customers contrasted with my internal anxiety and Brady's tapping, impatient foot.

"Maybe I should give you a piggyback ride. This is taking forever." He reached for the button again when the elevator doors hissed open.

I stepped inside and punched the third-floor button. An elderly couple sporting silver hair and too much polyester called for us to hold the elevator. Brady stretched a palm to the doorway and threw me a restless look. Once the doors shut, the man pressed the button for the second floor.

My brother eyed the buttons. "Four floors is a ridiculous amount of books," he grumbled quietly into my ear. "Who reads this much?"

He only wanted to goad me, so I let it go. As much as I loved literature, he tried to avoid it, preferring to watch the movie whenever that option was available.

At the second floor, home to the Red and Purple rooms, the couple exited. A slouchy teenage boy with his nose glued to his phone screen sauntered inside and poked the first-floor button, apparently unconcerned that the elevator was headed up. Judging by his Humpty Dumpty shape, taking the stairs wasn't his habit.

When the doors slid open at the Pearl Room level, only one customer browsed the shelves. The woman in overalls didn't bother to glance our way. I guessed the less-popular nature of the books in this room was a plus for clandestine meetings with chameleon Gargoyles. I couldn't help but slow my pace and cast a longing glance at the doorway to Powell's collection of rare books, which resided up here. That quarantined section was the reason I knew where the Pearl Room was located. Many times I'd entered the climate-controlled space and gazed at the changing assortment of first editions.

I sank onto the nearest bench, happy to get off my ankle.

"If I ever get a book published, you'd better come here and buy my book," I told Brady. "Buy all of them for all your friends. Start a book club." I chuckled at the absurd visual.

Brady sat beside me. "Nah, I'll just wait for the movie."

I rolled my eyes. "Well, I guess we'll have to sit here and wait for something to—"

"*Ahem.*" Someone cleared their throat but in the opposite direction from the lone customer. The woman in overalls turned and looked our way, as if we had made the sound.

Brady faked a cough behind his fist, playing along with the awkward moment.

I glanced around, hoping to look nonchalant. To my right, the mathematics section came to an end. A row of tall windows drenched a narrow hallway with sunlight that reflected off the white walls, making it hard to see without squinting. A velvet rope with an Employees Only sign blocked customer access to the corridor. At the opposite end, maybe thirty feet away, stood a door with matching signage. I blinked into the bright light and watched the Gargoyle materialize in front of the door, then disappear as his skin morphed into an imitation of the cream-colored metal.

After a little jump of surprise, I patted Brady on the leg and nodded in the Gargoyle's direction. We walked to the velvet rope. The other customer cast us a sidelong glance, and I felt about as subtle as a naked shoplifter. When she reached for another book, we ducked beneath the rope and walked casually down the passage and out of her sight. *Now you see us, now you don't.*

The closer we came to the door, the more the sunlight played against the contours of the Gargoyle's camouflage. It warped my perspective of the door as I noticed his outline shifting from one foot to another. It created an unsettling effect on my senses. And if the creature had ill intentions, he had chosen an ideal, remote spot for carrying them out. My palms felt clammy, and my nerves buzzed into high-alert mode.

"I'm going to remain concealed." The voice came from a few feet away.

"I'd prefer you show yourself," Brady said, keeping his voice low and even. "We don't trust you."

The Gargoyle's face and hands came into view, fading at the neck and forearms. The result was disconcerting—much worse than looking at him whole. "Better?" he asked.

"Fine." Brady gave a single nod. "Get on with it. We don't

have much time."

"Thank you for meeting me." He extended a floating hand. "I'm Tassitus."

My brother flicked his gaze at the hand. "Forget it. We're not friends and we don't plan on becoming friends. What do you want?"

The Gargoyle's face flashed with what I thought was disappointment. His almost human features made me oddly sympathetic toward him. I found myself imagining him with a head full of hair and a face free from those five bumps. He wasn't a bad looking guy with my mental makeover.

"Look, I understand your mistrust," Tassitus said, "and believe me, I'm putting myself at risk by making contact. I—I'm one of Malagruel's worms." His amber eyes looked at the linoleum, as if he felt ashamed to admit it. "But I haven't acquired a taste for his strain of nastiness. Still—"

"Get to the point." My brother spat out each word, his voice still low.

"I'm trying to give you some small reason to trust me. My point is," Tassitus looked from me to Brady, "I know where your brother is being held. He was captured only yesterday. By Malagruel, but with the blessing of the Trolls."

Footsteps sounded behind us. "Hey, I don't think you guys are supposed to be back there."

Brady and I whipped around to find Ms. Overalls standing in front of the velvet rope. Her lips pressed into a straight, disapproving scowl as if we had trespassed into her personal space.

Brady recovered quickly, looking her square in the eye. "Actually, our dad works here. We're surprising him for dinner." He was so convincing, I wanted to believe him.

She cocked her head. "Oh really?" The slanting sunshine glinted on a sparse, silvery mustache sprouting beneath her nose. I felt my lips contort into the same disdainful likeness as hers.

I threw in my own eager nod. "Yeah, he works in this back room. We can see him through the little window in the door. I can point him out to you if you want."

"No, because—" she pointed at the sign on the rope, "I'm not allowed back there. I obey the rules." The haughty look she gave us almost made me laugh. Thankfully, she turned with a huff and left.

"Close one," whispered Brady.

We turned back to the Gargoyle, who had defaulted to full camouflage mode. His face and hands mutated to visible. "Your brother has been placed in temporary custody among the Dark Dwarves, a compromise because Malagruel and Nekronok couldn't agree on who should keep him. But I'm trained to spy and listen." He looked down at his chameleon body. "This ability comes in handy. I've overheard the Trolls' plans to move King Brock to a high-security cell without Malagruel's knowledge. I don't know where your brother will be if that happens. But right now I can get you pretty close—close enough to find him—but we'll need to leave immediately. There's no telling when the Trolls may show up, especially since Malagruel has come topside today to spy on Joseph Marshall and hunt for the key to the sword."

My stomach lurched. I immediately crossed my arms, shielding my heirloom ring from the Gargoyle's view.

Brady glanced at me uneasily and shifted his weight. "What possible reason do you have for looking out for my brother's interests?"

"I can offer you no reason, if you are set on seeing me only from the outside. Like you, I cannot help who I am by birth. But I have my own ideas about right and wrong, and it places me at odds with my master." He wrung his hands and shifted from one foot to another. "I also know what it means to have a sibling who is different. The only reason I applied for a position in Malagruel's employ was to keep my sister alive. She is what they call simpleminded. In exchange for her protection, I was brought into service with Malagruel. Being a worm comes with certain clout."

I was too stunned to speak. Brady must've felt the same since, like me, he only stood there.

Tassitus' eyes glimmered with a hint of hope. "It's my understanding that your brother has some sort of mental or social challenge as well. Trust me, he won't last long in the horrors of a dungeon. Not with Malagruel and not with Nekronok."

"Take me to him." Brady's voice was so soft I thought maybe I'd imagined it. "Or do we need to make arrangements to meet up later?"

"We can leave right away."

I grabbed Brady's arm. "I'm coming too."

"No." He shook his head. "It would be too terrifying for Mom and Dad. They wouldn't know what happened to either one of us. You'll need to soften the blow. Tell them I'm going to help

Brock."

I nodded and gave him an impulsive hug. Deep down, I knew this decision would be costly—because every trip below had been costly. For all of us. But it had to be done.

Brock was in serious danger. Which meant the Flaming Sword of Cherubythe was still a target on the bad guys' radar. Which automatically endangered the Tree of Life.

I didn't know which of these things was worse. But I knew which one was most precious.

CHAPTER FOURTEEN

THE GARGOYLE REACHED FOR SOMETHING ON the window ledge beside him. "Slip this on and try to look official."

Brady glanced at the item. A Powell's Books employee badge on a lanyard. A raven-haired man with facial hair looked back at him from the laminated badge. *Trevor Malinak*, it read. "But I'm blond."

"It's not like he had time to design your fake badge," Sadie scolded. "I'm sure he grabbed whatever he could."

"Precisely." Tassitus held it up. "Now take it."

Brady grabbed the badge by the corner, wary of brushing against the Gargoyle.

Sadie's phone bleeped, and she dug it out of her pocket. "It's Uncle Brent. He'll be here in five minutes."

"We'll be gone by then." Tassitus gave Brady a hard look, his eyes narrow. "You ready?"

Brady gave a somber nod, then hugged his sister again. "I hope we're together again soon, sis. Pray I'm not too late to help Brock."

She nodded against his shoulder.

He pulled away, and she swiped at a tear. Her eyes reflected the same uncertain fear that swelled against his chest.

Tassitus touched Brady's arm. "We'd better leave. And please understand that I must stay completely concealed while we're in the building. I'll place a hand on you to guide you."

Brady felt an instantaneous wave of irritation. "You try anything stupid and you'll regret it." He secretly doubted his ability to take on a creature with near-invisible properties, but he'd fight tooth and nail trying.

The Gargoyle didn't look the least bit threatened, but he nodded. "Understood. Let's head for the elevator."

Sadie trotted to the velvet rope and peeked into the room.

"No customers in sight." She glanced at her phone. "And I should go too." She gave Brady a long look, as if trying to memorize him. With a soft cry, she turned and hurried away.

Brady clenched and unclenched his sweaty hands. He felt utterly alone and vulnerable the instant Sadie left his sight. It had all happened so fast. He didn't feel prepared for what he was about to face—whatever that might be.

Pressure on his arm alerted him to Tassitus' proximity. Brady followed the pulling sensation to the elevator next to the rare book room. His invisible guide must have poked the call button, because the small circle of light suddenly glowed. In under a minute, the two stainless steel doors slid open and spat out three college kids sporting various versions of Oregon Ducks collegiate wear.

Brady placed a protective hand over Trevor Malinak's badge and flipped it over. He felt far less conspicuous. Then, by his own freewill, he stepped into the deserted elevator with a Gargoyle. And although it might rank as the dumbest decision he'd ever made, Brady didn't see another option.

"Press the lower level button," Tassitus instructed.

Brady eyed the selections and found LL with an engraved plate below it reading Restricted. Employees Only. He pressed it. After a couple of stops for hitchhiking customers, the digital readout over the door read LL. The doors opened onto a concrete floor leading straight to a set of steel doors with a badge reader attached to the wall. Brady stepped into the vacant space and willed his hand and heart to steady themselves. He swiped the coded strip on the badge through the slot of the reader, wondering what sort of charges Powell's would slap him with if he was caught.

They'll probably throw the book at me. Brady snickered to himself.

"Act like you own the place," the Gargoyle's voice whispered as they walked through the doors.

Brady squared his shoulders and hoped he looked less like a deer caught in the headlights than he felt. They'd stepped into a wide hallway flanked with lockers on the left and restrooms on the right. Music thumped from a spacious lounge at the other end. Two girls huddled at a table, one a blonde and one with hair all the colors of the rainbow. They were glued to their phones and ignoring their lunch. The blonde looked up as Brady approached. She nudged her rainbow-haired friend, who quickly sized Brady up.

Brady gave a casual nod. "Hey."

"You new?" The blonde asked.

"Yeah, first day." *Please, God, let me be convincing.* He gave himself a mental slap. Should he be praying about his lying skills?

"I'm Hallie." The girl stood and stuck her hand out. "And this is Jazz."

Rainbow girl appeared bothered by the interruption to her social media forays. She stuck her hand out but didn't stand. "Hi."

"Good to meet you both." Brady shook their hands. "I'm gonna—"

"What's your name?" Hallie sipped her iced coffee. Jazz had returned to the world inside her phone.

"Brrr-o. I mean, it's actually Trevor, but everyone calls me Bro." He mentally bashed his head against the table top.

"Are you, like, a surfer or something? Sounds like a surfer name."

Brady chuckled nervously, aware of the urgent press of a hand on his spine. What did the Gargoyle expect him to do? Brush the girls off? "Nah. Nothing that cool." Well, why not something cool? "I—I only skateboard." At least that was truthful. *Skateboard like an unsteady idiot,* he thought.

"Sweet. Hey, we have another Trevor who works here. Have you met him?" Hallie smiled and sat back down.

"Yeah, I heard that." Brady shrugged. "All the more reason to go by a nickname, right?"

"Right." She picked up her phone but continued to look at Brady, lifting one eyebrow flirtatiously. "Hope to see ya around."

"Sure." He felt his face grow warm. "Me too."

He resisted the urge to hurry away and strolled past their table, as the pressure on his back directed him into a narrow hallway.

Behind him he heard Hallie say, "Sweet. Some guy brought Bigfoot to Pioneer Square. Told ya we should've eaten lunch over there today."

I took my time maneuvering through the store to the exit. Since going down the stairs didn't strain my ankle like going up, I plodded downward. Maybe if I was late they would circle around the block and give me a few more minutes to figure out how to explain Brady's absence. The dread of the whole day, topped off by this sudden need to return to the Tethered World, made my head pound.

I descended the last set of stairs and spied the woman in overalls talking to a store employee. Fortunately, she didn't see me, but she jabbed her finger at the staircase, and I knew precisely what she was pointing out. I made an about-face and zig-zagged through the orange level to the other set of stairs. At least the maze of books and people made for an easy escape.

Within a few minutes, I managed a complicated circuit to the correct exit. Uncle Brent's Suburban waited at the curb. Oh, well. Maybe it would be best to use the fast and furious approach, like pulling off a bandage. I left the bookstore and dragged my reluctant feet to the passenger door. Mom, Dad, Uncle Brent, and Sophie waited inside. My sister hopped out to give me space to climb past her seat into the back.

"Where's Brady?" She looked from me to the store.

"He's not coming." I dared not make eye contact with anyone for fear of bursting into tears.

"What do you mean?" Mom scoffed as I got in. "We're not going to leave him here."

"I'll explain." I plopped into the rear seat.

"Sadie, go back inside and find your brother." Mom pulled her phone out of her purse. "I'm texting him and telling him to get his butt down here now."

"That's not going to work. Trust me." I clicked my seatbelt in place. "He's not in the building."

"Good grief." Mom looked back at me and glowered. "Don't be so cryptic. It's been a long day. Spit it out."

There was no way that I knew to soften the blow, so I didn't bother trying. "Brady left to rescue Brock. He's headed to the Tethered World right now."

CHAPTER FIFTEEN

I GAVE THE FAMILY A RUNDOWN of our expedition from Pioneer Square to Powell's Books and everything the Gargoyle had told us. Of course, I got a lecture of epic proportions from my parents, which was no surprise. After that it was a silent, tense ride home. Uncle Brent didn't even attempt his usual lame chitchat.

It looked like I had a good chance of being grounded for life, beginning the moment Brady and Brock were safe. And Brady, of course, would be equally sentenced as my accomplice. Since solitary confinement in my room would prevent further life-threatening circumstances from sprouting up, it didn't sound half bad.

Uncle Brent turned into our neighborhood. "I'll drop you guys off and bring Nate and Nicole over later. That'll give everyone a chance to...decompress."

No one replied.

He pulled into the driveway, and we shuffled out. Only Sophie bothered to wave goodbye.

Mom stormed to the front door ahead of us, but Dad had the key. He said, "Ahem," and jingled the keyring. Mom stepped aside. Before unlocking the door, Dad turned and addressed us. "It's been a difficult day for all of us. But we can't allow the enemy to pull our family apart."

"I believe our kids have had as much of a hand in things today as our enemies." Mom's face contorted bitterly, glaring me down.

"And that, my dear, is false." He stepped beside me, placing his hand on my back. "Sadie and Brady may have made some decisions we disagree with initially, but after thinking through everything Sadie shared, I'm inclined to agree with what they did. It *is* Brock's life that's in peril, after all."

Mom dropped her briefcase and purse and covered her face, crumpling against the nearby wall for support. Her cries came out like desperate stabs of pain. I stepped back, trying to figure out what the sudden sound meant. Dad's arms went around her, and he rested his cheek on top of her head.

I grabbed Sophie's arm. "Let's give Mom some space."

We stepped into the grass, but Mom's hand shot out. "No!" She pulled away from Dad enough to look at us. "It's okay. I— I'm gonna be okay. You've done nothing to deserve what I said. Forgive me, girls."

Dad shifted away but kept an arm around her shoulder.

"I'm sorry, Liam." She leaned into his chest. "What Brady did was probably the right thing, but it knocked the wind out of me. After the disaster at the Square today, not to mention a summer of devastating blows to our family, I kind of feel like I can't take it another minute."

"I know. It feels that way to me too." He picked up Mom's briefcase and jingled the keys again. "We'll figure out what we need to do. Let's get inside and regroup."

Mom nodded. "I'm thinking Chinese for dinner."

Dad unlocked the door and pushed it open. "Perfect. We've got a take-out menu in the junk drawer."

My ankle was killing me, so I slipped out of my shoes as I walked through the foyer. Mom stuttered to a stop in the kitchen, a high-pitched yelp escaping her lips. The rest of us screeched to a halt behind her and followed her wide-eyed stare. Two Gnomes stood in the family room, their tiny frames barely as tall as the couch cushions. It only took a second for all of us to recover, then we rushed through the kitchen to greet our tiny friends.

Muscle and Mighty, two brothers and warriors who had protected us on our last two excursions, removed their hats and bowed deeply.

"Greetings, Larcens." Muscle replaced his hat first and smiled up at our family. He still wore the goatee I remembered from our recent visit, which helped me tell the two brothers apart. I couldn't suppress a grin at the sound of his familiar voice, deep yet somewhat frog-like coming from his little vocal chords.

Sophie crouched down in front of them. "What are you doing here? How did you get in our house? This is so cool." She offered each of them a fist-bump. The rest of us took seats on the couch and love seat near where they stood.

"We discovered perfectly fitted Gnome-sized doors inset within the larger ones." Mighty gestured to the door that led from our den into the garage. "They were not locked, so we let ourselves in. We prefer not to be out and about topside while there's daylight, you know."

Mom stood up again. "You're welcome anytime, of course. Let me get you guys a couple of chairs. Don't say anything important while I'm gone."

She trotted out of the family room and up the stairs. At least the Gnomes had improved her grumpy mood.

"You came in through our doggy doors. Guess it's good we forgot to latch them." Dad nodded toward the hinged flap that led into the garage. Another one, exactly like it, led from the garage to the side yard. "Thanks to the previous owners and their big husky, those doors are quite sizable."

"Yes. And we enjoyed getting acquainted with your four-legged friends. They followed us into the house." Muscle fingered his coffee-colored goatee. "They eventually lost interest and headed back outside."

"I can't believe they didn't try to use you as a chew toy." I shifted so I could rest my ankle on the coffee table. "Some guard dogs they are."

Mom returned with two small plastic chairs from Nate's room. She set them down behind the Gnomes.

"This is most unusual." Muscle eyed the chairs in wonder. "Why do you have furniture in such a size?"

"Our youngest son is about your size." Mom bit back a grin, and I knew she was choosing her words carefully to be polite. Nate had six inches and about ten chubby toddler pounds on these two.

The Gnomes situated themselves, looking pleased. Mom sat beside me on the love seat.

"Your dogs barked and tried to chase us," Mighty continued, "but since Gnomes can interface with animals, it did not take us long to calm them down."

"Like you guys did with the snakes." Sophie clasped her hands together.

Mighty nodded. "Precisely."

Dad leaned forward, resting his elbows on his knees. "I know you two didn't trek here to talk about animals. What can we do for you?"

The Gnomes took on pained expressions. I reached for my little book charm and zipped it along the chain around my neck. Though I had a good idea why they'd come, there was no avoiding the dread that accompanied such serious discussions.

Muscle sighed. "Unfortunately, we did not come with good tidings."

"We already heard about Brock," Sophie volunteered. "Brady's on his way to save him."

Muscle and Mighty blinked at us and then one another, clearly surprised.

"Sophie." Dad fixed her with a serious look. "Let them speak."

Muscle removed his conical hat and scrubbed his fingers through his wavy hair. Dark circles shadowed his eyes. "This happened only yesterday. How is it that you've heard the news?"

Dad waved his question off. "It's a long story. Go ahead and tell us yours first."

"Certainly." Muscle stood, which didn't make him much taller than when he was seated. "You see, Queen Judith has not been well. She suffered a stroke three weeks ago, which left her unable to walk."

"Oh, no." Mom pressed a hand to her mouth. "That's terrible."

"Truly." Muscle nodded. "This unfortunate development has left Brock to attend official functions without her. Yesterday, Brock visited Forest Ridge to speak at a memorial service. A statue was erected to honor those we lost during the siege that took place during your last visit. The one in which the Gargoyles used dragon fire to burn the ridge above Vituvia."

I nodded, remembering. Brady had been kidnapped in the chaos of the fire, though Brock was the intended target. The fallout had been ugly for Brady and left several of the Gnomes dead. So senseless. All of it. A hollow ache settled in my chest at the memory.

Muscle looked at his brother, then back at us. "Brock was to say a few words to honor and comfort the families of the fallen soldiers. In the middle of his speech, while he stood on the ridge, a Gargoyle swept down from the cover of a nearby tree and snatched the high king, carrying him away."

Mom dropped her head into her hands. Dad leaned back against the couch and smacked a palm over his mouth. I hugged Mom's shoulders and tried to push the visual replay out of my consciousness. I was so afraid for Brock I felt sick.

"So he's with the Gargoyles?" Fearless Sophie looked ready to grab the car keys and go after our brother, if it were that simple. "Sadie heard he was with the Dark Dwarves."

Mighty and Muscle looked startled by the news.

I thought I'd better jump in and explain. "We were in downtown Portland today because our arch enemy, Mr. Delaney, planned to introduce Bigfoot to the world..." I gave a brief overview of the situation—which included Brady discovering the tunnel—then launched into the press conference and our sighting of the Gargoyle. I finished off with the bizarre meeting with Tassitus at Powell's.

"Do you know anything about this Gargoyle, Tassitus?" Mom's fingers curled into fists on her lap. "Does any of this make sense?"

Mighty shook his head. "I am unfamiliar with that name. But we'd had no dealings with the Gargoyles until your last visit. I would find it unimaginable to trust one, however. Of course, I said that about Trolls in the past and then along came Chebar. We must place our trust in the Maker instead and pray this Gargoyle is sincere."

"Yes." Muscle smacked his palm against the plastic armrest of his tiny chair. "Indeed, we must. It will make a rescue much easier if Brock has not yet been taken to the Eldritch. As soon as we return, we shall dispatch special ops to survey the Dens of the Dark Dwarves."

"We'll come with you." Dad rubbed his palms together thoughtfully. "I'm not going to lose both of my sons to those monsters."

"I...I can't go." Mom's voice was soft but firm. She shook her head and a few more tears escaped. "It kills me to admit it, but things are unraveling at frightening speeds right here at home. Mr. Delaney exposed the Tethered World to the entire globe today. I must work on damage control as much as humanly possible."

I saw pride in Dad's eyes when he looked at Mom. "I agree. But don't despair, sweetheart. We'll divide and conquer, by God's grace."

Mom only nodded.

"I'm afraid there's more." Muscle bit his lower lip and laced his fingers together. "It has to do with the Tree of Life in the Garden Dome." He looked at Mighty, who nodded, encouraging Muscle to speak. Muscle's voice took on a sad but horrified edge. "It's unlike anything that's ever happened in the Tethered World." His gaze roamed across each of our faces. Dread etched his features and made my pulse quicken. "The Tree of Life is in danger of dying."

CHAPTER SIXTEEN

"IN DANGER?" I LOOKED FROM ONE Gnome to the other. "That's better than definitely dying, right?"

Mighty huffed a breath. "We're not sure if there's any difference. We are hopeful the damage can be reversed, but we've never encountered this problem before."

"To make it worse," Muscle said, raising an eyebrow, "the tree's condition is the result of a traitor in our midst."

"We've caught the traitor and placed him in custody." Mighty peered down his nose as if he could picture the culprit there in our den. "We haven't learned whether there are other accomplices, as he won't give up any information. And nothing we've tried has improved the condition of the tree."

Ollie nosed through the doggy door and came sniffing around the Gnomes.

"What did this traitor do?" Sophie patted her leg and called the little corgi over. Ollie jumped onto her lap.

"He hacked off large chunks of exposed roots." Mighty stood and paced between his chair and the coffee table while Ollie watched him, ears alert. "As you may know, the tree is behind a great wall that no one may breech. From the height of the viewing platforms, one may peek at the top-most branches stretching above the wall. The only other part that is exposed is a portion of the roots. Outside of the wall, where the guards have access, large roots twist between the rocks where the Flaming Sword of Cherubythe resides. Many of these roots have been removed."

I knew that wall. My broken ankle was a result of my fall off the top of it. I remembered the granite barrier, the mound of rocks, and the roots quite well. But I wasn't trying to climb the forbidden wall—I was trying to keep the Nephilim queen from doing so. She had lusted for the promise of perpetual life that a piece of fruit from the tree might give. Manipulating the Gnomes and myself, she pretended to be an ally to Vituvia but proved to be an enemy.

"I betcha a dragon tooth those plants Mr. Delaney is growing are from the Tree of Life," Sophie said with a glower. She looked dragon-like herself, and I half expected her to blast streams of fire from her nostrils.

"He said as much at the press conference." Mom rubbed her forehead like she wanted to erase all the bad news that had hit her between the eyes. "I've heard of people getting roots to sprout. But how do you know the tree is dying if you can't see it?"

Mighty and Muscle shared an odd glance, and Muscle nodded at his brother. Mighty clasped his hands behind his back and resumed his pacing.

"You see, there's one who lives within the garden. On the other side of the wall." He stopped and looked at us. "He's the Keeper of the Garden, and he's been taking care of it a long, long time. We call him the Dweller. He is both ancient and timeless. And he rarely interacts with the outside. With the exception of the annual Festival of the Sword, he keeps to himself."

"He stays in that garden, all by himself, every day?" Sophie's face was a picture of disbelief. "How boring."

"He's not one to complain." Muscle slid from his chair and stood beside Mighty. "All of his daily needs are met, and he has looked healthy and content on the few occasions I've seen him."

"How long is a long time?" I asked. "How old is this guy?"

"He's lived there since..." Muscle scratched at his goatee and looked uncomfortable. "Since the Maker moved our ancestors from the Garden of Eden to the Tethered World. Before the Great Flood."

I tried to comprehend the concept but failed. "What? That's impossible. Unless he's not human."

"He is quite human." Muscle nodded slowly.

My mind reeled through the impossible things that had rocked my world this summer. Had this person eaten from the Tree of Life? How else could he live forever? Or at least indefinitely.

Dad dismissed the idea with a wave. "Humans don't live for centuries. There must be more to it than that."

"Of course, there's more," Mighty said, picking up where

Muscle left off. "The scriptures mention this man in the book of Genesis. The twenty-fourth verse of the fifth chapter says, 'Enoch walked with God, and then he was no more.'" The Gnome let that sink in for a moment. "He was no more because the Maker brought him and fruit from the Tree of Life to the Tethered World. Enoch was to tend the tree and the garden until an appointed time in the future when the Maker shall need them both."

Brady roused to the sound of indistinct talking. Everything seemed indistinct, actually. His memory refused to cooperate and tell him where he lay. He felt like a mummy wrapped in fabric, which meant his eyes couldn't see and his breath felt suffocating. Panic swelled in his chest—until he recalled being disguised by Tassitus as a discarded heap of other rejected items after a long trek through Portland's underground.

The day before, Tassitus had brought Brady through the dark recesses of Powell's Books, into a little-used storage room where he finally materialized. Barefoot and sporting a black t-shirt and cargo shorts, the dude looked to Brady like an alien surfer. Brady decided he preferred alien over demon.

Dust and cobwebs lay like powdered sugar on crates stamped Books for Recycling. Brady wondered if Books for Decomposing might not be the better description. He could spy chewed corners and covers through splinters in the wood. The Gargoyle easily pushed a three-deep stack of the wooden containers out of the way to expose a squat, rusty door in the wall.

"Old vault." Tassitus pointed at the funky round knob with spokes radiating from its center.

The knob reminded Brady of a miniature ship's helm. He watched the Gargoyle grasp two of the spokes and twist the knob while giving it a yank. The door expelled a high-pitched groan as it swung open. Brady wasn't sure if he was more amazed by the Gargoyle's strength with the stacks of crates and the locked door, or the fact that this door actually existed and the Gargoyle knew about it. Either way, Tassitus' brute strength left an impression.

"Follow me." Tassitus waved Brady over. "This vault was compromised long ago and connects to antiquated passageways. Shut the door behind you."

Brady didn't move. Sealing himself into a black hole with a Gargoyle sounded like an idiotic idea. Tassitus disappeared into the opening while Brady stood there and second guessed himself.

"What are you waiting for?" The Gargoyle's golden eyes reappeared.

"Coming," Brady mumbled. He knew Brock had no foreseeable options for a rescue, which left Brady with only this rather idiotic one. He fumbled on hands and knees into the chilled, musty darkness, sealing his fate behind him by closing the door. Squeamish thoughts of rats and roaches scratched at his brain, but he heroically pushed them aside and crawled forward.

"Follow the sound of my voice," Tassitus said. "I can see in the dark." He guided Brady to something jagged and rough. "Careful, the back of this vault has sharp edges. It met with some dynamite years ago, from what I've been told."

Brady crept through the opening, wondering how the Gargoyle knew this but feeling too disconcerted by the all-encompassing void to ask. Without his sense of sight, he felt unbalanced and insecure. Tassitus kept up a soulful whistle for Brady to follow. The unfamiliar tune sounded sad and lonely in the utter silence of the passageway. Brady hated the despair that it stirred inside him. After several uncomfortable bumps into the cold, hard walls, he stopped long enough to dig his phone from his back pocket and activate the flashlight app.

Tassitus squinted and ducked behind his hand. "Guano! Don't point that thing at me."

"Sorry." Brady illuminated the recesses of the tunnel, his equilibrium happy to find its footing again. The cylindrical walls were pebbly and appeared to stretch into infinity. Every so often a circular opening perforated the passage, and he guessed there must be other tunnels that fed into this one.

He clamped the phone between his teeth as a sudden, panicked thought washed over him. What if they were inside some sort of sewer system? The obvious lack of moisture did little to suppress the alarm as he remembered being trapped inside a sewage aqueduct with Malagruel's other worm, Ophidian. Brady had nearly drowned in a flooding surge of water that swept through the culvert.

Although they hadn't been crawling on all fours for long, Brady wasn't sure his knees would ever forgive him. Up ahead, the Gargoyle had stopped by one of the connected openings and Brady plunged toward him, wincing.

"Down this incline and we'll be able to walk upright," Tassitus said. He waited for Brady to catch up.

"Hallelujah," Brady garbled around the phone between his teeth. He had fallen behind in order to remove his phone, wipe it off, and swallow his spit several times. Slobbering all over it was sure to short it out. Being able to see made it worth the delay.

They crawled into the short, gently sloping cylinder. It came to a stop in front of a rotting, round door that reminded Brady of a hobbit hole. An abandoned hobbit hole, anyway, since the door lacked any upkeep. His light shone through large chunks of missing, splintered wood. Tassitus popped the door open with a smack, and it swung out to reveal an uneven, filthy brick floor.

Brady stepped inside, grateful to stand but afraid to breathe. A snowfall of dust ebbed and flowed in the wake of the door's motion. The phone light's beam revealed ancient walls of brick and stone, pocked with boarded-up doors and smashed masonry. Brady wanted to explore its secrets even as his imagination went wild with who or what might be hanging out in a place like this. He sneezed.

"What is this place?" He sneezed again and pulled his shirt collar over his nose and mouth.

"The shanghai tunnels." Tassitus strode ahead. "You know, the Forbidden City."

Brady took it all in with wide eyes that blinked against the dust. "No, I don't know." Graffiti and trash littered the surroundings. It smelled earthy, like dirt mingled with the stale, uninspiring scent found in secondhand stores and antique malls.

"Just as well. Not a safe place. Now you only have to worry about vandals or ruffians. A hundred years ago, you humans had to worry about being kidnapped and forced into slavery on one of the ships docked on the Willamette River." He gestured to a series of compartments, some with bars still intact. "Former holding cells. The shanghaiers kidnapped able-bodied young men like yourself in Portland and then sold them to ship's captains. Nasty business. And during prohibition, the saloons simply moved into this underground city and set up shop."

Brady shivered, imagining himself forced into becoming an unwilling sailor. He glanced around, his mind boggled by the size and complexity of this vast network of tunnels and rooms, horrified by its evil history. It seemed the Tethered World wasn't the only underground place with a life of its own.

"This way." Tassitus turned into a shoulder-width passage. "We have to avoid the areas that host a series of tours down here. Fortunately, there are plenty of ways to get around if you know where to go."

Brady followed the Gargoyle over a pile of bricks and debris in the middle of the cramped passageway. As he clambered across the rubble, his hand fell on a pointed shard of pottery that would make a handy weapon. Though by now he felt somewhat comfortable with Tassitus, he liked the feeling of having extra protection in his pocket.

They traipsed through the broken, forgotten underground town for close to an hour, Brady rubbernecking in fascination despite the criminal past it represented. Tassitus finally stopped in front of a rectangular grate that had been moved enough to allow them both to slip through sideways.

It was downhill from there as they traveled out of the underground city and into crude tunnels deep in the earth. For several hours, it was rough going. The steep, constant angle began to wear on Brady's legs and they cramped up, slowing their progress. When Brady complained that he couldn't force himself to take one more step, Tassitus pushed him on for another hour. With the phone battery low, Brady alternated between following the Gargoyle with a hand on his shoulder—something that made Brady squeamish at first—and turning his light on to get his bearings.

At long last the two found themselves in what Tassitus called a collection cave. "Many creatures that sneak topside will grab whatever they can carry away in hopes of finding useful things. They'll stop in these collection caves and sort through their goods, discarding the items they don't want." He pointed at a heap of filthy cloth and crumpled cardboard boxes. "This is where you can safely rest for a few hours. Others might pass through, so you will need to be completely covered."

Brady had cringed at the idea of rats or fleas—or worse—that might cozy up to him among the leftovers. But his legs and eyelids gratefully gave way without resistance, and he had fallen asleep under the pile. Now his stomach growled like a wild animal, and he hoped he'd be able to escape the suffocating, musty old blanket that covered him and feed his neglected appetite soon.

"What was that sound?" Tassitus pulled the blanket away from Brady's face.

"That was my stomach." Brady squinted in the light of a lone torch that lit the room, which he now saw was about the size of a two-car garage. His lungs expanded gratefully, sucking in the unhindered air. "I'm starving."

Tassitus made what Brady guessed was an exasperated face. The nodules across his forehead made it hard to read his expressions. "That's right, you need a lot more food than we do."

"Yeah, like three well-balanced meals a day." Brady sat up and rubbed his aching back.

The Gargoyle straightened and cast his eyes about, as if he might locate something edible among the trash. "I don't have any food, and I don't know if we'll find something anytime soon. I'm sorry for the oversight."

Brady didn't like the sound of that. He stood, still groggy and with seriously sore knees from the previous day's crawling. "I guess it can't be helped."

"I'm afraid I shall need to bind your hands and feign that you're my prisoner. If anyone approaches, don't be shocked by how I might behave toward you." Tassitus picked up the blanket Brady had used and tore a few strips from it with his teeth. "We are bound to cross paths with others. I met a scrounging Leprechaun a few minutes ago."

Like I have a choice, Brady thought. "Sure. Whatever."

The creature wrapped the cloth around Brady's wrists. "It will be a long day. And when you're so weary of walking that you think you can't go on, we should arrive in the tunnels that feed into the Dens of the Dark Dwarves. And that's when things could get nasty."

CHAPTER SEVENTEEN

I DIDN'T LIKE OPERATING ON AUTOPILOT. Maybe because the term itself implied an enormous amount of trust while flying across the friendly skies at dizzying speeds—way scarier than a roller coaster in my book. Maybe because the term meant I wasn't in control. Either way, it was becoming our family's new *modus operandi* and took a lot of getting used to on my part.

But I had to admit, with a hint of pride, I was sliding into the autopilot mode with greater proficiency as the summer wore on. When my parents were kidnapped earlier in the summer, I had fumbled and fumed into action. When I was drugged and pressured into cooperating with the enemy, I had fought through the deception and fear, ready to die for what was right. Today, after learning that Brock faced a fresh round of danger and the Tree of Life was dying, I found myself eager to do whatever had to be done to get back to the Tethered World and make a difference. My family was working together like the proverbial well-oiled machine.

The chaotic day at Pioneer Square had morphed into a chaotic evening, topped off with the mind-blowing revelations from our Gnome friends about the probable demise of the Tree of Life and the role of Enoch, the famous biblical patriarch. That part, in particular, left me giddy with amazement. Thanks to all the other impossible things I now knew to be true, I was able to swallow that tidbit without a serious amount of choking.

The Gnomes told us Enoch's concern about the current condition of the tree that had brought him out from behind the wall and into the company of the Vituvians. Of course, the Gnomes were already aware of the damage to the roots and had arrested the traitor who hacked the roots to pieces, but the shocking state of the tree had left them in a panic.

Our friends tending the tree needed help. Brock and Brady needed help. The creatures being held captive at Mr. Delaney's house needed help—and we had the eyes of the world upon us, thanks to the earlier media circus. The only good news brought by the Gnomes was that our dear Aunt Jules and her husband Daniel had recovered enough to travel topside. But with Aunt Judith's recent stroke, Aunt Jules probably wouldn't come home anyway.

It exhausted me to think about the entirety of the mess we found ourselves in, but there was no time for rest or even contemplation. Action was required, and the clock was ticking.

Like a bomb.

Uncle Brent brought Nate and Nicole home and then insisted he wanted to stay and help figure things out. After sharing a couple of frozen pizzas—easier than ordering Chinese food—and holding a strategy session around the table, Dad and the Gnomes reached a consensus.

"It's settled." Dad took a long slurp of his root beer. "I'll distract Joseph at the front door while you two stealth warriors do your thing to rescue your Gnome friend and the elf. Then late tonight we'll sneak into his yard and head below ground through the tunnel. The girls will stay here and help Amy put out any fires but remain on standby to the Tethered World."

We pushed away from the table and reached for our plates. The Gnomes sat on tall bar stools that we had scooted next to the breakfast table.

"I'm going with you."

We turned incredulous eyes on Uncle Brent. Mom plopped back down. Or maybe her legs gave out. "You'll go *where*?"

He fidgeted with his paper plate and appeared equally shocked by what had slipped out. "I'm going with Liam to the Tethered World."

I blinked at the silvery moonlight that pooled across my pillow. Was that the screech of the sliding door being opened? Shifting onto my elbow, I listened, watching my curtains flutter like lazy wings in the breeze.

Yes. Another sound like a squeaky brake pierced the quiet night. My room was situated above our back patio, in line with the door. The noise made my pulse kick into gear, guaranteeing no more sleep for the night.

I was astonished that I'd fallen asleep at all after the excitement of the evening. This included a successful reconnaissance mission, in which my dad had the pleasure of getting into Mr. Delaney's face for a spell, tearing him up one side and down the other with threats of legal action—or fist action—if he continued to implicate me as some sort of ambassador in his sickening celebrity agenda. While Delaney was distracted, the Gnomes sneaked inside, although they refused to say how. They freed their two friends, unplugged the contraption keeping the dead Yeti from decomposing, and drugged the Leprechaun with a big puff of their magical mushroom powder to the face, along with a dose in Mr. Delaney's steaming cup of coffee. They detected no sign of Sargon anywhere.

In the meantime, Uncle Brent had made a run home to get various tinctures and fertilizers he thought might benefit the injured tree. He had his own natural pharmacy growing throughout his yard and distilled in tiny amber bottles in his cupboards. Unfortunately, Aunt Val wasn't optimistic about, well, anything to do with the Tethered World, but Uncle Brent said they'd have to work it out when he came back. He called his work and got time off for what he labeled a family emergency.

Sometime during the night, the Gnomes intended to return to Mr. Delaney's. They would slip over to the security guard's car, where the rent-a-cop continued his overnight vigil, and blow fistfuls of mushroom powder into his open window. Once the man was thoroughly out, my dad and uncle planned to creep into Delaney's back yard and descend into the tunnel.

I lay in bed, listening. The sound of activity outside my window meant their strategy was underway. I padded to my window seat, attempting to look down into the yard. I could hear Dad hushing our excited corgis, and then the side gate clinked as they left. With that, they were headed to the Tethered World.

And I'm not. That thought stabbed me with panic. I didn't want to stay. I couldn't. Images of my brothers, my aunt and uncle, my Dwarf and Gnome friends, and, finally, Xander, jostled for priority in my brain. How could I possibly stay here and bide my time? Besides, if I was gone, there would be no cameras stuck in my face, forcing me to pretend to be some ridiculous ambassador. Mom had already fielded half a dozen phone calls wanting to interview one or both of us.

I floundered around in my closet for jeans, a t-shirt, and a hoodie. A pair of tennis shoes and a quick braid meant I was ready. Wait! I grabbed the ankle brace and popped off my shoe, wriggling into the supportive elastic. Then I scribbled a note for Mom—boy was she going to be furious—and crept into the hall. Outside my parents' room, I hesitated. Mom had planned to see Dad and the others off. A faint light filtered under the door. Her bed creaked and the light disappeared with a faint *click.*

Expelling an uneasy breath, I tiptoed past their door and headed downstairs to the kitchen. In the privacy of the walk-in pantry, I stuffed a handful of granola bars in the pouch pocket of my hoodie and latched an LED flashlight to my belt loop. My hasty plan was to let Dad get deep enough into the tunnel so that, when I caught up, it would be too far to send me home.

I found a reusable water bottle tethered to a lengthy strap. I filled it and hung it across my shoulders. Part of my brain wondered who I was and where the old Sadie might be hiding. This sneaky, adventurous seventeen-year-old certainly didn't resemble the girl I had been at the beginning of summer.

From the den, I slipped into the garage, locking the door behind me. I prayed I was doing the right thing—and wondered what I'd do if it wasn't.

Stepping from the garage into our side yard cranked the wattage on my pulse. After gulping several calming breaths, I headed for the driveway to spy on the rent-a-cop. He snoozed on, much to my relief. I hoped that Mr. Delaney was out cold too.

The side gate stood ajar, a tuft of grass keeping the latch from catching. I pushed it open and kept close to the side of the house, peering around the back corner. No sign of anyone. The greenhouse, shed, and horse trailer sat exactly as Brady had described. And there, crouched in the moon-drenched yard, was a square, metal hatch, yawning wide, ready to swallow me whole.

The troll stared at the ceiling from his cushioned palette on the floor. Thanks to that ridiculous Topsider, Joseph Marshall, new opportunities had presented themselves. His father, Chief

Nekronok, was beside himself upon hearing how well the press conference had been received. Now the chief would busy himself with a new uniform and a good grooming in anticipation of his topside debut. Probably wouldn't be long before he dropped the title of chief and declared himself king of the world.

At least Nekronok's new diversion meant his ever-commanding gaze would be off his son, at least for a while. And hopefully off the young king who had been captured. The Troll had plans for that boy.

The temporary reprieve made him grin. He could deal with a little breathing room from his father. Being one of Nekronok's sons translated to far too many expectations and overtures.

You will do this.

You're expected to do that.

If you want a portion of the power, you must demonstrate yourself worthy.

Do you want this more than your brothers? Prove it.

His father had no problem pitting his sons against one another. He'd threatened more than once to let them fight to the last son standing in order to name his successor. And with eleven sons in the running, that could take a while.

Of course, tradition dictated that the eldest son would be the natural successor. But at his core, he doubted that this would be the method his diabolical father would use to name the heir. The chief had many years left to rule with brute force. Years to tighten his grip on his sons' lives and make them miserable.

And if Nekronok got his greedy hands on a piece of fruit from the Tree of Life, he might never need a successor. Such a concept made the Troll willing to resort to whatever means necessary to remove his father from power. He must bide his time and wait for the right opportunity.

Until recently, he had cared little for the iron fist of power. He would rather assist in the governing of the realm and allow other, more brutish Trolls to wield the sword. A partnership of sorts might have entered the discussion—a Craventhrall democracy, perhaps.

All of his overtures to jockey for such a position were ignored or dismissed, even mocked, by his father. He was losing patience with the lot of them and could see that the others couldn't separate the brains from the brawn.

But things finally were changing. The past three months

had ushered in exciting possibilities for Craventhrall and profound opportunities to impact the Land of Legend, the Tethered World, and the topside world at large. His ambitious strategies needed to change with the times. If he didn't adapt, he would watch this historical opportunity pass him over in favor of one of his brothers.

Or worse yet, it might even stay in the greedy, tyrannical claws of his father. Such an appalling possibility had prompted the Troll to ensure that Nekronok would never obtain a piece of fruit from the Tree of Life. The last thing the Tethered World needed was a never-ending reign by His Worshipful Master. But he knew he could run things much better than his father ever could, both below ground and above.

Adapting to the times had the unfortunate, distasteful side effect of making unsavory alliances. The worst, thus far, was partnering with the fiendishly foul Malagruel. But when opportunities presented themselves, one must seize them, whatever the cost. One pivotal play awaited; he must grasp it and use it as his impetus. Regardless of the compromise to his personal ethics, he had to make it happen.

For him, the end result always justified the means.

CHAPTER EIGHTEEN

BRADY SHIVERED IN THE DAMP, CHILLY tunnel. He longed to rub his hands over his arms to generate warmth, but his wrists were still tied together. The upside to freezing was that it took his mind off the gnawing hunger that hollowed out every bit of space beneath his ribs.

While he and Tassitus traversed the tunnels, Brady waffled between anger at himself over how he had waltzed right into this trap and a flimsy sort of hope that they really were on their way to help Brock. It was a stalemate in his mind, and neither side was winning.

The sound of footsteps made Tassitus stop and press Brady against the wall behind him. The *thunk-thunk-thunk* of large feet approached from around the curve in the passage. The Gargoyle quickly gestured for Brady to lie on the ground. "You've passed out," he hissed into Brady's ear.

Brady complied, lying down at an angle that allowed him to peek between slitted eyelids at who or what was coming toward them, his heart hammering at all the grim possibilities. They hadn't passed anyone in the poorly lit tunnel since they'd left the place where Brady had napped, so he'd half expected to trudge on indefinitely in silence. Tassitus had refused to talk since voices carried so well in the passageways.

Out of the gloom appeared a wide, waddling Stygian. He jumped, startled, at the sight of Tassitus and his prisoner. "What've we here?" asked the pasty-faced Dark Dwarf. He scuttled over to them, peering over his large, fleshy nose at the Gargoyle and his captive.

"Bringing this Topsider to Prince Malagruel, sir." The worm bobbed his head at the Styg. "I'm afraid he's fainted from fright. Makes for a slow trek through the tunnels, dragging him like this."

"Ya don't say." The Dwarf sounded like he had a stuffy nose. He squatted and inspected Brady, giving him a poke in the ribs that made Brady catch his breath as he tried not to squirm. "He's a fresh catch, this one."

"Yes indeed," Tassitus agreed. "Don't suppose you could tell me how much farther 'til we reach your dens? I'm unfamiliar with these particular tunnels."

"Sssure." Nasty Styg spittle spattered Brady's face. It took everything in him to keep from cringing.

The Dwarf stood and placed his meaty hands on his lower back, arching into a stretch. "I'll do yas one better. How's about I's help ya carry the bloke? I's gonna look for some mushrooms for my pipe, but I's can do that later. Name's Glump. Never met a Gargoyle befores."

No! Brady silently pleaded. The thought of pretending to be deadweight sounded awkward and uncomfortable.

"That's quite a generous offer, my good dwarf." Tassitus stuck out his hand. "I'm Tas—uh—mania." He pumped the Dark Dwarf's arm in greeting. "Tasmania. Good to make your acquaintance."

Brady stifled a smirk over the fake name. But he also decided he should wake from his fake stupor to avoid the whole mess of getting dragged through the tunnels like a sack of rocks. He moaned and mumbled, "Where am I?" working hard to make his voice sound convincingly weak. Blinking through squinted eyes, he caught the Gargoyle's disapproving glare.

"Oh look," Tassitus said, pointing at Brady. "He's losing consciousness again."

The last thing Brady remembered was seeing a black fist firing toward his head.

I peered down into the pit and took a tentative step. Crude stairs delivered me from the lunar-lit evening into a literal black hole—not the kind in outer space, but the kind that would smother me in its depths like I'd been buried alive.

Afraid Mr. Delaney would spot my bright flashlight from his house, I kept it off until I walked far enough into the pit to feel it was safe. The passage sloped at a swift angle and was too low for me to stand in. How had a gargantuan Troll made it through? Obviously on his hands and knees.

Once I lost sight of the faint square of moonlight from the yard, I unhooked my flashlight and fumbled for the switch. Before I could turn it on, a glow from farther down the tunnel made me hesitate. Darn it! Dad hadn't made it very far at all. Maybe they'd had trouble with the lock on the trapdoor. I would have to linger out of sight temporarily. Maybe I could stay far enough behind to follow their glow but keep out of view.

I walked toward the light. Soon the tunnel opened up, and I found I could stand. But the pale gleam didn't grow fainter as they moved ahead—instead it became brighter, like they were headed back. Had they forgotten something?

If I didn't scram, they'd spot me. I turned and ran. In my hurry, my foot skidded across the loose, pebbly dirt and slipped right out from under me. *Smack.* Down I went in a painful face plant. So much for subtlety. I groaned and felt my nose for blood as I struggled to get my feet beneath me. Footsteps hurried toward me. I glanced back, and a blinding flashlight beam caught me in its glare.

"What's this?"

The voice didn't belong to my father or my uncle, and it definitely wasn't a Gnome. But I recognized it. I pressed an angry fist to my forehead and sat back on my heels. Busted!

"Well, if it ain't the Ambassador to the United Dynasty of Thrall." A wheezy laugh followed. "Fashionably late to the party, I see."

I pounded my forehead several times for good measure and glared up at my nemesis. His light drowned me in its blue-white brilliance, like a police spotlight targeting a criminal.

"Vengeance is sweet. Or maybe it's karma." The pool of light grew bigger as Mr. Delaney approached. "Funny thing happened earlier tonight. Somehow my myth collection escaped. Next thing I know my alarm is sounding 'cause someone broke into my tunnel."

The short, stout man seemed to tower over me, but I looked away, as much to avoid the blinding light as to avoid looking at the man I despised.

"Ain't sure who the tunnel rat was, since a man my age doesn't move very fast. Of course, it won't be long 'til that changes. Got a whole slew of those miniature trees growing, and I can guarantee I'll be the first to benefit from their magic. Then I'll be unstoppable."

"You're a diabolical, greedy man." I couldn't see him with

his light shining directly in my eyes. I put my hand up to shade them. "Your stupid plan is killing—*killing*—the real Tree of Life in Vituvia. But what do you care?"

"Very little." He grunted. "I've got my own stash. Now get up. We're going to head to my place for an overdue chat about what you're going to do to help my cause."

I heard the unmistakable sound of a gun being cocked— next to my ear. I jerked my head away. A glint of metal hovered near my forehead. Mr. Delaney lowered the light to the ground, which gave me a clearer picture of my predicament—not that I was about to underestimate how precarious things had suddenly become.

"Stand up." The gun barrel twitched, pointedly.

I stood.

"Hands in the air," Mr. Delaney ordered. He wore a striped robe tied around his ample belly, giving him a cartoon-like appearance. "Walk slowly up the steps and into the back door of my house."

Within a few yards, I had to hunch over again where the tunnel shrank. To buy time, I slowed down. Should I cooperate? Like a punch to the throat, I remembered the note I had left my mother. No one would be looking for me if Mr. Delaney decided to keep me captive until I cooperated.

My mind reeled, weighing whether I should run like a bat out of the underworld and take my chances. I was an asset. He wouldn't shoot an asset. The odds were stacked in my favor for sure.

At least, that's what I hoped.

CHAPTER NINETEEN

BRADY BLINKED. HIS SURROUNDINGS CAME INTO view upside down, his head lolling backward. The unnatural perspective nauseated him. He closed his eyes, trying to decipher what was happening. He and Tassitus had come upon a Stygian...and then?

He couldn't remember.

Brady lifted his heavy head. Tassitus carried Brady's upper body like a woman carries her purse: the Gargoyle's arm was threaded through Brady's two arms that were still lashed together at the wrist. He glanced ahead to see that his ankles now rested on the short but sturdy shoulders of the Stygian. The creature's back was to him as he lurched along, guiding them through the dimly lit passage.

"...boasting about his son training with the army of Trolls," the Dwarf was saying.

Carefully, Brady leaned his head back and looked up. Tassitus met Brady's gaze with a subtle shake, indicating that Brady needed to continue to act unconscious. Though unsure how long he could manage the uncomfortable position, Brady complied. Keeping his eyes closed would be key to keeping his vacant, hungry stomach from lurching.

"So you're not in favor of joining forces with the Trolls?" Tassitus asked.

"Bah! I've no interest in politics." The Styg shrugged. "As long as I's my pipe and grog and knows the fine love of my wife, what do I care? Which is why his blabbing on about the boy drives me wally."

"I see," said Tassitus. "But he's not in Craventhrall, you say?"

The Dwarf made a production of clearing his throat and spitting. "Why do ya care? Does this Topsider here have something to do with the boy king?"

"Him? Nah." Tassitus chuckled. "This one's a trespasser. Ran into him farther up in the tunnel."

Brady noted that the Gargoyle evaded the Dark Dwarf's other question.

"Whaddya plan on doing with the lad anyway?" The Stygian slowed and shifted direction. "Need to take a left here."

They went left. Brady didn't know how much longer he could tolerate the pain in his arms, legs, and neck, but he gritted his teeth and prayed for strength.

"Figured I'd take him to Malagruel," Tassitus said, "and see what he wants to do with him."

Brady's eyes popped, and he gave Tassitus a hard stare that the Gargoyle ignored. Although Brady didn't know whether Tassitus was serious or blowing smoke, his internal alarm rattled.

"Ingratiating yourself to the big guy, huh?"

"Can't hurt." Tassitus glanced down, his face unreadable in the gloom.

"Might hurt the Topsider, though." The Styg wheezed out a laugh.

Brady had had enough. Physically, at least, he could take no more. He squirmed enough to let the Dwarf know his cargo was awake. Tassitus gave Brady an impatient glance. Apparently, the Gargoyle had never experienced being carried around like a dead deer.

The Dwarf came to a stop. "What's going on back there?"

Brady moaned. "Please, let me walk. It'll be easier on all of us."

Tassitus sighed and lowered Brady. "Stand up and shut up."

The Dwarf dropped Brady's legs like inanimate objects devoid of feeling pain.

"*Ugh.*" Brady winced but clambered to his feet.

Tassitus glared and stepped in front of Brady, yanking the bonds around his wrists. Brady couldn't quite read the vibe. The Gargoyle seemed genuinely angry at him, but for what? Again, fear whispered to Brady, *You've walked into a trap, you fool.* The only competing voice was the one in his stomach.

The three trudged on in a grim silence that was broken occasionally by the sound of the Dwarf hacking and spitting. The further they went into the tunnel, the more intersecting tunnels presented themselves. Brady doubted that Tassitus would've known which passageway to take without the help of their pasty-faced tour guide. But maybe all the tunnels eventually ended up in the same spot.

Hours later, placing one foot in front of the other began to feel as impossible as flying. *How much longer?* he moaned to himself. But soon more Stygians began to frequent the tunnels. The first two Dark Dwarves, a male and female, stopped to gawk as much at Tassitus as at Brady. The next one spat at them without slowing a step, hitting Brady square in the chest.

Another passage brought the travelers into a cavernous space buzzing with Dark Dwarves. The enormous, arching cave made Brady think of an old-fashioned big top carnival full of activity. Fabric booths showed off a variety of items. Some, like a pile of worn, mismatched shoes, had obviously been pilfered from life topside. Countless torches encircled the space, stretching along the rough-hewn walls and out of his line of sight. Irregular openings in the smoke-charred ceiling allowed the smoke to escape.

Brady gaped at the many clusters of Stygians, including numerous children, busily eating, bartering, laughing, drinking, and even arguing. The mouthwatering smell of roasted meat mingled with nearby pipe tobacco and tortured his starving stomach.

Glump led them to an enormous blob of flesh wearing a turban and seated in a chair. Brady guessed from the chair's elaborate carvings and plush cushions that this Styg must be important. An embroidered vest gaped open across rolls of grey flesh. His belly protruded over his silky harem pants, punctuated by two thick, calloused feet. A handful of other Stygians sat on cushions on the ground, obviously fawning over their version of Jabba the Hut.

The Styg sized up Brady without removing his blubbery lips from the stem of an ornate, swooping pipe. The presence of Tassitus didn't faze the Styg. It was Brady he appeared to be interested in.

"Do my eyes deceive me, or is this the so-called king that was recently captured?" The turban-headed Styg had a high-pitched voice that sputtered out of his throat as if he were gargling.

Glump knelt and bowed his head, exposing a large, hairy mole on the back of his neck. "Oh great Oradini, I's come upon this traveling Gargoyle and his prisoner in the far depths of the tunnels. Tasmania, here, works for Prince Malagruel and hopes we's might keep this prisoner for him until he can arrange to have the fella moved."

The big blob drew on his pipe. "You don't say."

The Styg glanced at Oradini, then looked back down at the ground. "I believed you knows what is best to be done, so I's brings them to you."

One of Oradini's eyebrows arched high enough to shift the turban on his head. "I ask again, is this not the captured king from Vituvia?"

Tassitus stepped forward, hesitated, then knelt as the Dwarf had done. "If I may, Your Excellency?"

"Enlighten me, please." The fat Stygian gave a gesture of encouragement.

The Gargoyle placed a hand on his chest and gave a little bow. "Thank you, sir. This Topsider is not the Vituvian king-to-be. He is the king's twin brother, Brady Larcen. If it pleases you, may I leave Brady in your charge while I make arrangements with my prince?"

Brady's lungs felt short of oxygen. Teeth gritted and jaw flexed, he could only berate his own stupidity for delivering himself—signed, sealed, and delivered.

"I's thought you didn't know this boy." Glump scratched at his nose and scowled.

Tassitus shrugged. "Safety measure. Didn't need any undue attention."

Oradini lowered his pipe and exhaled two streams of smoke from his wide, flat nostrils. "I can make better arrangements than what you're requesting." His thick lips stretched into a sickening grin. "Let's put this Topsider in the crypt with his brother."

My feet pounded across Mr. Delaney's lawn. I lost traction on the dewy blades as I rounded the corner, slipping sideways. A startling *pop* split the night. Simultaneously, the bottom of a fence slat shattered. This guy was nuts!

I righted myself, sprinting for the gate. My jittery fingers fumbled with the latch. I finally unhinged it and darted out, risking a glance over my shoulder as the gate swung closed. Mr. Psycho had just rounded the back corner of his house. I was halfway down the driveway when another loud *spat* hit the wooden fence behind me. It was disconcerting how the shots seemed to come from far away, or maybe different directions. A remote location of my brain decided he must have a silencer on his pistol, though it was anything but silent.

Dashing across the street, I flew to the side door that went into our garage. Locked, of course. And I hadn't bothered to bring a house key when I set out on my expedition.

Shouts from across the street alerted me to the fact that Delaney was trying to rouse the drugged rent-a-cop. Crouching down, I finagled myself through the doggy door, thankful for my narrow body. The flap had a latch on the inside, and I stooped to secure it, more to keep out the gun than my overweight neighbor.

When I knelt to crawl through the doggy door leading into the den, I heard the croaking voice of Mr. Delaney calling outside, "Check the backyard."

Clambering inside, I crawled to the couch and peeked through the vertical blinds. The plastic slats rattled in my fingers, and I drew back. In a moment, a circle of light swept the length of the window, causing me to press into the couch cushions. Fortunately, Ollie and Mindy-loo were in a flat-out frenzy, barking and yelping from their kennels.

How far would that man go to catch me? Surely not to the point of breaking and entering. Delaney wouldn't jeopardize his new-found fame by doing something worthy of calling 911, would he? Then again, he did shoot at me.

After several minutes of trembling on the sofa, I dared to glimpse what was happening outside. The dogs continued to bark, but they always took a while to wind down once they started. Not seeing the beam of a flashlight, I felt a bit braver and opened the blinds to see better.

Behind me the floor creaked.

I whipped around and found my mother, standing with her arms crossed. "You mind telling me what on earth is going on?"

CHAPTER TWENTY

I SLUMPED OVER A BOWL OF cereal, miserable beyond belief. The rush of running for my life now gone and the sleepless night tapping me on the shoulder, I stared at the tabletop through bloodshot eyeballs burning from their puffy, pink lids. That condition had been caused by an intense round of bawling said eyeballs out once I'd faced my mother a couple of hours earlier.

First I had cried from relief, then I'd cried harder when she found the note and learned of the danger I'd placed myself in. Mom was spitting mad at me *and* Mr. Delaney—compounded by discovering a bullet had grazed the outside of my leg. It had torn my jeans and left a bloody streak in its wake. In the rush of the moment, I hadn't felt anything.

When my irate mother, the former nurse, got hold of it, she had little sympathy—or gentleness. I think she took pleasure dousing it in alcohol and watching me writhe through the pain as it burned. Her fingers smeared ointment on the scrape with a vengeance before she slapped a large bandage strip on it.

Now Mom was fuming around the kitchen giving me the "serves you right" lecture. She had no recourse against our nut-job neighbor for shooting at me because I was trespassing on his property.

I shoveled flakes and granola into my mouth in slow motion, thinking of everything I was missing. Would Dad be able to get to my brothers? What about Brady? Had he managed to find Brock? And how was it going with that Gargoyle? I sure hoped Tassitus was as trustworthy as he appeared.

After the ridiculous things Mr. Delaney said about his little trees, I hoped Uncle Brent would be able to save the real one. If our nefarious neighbor had the monopoly on such a powerful plant, it could be a worldwide nightmare.

I had only learned of the tree's existence at the end of our last visit to the Tethered World, but I'd spent a lot of time thinking about it since. Although it wasn't the actual tree that had grown in the Garden of Eden, it had sprouted from a seed produced by the original tree—which made it one and the same, as far as my knowledge of fruit trees went.

This tree was mentioned in the first and last books of the Bible, which to me demonstrated its supreme value in God's sovereign plan. Even now, it played a central role in the Tethered World. The Flaming Sword guarded it, and Enoch himself, a man who had never tasted death, cared for it. Enoch! My mind was officially blown.

But right now my body and emotions were in meltdown-recovery mode. I slurped the last of my milk and face-planted on the couch. Mom had stormed upstairs with a promise to pick up where she left off. I figured I'd better hang around and take my punishment. Hugging the throw pillow, I tried to strangle the uncertain limbo that I felt. For once in my life I needed action. Craved it. If I'd timed things differently last night, maybe my plan would've worked. Instead, I was stuck babysitting an evil neighbor with no means to stop him, as far as I could tell. While we looked on, he would continue to schmooze the media, grow his little trees, and operate a clandestine underground tunnel. And what could we do to stop him? Our hands were tied.

Maybe Mom could downplay things in the media to minimize the impact topside. But the real problems were happening in the belly of the earth with my brothers, the sword, and the tree.

I touched the ring on my finger and whispered a little prayer that I could do something productive before I drove myself crazy with worry and curiosity. And if I didn't learn to be anxious for nothing, I might jeopardize everything. Last night was a painful example.

Mom made her presence known with a sigh as she sank into the nearby recliner. "You should've done your sleeping last night. Damage control starts today."

With effort, I turned to face her. "What do you need me to do?"

She pinched the bridge of her nose and squinted. "Wish I knew. Reporters could be at our door any minute. I'm going to contact that Professor Ferrell and find out what he's learned about the saplings."

I was relieved to see Mom back to her calm, collected self,

although I knew if I brought up the subject of leaving I'd be back in the dog house. "What do you think the tests will show?"

"I've no clue." She shrugged. "Botany isn't my field. I'm hopeful that the only thing special about the Tree of Life is the fruit. If so, that buys us plenty of time to deal with them." She stood up and left the room without another word.

I buried my face in the pillow. Fighting? Yeah, probably not the kind we had been involved with earlier this summer. It would be more like a battle of wits, topside.

And right now, my brain was fried.

Things looked a smidge better after I took a hot shower, but my sunnier outlook didn't last long. I brewed myself a giant mug of coffee, cupping its caffeinated comfort with grateful hands. Too tired to retrieve my iPad or phone from my room, I opened the day's edition of *The Columbian* that lay on the table. I figured damage control would begin with whatever was buzzing around the news and social media.

Although it didn't make the front page, thank heaven, I still cringed at the lengthy, prominent article about the events in Pioneer Square on page three. The writer kept a skeptical tone throughout the piece, questioning whether the two men called up on stage to inspect Sargon had been planted in the audience. But she admitted she didn't have a theory for explaining such a convincing Sasquatch. In regard to the saplings, she scoffed at Delaney's promises and doubted the tests performed would be unbiased.

A full-color photo spread displayed the chronological circus. Unfortunately, there was a big, fat, close-up of me holding the microphone and looking petrified. The caption beneath read, "Sadie Larcen claims to have visited the world where Joseph Marshall's creatures exist." The writer's mention of both my mother and me in the article was colored with skeptical words like contends, professes, and maintains. The writer pointed out with apparent amusement that my mom was booed off the stage.

I dreaded getting on Facebook and reading all my friend's questions and finding myself tagged in this dumb newspaper article. My mother's Bigfoot obsession wasn't a topic I'd ever embraced or talked about willingly. This summer, though, I had gained a fresh appreciation for what she did, and I no longer shied away from it.

Still, here she was, and here *we* were, in the eye of an unfavorable media hurricane. Not my favorite place to be.

"Sadie," Mom called from her office, "come here. *Quick.*"

Ignoring the knot in my stomach, I trotted to her office. An email filled her computer screen. Mom leaned on her elbows, staring at it.

"What's wrong?" I knelt beside her chair and looked at the monitor.

She rotated it toward me. "Read this."

Curious, I leaned in and read,

> *Dear Mrs. Larcen,*
>
> *I saw the broadcast from Portland's Pioneer Square yesterday and watched with fascination. The subject matter is important to my family. Of particular interest was the ring your daughter was wearing when she spoke. I have important information about that ring that I need to share in person. Forgive me for using the Internet to contact you, but your blog was the only way I could find to get in touch. Please let me know when you are available to meet. What I have to say is of extreme importance and should only be shared face-to-face. Call me at the number below, and we can arrange a time to meet.*
>
> *Sincerely,*
> *Mystique Malakoff*

CHAPTER TWENTY-ONE

BRADY SAT ON A STUMP IN his cell, spooning a watery concoction into his mouth. It appeared to be mushroom soup but without the "cream of" part. Too famished to be picky, he sopped up the brown broth with a crusty roll. He stuffed the last bite in his mouth and set the bowl between his feet.

Other than the stump, everything else in his cell—which was nothing more than a rough-hewn pit—was rock. The only way out was a rope ladder that connected to the opening, but it had been pulled out once Brady descended. Faint illumination came from the golden glow of the crystal-dome sky that lit the Tethered World. The pitiful amount of light only made his forlorn predicament seem worse.

A Stygian guard had escorted Brady to the rocky pit after Oradini assured Tassitus that Brady would be taken to where Brock was being held. The crypt had sounded creepy and zombie-like—two of Brady's least favorite descriptions. But if Brock was in such a place, Brady didn't want him there alone. If Brady couldn't rescue his brother as originally planned, at least they would face trouble together.

Brady heard a noise, something stirring up above. The ladder cascaded down, and the dark form of Tassitus descended. Brady got to his feet, and the two were eye to eye in the cramped space. Brady couldn't hide the contempt he felt for the lying Gargoyle. He wondered if he could take the worm down.

"Allow me to explain," Tassitus said, as if aware of what Brady was contemplating.

Brady pictured his fingers encircling the Gargoyle's neck and giving him a good choking. "I see what's happening plain as day."

The worm shook his head and kept his voice low. "It's not

what it appears." The nodules on his forehead scrunched together. "Though I've got a plan in mind, there are many variables that affect how this plays out."

"Yeah, like you turning me over to the Dark Dwarves."

"No, no—this is temporary." The Gargoyle lifted his hand like he meant to pat Brady on his shoulder, then thought better of it. "First of all, forgive me for punching you as I did. I needed information, and the Styg would not speak freely in front of a Topsider. A conscious one, anyway."

Brady slightly decompressed. "So now what?"

"Now, you must be patient with me. Getting an audience with Oradini has taken the guesswork out of your brother's precise location, so that is a benefit. Unfortunately, it also placed you in their custody."

"You're telling me." Brady felt anger pulsing at his temples. "And what happened to trying to get my brother out before Nekronok had a chance to move in? You don't seem to be in a hurry now."

"Shh!" Tassitus pressed a finger to his mouth. "Please, we don't want to be overheard. Oradini claims that both the Trolls and Malagruel must go through him to get to your brother." Tassitus leaned in to Brady. "And there hasn't been any contact since they delivered him here, which means we have a little more time than I thought. I must report in with Malagruel before he gets suspicious of my absence. But I promise to work on a plan of action. Okay?"

Am I going to trust this guy again, like an idiot? Brady attempted to study Tassitus in the murky light. His ebony skin melded with the shadows, but the Gargoyle's amber eyes glinted with an openness Brady hoped was sincere. He blinked long and deliberate, summoning a measure of calm. "It's not like I have a choice, is it?"

"Not at this point, unfortunately." Tassitus glanced at the hole in the roof. "I've arranged to accompany you tomorrow so I will know where to find you. And I've impressed on Oradini the importance of treating you well, since you are, technically, Malagruel's prisoner."

"That's precisely what worries me."

Ignoring the comment, the Gargoyle pointed to the floor. "Try to get some sleep."

I looked at Mom, who was staring at her screen. "Whoa, that's a weird email. And who has a name like Mystique, except in the movies? Sounds totally fake."

"Forget her name. What on earth could she have to say about your ring? This is out of left field." Mom leaned her chin on her hand and scanned the email again.

I felt a quirky sense of dread, knowing where this conversation might end up. Mom turned from the monitor to me. "Is there something you haven't told me about Aunt Jules' ring?"

I willed my face to give nothing away.

"What is it?" She was reading me like a text.

"I don't know if I should tell you. It's dangerous."

Mom's eyes softened. "Aunt Jules' ring is really the key to the sword." It wasn't a question. I nodded. She covered my ringed hand with her own. "It's okay, Sadie. I guessed as much when she gave it to you. Why else would she pass on her wedding band when she had finally reunited with her husband?"

"I didn't want to take it." My hand slid from beneath hers, and I looked at my ring with its wavy, vine-like circle. "She said I didn't have any say in the matter—that she'd prayed about who to pass it on to for some time. When she told me all this, I had no idea the key was actually her wedding ring. Anyway, when she gave it to me, I didn't want to tell anyone else because it would only put others in danger. Seemed safer for everyone to assume I had inherited an antique ring."

Mom offered a sympathetic nod. "That's why I didn't question it. Not because of the danger, but because I didn't want you to feel the weight of placing anyone else in harm's way." She squeezed my hand. "Still, what could this Mystique person want to tell us? How much could she possibly know?"

A loud knock on the front door interrupted our discussion.

"Great." Mom stood up and headed toward the door. "The first of many kooks has arrived."

I heard the front door open and the hum of muffled conversation. My gaze flitted to the computer screen, and I read through the email again. *Does this person know how significant this ring really is?*

Mom peeked her head into the office. "Hey, I think you should come here."

CHAPTER TWENTY-TWO

"BROCK, IT'S ME." BRADY TOUCHED HIS brother on the shoulder. Brock continued rocking back and forth, perched on a large rock in the damp cave. Brady knelt in front of him, exhausted from his journey but thankful to be with his brother at last. "Hey bro, I'm here, and everything's going to be okay."

Brock stopped rocking and looked at his twin. "I don't like it here."

"Me either." Brady offered a reassuring smile. "But at least we're together. We can get through this as long as we've got each other, right?"

"It might be hard." Brock grasped his knees and resumed rocking. "Trolls and Gargoyles are the enemy. They're not nice. They want the sword and the tree."

Brady nodded. "You've got that right." He stood and paced the narrow, confining space, dodging rocky obstacles in his path. The ceiling dipped low and swooped upward suddenly, revealing pointy stalactites. They dripped their mineral-rich water to form smaller, rounder stalagmites, making the cave look like a mouth full of teeth. The rocky hollow yawned deep toward the back, but the lone torch outside the cave didn't cast its light deep enough for Brady to investigate.

After an arduous journey through the Dens of the Dark Dwarves, Brady could see why the Stygs had dubbed this underground chamber the crypt. The narrow passageways smelled of sulfur and were so numerous, they reminded Brady of the ancient Roman catacombs he had studied. Add to that the stalactites and boulders, the odd drop-offs that suddenly opened up on either side of the tunnel, threatening to swallow you with one misstep, and strange, echoing noises that sounded like victims of torture screaming in pain—and you had a frightening, formidable fortress.

The Dark Dwarves must have had a lot of faith in the impenetrable nature of the place. They hadn't bothered to post a guard outside the barred door of their cramped cave. Brady didn't see how Tassitus would remember the way to their cell, let alone what he could do to break them out. And if he did, how could they escape through the tunnels without getting lost? Brady's heart sank, weighted down by hopelessness—and he still had doubts about the Gargoyle's genuine interest.

He had considered telling the worm to contact Chebar for help. But doing so might compromise the Troll's careful cover and make a bigger mess of things. At least he and Brock were together. That much had taken place as promised, and Brady would have followed Tassitus here for that benefit alone.

"I'm hungry." Brock stood up, unfurling his blue Vituvian tunic and pants, which had become a crumpled, filthy mess. Brady wished he had something to offer his brother besides empathy.

"Me too. Let's hope they don't forget to feed us." Brady groped for his phone, wanting to use the flashlight. Then he remembered it had disappeared when he was dragged through the tunnels unconscious.

Brock wrung his hands. "Queen Judith is sick. I'm supposed to help her. I can't help her from here. I'm supposed to help her." Brock's voice rose with anxiety.

With a gentle touch, Brady tried to head off a Brock-sized meltdown. "It's okay. You can help her when we get out of here. She'll understand."

Brock shook his head in rapid-fire motion. "I'm supposed to help. I can't stay here." He flung Brady away and lurched for the bars on the cell door. With a primal screech, he rattled the metal on its hinges.

Brady wrapped his arms around his brother from behind, pulling against his shoulders, but he couldn't tear Brock free. He was shocked by the strength his brother had cultivated during his summer of training. Brock switched tactics and slammed himself against the bars. He banged his head repeatedly on the door.

"Stop it, Brock. Let go!" Brady pulled for all he was worth. His brother maintained his grip but couldn't reach the metal with his head. He screamed and tried to bite Brady's arm.

"Quit it, Brock, or you'll regret it." Brady clenched his teeth, his mind reeling. How would his dad handle Brock? Brady's fist ached to temporarily put Brock out of his misery. One well-placed punch could keep his brother from hurting himself or the both of them.

"No, no, no!" Head shaking, Brock's arms exploded up and back, flinging his brother to the ground. He turned his tear-spattered face to Brady. Suddenly Brock dropped to his knees and clasped his hands. "I'm sorry. I'm sorry." He rocked his body and squeezed his eyes shut as if trying to block out everything. "I lost control. That's bad. I'm sorry."

Brady rolled onto his knees and crawled to his brother. "It's okay, Brock. I'm fine. It's fine. I'm here." He tasted his own salty tears, aware that this was the first time Brock had apologized for an emotional outburst without being prompted by their parents. The Tethered World was changing his twin. Changing the whole family.

"I'm sorry." Brock covered his wet face with his hands, and Brady wrapped a tentative arm around him. Brock didn't pull away. Instead, he hugged Brady back.

I stepped out of the office at the same time Sophie came clomping down the stairs. Nate and Nicole were on her heels, squealing as they chased her. Sophie grabbed the decorative knob at the bottom of the bannister and swung around the end like a fireman on a pole. The other two hit the tiled foyer and slid, bowling-ball-style, to Mom's feet.

Her hand was on the front doorknob, and she looked down disapprovingly. "Up!" She snapped her fingers. "You two into the backyard to play."

Sophie skittered to a stop next to me. "What's going on?"

I shrugged. "Someone's at the door."

The two little ones ran through the kitchen to the backyard. Mom watched their retreat, then her eyes settled on me with a look I couldn't interpret. "This guy asked to speak with you." She nodded toward the door. Before I could protest, she added, "He's not a reporter. I think we should hear him out."

She pulled the front door open to reveal a young man with sandy hair and heavy stubble.

Sophie and I stepped up beside Mom to have a better look. I couldn't help but notice the guy's hazel eyes and thick, make-ya-sick eyelashes—every female's dream lashes. Why didn't girls ever have a set of lashes like that?

"Hi." He grinned at us. "Sorry to stop by unannounced. Name's Erik Cooper." He stuck his hand out, and I shook it. "Thanks, Mrs. Larcen, for allowing me to speak to your daughter." He reached for the folded newspaper he had tucked beneath his left arm and opened it. I recognized the article from *The Columbian* that I had been reading that morning. The guy—Erik—pointed at the photo of me. "I couldn't help but notice the ring you're wearing in the photo." His gaze skimmed to my right hand, and I stuffed both hands into my jeans pockets. "I see you're wearing it now."

"Yeah. So?" I glanced at Mom. Her mouth was set, eyes wary. Was this guy connected to the Mystique lady? I assumed she was a lady with that name anyway. Surely Erik wasn't short for Mystique.

He shifted his weight and gave me a sheepish grin. I'll admit, he was charming, but I resisted the urge to swoon and met his eyes with a steady gaze.

"I've seen that ring before." He sounded like he was choosing his words with care. Another shuffling of the feet and then, "Would you mind if I came inside?"

Mom stepped in front of me in a protective gesture. "It's been a crazy couple of weeks, with too many people calling and knocking on our door. Forgive me for not being more hospitable, but I think you need to get to the point."

Erik looked taken aback but cleared his throat. "All right. I understand."

Realizing where this conversation might go—down the path to the truth about the ring—I asked Sophie to go find something else to do.

"Why?" She looked wounded, forever hating to be just young enough to miss a lot of the action and important discussions.

Mom snapped her fingers, a favorite gesture when making a point. "Go on, Soph."

Once clear of my sister's prying eyes, I pulled my hands from my pocket and clasped them behind my back. His eyes glimmered with something unusual when he tried to glimpse my ring. Something...alive? Something greedy?

"Are you any relation to a Mystique Mala—uh, Malakoff, maybe?" Mom said, standing her ground at the door. "I got an email from her about the ring this morning."

More shifting of his feet. "Oh, uh, Mystique. Um, yeah. She's my—my mother. She wanted me to come by," he added quickly.

"Okay." I got the impression he was lying.

"Your mother?" Mom cocked her head. "I thought your last name was Cooper."

He pressed his lips together and I could practically see him casting around his brain for a convincing lie. "My mother re-married."

Movement in the nearby shrubs caught my eye. Erik followed my darting glance, pivoting around as if he might yell, "Aha!" It happened quickly but felt awkward and paranoid all at once. I wasn't sure what to make of what I thought I saw or how Erik reacted to it.

He tried to recover his flustered movements by coughing with his fist in front of his mouth. Mom and I exchanged confused looks. "I thought I saw something. Did you see something?" He jerked his thumb at the shrubbery.

"Probably one of my dogs." I waved it off like it made perfect sense.

"Dogs." He nodded. "Like I was saying, I've seen your ring before."

"You definitely said that. And your point?"

In the bushes behind Erik, a metallic shape showed itself between the branches of our rhododendron bush. I tried not to react to the sight of a cylindrical Gnome hat, followed by a set of bright cobalt eyes. Crouching beneath the Gnome was a slimmer face with pointed ears. An Elf. Probably Mr. Delaney's former prisoners. They slipped back into the foliage, there and gone so fast I might have imagined them from lack of sleep.

Erik reached a hand to his throat where he fumbled for something beneath the collar of his shirt. "My point is that I've seen your ring before because." He pulled out a gold chain. "I have one exactly like it."

CHAPTER TWENTY-THREE

ERIK UNCLASPED HIS NECKLACE AND DANGLED it in front of me. A gleaming gold ring hung from the chain. I gaped in astonishment, my heart rattling around in my ribcage. Mom gasped and leaned in for a closer look.

Aunt Jules had told us the other key was long lost. Then Malagruel claimed to have found it. Yet here it was, mere inches from my face and a perfect match to the one on my right hand. Who was this Erik guy?

"As you can see, this looks a lot like your ring in the photo." Erik hiked it closer to his own face and studied it. "I wondered if I could examine your ring to compare."

I shoved my hand into my pocket again. Something smelled funky, and not the good kind of funky. In my peripheral vision, a tiny head peered out from the shrubbery. My gaze slid to my feet, then slowly made contact with the petite features and leaf-shaped ears of the Elf. He moved his head from side to side in a slow warning gesture. I wondered if my mom was paying attention, but I couldn't risk checking.

I didn't know what to make of this situation, but I knew one thing for certain: I instinctively did *not* trust this Erik dude.

He held out his hand, palm up. "Would you mind if I take a look?"

"Yes, we do mind." Mom lifted her chin. Maybe she sensed the same funkiness. "Where did you get your ring? I'd like some background."

Another odd look twitched across his features. It reminded me of someone, but I couldn't place who.

"It's been in my family for generations. My mother, Misty, passed it on to me. Recently." He looked at my hand buried in my pocket, as if he had x-ray vision. "How did you get yours?"

"Right now, we're the ones asking the questions." Mom

shifted closer to me, and I had a sudden flash of another face. The one I couldn't place a moment ago. It was seared into my memory with a different set of features. But the expression behind the eyes was a perfect match.

"You're right, Mom." I hoped my voice sounded calm and my face remained neutral. My insides were convulsing, and my mind churned at the implications of the situation. "How about you let me look at your ring first, and I'll let you know if it's the same."

Erik's posture stiffened, and his jaw flexed, then relaxed. "Sure, sure." He nodded and held out the chain toward me. Although I didn't think he knew that *I* knew who he was, part of me feared reaching out. What if he grabbed me?

Before I could attempt anything brilliant or brainless, Mom reached for the necklace. Erik clamped her wrist with his free hand and twisted her arm behind her back before I could blink. He wrapped his other arm under her chin in a headlock. Mom gasped, her eyes wild. I froze, unsure what to do. The Gnome and Elf stepped out of the bushes behind Erik, weapons drawn.

"Look, I don't want to hurt your mother but I will." He flexed, tightening his hold around her neck. "Let me see your ring."

The Gnome and Elf were edging closer, but I didn't tear my eyes from the creep in front of me. The necklace dangled beneath the man's wrist, the ring resting on Mom's collarbone.

"Okay, okay." I nodded and withdrew my hand, holding both hands in the air in a show of surrender. "Here, look."

"Don't do it." Mom drilled me with her eyes.

Pretending to allow him to inspect the ring, I moved my hand closer to his face.

"Stay back, Sadie," Mom pleaded.

With a quick swipe, I snatched his ring and yanked the chain from his fist, lobbing it between him and the doorframe. The Elf caught it and disappeared, literally invisible, before a stunned Erik could see what had happened. He cursed and yanked my mom's arm higher, swiveling to see what I'd done with it. Mom yelped. The Gnome advanced, gripping his weapon.

"Let her go!" The small but mighty Gnome brandished his sword—a dagger to us humans—his bearded face contorted with anger.

Sophie gasped from behind me. I glanced back and gestured for her to keep away.

Erik released Mom's twisted arm, only to tighten his stranglehold on her neck. "Get back or I choke her to death." His savage gaze scoured the ground, then looked from me to the Gnome, turning his back. "Where's the ring?" *Where?*" His ferocious voice made me recoil.

Mom writhed in his grip, clawing at his arm. He staggered backward, stumbling into the threshold. He reached his left hand to the doorframe to steady himself, his fingers slipping into the space beneath the hinge.

I stepped away and slammed the door as hard as possible. There was a sickening crack of wood and bone. The heavy door popped open with a shudder and Erik doubled over, clutching his hand with a screech. Mom slipped out of his arm and fell onto her backside right inside the door. Erik's head butted her square in the face. She reeled backwards, hands flying to her nose, blood blossoming through her fingers. My sister rushed to her side.

I looked up in time to see Erik transform. The good-looking, sandy-haired man with the dreamy eyelashes evaporated like water on hot cement. His suntanned skin dissolved, and a charcoal leather exterior suddenly filled the doorframe as he straightened, still grasping his fingers. I hadn't forgotten the scar beneath that bulging, watery eye. Unforgettable from his yellowed fangs to his black wings to his taloned feet, before me stood the gruesome, bat-like Gargoyle that had pretended to be my father a month before.

A hissing sound jerked my attention from his face to his leg, where what looked like a snake slithered along his thigh. I instinctively shrank bank with a gasp. The last time I saw Malagruel's snake-like tail, it had been falling from the sky in the heat of battle. Apparently, Gargoyle tails grew back, like lizard tails. This new one needed a lot more growth to return to its former glory, which had been long enough to wrap around my body like a rope.

"Ah, it is none other than my darling daughter." Malagruel stepped toward me, ducking slightly to see beneath the top of the doorframe.

"Sadie!" Sophie sounded horrified.

I didn't know what to do. Mom struggled to get onto her elbow while still clamping down on her gushing nose. I couldn't shut the door and lock the big bat out because her legs were in the way. Not that it would offer much protection. "Sophie, help Mom get up." My voice was hoarse with fear. Sophie reached for Mom's arm.

The Gargoyle placed his injured hand on the doorframe and reached out to me with the other. "Give me that—*ugh!*" His leathery hand swiped at me as he tumbled forward and crumpled onto his knees across Mom's legs. Mom and Sophie screamed, while I jumped out of the way. Malagruel clutched his ankle, cursing and foaming at the mouth with rage.

The Gnome stood behind the writhing demon and raised his bloodied sword to strike again. Malagruel looked over his shoulder and donkey-kicked the Gnome out into the yard with his uninjured foot. The little creature sailed down the walkway and bounced into the grass, where he lay unmoving. Then Malagruel gasped and arched his back as if he'd been stung there. I looked around, confused. The Gargoyle snarled and jerked sideways against the doorframe. There was the Elf, his bloody sword in his hand, running away from Malagruel's side and toward the listless Gnome.

Mom was trapped under the injured bat. I crouched and shoved my weight into the Gargoyle's side, trying to lift him off her. A guttural growl exploded from his throat. He grabbed my waist and flung me over his shoulder.

"Sadie!" Sophie's voice was desperate.

Malagruel stood, favoring one leg. Hanging upside down against his winged back, I had a close-up view of his sliced Achilles tendon and the fountain of blood trailing across the cement. My hand felt wet where I pressed against the stab wound from the Elf's sword.

Two fangs and slitted pupils filled my vision. "It'sss me, Sssadie," the snake tail hissed.

I shrieked and batted the viper away. "Sophie! Help mom get out of here."

"Sadie, I'm scared." My sister was crying, and it made my heart hurt.

"Get something to stop the bleeding! Don't worry about me." My charm necklace dangled around my chin and caught in my mouth as I tried to speak.

The snake recovered from the smack down, fangs bared and glistening. I still had two faint scars on my cheekbone from our last encounter. *Not today, you monster.* With agility that surprised even me, I grabbed the snake right behind the head, taking control as I'd seen my brothers do with snakes found in our yard. My other hand encircled his scaly body as well. Keeping my arms rigid, I fought against its muscular, thrashing form with my clamped hands, praying it wouldn't twist from my grasp.

Malagruel limped into the house, carrying me like a sack over his shoulder. Blood spurted onto the floor with each bit of pressure placed on his foot. It pooled onto the tile, spreading to where Mom's nose had left a sizable puddle. The entryway was a bloodbath. I prayed desperately that Nate and Nicole would not come inside and see the gruesome sight—let alone the Gargoyle.

Gripping the snake, I risked a glance at my mom and sister. They had recoiled to my right, staring at the towering, bleeding beast with horrified faces. Mom pressed a rag to her nose; blood streaked her face and hands. Then she lunged at Malagruel and shouted, "Let her go!"

I braced myself, willing my fingers to stay clamped on the viper, but the impact never came. Mom slipped in the blood, landing with a frustrated yelp at the monster's feet. I felt Malagruel's amused chuckle beneath my body, and it made hopelessness swell inside my heart. I didn't see how this situation could have a happy ending.

In an instant, the Gargoyle pivoted his enormous foot so that his talons encircled Mom's thigh. He pointed at Sophie. "You, get a long strip of cloth to bandage my ankle. If you don't cooperate, I will use my talons to dissect your mother right here."

Sophie's footsteps, and cries, retreated.

"Make sure the little ones stay outside!" I hollered after her. My arms and fingers ached to maintain their grip on the slithering tail. The thing seemed to sense my trembling limbs and fought harder. I closed my eyes and prayed desperately for strength.

"Get...out...of my...house." Mom's voice was weak but fierce.

Another chuckle rumbled through Malagruel's chest. "You're in no position to order me around, woman. This could've been a harmless visit, had you cooperated. Now it looks like your darling daughter and I will take a little trip to the underworld."

"No. *Please*," Mom begged, her despondent voice an echo of all the emotions inside myself.

The Gargoyle expelled an evil laugh. "And don't waste your

time trying to find her. I kept the old man out of sight for nearly forty years."

CHAPTER TWENTY-FOUR

BRADY WOKE TO THE SCREECH OF metal on rock. It was only the sound of the cell door, he'd learned. Rubbing his eyes, he sat up. Brock didn't stir.

Relief warmed his chilled body. Chebar! He smiled up at the ginger-brown Troll and stood, knowing he must hide his eagerness. Chebar had risked much to help Brady's family, and he didn't want to jeopardize the Troll by doing something stupid.

Chebar nodded, his dark eyes friendly beneath his heavy brow. He glanced over his broad shoulder, checking whether he'd been followed by a Dwarf. He leaned close to Brady. "Are you well?"

Brady nodded and kept his voice soft. "I might die from either the cold or boredom. But no one bothers us beyond our daily bowl of soup."

"Craventhrall is buzzing with the news that the twin kings have been captured. Had to see it for myself."

"It's true." Brady spread his arms wide. "Here we are. I stupidly trusted a Gargoyle who told me he would help me get my brother out of here. Instead, he delivered me to the Dark Dwarves, and they put us in joint custody. The worm insists he's trying to figure out how to spring us, but I'm not holding my breath."

"A worm? He works for Malagruel?" Chebar tugged his pant legs up and sat on a chunk of rock.

"Yeah. Tassitus. Do you know him?"

The Troll looked thoughtful. "No, can't say I do. But I'll keep my eye out."

Brady shrugged. "At least Brock isn't stuck here alone, so I don't mind."

"I'll do what I can to get you out."

A tiny bit of optimism surfaced. "Thanks. And who knows, maybe this Tassitus fellow will come through. I mean, look at you." Brady gestured at the Troll. "You're not like the other Trolls. Maybe he's not a typical Gargoyle."

A strange look rippled through Chebar's features. "I'd find that hard to believe where Gargoyles are concerned."

"Yeah, not likely." Brady glanced at his sleeping brother, curled on his side, one arm bent beneath his head. "How did my brother get here, do you know? He would only say that he flew from the mountainside."

Chebar nodded and told the story of the memorial service on Forest Ridge. "Spies had been scouting the area for a couple of weeks, looking for a way to start trouble. My father and Malagruel agreed they needed to use any opportunity to regain some leverage. But Joseph Marshall wasted no time carrying out his plans topside. They wanted their own ace-in-the-hole, as you say, to stay on equal footing with that man. Marshall has his own agenda and doesn't really care if we are prepared for what he's planned."

"He's up to all sorts of crazy things, that's for sure." Brady rehashed the dead Yeti, the captured creatures, and the press conference with the promise to deliver the fountain of youth through the sprouting trees. "He also forced Sadie to speak and had one of your brothers parade himself for the media."

Chebar pressed his fists together at the knuckles. "Sargon! I heard about that. He's the second oldest, after Rooke. Loves to be the center of attention."

"He made quite an impression. My mom, on the other hand, was booed off the stage." Brady shook his head remembering. "So, what have you heard about the Tree of Life? What'll happen if our neighbor's little saplings fall into the wrong hands? Well—I guess they already have, in a way."

The Troll leaned his forearms onto his knees and looked at the floor. "A lot of rumors surround the tree." His voice was so quiet that Brady had to concentrate to make out his words. "It's always been heavily protected and so mysterious that much of what is said may not be true. A fountain of youth, a cure-all, a way to immortality. With so much conjecture, the focus has been on the Flaming Sword. *That* is a real, solid object with tangible by-products we see every day. We know it is powerful. We know it allows the Tethered World to have light. 'He who possesses the sword possesses all' is one of my father's mantras. Until recently, the Tree of Life felt like a bonus that came with the sword. But Queen Estancia's fixation on the tree seems to have made an impression on both my father and Malagruel. Now they speak of the tree as if it's the ultimate prize. One they can't attain without taking control of the sword."

"It's like they're one and the same." Brady chewed on his lip.

"Exactly." Chebar dropped his voice even lower. "Now the two of them are in an unspoken competition. Whoever sinks their teeth into its fruit first becomes the immortal ruler of all."

While Sophie looked for something to wrap Malagruel's ankle, I continued to hang upside down with a death grip on his writhing tail. Thankfully, the creepy thing seemed to be getting tired as well. Mom was berating the beast while pounding his leg with her fist. Her clothes and skin were sticky with blood, and the whole scene felt to me like it was straight out of a horror movie. How I longed to hear someone yell, "Cut!" and stop the nightmarish scene.

The Gargoyle swayed beneath my weight. He released my mother, stumbled toward the stairs, and sat, allowing me to slide awkwardly off his shoulder. I involuntarily caught myself, releasing Malagruel's tail. His enormous hand snatched my wrist, encircling it with a grip as strong as any handcuff. "I'm not letting you get away again." His voice had weakened, which I took as a good sign. Blood loss must be taking a toll. "Key or no key, you're going back with me. You're going to help me get fruit from the Tree of Life, or I shall kill every last member of your family."

I glared at him, steeling myself to look directly at his grotesque face. "I thought you were interested in the sword."

He tugged me closer, where I could smell his sulfurous breath. It made me gag. "I will have both. My current condition makes the fruit a little more pressing."

Sophie returned, holding a strip of plaid fabric. Nate's room had curtains made from the same cloth.

Mom had managed to get to her feet on the slick floor. Her chest heaved in rage, fists curled at her sides. "Let her...go."

Malagruel didn't seem to hear her. His crazed eyes cast about, searching the floor. "Where's my key? What did you do with it?" He lifted my ringed hand to his face and took it in with lusty satisfaction. I kept it balled in a tight fist. "At least I still have *one* ring."

"I'll never let you have it." I struggled to tug free of his vise-like grip. He grabbed my fist with his free hand and tried to uncurl my fingers. His efforts were surprisingly feeble. I realized he had several broken fingers thanks to the door slamming episode, which left him little to work with.

Mom grabbed the fabric from Sophie. "Here, let me bandage your ankle." Her footsteps spattered drops of blood on the slick floor as she approached him cautiously, as if he were a wild animal. "Just let go of Sadie."

Malagruel didn't acknowledge her. He only mumbled, "Give me the key," with each attempt to open my hand. He sounded desperate and exhausted. Panting between words, he soon faltered and, to my shock, slumped back onto the stairs, releasing my wrist. His mouth gaped open and closed several times, like a fish out of water. His hateful, helpless eyes drilled me.

My legs wouldn't listen to my brain, which told them to run before he got his second wind. Then his gaze slid up to the ceiling and his head slouched to the side ever so slightly. I heard him wheeze out an interminably long breath.

I stared.

"Is he...?" Sophie moved closer.

"I—I don't know." Head to toe, my body felt jittery and disconnected. I could hear my pulse throbbing between my ears.

Mom clutched my arm. "Oh Lord, please let him be dead."

Sophie picked her way across the wet tile to peer through the banisters at the Gargoyle. I marveled at her courage for the hundredth time since the summer began. We were all a big, bloody, out-of-breath mess. Crimson smudges dotted our clothes and skin, and a slick, slimy puddle crept over the tile and pooled in the grout. The front door was open, exposing the whole scene to anyone who might pass by, and I wondered how much our spying neighbor had seen. I pushed it closed.

Mom reached a tentative hand to grasp the Gargoyle's limp wrist. "I don't know if his pulse would be in the same place as ours." She gingerly climbed a couple of steps alongside his body and slipped two fingers against his neck, cringing. Her nose had finally stopped bleeding.

I held my breath, hoping for good news.

Mom gently prodded both sides of his throat. "He's gone."

Relief pummeled me. I sagged against the wall and watched

as Mom closed the lid over his bulbous eye. *Dead.* It was hard to believe I was so eager to embrace the word. Context is everything.

"The Gnome!" I sprang away from the wall at the thought. Sophie jerked the door open and reached his sprawling, limp body before I did. We both knelt and felt his skin, which was already cold.

"No!" Sophie's cry was bitter. "He's dead."

Ugh. The word that had brought such comfort a moment before now rang with the pain of loss. We didn't even know the little fellow's name, yet he had died saving us.

I placed my hand on Sophie's shoulders. "Why don't you bring him into the house so we can clean up? Mom will help us figure out what to do."

With robotic movements, Sophie scooped the Gnome into her arms. His bloody sword remained in the grass. Wiping the blade, I tucked it into my belt loop, like the daggers I had carried in the Tethered World. His conical hat lay several feet away. I retrieved it and followed my sister back inside.

I had no sooner closed the door than I heard the high-pitched wail of police sirens. Mom and I looked at each other in alarm.

Sophie turned, hugging the petite body to herself. "Oh yeah! When I went to find a bandage, I called 911."

CHAPTER TWENTY-FIVE

"SOPHIE! THIS ISN'T EXACTLY A POLICE matter. How are we going to explain this?" Mom dashed into the guest bathroom built beneath the stairs, reappearing with an armful of towels. She tossed them on the floor. "Start mopping."

"I'm sorry." Sophie stood there, clutching the Gnome, eyes round and watery. "I just knew we couldn't handle that beast by ourselves."

"Of course, honey. I'm sorry." Mom wrapped my sister in a quick hug. "Good thinking. You better hide the Gnome in the closet for now."

Mom hurried to a pile of clean laundry dumped on the sofa in the living room and pawed through it, pulling out a clean T-shirt and a pair of sweats. She peeled off her bloody clothes, and yanked the other ones on. "Glad those blinds are closed. How's my face?"

"Still a mess." I looked out the peephole. "They're getting out of their car."

Mom disappeared into the bathroom again, and I heard the faucet blasting water. "Okay, listen," she called. "Sophie, go out back and stay there. Don't let Nate and Nicole in this house. Stay outside until one of us comes to get you."

"Got it." Sophie grabbed several towels and tossed them into the guest bath on her way outside.

Mom rushed out of the bathroom, her face glistening and clean, though her nose looked swollen. "Get a large blanket and cover this creep up. We'll move him, somehow, after I get rid of the cops. Then do what you can to get the rest of this blood off the floor—but we'll probably never get it out of the carpeted stairs."

Mom opened the door and stepped outside. How was she going to explain the blood on the walkway? I ran to the linen closet and pulled out the large, raggedy quilt we used for the dogs in the winter, not wanting to contaminate anything decent. I shook it out and draped it over the still figure of the Gargoyle. Before tackling the floor, I couldn't resist a quick peek outside.

There was no mistaking the thick, caterpillar unibrow of one of the cops. I blinked. Officers Unibrow and Barbie—I couldn't remember their real names—had awakened me that fateful night I learned my parents had been kidnapped. Thus began my bittersweet association with the Tethered World. Not that they knew anything about the place, but those two would forever remain the starting point of the secret life I had uncovered at the beginning of summer.

Oh no. The three of them were strolling toward the front door. I dashed into the guest bath and plunged a hand towel beneath the faucet. Diving back to the tile, I shifted into cyber-Cinderella gear and scrubbed at the grout and tile. Pale pink streaks remained like a thin varnish, but they blended with the tile's marbling well enough.

Another peek revealed they were right outside the door. They seemed to all be looking down, likely at the blood on the front walk. I tossed the towel behind a potted plant in the living room and surveyed the entryway, satisfied that "bloodbath" wasn't going to be the officers' first impression. It was the bulky figure under the quilt that looked alarmingly suspicious.

What to do? What to do?

Circling to the peephole, I found Mom waving goodbye and Unibrow and Barbie heading to their cruiser.

"Hallelujah!" I mumbled at the door.

Mom slipped inside and gave me a that-was-a-close-one look. "Whew."

"How did you get rid of them?"

"A lot of fast talking." She ran her hand through her hair. Blood still rimmed some of her fingernails. "Told them I got hit in the nose with the slamming door—hence all the blood on the front stoop. Said my daughter freaked out and called 911."

"Wow. Good thinking."

"Yeah. They knew who I was, I guess from the press conference. They were more interested in what I thought about our neighbor's Bigfoot claims than my bloody face."

I remembered their skeptical interest in my mother's hobby the night they came to our house. Officer Unibrow had wondered if my mom had ever seen "him"—as in Bigfoot.

Mom puffed a long breath with inflated cheeks. "Now, what to do with this giant Gargoyle? I don't know if we can lift him on our own."

I cocked an eyebrow. "Did you ever imagine you'd need to string those particular words together to form a sentence?"

She chuckled. "Not exactly."

"I don't see how we can move him without Brady or Dad. Dead weight is difficult enough, let alone seven or eight feet of it."

"Well, we can't leave him here. It's a miracle your little brother and sister didn't wander inside in the middle of that nightmare." She shook her head. "I can't imagine trying to help them through such an ordeal."

"How about the sled?" I scratched my head, thinking through the logistics. "If we can heft him onto the sled, we could slide him upstairs into Brock and Brady's room."

Mom nodded. "That might work. I'll lock the bedroom door, and we can start digging a hole in the backyard or something. If he stays in the house too long, he'll decompose."

I gave a half-hearted grin. "Another sentence I'd never predict any of us would need to say."

Chebar placed his hands on his knees and stood. "Before I leave, I want to tell you what to expect. Your brother was brought here as a compromise. Both Malagruel and my father want your brother under their own control. Malagruel wanted to bring your brother—and now, of course, it'll be the both of you—to Abaddon, the place where the Banished dwell. He believes the Gnomes wouldn't dare attempt a rescue if your brother was there." He shook his head. "Trust me. That place is not fit for humans. Or Trolls. You saw the state your uncle was in when the Dwarves discovered him."

"Why drag my brother anywhere? Why don't they kill him?" Brady got to his feet and buried his hands in his pockets.

"It's all about leverage. The Vituvians will restrain their retaliation if they know their king is alive. They will negotiate. If Brock dies," the Troll glanced at Brock's sleeping form, "there's no reason for them to hold back. Certainly no reason to negotiate over the sword and the tree."

"Do those giant bats actually fear the Gnomes? They outsize

them like elephants to mice. Plus, they have the muscle of the Trolls at their side." Brady raked a hand through his hair. "I don't get it."

"They fear the power of the sword." He stepped closer to Brady. "The sword enhances the might of those who control it. Why else would the Gnomes be able to keep it under their thumb for thousands of years? There have been other attempts to steal the sword or attack the tree, but always the Vituvians miraculously prevail. Through some perilous times, let me assure you."

"Sounds more like God's protection, if you ask me. So what makes them think they have a better chance to steal it or get to the tree this time around?"

"Your brother has access to both the sword and the tree. And for the first time, the enemy has access to a Vituvian monarch. Both the Banished and my father are betting the Gnomes will concede to Brock's wishes if he can be forced to do their bidding. As loyal subjects, the Vituvians would obey him."

Brady shook his head. "I doubt they can force him to do anything like that. Besides, he doesn't have the keys to unlock the sword, even if he wanted to."

"If my father or Malagruel can strong-arm your brother into handing over his kingdom to their rulership, they won't need the key. They would simply take over Vituvia—not without heavy bloodshed, of course. The citizens won't take it lying down."

"And if they can't strong-arm Brock? Which is where my money would be. No Brock, no key. No chance at success."

Chebar flexed his jaw, his eyes glinting with something cold. "There is another way. Let us hope it never comes to that. But in the hidden, arcane laws that govern the Tethered World, there *is* a way to remove the sword without the keys."

Brady's throat tensed, unsure if he wanted to know. But he had to know. "How?"

Chebar gave a long, deliberate blink. "If the blood of a Vituvian monarch is shed upon the stone and fills the keyholes embedded there, the Flaming Sword of Cherubythe will be released."

Brady stiffened, his eyes flitting to his brother. "What? No. *No.* That can't be. Why would such a thing be possible?"

"It is a horrific anomaly." Chebar grimaced. "And one we must guard against."

The cavern seemed darker than ever, its walls pressing in.

The stalactites threatened to impale Brady through his skull—a welcome possibility compared to the horror movie that played in his brain. He imagined his helpless, innocent brother being sacrificed at the hands of his enemies. Never!

"This arcane truth," the Troll said, shifting closer, "is knowledge I've gained from studying ancient documents related to the founding of this land. But my father is a clever, well-studied Troll, so we must assume he also knows of it."

Brady felt sick with dread. He could only nod.

"Now listen." Chebar glanced back at the door again. "My father plans to secretly move you and your brother to Craventhrall without telling Malagruel. Relations between the two are strained since Queen Estancia died and their original plans were dashed to pieces. He's far less motivated to share the governorship now that he has his sights set on fruit from the tree. And he's enraged that both you and your sister escaped from Craventhrall. He will avenge such humiliation, and he will personally transfer you and your brother to his private dungeon to ensure nothing goes wrong."

The cool, damp air chilled Brady. He shivered. His mind wanted to shut down. Shut off. Drown in sleep and wake up at home with his brother sprawled on the opposite bed. He pushed the unrealistic thoughts away.

He had to fight. Had to be alert and prepared. "I'm really hoping you have a plan."

"Absolutely." Chebar's face glazed over, hard and spiteful. "I'm going to assassinate my father."

CHAPTER TWENTY-SIX

MOM ICED HER NOSE WHILE I rummaged through the garage for the sled. We didn't get much snow in this part of Washington, so our sled collected a lot of dust and was hidden behind layers of obstacles that concealed its whereabouts.

I finally spied a bright red runner beneath a piece of plywood Brady used as a skateboard ramp. I freed it from its plywood prison and took it to the door. Snatching a greasy rag, I smacked at dust and cobwebs clinging to the metal and wood.

Once inside, I set it at the foot of the stairs. "Got it!"

Mom stepped out of her upstairs bedroom with wet hair slicked back into a ponytail. Her nose was a neon sign that looked like an advertisement for plastic surgery.

"What happened to icing your nose?"

"First things first. My hair was disgusting and matted with blood." She sauntered down the steps, stopping right above the lumpy quilt. "Let's get this over with. I've got my doubts that we can manage Malagruel's heavy bulk, but I want this demon out of sight—and hopefully out of my house—ASAP."

I tugged the blanket off the dead Gargoyle. Mom and I gasped.

He had turned to stone.

"Whoa..." I blinked, wondering if my eyes were playing tricks on me. Malagruel lay precisely as he had when we covered him up. Shoulders against the carpeted stairs, his leather vest—still leather—flopped open on one side. His knees were somewhat curled and twisted to the right, his gnarly talons clamped together like they were grasping for prey. And his left ankle still gaped open where the late Gnome had struck him. That Gnome had one sharp sword.

Mom whistled long and low. "Well, I guess this solves the decomposing problem."

"Yep." I puckered my lips, wondering how we'd move a giant block of stone *up* the stairs. "Maybe we should rethink taking him up. How about out?"

Mom sputtered. "I don't exactly want to make yard art out of him."

"Of course not. How about taking your frustrations out with a sledgehammer?" I mimed pounding on his head. "That's what I'm thinking."

A smile pulled at Mom's mouth. "As long as I can take the first swing."

"Hang on." I held up a finger then dashed back to the garage. A sled would likely scratch up the tile and wouldn't slide across the cement with his weight. We needed wheels.

I returned with Brady's skateboard and a couple of Dad's little-used dumbbells to brace the wheels. Mom and I stood on either side of the beast, taking hold of a stone shoulder. I found the rough, grey stone much more appealing than the charred leather hide.

We tipped him up in unison and both gasped in surprise. The dude weighed much less than we expected. I could have almost picked him up myself. "Did he turn into a giant pumice stone or what?" I asked, noticing that his surface looked rather porous.

"I don't know and I don't care." Mom grabbed the body by one arm. "But thank God we can actually get him out of our house. I was pretty worried that he'd be too heavy."

We lowered the Gargoyle onto the skateboard. He resembled a dead cockroach, legs sticking up in the air at odd angles.

"Guessing you want to smash him to smithereens in the back yard? Should I tell Sophie and the others to go in the garage or something?"

"Nope." Mom pointed. "Out front. Let's hope, for once, Joseph Delaney *is* watching. Maybe this will be a warning to him."

Disembodied, amber eyes glowed in the shadows. Brady jumped, sloshing his soup, at the sight of the gleaming orbs outside their cell. Tassitus had returned, as promised.

"Oh, it's you." Brady willed his escalating adrenaline to return to the shallow end again. He set down his half-eaten bowl of soup and stood.

Brock glanced up from his meal, watching Tassitus unbolt the door and step inside. He lowered his spoon and fixed the Gargoyle with a wary stare. Brady wondered if his brother's fear came from his innate ability to read people's character or simply from the fact that Tassitus was a Gargoyle.

Tonight the worm was shirtless but wore a pair of camouflaged board shorts he'd surely nabbed topside. They made him look even more human and less intimidating—as long as Brady didn't focus on the Frankenstein knobs across the guy's brow bone.

Tassitus offered the brothers a curt bow. "How are they treating you?"

"All right." Brady shrugged. "They pretty much ignore us. The guard seems freaked out to have anything to do with us. And they feed us a bowl of soup once a day whether we're hungry or not."

"Only one meal a day?" The knobs pressed together. "I'll speak to them about that. The Stygians are very superstitious about this part of the mountain. A deathtrap built by monsters, they say. They pay the guards double to do half as much."

"Monsters worse than Stygs or Trolls or, no offense, Gargoyles?"

"Apparently so. The crypt is as far as the Dark Dwarves dare to penetrate into this part of the mountain." Tassitus stepped closer, and Brock stepped back. "Listen, I wanted to discuss what I've learned. It's proving difficult to get you out without marching you in front of the guards. Nekronok and Malagruel made it clear that Brock was not to be moved without their express consent."

"What? You thought it was going to be easy, and now you realize you got it wrong?" Brady couldn't help the heavy sarcasm that seeped into his words. He didn't need more disappointing news.

The Gargoyle dropped his gaze. "Forgive me. I knew it would be challenging, but now it looks impossible. They only let me back here to visit because I brought you here myself."

"Why can't the three of us just walk out?" Brady pointed at the door. Anger and helplessness simmered together inside. "There's no guard stationed here. We can head the opposite direction and figure it out as we go. Anything's better than sitting here, waiting on Nekronok."

"It isn't that simple. We would need to get to safety, and it would be certain death to run deep into the mountain." His voice was quiet and sincere. "Besides, that passageway ends right beyond your cell. The only way out is through the guarded door." When Brady didn't reply, the Gargoyle went on. "I've been lurking about Craventhrall, trying to learn what I can. Malagruel hasn't returned since our escapade in Portland. I didn't have time to check for him in Abaddon, but all of his advisors are waiting on him in Craventhrall, so I believe he's still topside."

"Which means?"

"I'm not certain." The Gargoyle stuffed his hands in his pockets. "Hopefully it means you only have to worry about Nekronok. That's where things get sticky. Against Malagruel's knowledge, Nekronok plans to move you both to Craventhrall. Tomorrow."

Brady didn't let on that Chebar had already shared this information. Still, he shuddered, remembering the horrors of solitary confinement at the Eldritch. "In that case, I'd rather stay here. But they probably don't want my input." He glanced over at Brock and saw that his brother had finished his own soup and was starting on Brady's neglected bowl. "Dude! That's my—ah, that's fine. Go ahead." He didn't have the heart to tell his brother to put it down.

Tassitus went to the barred door and stepped into the doorway, where he could look out in both directions. Then he stepped close to Brady and whispered, "The chief himself will be escorting you with some of his sons. They plan to take the deep passageways. Nekronok won't risk bringing you across the valley to Craventhrall. He's afraid the Gnomes or Dwarves of Berganstroud may ambush them and rescue you."

"Ambush? Like in Vietnam?" Brock came over to where they stood, suddenly interested in the conversation.

"Something like that." Brady glanced from his brother to Tassitus. "Brock's a war aficionado."

The worm nodded. "Yes, that kind of ambush. Nekronok won't take the risk. He sent scouts to map the way through the tunnels today. Assuming they return, you will be moved tomorrow."

"Assuming?"

Tassitus raised his knobby brow. "There are legitimate fears about the tunnels on their side of the mountain as well."

"Then why did you come today? Wanted to get the bad news

off your chest or something?" Brady gave him a skeptical look.

The Gargoyle looked away and shifted his weight. "I understand how this situation must look. Believe me, I did not intend for you to be in this crypt with your brother. I only wanted you to come with me while I knew of his whereabouts. Things unraveled before we made it far enough to form a plan. But if you wish to protect your brother, I can only pray you will listen to what I'm about to tell you and take it to heart."

Brady gave a wry laugh. "Pray to who, Beelzebub?"

A look of shame darkened the Gargoyle's face. "Let me share something with you, Brady. Until this past year, I was as vile as Ophidian or Malagruel. To be appointed as one of Malagruel's worms, I had to prove myself by competing with other potential worms. I had to do some despicable things. I must have been the most despicable because I earned the position."

He sat down on a rock, his voice sorrowful. "Since moving to Malagruel's quarters and gaining access to his library, I've spent a lot of time reading. I discovered an old, neglected *antiquus scriptum*—a Bible—that I've studied voraciously. It's altered my understanding of everything."

Brady was stunned. Could these creatures change their natures? Of course not. But God could cause them to change. Maybe Tassitus was proof.

"It's my wish to do what is right," he went on. "I've petitioned the Maker to show me how I can help you. Unfortunately, it doesn't involve my leading you both to freedom, though I'm actively seeking a way to do so, even now. But I've overheard things, and I believe I have a plan."

CHAPTER TWENTY-SEVEN

AFTER REDUCING THE STONE MALAGRUEL TO a pile of chunky rubble in our front yard, and disposing of his leftover clothing, I took a long, scalding shower. It was my goal to scrub every last speck of that loathsome monster from all bodily surfaces, with the exception of the bullet-grazed scrape on my leg.

Properly dried, deodorized, and dressed, I headed downstairs, ready for lunch. Dark blotches on the carpeted stairs made me pause. Malagruel's blood seemed to glower up, as if to say, *You'll never be able to erase me from your life.* I would locate a can of rug cleaner and use some elbow grease on the steps as soon as I finished eating. The tile also needed proper scouring.

Tap-tap-tap.

A weak knock made me cock my head. It sounded like it came from the front door but was suspiciously faint. I drew near to the peephole, guessing it must be a curious but shy fan from yesterday's press conference.

Looking out, I couldn't see anyone.

Tap, tap...tap, tap, tap.

The knock was louder this time. I felt the vibration of the door against my cheekbone pressed against the peephole. But no one was there. No one tall enough to be seen, anyway.

"Good news, hon." Mom came out of her office, holding an icepack to her nose, as I reached to unlock the door. "Oh, was that the door? I wasn't sure."

"Yeah, I think so." I pulled it open, and there stood the diminutive form of the Elf who had helped fend off Malagruel. His large, oval eyes looked up with a mixture of awe and curiosity. They were lavender. "Oh! Hello," I said. "Won't you come in?"

He blinked several times, then jumped onto the threshold

of the door. Though I'd had glimpses of the Elves of Willowmist in the Tethered World, they were brief at best. The shy Elves popped in and out of view spontaneously, preferring to stay invisible more often than not.

Seeing this little guy was fascinating. His skin was weathered, the way a worn leaf looks come late autumn, almost transparent between the network of veins. His oversized nose and chin poked downward, in the opposite direction from his large, pointy ears. Although his limbs were proportionate, his head was as wide as his shoulders, like a real-life bobble-head with thinning grey hair. His sword was sheathed in a belt, attached to high-water red pants, worn through on both knees. A supple leather pouch hung from the belt, opposite his sword. He sported a navy cardigan with tiny acorn buttons and brown elbow patches. His sleeves were too short, exposing his incredibly narrow forearms, no bigger than a pencil. He wasn't any taller than a bowling pin.

All in all, I wanted to keep him.

He walked silently past me into the foyer, barefoot. With an arm across his belly, he bowed dramatically, then spoke in a high, raspy voice. "Greetings, Larcens. Lark here, at your service." Standing straight again, he took in both Mom and me with his steady gaze. "I saw the mountain of rock in your front lawn. I'm wholly pleased at the demise of the Banished. May I remark that annihilating his image entirely was a brilliant ending to his story."

I grinned at his choice of words.

"Why thank you." Mom curtsied. "That was Sadie's suggestion."

He bowed to me directly. "Indeed, Princess Sadie's bravery and wisdom are legendary."

I sputtered, not wanting to laugh in his face but scoffing at such a description. "I don't know about that, but it's kind of you to say. We were more than happy to obliterate the Gargoyle. And we also thank you for helping to take him down."

He tilted his head. "Ah, well. We each do what we can." He pointed at Mom's colorful, swollen nose. "My apologies for not stopping the brute before he clobbered your face."

Sophie walked into the foyer. "Mom, I think we're out of jelly..." Her eyes lit up at the sight of the Elf, and she let out a squeal. "Ooh! It's you! You're the Elf that Mr. Delaney stole. I remember you from yesterday."

He made a sour face. "Worst week of my life. Your friends

Muscle and Mighty were a welcome sight for my poor eyes yesterday. They are the reason Prussell and I stayed around to help your family. I would've returned to the Woods of Willowmist straightaway if not for their insistence."

"We're certainly glad you did." I knelt down so he wouldn't have to look up so far. Mom and Sophie did the same. His sword, I noticed, was actually a paring knife stuck into his belt. He must've pilfered it from Delaney's house once he escaped. "And you have the other key—I mean, ring, too. Correct?" I mentally smacked myself in the head. Sophie didn't know about the ring. Maybe she wouldn't catch the slip. *Fat chance.*

He nodded and patted a lump in the pouch attached to his belt. "Safe keeping."

"Perhaps I should take it." Mom held out her palm. "We have a place to lock it up."

Sophie looked from Lark to Mom to my hand. Her wheels were turning so fast they were coming off their axle, but I avoided looking in her direction.

The Elf shook his head vigorously. "Oh, no, no, no. Never, ever. It's dangerous enough to have the keys in such close proximity. It would be borrowing trouble for one family to protect both of them."

My face fell at the same time that Sophie's eyes popped. The cat was officially out of the bag and in the litter box. She snatched my wrist, and I reluctantly met her gaze. "So this is—"

"Yes." I cut her off. "Let's leave it at that."

Mom cleared her throat. "Thank you, Mr. Lark. That's good information." She lowered her voice. "Listen, I'm afraid I have some sad news about your friend Prussell."

His pale violet eyes clouded. "Yes. I saw for myself after that beast kicked him. Though I'd only met Prussell after we were captured and thrown together, his companionship was of utmost comfort to me." He looked around. "Where have you taken him?"

"I've wrapped his body in a sheet," Sophie said. "He's in my closet."

Lark nodded. "Transporting him is one of several things we need to discuss. It looks like the Maker has left the job to me."

A mournful wail radiated from the kitchen. Nate was clearly unhappy. Sophie stood, but before she could react, Nicole dashed into the entryway.

"Mom! Sophie was supposed to make us—oh, there you are, Soph. What are you..." Nicole's chestnut eyes fell on the Elf. She blinked several times and took a step back, sucking in her breath. She clamped her hand over her mouth and, with a giggle of wonder, turned round eyes on Mom.

"It's okay, Nicole. This is our new friend Lark." Mom introduced him like Nicole knew all about the secrets we'd been trying to hide from her all summer.

Lark bowed low. "What a pleasure it is to meet such a fine young lady." He pulled open his drawstring pouch and rummaged around its insides, retrieving a polished acorn. He offered it to Nicole. Her eyes shimmered, and she stretched out her hand. Lark placed it ceremoniously on her palm.

Another screech from Nate broke the magical moment. For me, anyway. I trotted into the kitchen to see what he needed. The poor kid had climbed onto one of the spindle-back chairs and gotten one of his chubby legs lodged between two spindles.

"I gotcha, little man." Grabbing beneath his arms, I lifted him so that his leg slid up to where the spindles widened, pulling him free and into my arms. "All better."

Before we could walk out, the others walked in. Mom gestured to the den. Nate's two tiny chairs had remained from the Gnomes' visit the day before. Lark pulled himself up into one of them, a bit challenged by its size since he was shorter than a Gnome by several inches. Nicole flitted past the coffee table—only because she couldn't fly, no doubt—and sat on the floor beside the Elf, grinning. I was amazed by how readily she accepted his presence. No balking or questioning his existence, only delight.

After Nate shifted and smeared crumbs on my leg and wiggled around a bit, he noticed Lark sitting on his own little chair. He bounced and pointed. "Baby man."

We all laughed, except for Lark. But his eyes crinkled like he wanted to be a good sport. "This won't take long, friends." The Elf steepled his fingers and looked down his arrow-like nose. "Time is not on our side, so we must move past the niceties and talk business."

I leaned over to Mom. "You want me to take Nate and Nicole outside while you talk to him?"

She shook her head. "It's getting too difficult to keep our life here separate from life there. They're going to find out sooner or later anyway."

"I hope you fine folks are ready to take a trip." He took the time to look at each one of us. "Tonight Odyssey, the dragon, is coming to fetch you."

CHAPTER TWENTY-EIGHT

I CHECKED THE WEATHER FROM MY phone. The cloudy afternoon held promise for a hazy night. In fact, a weather icon blinked with a hazard warning for heavy fog. Without it, Odyssey wouldn't be able to retrieve us. I didn't understand how Lark could arrange for the flying reptile to come on such short notice, but I'd learned to stop questioning everything I didn't understand. For all I knew, the Elf arranged for the weather to cooperate as well.

Since Aunt Val flat-out refused to keep Nate and Nicole after our last lengthy trek, they would be coming too. With the little ones in tow, Mom preferred to utilize the Meadow Faeries for travel. They had been our ticket back to the Tethered World on our second visit. Our dear Gnome friend Reiko had taken us to a secluded meadow where the tiny, effervescent Faeries had come and whisked us away in their cyclone.

Unfortunately, Lark had no way of contacting the Faeries from topside. This left Mom with the dilemma of how to best secure Nate for the flight on the dragon. Scrawny Nicole posed a bit of a problem as well. We also needed to transport poor Prussell's body securely below.

Both Nicole and Sophie barely left Lark's side. They talked him into a game of hide and seek and even a tea party. He seemed to genuinely enjoy their playful curiosity. Meanwhile, I fielded questions from two different reporters who'd come by unannounced, doing my best to be truthfully obtuse.

Before dinner I changed into proper traveling-to-the-underworld attire—lace-up boots, jeans, long-sleeved t-shirt, and hoodie. Braiding my hair in the mirror, my mind fluttered over to Xander. Would I have an opportunity to see him? Would he suspect I was coming and be looking for me?

Although we finally admitted our feelings to one another on

my previous visit, we also agreed there were many obstacles standing in the way of a lasting relationship. Not the least of which included my age and place of residence. And, although I had added a seventeenth candle to my birthday cake three weeks earlier, it had zero effect on either obstacle for now.

Lark felt certain that the best way to keep our family's secrets below ground was for us to get down there ourselves. Otherwise, we were enticing Trolls and Gargoyles to get involved with us here, as the events of the day had proved. And that would surely expose more of the Tethered World to the media. Notoriety was exactly what those creatures, and our neighbor, craved.

In order to curb the damage Mr. Delaney could do, we needed to intervene with the events happening below, rather than add to them up here. Delaney couldn't play us in the media if we weren't around. He'd already lost wind from his sails by losing the Elf and Gnome he had captured. And, according to a phone call Mom made to Dr. Ferrell, there wasn't anything special about the properties of the saplings from the Tree of Life. After testing their bark, wood, and leaves, he had come up empty. The power of the tree must reside in its fruit. Since it would be years before the saplings would bloom, Mr. Delaney's science project wasn't a crisis that needed our immediate attention.

The tree itself, however, needed us to intervene quickly. I hoped Uncle Brent was having success on that front.

It looked like all our neighbor had going for him now was a dead Yeti. Not that his tunnel couldn't deliver more problems to the surface, but that was part of what we were going to try to prevent from the other end. It all made such sense, I don't know why we didn't take this approach at the outset.

I leaned into the mirror and moved the clasp on my charm necklace to the back of my neck. A very different me looked back. The beginning-of-summer me feared and resisted what the end-of-the-summer me now anticipated. Last night, I nearly got shot trying to get to the place I had dreaded traveling to in June. And for some reason, Xander cared deeply for both of the Sadies he had known. And both Sadies had a hard time forgetting about him.

My ring glinted in the mirror. Should I disguise it? The doorbell rang while I was digging through a basket of gloves, hats, and scarves in my closet. My fingerless gloves, rarely used, sat at the bottom. I stuffed them into my hoodie's pocket.

By the time I got downstairs, Mom had opened the door. She stood in the center of the foyer looking amused while Aunt Val paced a fidgety circle around her. "I might reconsider," Aunt Val was saying, wringing her hands. "I feel so guilty for saying no. But I can't commit to another long babysitting stint. I realize you guys were in grave danger or something, but I felt like you took advantage of me."

Mom reached for Aunt Val's hand, pulling her to a stop. "I totally understand, Val. I can't tell you how terrible I feel about what happened, and it's very generous of you to consider watching them again. But there's no way for me to guess how long we'll be gone. I hope it's short and sweet, but this place is unpredictable."

"That's what Brent keeps telling me." Val squared her shoulders and tossed her wavy, blonde hair over her shoulder. "I can't help but be skeptical about a place I've never heard of until this summer, even though Brent and the rest of you insist you've known about it all along. How do you think that makes me feel? And what on earth happened to your poor nose?" Without waiting for an answer, she stretched out her arms. "Am I supposed to embrace this untamed land with open arms? It sounds crazy. No offense, Amy, but your Bigfoot blog always seemed a little out there. Now the whole family is chasing them down and hanging out with—oh my word!"

Sophie, Nicole, and Lark had walked into the entryway in the middle of Val's tirade. She froze, her eyes locked on the little Elf.

He bowed. "M'lady."

My aunt's eyeballs rolled back, and her head tilted at an odd angle. She looked like she might faint.

I rushed to her side, catching her in my arms when she went down. "That was supremely perfect timing, you guys."

Sophie and crew stood blinking, mouths open. Mom sputtered a laugh and helped me get Aunt Val's lanky body to the couch. "Whew! That was funny." She fluffed a blanket over Valerie. "If I hadn't been so entertained, I may have been insulted."

"Is she okay?" Nicole tiptoed over to peer at our aunt. Sophie and Lark followed.

"She'll be fine." Mom placed a hand on my little sister's head. "Why don't you go get a glass of water?"

"Are you going to throw it in her face like in the movies?" Nicole sounded awed by the prospect.

Mom cracked up. "No, silly. She may want a drink when she wakes up. She did a lot of talking. My ears are still sore."

"I heard that," Aunt Val mumbled. Her eyes fluttered open.

"Well, it's true." Mom knelt beside her. "That was quite an earful. But I thought it was hilarious." She offered her hand. "You want to sit up?"

"Sure." Val gripped Mom's forearm and pushed upright. Catching sight of the Elf, she did a double take. "Is—is that...?"

"This is Lark." Mom gestured to the little guy. "He's a genuine, real, Tethered World Elf."

Aunt Valerie blinked like she might be hallucinating. "Nicole, sweetie, I'll take that glass of water." She didn't remove her gaze from the smiling Elf, who wiggled his fingers in greeting. "And Amy, why don't you let me take the little ones after all. No need to hurry back."

"Where in the depths of Hades is Malagruel?" Nekronok stormed into the Troll's quarters. "The two of you have been awfully tight lately. What do you know about his whereabouts?"

The Troll stood in his father's commanding presence. How did Nekronok know that he'd been to see Malagruel? But of course he knew. The stinking Gargoyle was likely the one to broadcast the news if he saw it was to his advantage. The Troll needed to play cool and indifferent.

"I've not seen him, Father." He kept his face neutral. "Talk among the Banished is that he traveled to watch the proceedings topside. Hasn't been heard from since. Have you questioned his worms?"

Nekronok strode to the window and looked out, his bulky arms crossed. "I spoke with one of them yesterday evening." His voice was even but tense. "Ophidian has no idea where the other worm, Tassitus, ended up after the press conference. Malagruel had important business to tend to before he would return. But he has not been heard from."

"I had no idea he went topside until today," the Troll lied.

Nekronok pivoted slowly, his face twisted into a fierce scowl. "You knew very well he would be there, watching from afar." He took several menacing strides, closing the gap. "But here's what you probably *didn't* know. Malagruel's important business involved getting his hands on the other key. He'd concocted a fool-proof plan to get it, or so he assured me."

"Another one of his plans? His last one didn't turn out so well, though I suppose that's Ophidian's fault for capturing the wrong Larcen boy." Although the Troll was a bulk of muscle in his own right, he still felt inadequate in the presence of his father. The chief stood taller and broader than any other Troll in Craventhrall.

His father's fingers curled into fists of anger. "He was certain that if he had the actual ring to show the Larcens, they would be willing to offer their ring—their *key*—for comparison. Of course, this was under the guise of his shapeshifting prowess."

The Troll's eyebrows shot up. "So you gave him the ring?" He knew as much but couldn't pass up the chance to take a jab at his father's self-proclaimed inerrant wisdom.

"Yes, I did." Nekronok seized his son's tunic shirt by the collar, spittle flying as he spoke. "Malagruel brought the ring to me as you well know. That's how this whole alliance started between our clans. I couldn't very well refuse to give it back when he was offering to capture the second key."

"Of course, Father. Of course." He needed to diffuse the situation before he found himself on the receiving end of a fist. "And being in possession of one ring does us no good. That makes perfect sense."

His father took a deep breath and released him. "Precisely." He stuffed his hands into the pockets of his trousers. "Which means we have several problems on our hands. Where is the blasted bat, and more importantly, the key?"

"Perhaps the Larcens aren't cooperating."

"For once, that's what I hope." Nekronok closed his eyes and shook his head. "Otherwise I've been played like a fool. If he has both keys and heads to Vituvia...How did I not see this coming? It's more important than ever to get those prisoners moved from the crypt to Craventhrall."

"Agreed." The Troll flattened his rumpled tunic where his father had creased it. "Tomorrow, correct?"

Nekronok lifted his chin. "Yes. Tomorrow. I won't rest until the Vituvian king is under my roof and the ring is back in my possession."

CHAPTER TWENTY-NINE

WITH NATE AND NICOLE TAKEN CARE of, preparations for our trip moved quickly. It was a difficult goodbye for all of us, since the last time we left the two of them it became such an extended time away—as Aunt Val pointed out several times before she left with them in tow.

Sophie and I knew what to expect on our dragon voyage and anticipated it with nervous excitement. Nervous from my perspective, excited from hers. Our first and only experience flying on the graceful beast left me blacked out with fear for the majority of the ride. I hoped to face it with much more courage this time around.

Since our supplies were routinely lost or stolen or had proven useless on previous journeys, we stuck to one backpack with bottled water, granola bars, jerky, and flashlights. And a roll of toilet paper, of course. Mom added a pocket knife for good measure, but I wished we had a semi-automatic gun we could stash in there as well.

Mom left Sophie, Lark, and me to tidy things up while she ran Ollie and Mindy-loo to the nearby kennel. She returned with a sack full of burgers. "Since we've basically snacked our way through the day, I thought we should gobble something more substantial before we leave."

She didn't get any arguments from me.

Lark nibbled and tasted the various layers in his first ever burger. Sitting on the table top, he chewed politely, his features morphing from delight with the tomato to dubious with a mouthful of meat. Evidently, he preferred whatever Elves normally eat. Mushrooms, I think. Everyone in the Tethered World seemed to have a fondness for fungi.

"Did you ever call that Mystique lady about her cryptic email?" I asked between bites.

Mom shook her head. "I don't trust her after what happened today. I don't know if she and Malagruel were in cahoots or if, somehow, the Gargoyle himself sent me that email." She waved off the notion. "Forget it."

Before we finished, Lark bounded to his feet with one fluid motion. "My ears are tingling. Odyssey draws near."

We finished eating in haste and readied ourselves for the journey. I volunteered to carry Prussell's body back to Vituvia in Nate's toddler carrier, the kind that straps on like a backpack. At least, I tried to tell myself it was a privilege, rather than kind of creepy. Once I slipped into the shoulder straps, Mom carefully lowered the wrapped body into the padded carrier and buckled him in.

We also dug out an old baby sling for Sophie to wear. Poor Lark would have to endure the humiliation of being swaddled in the fabric to travel securely on the flying dragon. Sophie fitted the single strap across her body from one shoulder to the opposite side of her torso. Lark climbed from the table into the folds of cloth, shaking his head and mumbling to himself.

"Think of it as an Elfin hammock." Sophie held the fabric wide while he arranged his legs.

"I shall not be lying down," he said. "I plan on enjoying the view." His eyes barely cleared the top of the sling until he pulled it down and hooked his elbows over the top, securing it beneath his armpits.

The room rippled with a sonorous boom. Nearly imperceptible to the ears, it ricocheted around my insides. We exchanged anxious glances. From the pocket of my hoodie I withdrew the fingerless gloves and poked my hands inside.

Mom reached for the backpack of supplies and pulled it onto her shoulders. "This is it, kids. Let's lock up and leave."

Outside, the fog smothered us like creamed gravy. It swirled in lacy patterns around our bodies as we made our way into the backyard, arms outstretched lest we walk blindly into the beast.

Two round, golden discs glinted all of a sudden, startling me to a standstill. Slitted, reptilian pupils checked us out between slow blinks, moving closer to where I stood. The fog feathered away enough to expose an ebony snout flecked with silver on a head the size of a refrigerator. If I hadn't already encountered this gentle giant—with fear and trembling and fainting—I would have had the same reaction all over again. Even now, my nerves jittered right below the surface, sending butterfly spasms into my stomach. Facing this creature meant a jolt to reality I'd probably never get used to.

"Odyssey!" Sophie whispered into the mist as she curtsied. "We meet again, O great star treader." She liked to wax poetic and medieval whenever he was around.

"Indeed." Odyssey's deep bass voice resonated in each of our minds simultaneously. *"I've eagerly awaited a reunion with the brave Larcen clan. Your exploits have been expounded on throughout the realm."* His colossal mouth tilted up and crinkled his eyes with a smile.

Our exploits? The realm? I couldn't imagine being talked about in such a way, but that was terrifically cool.

Lark waved his little limbs to be seen. "You will have one Elf—*me*—and one beloved Gnome who sacrificed his life for the cause riding with you," he said in a commanding tone. "No showing off or trying anything tricky. Is that understood?"

Odyssey looked amused but nodded. *"I am always careful with my passengers. Now, if you please, let us fly high while the fog is in our favor."*

We moved past his watchful gaze and down the length of his powerful neck. Sophie and I did, anyway. Where was Mom? Turning, I glimpsed Mom's quaking body through a break in the fog. She hadn't met this behemoth yet.

I trotted back to where she stood, eyes round with either fear or disbelief. "You okay? I know he's ginormous, but he's sweet and gentle. He even has a sense of humor." I slipped my hand in hers and offered a reassuring squeeze.

She shifted her gaze from Odyssey to me. "He's much bigger than I imagined."

"Come on, Mom, you don't want to jeopardize your status as the Faery Blogmother, do you?"

Expelling a long breath, she squared her shoulders. "No, that's not my style. I can do this."

"Atta girl." I led her around to Odyssey's side, shaking my head at the irony. Last time, Aunt Jules was giving me a pep talk while I had a nervous breakdown. My, how times had changed.

We climbed up his front haunches and situated ourselves between the leathery humps along the ridge of the dragon's back. Sophie sat in front and Mom in the middle. I figured she would feel more secure sandwiched between us.

"It is an exquisite night for flying, friends. Please, keep your seat belts fastened and your trays in an upright position for

takeoff."

We giggled. Where had he learned the flight attendant spiel? Odyssey unfurled his wings and leapt gracefully into the night. Instinctively, I held my breath and squeezed my eyes shut. There were altogether too many similarities to riding roller coasters. My stomach lurched as he propelled upward at a steep angle. I clutched the large hump in front of me and squeezed my legs against his scaly back. Once Odyssey reached his cruising altitude, it would be smooth sailing—with a spectacular view of the heavens.

But getting there without blacking out again would require steeling my nerves and, to be honest, keeping my eyes glued shut while reciting the Pledge of Allegiance. Repeatedly. Yeah, one of those weird childhood rituals that I still found comforting. Don't judge.

After what felt like half an hour but was probably closer to five minutes, Odyssey leveled off. I peeled my eyelids open. *Brr!* I had failed to dress appropriately for flying the friendly skies in a convertible airplane. How had I forgotten how frigid it was at five thousand feet? With one hand, I fumbled for the hood that flapped behind my head, dueling with my long braid. My teeth chattered, but the splendor of the Milky Way easily distracted me.

Above the fog, the night sky glistened. I had become a satellite caught in the orbit of the earth, a tiny rhinestone among millions of diamonds. And our Creator had crafted each of us individually and knew us by name. I smiled, feeling connected to the fabric of history in a way that stirred me to tears. Or maybe it was only the cold wind pressing tears from my eyes. It didn't matter. Fresh faith in the One who watched over me, whether in the depths of the earth or the heights of the heavens, melted my cold fear of the unknown.

Up here, it was easy to believe that all of our problems were as tiny as the specks of light from the city below. I relaxed against Odyssey's hump. The Gnome's carrier rested on top and pressed him high against my back. Prussell would never again enjoy the beauty that surrounded him. It made me sad. Did Gnomes go to heaven? Did they have a soul? The questions stirred new insecurities. An awful lot of them were giving their lives for our family and for their Maker.

Odyssey banked sharply to the left, pulling my thoughts back to the here and now. Sophie twirled one hand over her head like a lasso while I white-knuckled the hump in front of me. Mom, as far as I could tell, hadn't moved a muscle since takeoff. Once the dragon straightened out, I knew we were getting close to the scariest part of the ride. Remembering how freaky it had been when we last spiraled down and zoomed up into the lair at Beacon Rock, I began to lose my nerve.

A hand suddenly clamped over my face. I froze, mind scrambling to make sense of it. I tried to scream but got a mouth full of salty and sour.

"Be still and be quiet," a voice hissed in my ear. *"If you don't do exactly as I say, you will be forced to take a deadly dive into the river below."*

CHAPTER THIRTY

BRADY GNAWED THE SKIN AROUND HIS thumb like a starving beaver. Although he stared into the shadows, the only things in focus were fearful images of what might unfold once they left the cell. No matter how he scoured the logic behind Chebar's conspiracy, and the safety net that Tassitus had proposed, the future promised to be painful and dangerous at best.

He studied Brock's profile, watching him rock to music that only he could hear. The familiar, rhythmic motion calmed Brady's internal chaos but also constricted his throat with the threat of emotion. He marveled at Brock's composure and realized the only one on the verge of a meltdown was himself.

Brady got to his feet, annoyed by the tremors that seemed to radiate from his core like the epicenter of an earthquake. He tried to tell himself it stemmed more from hunger than panic. He reached a hand to the nearest stalactite to steady himself.

His brother glanced up, now motionless, and offered Brady a hint of a smile—as if he sensed the tension coursing inside him. Brock held Brady's gaze and stood, his placid features a peculiar mirror that revealed opposite emotions on the same face. His direct gaze distracted Brady's dark thoughts, making Brady pause to consider Brock's unusual disposition. His brother had rarely looked at him with such purpose.

"I'm not scared anymore." Brock's voice was matter-of-fact. "Aunt Jules says when we seem to have no choice, we can trust that the Maker has made the right one for us."

Brady inhaled the truth of these words, wrapping his arms around his middle as if to cloak himself in Brock's bold assurance. When did his brother become the one to dispense such wisdom? What was it about this place that called through the veil of autism and allowed a deeper part of Brock to answer?

Before Brady could grapple with the question, the door that

led into the passage to their cell squawked in the distance. The sound cranked up the adrenaline, but Brock's lingering words brought back a needed measure of faith. Why hadn't he noticed its absence in the first place?

If it was time to leave, then he needed to pull himself together on the double. He closed the gap to give Brock a fierce, quick hug, hoping the physical touch wouldn't make him retreat once again. "Aunt Jules was right." He kept a hand clamped on his brother's shoulder. "*You're* right. And that's exactly what I needed to hear. We can trust the Maker and be thankful we've also got each other. We're not alone."

"I've got your back."

Brady chuckled, wondering what the Gnomes had done with the withdrawn version of Brock. "And I've got yours, dude. You remember the plan once we leave?"

"Stay by you," Brock repeated. "Follow you. Don't speak unless spoken to."

Brady offered a fist bump, thankful that Brock knew the drill. "Yep. Pretty simple. We've got this."

"Breakfast." The stout guard appeared outside their cell. He slid two bowls under the door.

"Really?" Brady crossed to the door and picked up the bowls. Hope revived that Tassitus could be trusted. Hadn't he said he would see about getting them more food?

The brothers had only swallowed a few spoonfuls of tasteless mush when the guard returned. "You are being ordered to leave the crypt." He fumbled with the lock. "At once. Leave your food and follow me."

So this is it, Brady thought, standing alongside Brock. The day held promise for some major developments. Between Chebar's mutiny and Tassitus' covert advice, it was a day that might free them—if it didn't kill them first.

With a sudden swoop that left me gasping for breath, Odyssey descended through the clouds and up into his lair inside the monolith called Beacon Rock. The terrifying plummet made me shake from the adrenaline rush and blast of cold air. It provided an excuse for my aloof, disjointed behavior once we landed.

Behind me, unseen, sat Ophidian. Best I could guess, he

had slinked aboard with us in the fog and waited until we were near our destination to reveal his presence. He knew what Mom and I had done to Malagruel. He'd seen his master's pulverized remains in our yard. Since Malagruel hadn't returned to the Tethered World, Ophidian the faithful worm had come for him.

And now, he vowed to avenge the death of his prince. The worm demanded to know what happened to the key that Malagruel brought with him, and warned me to obey his whispered instructions if I wanted to protect my mother and sister. He gave me an earful of seething instructions while his hand smothered my mouth so I couldn't talk or scream.

"The Gargoyles have strategized for years to get our hands on the key that would unlock the power of the sword and grant us the Tree of Life. We won't allow a family of Topsiders to stand in the way. We are so close! You will either help the cause or be eliminated from the equation altogether. Understood?"

With his sandpapery hand pressed against my face, all I could do was nod.

Phosphorescent flecks in Odyssey's skin provided a sparkling, violet glow in the cavernous space. Folding his magnificent wings, he lowered his belly to the ground with a loud grunt.

"Whew!" Sophie slid down his ribcage. "That's the coolest thing *ever*. Coolest and coldest, actually." She rubbed her arms and bounced up and down.

"Holy guacamole." In front of me, Mom shook her head like she was coming back to life. "I think I'm in shock." Her rigid posture deflated. "My senses were positively overwhelmed. In a good way. Cleared up my headache." Her hand found my leg, and she attempted to twist around, her backpack making it difficult. "You okay, Sadie girl? If you hate roller coasters, then I can only imagine your utter dismay after all that."

"Yeah." My constricted throat made my words a bare whisper. Invisible fingers encircled my arm and squeezed, reminding me of my predicament. "I'm fine."

Mom swung her leg over the hump and dropped to the ground.

"Dismount and act natural," Ophidian snarled softly. *"Once we get into the tunnels, I expect you to discuss the key. I want to know precisely where to find it."*

I gave a subtle nod, my mind working out a way to rid myself of this parasite without endangering my family. I slid off and landed with a tweak of pain in my ankle. Beside me a quiet *thump* proceeded my own footfall, only noticeable because I was listening. Could the dragon feel the extra passenger or was his thick, calloused exterior more like armor than skin? Darkness rippled to my right. With my peripheral vision, I could see the worm in an odd, distorted way. The Gargoyle's chameleon skin melded with the shadows and stone with astonishing precision.

Odyssey's tree trunk neck curved so that his colossal head looked our way. *"Shall I warm you up, my friends?"* He boomed into our collective brains.

"Yes, please." Sophie still bounced on the balls of her feet, though I'd guess it was more from excitement than the chill.

"Stand back."

We moved to the far side of the cave. The dragon lifted his snout toward the ceiling and hissed a short blast of flames from his nostrils. The flash of light blinded me for an instant. As my vision returned, a downdraft of heat settled around me like an electric blanket.

"Perfect!" Mom removed her backpack and shook out her shoulders. "Thank you."

"Roots and fruits! Why didn't someone tell me I'd become an Elven icicle?" Lark's voice piped up from Sophie's direction.

My sister looked down at the fabric carrier and pulled the top open like a pouch. "You okay in there?"

The Elf popped his head up, scowling. "That was the worst experience of my life. I suppose I should thank you for placing me in this ridiculous sling and saving me from death by frost bite."

"Um, you're welcome?" Sophie giggled then trotted up to Odyssey's watchful eyes, placing a hand on the gnarly hide of his snout. "I'm so glad we got to take another ride with you. I've prayed that we would meet again."

Odyssey's eyes squinted with a dragon-size grin. *"I, too, have prayed for this, young Larcen."*

"Sadie, you wanna take that carrier off your back and stretch before we trek down the tunnels?" Mom pointed at my back. "I'll help you."

There was something about the way the carrier pressed its padded bars against me that made me feel insulated and protected from the monster lurking in the dark. I shook my head. "I'm good."

Mom stepped closer, her eyes narrowing as they skimmed

my face. Her brows creased. "You sure you're okay? Are you feeling nauseated from the flight?"

I attempted a lopsided smile. "I'm fine."

"You're speaking in one-syllable words. That's not like you."

"It's all good, Mom."

"See." She gestured at me but winked. "Okay, I'll leave you alone."

Sophie assisted Lark to the ground. His sword-a-la-paring-knife glinted at his hip, and I recalled how the Elf had used it to stab Malagruel in the back. I'd keep an eye out for the opportunity to use it on the worm.

The pocket knife! It was stored in the side pocket of Mom's backpack. The pack slouched near her feet, its unzipped mouth gaping open. Mom withdrew three flashlights and passed them out. Dad and Uncle Brent had taken the more useful headlamps.

Kneeling beside the pack, I milled around on the inside for a moment, unscrewing a bottle of water and taking a sip. Since Ophidian was undoubtedly watching my every action, I kept my hands moving in and out of pockets like I was double-checking our supplies.

My hand dipped into the side pocket and felt the weight of cold steel. I fingered it beneath the cuff of my sleeve, withdrawing my arm in an upward motion that slid the knife to the crook of my arm.

"Looking for something?" Mom squatted beside me.

"No. I needed a drink and took a peek at what we brought. I didn't see what all you packed." That was true. I hadn't known about the hand sanitizer.

She zipped the top closed, and we both stood. I was careful to keep my arm parallel to the floor.

"It is time to embark on our journey." Lark rested his hands on his tiny hips, looking fully in charge. "Once we descend through the base of Beacon Rock, I should be able to call up the Faeries to expedite the remaining distance."

"Terrific!" Sophie clasped her hands then spun toward Odyssey. "Second tunnel from the left?"

His humungous head bobbed once with a simultaneous blink. *"Correct."*

The soft glow of the dragon's granite-flecked skin reminded me of a sparkling parade float. Perhaps one meant to look like a mountain range, the way his ridged back curved and peaked against the smooth wall of the cave.

The four of us gathered before him. A few steps away from Odyssey's pooling incandescence, a black void sliced into the darkness, reminding me that I was being watched. I turned my back on it.

"God speed. God guide. God protect." He conveyed the same blessing I remembered from our first visit.

"Thank you." Mom brushed the side of his snout with her fingers. "We need God to do all of that for us if we're to survive."

Sophie curtsied low and solemnly. "We are grateful for both thy help and thy blessing, O ancient Odyssey." The kid was born in the wrong era.

"That means thanks for everything in modern English," I offered.

"So, this tunnel?" Mom clicked on her flashlight and pointed the beam to the second of four tunnel openings.

Sophie turned on her light. "Yep!"

Dread congealed in my blood, sapping my former anticipation. I stuffed my hands in the pockets of my hoodie, allowing the knife to tumble into the flannel lining. At some point, I needed to know precisely where my enemy stood so I could deliver a fatal stab. One shot was all I'd get. An angry, wounded Gargoyle would be a disaster.

I heard a hiss in my ear and smelled foul breath. *"It's time for your magnanimous cooperation, Princess Sadie."* Clammy fingers clasped my arm and guided me behind my mom and sister. *"Remember to steer the conversation toward the key, or there will be some tragic accidents in the slick slopes of the tunnels."*

Ignoring him, I watched Lark scurry to the front, his pouch jostling against the blur of his legs. It would be all too easy to speak of the key and its whereabouts. Ophidian could snap the little Elf like a twig. Once he discovered the key was actually the ring in the pouch, he'd take the one off of my finger as well—probably with my finger still attached.

Somehow, I needed to appease this monster so he wouldn't hurt my family, while trying to keep the truth from being exposed. And in between that exciting tightrope walk, I had to find a way to kill the brute.

CHAPTER THIRTY-ONE

THE STYGIAN GUARD LED THE BROTHERS into a yawning, bleak space. Devoid of rocks and stalactites, its circular perimeter was rimmed with multiple openings, like spokes on a wheel. Across the poorly lit cavern Brady saw six hulking figures. Their Neanderthal heads and hairy silhouettes left no question about what kind of creatures they were.

The Dwarf pointed to a sphere of light in the center of the room. An opening in the vaulted ceiling provided a skylight effect, allowing the crystal dome to shine a cylinder of light into the dark. Brock and Brady stepped into its brightness, which lit them like a spotlight. Brady felt vulnerable. Like a target. He didn't care for the advantage the Trolls had in the shadows.

Then four of the six Trolls stepped forward. Nekronok, Rooke, Sargon, and Chebar stopped a couple of yards from the brothers. Brady hoped his face remained neutral at the sight of the chief Troll. Their last encounter had been quite unpleasant, leaving Brady unconscious.

Nekronok stepped in front of his three sons. He wore a plain black vest and loose drawstring pants over his salt and pepper fur. The strange insignia that many Trolls had branded into their skin was stitched onto his vest, over his heart. A sheathed sword was buckled to his side. He glared from Brock to Brady.

"Well, if it's not a couple of those slippery Larcens." A bitter chuckle rumbled in his chest. "What is it you Topsiders say? If you want something done the right way, do it yourself?" Another stride and he towered over them. "I'm here to personally ensure nothing goes wrong. And I brought reinforcements."

The other Trolls stepped forward. Brady looked back at their cold, forbidding eyes with a flat expression. He hoped Brock was able to do the same. Chebar, ever playing both sides, looked as cold and calculating as his brothers. Brady couldn't help but imagine himself as a second string high school football player facing the bulk of the defensive line from the Seattle Seahawks. A defensive line armed with swords.

"Have you nothing to say for yourselves?" Nekronok looked the brothers up and down, circling them with a hungry expression. "There are no last-minute rescues in these cryptic tunnels. No puny Gnomes, no foolhardy Dwarves, no Nephilim warriors. You two are at my mercy." He completed his circle, then seized them both by the neck, pinching with his lanky fingers, lifting them from the ground. He leaned his ape face into theirs and shouted. "And I have no mercy!"

Lights blinked on the edge of Brady's vision. His head felt like it might pop off. He pointed his toes to the ground, trying to gain purchase. Nekronok released them, causing the brothers to knock foreheads as they landed.

"Guards!" Nekronok barked.

From the recess of the cave the other two Trolls stepped forward, sporting a sword on each hip. In unison, they crossed their arms and grasped the hilt on the opposite side of their body. With a metallic zing, they unsheathed their weapons—short, curved scimitar blades—and crossed them in an X in front of their bodies.

Brady wondered how Chebar would pull off any sort of assassination attempt with two ninja Trolls and two loyal brothers in the mix. He flexed his jaw, feeling that Chebar's plan held little hope.

"Another son, Grym, is meeting with insurgents from Vituvia and Berganstroud this afternoon." Nekronok spoke through a clenched smile. "He shall give them a letter with my clearly stated demands as well as my explicit methods of torture should those demands be refused. But I expect that once they learn that both keys are in my possession, they will be wise enough to concede." He leaned his head close to theirs and whispered, "The fall of Vituvia shall be great and to the uttermost. I can practically taste the victory now. It shall taste like the fruit of immortality from the Tree of Life."

Brady and Brock said nothing.

Lark led our small brigade through the tunnels. I fell in at the back, with Ophidian stealing along behind me. Our strides quickly overtook the Elf, so he agreed to ride in the sling. Like a sailor in the eagle's nest of a ship, he navigated our way through the current of stone corridors.

Since no one conversed or made small talk, I didn't either. I hoped that the mood set by the others would provide the justification for my own delayed chatter. Within ten minutes, however, the worm took to jabbing me in my back every few steps.

"Ouch!" One painful poke made me yelp.

"What's wrong?" Mom turned and looked at me.

I shook my head. "Nothing. I'm okay."

"That didn't sound like nothing."

"Only a tweak in my back. It's better now."

She nodded, then narrowed her eyes. "What was that?" Her gaze searched the space behind me.

I stepped aside and her flashlight fell on a chunk of rock sidled next to the wall that, I knew, hadn't been there a moment before. "Weird, I thought I saw something." Her light flitted back and forth then returned to the rock. "Funny. I don't remember passing that. Guess everything looks the same after a while."

The outburst made Ophidian ease up. It was several minutes before he made his dislike known.

"*Speeeak.*" His voice was no more than a wisp of breath, and I wondered if I imagined it.

What should I say? There was no way I could give away the key's whereabouts. But neither did I want to be responsible for injuring my mom or sister.

"How much farther, Lark?" That was a start.

"Quite a bit. Didn't you say you came this way before?" he called back.

Sophie tossed a glance my way. "We've only been in here for like thirty minutes. We walked for hours, don't you remember?"

"Yeah, I just thought Lark may know a shortcut, that's all." I fingered the knife in my pocket.

"Actually, I do. But it would cause you all to get wet and slimy and cold."

"Yuck." Sophie scowled. "How much time do you save in exchange for getting so gross?"

"Perhaps a couple of hours."

We all stopped. Sophie turned the Elf to face Mom and me.

His brow furrowed. "Why are we stopping?"

"A couple of hours is significant." Mom stepped closer to the pouch. "Care to elaborate?"

He shrugged. "Well, since we aren't going all the way to the roots of Beacon Rock, it probably saves less than two hours."

"That's time that could be better spent, I'm sure."

"For certain, m'lady." Lark offered a curt nod. "And the sooner we can part ways with our keys, the better. I'm not at all comfortable with them in the same vicinity."

I pressed my lips together like it might stop the despondent panic swelling in my chest. The beans had been spilled. It was too late.

"Beware!" Lark said. "Once you take the rapid route, you may wish you had walked."

"Perhaps." Mom fiddled with the straps on the backpack. "But let's hear what it is."

Lark's pale, violet eyes skimmed around the roughhewn walls and ceiling.

"Dwarves of old dug these tunnels. The first thing they burrowed out of the rock was a channel that provided an efficient method for removing the stone as the passageways were constructed. Using the trickle of ground water, they bored a steep channel into Beacon Rock that provided a slick incline for the avalanche of rock they would remove. Smaller channels fed into the main one."

"A granite water park!" Sophie's eyes glinted. "Sounds fun."

Lark clicked his tongue disapprovingly. "With disuse, the conduit is a gooey funnel of algae. It will make a cold, wet mess of every inch of you. And me too, I might add."

As unappetizing as it sounded, there would be no chance of conversing about the key or anything else while zipping through an ancient water slide. "I'm in."

"Please, Mom?" Sophie clasped her hands together.

"Yeah." She nodded. "Absolutely. Lead the way."

Lark looked dubious. "As you wish."

It took about twenty minutes to find the nearest artery. Ophidian kept to himself as we wound our way to it. His silence made me both relieved and nervous. What was he up to?

The opening had been sealed with a rock that didn't quite fit. Sophie, Mom, and I scraped up our fingers and chipped our nails trying to get a collective grip to heave it out of the way. At last it tilted up. We let it tumble while jumping clear of a potential foot crushing.

A rank, noxious smell assaulted us. I cringed and shrank back, gagging. Maybe this wasn't a good idea.

"Ugh!" Sophie wrinkled her nose and slapped a hand across her face. "Rotten eggs."

"That would be the algae." Lark tossed his hands up. "I told you this would not be pleasant."

Mom peered inside with her flashlight. "I don't care about the smell as much as whether this will work." She turned to Lark. "How do we know the opening isn't blocked, full of lefto-ver rocks and debris?"

Lark shook his head. "Because the Dwarves still use it on occasion. That's how I know what condition we shall all be in when it spits us out at the other end. I've seen the Dwarves."

"Good enough for me." Mom gestured to Sophie. "Would you like to lead the way, O fearless child of mine?"

"Sure." She rubbed her hands together in anticipation.

Mom placed her hand on my arm. "And you next. I feel bet-ter sending you two off together."

"Okay." I wondered, again, where Ophidian lurked. No doubt he was sizing each of us up, calculating his what, when, and how.

"A great pit of sand awaits at the bottom. But it isn't entirely clear of rocks, so it may be a harsh landing." Lark sank into the folds of the fabric sling, covering himself entirely. His muf-fled voice called, "And try not to squish me. I surely would not survive."

Sophie giggled. "I wouldn't dream of it."

It occurred to me that the lump on my back wasn't a per-manent part of my body. I had better take care of poor Prussell or he'd be in worse shape than merely dead, if that was possi-ble. With a happy groan, I slid my shoulders free of the pack. "I should wear this on the front side for the trip."

"Good thinking." Mom did the same with her backpack.

"See you at the bottom." Sophie swung one leg over the bar-rier, straddling it. She looked down, shining her light. "Wow. That's super steep."

The hesitation in her voice made me certain I'd find the sight terrifying. She didn't seem to have a fear of doing her own stunts. Wrapping her arms around the sling, she adjusted her grip on the flashlight, then shifted her other leg into the hole.

"Oh, be careful!" Mom shot her hand out.

My heart leapt at the same time Sophie did. She yelped ex-citedly but the sound was gobbled down with her. I walked over and peeked inside. My flashlight beam spotlighted deep green filaments, slick with a steady drizzle of water from somewhere up above. The grassy goop shifted and trembled as if trying to make up its mind which way to flow. The severe tilt made me gasp. It was practically vertical. I lifted my head and closed my eyes. This was not something I could think about or back away from.

"You okay, hon?" Mom grabbed my hand. "I know this isn't your thing. But I really don't want Sophie down there by herself for long. Can you manage?"

I nodded and hugged Prussell securely to myself like he was my lifeline. Sitting on the edge of the precipice, I swiveled so one leg and then the other dangled into the opening. With my eyes squeezed tight, I put a death grip on my flashlight.

Then, I pushed off the side and died a thousand deaths.

CHAPTER THIRTY-TWO

SKITTERING SOUNDS IN THE TORCH-LIT shadows made the skin prickle across Brady's scalp. His eyes darted about. Whatever made the noise had to be rodent sized. He stole a glance back at his brother. Even in the dim light he could tell Brock's face wore a mask of indifference. Brady willed his own strained nerves to settle into a similar expression.

They'd been walking for close to an hour, by his estimate. Before venturing into the tunnels, Sargon had tied his and Brock's hands behind their backs and threaded a chain through their wrists and between their legs, forcing them to walk single file. The chain was manacled to Sargon's wrist in front of Brady, and to Rooke's wrist behind Brock. Nekronok came next, his watchful eyes surveying the prisoners. One of the ninja Trolls brought up the rear. Chebar held a torch, the only source of light, in front of Sargon. The other ninja Troll led the way, a sword in each hand.

The tunnels in this part of the mountain felt different. Alive. Before Brady's ears picked up on the scurrying footfalls, he had the sensation of being watched. As if the high stone walls had eyes. The walls soared upward into the darkness, and the granite passageways seemed to shift, closing in at times, then suddenly loosening their grip. But he knew it was actually the play of torchlight and shadows teasing his perception. At least, that's what he told himself.

At first, Sargon and Rooke played a tedious game of tug-o-war with the chain. The boys were jerked to and fro, tripping and toppling and scrambling to keep up. The Trolls mocked and swore and spit at the brothers. But from the intersection of one tunnel to the next, the atmosphere changed. The Trolls must have sensed it too, because they stopped yanking them around and fell silent, their squared shoulders and swiveling heads indicating they were on alert.

Something darted across Brady's path. He stutter-stepped and sucked in his breath.

Sargon stopped and turned with a sharp look. "Seeing things? You know these tunnels are haunted, don't you?" He grinned, sly and conniving. His yellowed fangs contrasted against his brown, leathery face. His gaze flicked past Brady. "His Worshipful Master hopes he is impervious to the rumors. As am I."

Brady continued to gaze into the void, not meeting Sargon's eyes.

"Enough, Sargon," Nekronok barked. "Proceed."

They plodded ahead. Brady hadn't taken a dozen steps when some sort of vermin launched itself onto his leg. A grubby-faced imp clawed up Brady's thigh, baring its pointy teeth and growling. Instinctively, Brady launched himself at the wall, squashing the creature until it let go. It landed with a yelp, covering its sparse, spiky hair with its hands and hissing up at Brady. It scurried along the wall and out of sight.

Rooke expelled a wheezy laugh. "Rotten little Goblins living in these parts. Good thing you didn't let him get to your face. Would've clawed your eyes out."

Brady shuddered on the inside. Such a thought made his stomach lurch, reminding him of Uncle Daniel, who had lost one of his eyes while in captivity. Maybe the Gargoyles had employed the nasty Goblins for their acts of torture.

The Trolls continued on. The passage took a sharp left turn and widened. Distant groans and sounds of sobbing whispered on a hint of a breeze. No, not sobbing. Laughter maybe. Sometimes the two could sound remarkably alike.

They rounded a curve, and the eerie sound grew in volume. Another Goblin appeared, its back to the wall as they passed. Dark orbs peered up from its sallow, taut skin. Its belly protruded like the bellies of malnourished children Brady had seen in pictures. About the size of a Gnome, the creature had impossibly skinny arms and legs and wore no clothes. This one must've had a friendlier disposition. It smiled a zigzagged grin, like a poorly carved jack-o-lantern.

Brady watched it warily from the corner of his eye, relieved when it stayed put. But as the disquieting sounds grew, so did the frequency of Goblin sightings. They passed several clusters of Goblins scratching and screeching like stray cats in a brawl. Other Goblins on the fringes cheered their angry counterparts, fists pumping in the air.

Brady covered his ears at the same time Brock covered his own. Something about the cave's acoustics made the sound warble in a continuous, piercing loop.

Another Goblin dashed in front of Chebar, and the Troll stumbled. "Next time I'll step on you, ya big tunnel rat." He pointed the torch down and waved it from side to side. It quelled the commotion as they passed more Goblins.

Brady focused on Chebar's back, wondering how his assassination might go down. Would he toss all the bad Trolls in a hole with a bunch of hungry Goblins? Chebar hadn't offered any details, but he had sounded certain that he could pull it off. Brady couldn't picture how a solitary Troll could take down Nekronok in front of the others. Besides, assassinating Nekronok would put Rooke next in line for leadership of the clan, and he was as nasty as his father. But even with Rooke somehow out of the way, there was Sargon. And where did Grym, the one delivering the note from Nekronok, fit into the lineup?

Brady thought Chebar would make an excellent leader, but the Troll didn't seem to have his sights set that high. Probably because it was a long climb up the family ladder. Being number six meant a lot of brothers stood between him and the seat of power. And if he pulled off his mutiny, the others would no doubt take their revenge. Which left Brady to ponder why Chebar would do such a thing in the first place.

The Tree of Life, of course. Nekronok wanted ultimate power for an infinite amount of time. That alone was reason enough to get rid of him, especially if he had both of the keys, as he claimed. That news had startled Brady. How had the big ape gotten his paws on their great aunt's key? Since she had stayed in Berganstroud to be with Uncle Daniel, maybe the enemy had managed a thorough raid of her beach house in Oregon, something they had managed once before. Why hadn't his parents removed the key to a safer place before such a travesty could happen?

"Ouch!" Something slammed into his shoulder, obliterating his thoughts. Gibberish yowls squawked in his ears and needle-like fingers clawed at his scalp. Brady spun and writhed, helpless to do much with his hands constrained. The slack in the chain wrapped around his leg as he twisted and hurled his upper body forward in an attempt to fling the little demon away.

He caught sight of Rooke, watching and laughing, and his

anger burned hotter than the pain. Brock stepped into view and Brady stilled, sensing his brother's intent. As the Goblin latched a claw onto Brady's ear, Brock head-butted the creature, sending him into the wall. Before the imp could recover, Brady was standing over it, Brock at his side. Brady pressed his foot against its little body until, *pop*, it burst like a balloon. The boys jerked back. Greenish-yellow goo puddled where the Goblin had been.

Brady gaped at it, blinking, gasping for breath. Blood trickled down the side of his face and splattered onto the ground.

Light and shadow flickered in front of me whenever I dared to open my eyes. Careening through the steep tunnel left me both petrified and in pain. My body slid and bounced and slammed against the stone, with none of the safeguards or smooth surfaces of a waterslide park. Flashes of myself plummeting down the face of the Eldritch mingled with my present terror. If only Xander could snatch me away from this free fall as he had that one fateful day.

"*Oomph.*" I came to an instant, jolting stop. I gasped, somewhat surprised to be alive.

"You need to get out of the way pretty quick or Mom will land on top of you." Sophie tugged at my arm while I sat still and blinked, senses in shock. "Come on!" She tugged again, and I gained the presence of mind to cooperate.

I stumbled to my feet and shuffled through the deep, shifting sand, away from the chute. My limbs wouldn't support me, and after a few yards I collapsed like a rubber chicken, aware of a hunk of rock poking my rib. But it was a solid, unmoving hunk of rock, which meant I was no longer being flung through that stinking, paralyzing pipeline.

Rolling from my side to my back, I was happy to find that I hadn't lost my white-knuckled grip on my flashlight. And poor Prussell seemed to have made it through in one piece.

Sophie giggled, and I found her with my beam of light. "Ugh, Sophie. Don't tell me you enjoyed that. What's so funny?"

She knelt a few feet away, pointing her flashlight back at me. "You are! You should see yourself."

In my delirium, I hadn't paid attention to her pitiful state. She looked like the Loch Ness Monster. Algae coated her like a layer of pond scum. I couldn't suppress my own amusement, laughing with her because I knew I looked the same.

Something moved against her chest. Poor Lark emerged from the edge of the carrier, his face a picture of mortification. Although he seemed to have fared much better than Sophie or me, a blob of green lay across his forehead resembling a bad comb-over. I laughed harder.

He looked from me to Sophie, and chuckled.

"Wait!" Sophie shot up, a stricken look on her face. She gestured toward the exit of the slide. "Where's Mom?"

CHAPTER THIRTY-THREE

BRADY WILLED HIMSELF TO BE INDIFFERENT to his bleeding ear and other painful scratches that stung. The Trolls would only taunt weakness. They'd been quite entertained by the whole episode, roaring with laughter when the creature exploded into a puddle of green goo.

What would Brady have done without his brother's help? Growing up, he had always felt Brock needed him. Lately, he realized more and more how much he needed Brock. And, oh, how thankful Brady felt that the two creatures chose to attack him and not his twin. Brock hadn't been injured. He was to be high king, after all. And as a Guardian of the Sword, Brady had taken an oath to protect him. Actually, he realized, that was a promise he'd been keeping to Brock since they were small.

The idea that more terrors awaited in the bowels of the mountain was enough to ignite burning fear in Brady's heart. He silently prayed for strength, and that his brother would be safe, no matter what. When Brady had been at his lowest, sick and alone and forgotten in the depths of the Eldritch, the Lord had remembered him. He had made a way of escape when things looked impossible.

Brady chose, now, to remember that.

Hordes of Goblins clamored alongside the travelers, their numbers increasing. Chebar's method of holding them at bay with the torch could only do so much. Ninja Troll number one, at the front, began slicing and dicing them as they skittered and leapt in front of the travelers. Like some sort of sick video game come to life, the Goblins detonated into sticky, yellow globules. Nekronok and his sons drew their own swords and tallied their kills. The weapons didn't deter the Goblins but rather seemed to entice them. They dodged and dashed and tried to trip the Trolls up. Some Goblins survived, others did not. The ground became sticky with their residue. A nauseatingly sweet smell wafted from the aftermath, kicking Brady's gag reflex into gear.

Relief washed over him when the passageway opened into a cavernous space, similar in size to the one in which their journey began. Several perforated openings in the soaring ceiling bathed the space in a hazy, golden glow and the blissful benefit of fresh air. Stalactites and stalagmites formed tremendous sets of fangs, some with their points touching.

Goblins climbed and clung to the conical formations like cavities. Others clumped in corners or argued in their strange gibberish here and there. The chatter and clamor quieted in slow succession as the Trolls and prisoners penetrated the room.

Brady noticed the granite floor came to an abrupt end in another ten yards. A rickety rope bridge spanned a gaping chasm. He gulped. The thought of traversing that tenuous, twined excuse for a bridge was almost worse than facing the Goblins. That flimsy thing didn't look like it could support someone his size, let alone the Trolls. What would they do?

The feisty imps scurried about in the shadows while others jumped from their perches and surrounded their group. Chomping their razor-like teeth and shrieking like banshees, the sea of Goblins moved alongside the travelers but did not attack. The creatures seemed to be ushering the eight up to the edge of the precipice.

A deep, belching voice shouted from across the chasm, "What do you intruders have to do with Mudgeon, the great Goblin god?"

Brady, who now stood beside his brother in the clustered group, flinched at the unexpected sound.

Ninja number one performed quick, flashy maneuvers with his swords. He swirled and crossed them like batons, then took a knee, stabbing the weapons at the ground in a simultaneous *poing!* "Your Greatness," he bellowed, "we are from the house of His Worshipful Master, Nekronok. We wish to deliver prisoners to our lord by requesting passage through your splendid realm."

Interesting. This soldier did not let on that Nekronok was one of the travelers. Brady shifted, trying to see this so-called god of the Goblins. Across the bridge, he glimpsed movement behind one of the stalagmites. As he watched, a large, lumbering monster came into view. An egg-shaped vision of repugnance, he waddled on fat, stubby legs, too short for his body. In contrast, long, lanky arms with swollen, knobby elbows ended in hands that dragged on the floor. Brady stood too far away to make out facial features, but he had the general impression of a toad with bulging eyes.

"Without payment, it is impossible to pass." Mudgeon clasped his hands together and rested them on his ample stomach. "And without payment it is impossible to go back the way you came. I shall be forced to make a meal of each one of you and spit your bones into this great fissure in the rock."

"Your Greatness," shouted the Ninja Troll as he stood and sheathed his swords, "we have brought payment." He jingled a pouch on his belt. "If you will permit me to cross the bridge, I will pay the price you demand."

Brady studied Nekronok. The Troll's jaw flexed, fingers twitching on the hilt of his sword. Brady hoped the arrogant tyrant wasn't about to start something with this horde of Goblins. Besides the fact that he and Brock were chained and fairly helpless, the Trolls themselves were tremendously outnumbered, even if they did tower over the imps.

A half-dozen Goblins swarmed near Mudgeon's feet. He punted one unlucky imp into the abyss. "Since you have disturbed my breakfast, it shall cost you twice the sum."

"Fat, impotent, slug," Nekronok mumbled under his breath. "We don't need this delay."

Ninja number two stepped up beside his counterpart. "We are prepared to pay this price, O great Goblin god."

Mudgeon placed his fists where his hips should have been. "Very well. One of you may cross with both of the payments."

Ninja two handed his pouch to ninja one. He eyed the bridge with a wary eye. "Best of luck."

The Troll stuffed the pouch into his belt and walked to the rope bridge. His fingers encircled the first of many rough cords that swooped from the heights of the ceiling and formed a narrow V shape. They met in the middle and knotted together along another rope that spanned the gap.

With tentative steps, the soldier placed one oversized foot after the other on the central rope. The cords quivered and creaked. Whether from the strain of the Troll's weight or from his shaky nerves, Brady couldn't tell. As much as he disliked this enemy soldier, he found himself rooting for the big ape to make it.

At long last he did. Brady and the other Trolls released a collective breath. They watched the monster dump the pouches on a nearby rock and pilfer through them. Though the glimmer of gold caught Brady's eye, there were other items that he couldn't make out. Mudgeon took his time inspecting the loot.

Nekronok and Rooke grunted and shifted impatiently. Sargon glanced at them. "It'll work. It has to."

"It better." Nekronok's voice was low and bitter. "Grist knows to take the beast out if he doesn't concede. But I don't need a Goblin uprising with everything else going on. It'll make life easier if Mudgeon takes the bribe."

That news made Brady's anxiety level drop a notch. He was relieved to know the plans did not include a Goblin apocalypse.

Mudgeon tottered back to the edge. "Good to see that Nekronok is a generous neighbor. Send him my heartfelt thanks whence you return." He pointed a bony finger at the chief himself. "You. The tallest Troll. You and your grey companion may cross next."

Nekronok raised an eyebrow at Rooke.

"It seems best to go along with it, Father." Rooke spoke in a low voice and nodded at the bridge. "I know you are not accustomed to being told what to do, but we cannot disclose your identity."

The chief inhaled through flared nostrils and stepped up to the ropes.

"After you." Rooke gestured to the bridge.

Nekronok grabbed the ropes and gave them a quick yank, testing them. With less hesitation than the ninja, he threaded his way across the swaying bridge.

At the halfway point, Mudgeon pointed at Rooke. "Let's get on with it."

Rooke stiffened. "Sire, it seems more prudent to wait until he crosses."

"Cross, I say, or our deal is void. And those two measly prisoners need to get ready to cross after you."

Without being told, Brady and Brock shuffled their fettered bodies behind Rooke. The pewter-colored Troll didn't bother giving them his usual smug glare. Grabbing the ropes, Rooke placed one foot on the already straining cords and grimaced. Shaking his head, he muttered, "If there's a God, I hope he helps us."

In no hurry to test the mettle of the bridge, Brady decided to wait until they were told to add more weight to the creaking structure.

When Rooke was far enough into his trek that Brady expected to be ordered on board, something snapped. The cords gave way in a sudden collapse. Brady lurched back from the brink with a yelp that almost yanked Brock off his feet. In a blur of rope and fur and limbs and screams, the entire contraption plunged into the great rift of rock. He heard the tangled mass crash into jutting chunks of granite and land with a distant thump.

Brady's head spun and his heart rammed against his chest. Brock shook his head. "There was too much weight on the bridge," he said.

"Definitely." Brady inched to the ledge and peered into the fragments of shadow and light below. The chasm narrowed as it descended. Loose rocks continued to tumble and crash against the ragged surface. At the bottom, splayed and contorted and still as death, lay Chief Nekronok and his son.

"Well, there we are," shouted Mudgeon from across the gap, a bloody dagger in his hand. He stood over Grist, the ninja Troll, who was sprawled headlong and bleeding. "These Trolls will make a delectable feast for my upcoming nuptials." He flung the dagger so that it flipped and landed deep in Grist's back. The wounded Troll arched, crying out, then went limp.

Brady looked from Chebar to Sargon, wondering what they planned to do.

Mudgeon brushed his hands together. "Pleasure doing business with you fine Trolls. Payment accepted."

"Thank you, Sire." Sargon bowed. He turned to Chebar and offered his hand. "And a pleasure doing business with you, brother."

Chebar clasped it, caught Brock's eye, and winked.

CHAPTER THIRTY-FOUR

I SCRAMBLED TO MY FEET, LEAVING Prussell in the sand. Mom should've come through by now. Sophie and I moved closer to the exit, our ears straining to hear. We clasped each other's cold, gritty fingers. My whole body shivered.

Mom shot out of the hole head first with a thunk.

"Mom!" Sophie and I rushed to her side, helping her to roll onto her back. She groaned and spit, her eyes clenched tight against a coating of sand. Her poor face had taken another pummeling.

I knelt and stabbed the handle of my lit flashlight into the dirt, looking in vain for something, anything clean to use to brush the sand from her eyes. Green slime coated her entire front, and globs of the stuff caked her ears and clumped in her hair. On top of it all was a fine coating of dirt, like she'd been frosted then rolled in powdered sugar.

"Let's get you cleaned up." I squeezed her shoulder.

"Okay."

Sophie crouched and brushed grit from Mom's hair.

"Let me pour some water across your face. Hang on." Glancing around, I looked for the pack of supplies. "I don't see the backpack. Did you forget it?" My heart sank. There would be no going back to retrieve it.

She shook her head. "Before I climbed in"—she spat and sputtered, then used the inside of her shirt to wipe her mouth—"I was attacked by a Gargoyle."

"What?" Sophie bolted upright, her hands in fists.

My gut twisted. I assumed the creep had come down behind me at some point and now lurked in the shadows.

Lark poked his head out of the baby carrier slung across Sophie's chest. "A Gargoyle?"

"Hang on." Mom sat up, raking slimy strands of hair away

from her face while keeping her eyes closed. She pulled her arms inside her T-shirt, then spun it around her neck so it was backwards but fairly dry. Plunging her head inside, she wiped her face. "Ow. That hurts my nose." She emerged with swaths of skin visible through the glaze of green. She opened her eyelids carefully, blinking several times. "Whew."

"Take your time, Mom," I said, horrified that she had been alone with the Gargoyle. Should I have told her?

After a few deep breaths, she seemed to relax a bit. "I was getting ready to climb the ledge when something jerked me back. This awful, black thing appeared out of nowhere. He looked like a-a salamander. He wrestled the pack away and demanded the key. Started unzipping it and dumping out the contents. While he scavenged through it, I dove headfirst into the chute to get away." She made a gagging face and shook her head. "That's the grossest thing I've ever experienced."

I looked around, trying to spy the creature in the shadows, hoping to see that ripple of air that tattled on his presence. The space was too large to see anything.

"Listen." I leaned in to Mom and Sophie, wrapping my arms around myself for warmth. "That Gargoyle has been with us since the house—"

"What?" Mom grabbed my knee.

"He came looking for Malagruel and saw what was left of him in the front yard. Of course he's livid, and he knows the key is missing. He hopped on Odyssey when we did, doing that shapeshifting thing so we couldn't see him. Next thing I knew, I had his hand around my mouth, and he was whispering to me to do what he said or he would hurt you guys. He wanted me to talk about the key so he could find out where it is."

Lark clapped his hands on his head and shook it. "No, no, no. This is terrible. Thank the Maker we didn't put it in your pack." He grasped the sack attached to his belt as if to ensure the ring hadn't moved.

"Believe me. I know." I dropped my voice. "At least now I don't have to keep it a secret. It's Ophidian, the same worm that kidnapped Brady last time we were here. Be careful about what you say. He may be listening even now."

As if expecting him to answer, Sophie spun around, her eyes darting about. When nothing happened, Mom got to her feet. "I think we need to get out of here as fast as possible. If that creep is still searching through our things, which I doubt, I'd rather not wait around for him to catch up."

"We're in the realm of the Tethered World now." Lark swept his arms open. "I can call up the Faeries from here. No telling how long it will take for them to come, however."

"What can we do to help?" Sophie looked down at her pouch full of Elf.

He shook his head. "Not a thing. I must call them with my pipe flute." From an inside pocket of his coat he withdrew a slender wooden instrument, no bigger around than a drinking straw. Seven tiny holes riddled the top of the intricately carved piece that he placed between his lips. The lilting, tittering tune he played brought a smile to our faces. At times, it soared to an earsplitting frequency, much like the sound the Faeries made when they whirred around our bodies to transport us from one place to another.

The tune dipped and chirped and swooped for several minutes, and I started feeling jittery. I was certain Lark was broadcasting our presence to Ophidian and any other nearby creatures.

When he finally finished, Sophie applauded. I leaned over and picked up my flashlight. "Should we wait here?"

Lark nodded. "Yes. My melody explained to them where they shall find us and that we need to be delivered to Vituvia."

"Cool! You can do that with music?"

"Of course, Princess Sophie. Music is a universal language, is it not?" Lark placed his pipe flute back in his coat.

Mom rubbed her arms and shuddered. "I vote to huddle close together and try to stay warm while we wait." She shifted closer to Sophie and waved me over. "You certainly didn't exaggerate our current condition, Lark."

"I'd better get Prussell. Wouldn't want to leave him here on accident." Replacing the baby carrier on my back, I sucked in my breath. His weight pressed my cold, wet shirt against my skin. I hurried back to where the others clustered together.

My gaze scanned the shadows. I didn't see any signs of the Gargoyle, but my money was on him being somewhere nearby. He wanted the keys and knew they were with us. But the silence was almost harder to bear than the way he had shadowed me earlier. The question was whether he had come through the chute before or after I told the others about him.

Although my gloves were soaked and coated with scum, I was thankful I'd had the presence of mind to keep the ring covered. I blew hot air onto my fingers and hoped the Meadow Faeries would arrive soon.

"Lark," Sophie whispered, "is the Tree of Life really dying?"

The tiny creature let out a long, sad sigh. "That is what my kinfolk have heard from the Gnomes. They were in quite an uproar in Vituvia at the time I was snatched and taken topside."

"What will happen if it dies?" Sophie chewed her lip.

"I've pondered that question myself, young Larcen." Lark hooked his elbows over the fabric and rested his chin on his hands. "I believe it is a question of how intertwined the tree is with the sword. Is the sword dependent on the tree, or is the tree dependent on the sword? Does that question have any relevance because they are one and the same?"

"Sounds like no one knows." Mom used a shard of rock to clean beneath her fingernails.

"Precisely."

He sneezed, and we all said, "Bless you."

"Thank you." He offered a little bow. "Though there have been past attempts on the sword, there's never been a problem with the health of the tree until now. I believe the tree is a power source for the sword. Much like your electricity, the Flaming Sword is plugged in, if you will, to the life of the tree."

"So, if the tree dies..." I hated to finish the thought.

"The sword dies with it."

Sophie frowned. "And if that happens?"

"The Tethered World will plunge into darkness and chaos. It will be overrun with evil."

CHAPTER THIRTY-FIVE

BRADY HAD NO TIME TO PROCESS what he had witnessed. Chebar, Sargon, and the remaining ninja Troll ushered Brady and Brock to a nearby wall of sloping rock. The soldier slashed the brothers' bonds, and they eagerly rubbed their raw, burning wrists.

"Start climbing." Chebar pointed to Brock. "Head toward the opening in the ceiling above."

Brock blinked but didn't move.

"Let's go." Chebar looked from Brock to Brady, brows furrowed.

Come on! Brady willed his brother to cooperate. Thankfully, Brock began to climb. Without a word, Brady followed. A few Goblins lingered close but didn't interfere. Traversing the steep slope, Brady rehearsed the assassination. The whole thing had been a setup. And Sargon and the second soldier were complicit with Chebar. In one fell swoop, the leader and his successor had been eliminated. Did this mean Sargon could be trusted? Brady doubted it, since Mr. Delaney had been working with him topside.

Still...Nekronok and Rooke no longer posed a threat. What a relief! So what awaited them next? Brady guessed he'd find out once they climbed out of the gaping skylight above.

Soon the five of them stood on top of a desolate hill. The holes in the ground, which were the openings that provided light for the Goblins, would be dangerous to an unsuspecting traveler. The creatures probably enjoyed a few gruesome meals dining on the poor souls who had the misfortune of falling through.

The glowing geode sky stretched from one horizon to the next. The radiating light felt oddly dim. Was it dusk already?

Brady had had no way to keep track of time inside the dungeons but had assumed that their trek through the tunnels began in the morning, a few hours before. Still, he warmed at the familiar sight, thrilled to be out of the tunnels and in the vast, open air—even if it was well below the earth's surface.

A smile settled on Brock's lips, hinting that he felt the relief of it as well.

The Trolls busied themselves scanning the horizon. Brady noted the distant hills that snaked in front of the looming, chiseled Berganstroud mountain range. The towering point of Mount Thrall jabbed like a gnarled finger against the amber sky. Brady hoped Chebar's plan didn't involve going back to the Eldritch, Nekronok's creepy palace carved into the face of Mount Thrall.

Chebar pointed. "Here they come."

Brady followed the Troll's line of sight. Three distant specks hovered over the ground, growing in size and shape as they came closer. Based on their massive wingspans, Brady thought they were hippogriffs—those mythical half-eagle, half-horse oddities used by Trolls for transport.

As the winged anomalies circled to land, Brady realized that one of the three was a griffin—half eagle and half lion. He remembered that Rooke had ridden a griffin on Brady's last unfortunate visit.

The beasts touched down with graceful ease, trotting to a stop.

Chebar took Brock by the arm and helped him into the saddle strapped to one of the hippogriffs, then climbed up behind him. Brady mounted the griffin with Sargon's assistance. The conglomeration of eagle and lion made the creature shorter in stature than the hippogriff and easier to mount.

The ninja Troll started toward the other hippogriff but made a sudden beeline to the opening that the five of them had climbed out of. He drew his sword.

"What is it, Thiago?" Chebar grasped the hilt of his sword.

The soldier held up a silencing hand and raised his scimitar. A set of small, filthy fingers grappled the edge of the hole, followed by a foot. As the Goblin attempted to haul its rotund body up and out, Thiago's blade whistled through the air and punctured the imp, leaving a telltale puddle of slime.

"Let that be a warning to the rest of you," he hollered into the opening. He made a face at the gunk on his sword and scrubbed it across a nearby shrub. He strode back to the hippogriff and mounted. "We don't need those Goblins spooking the griffs."

Brady caught Brock's eye as their respective griffs took to the sky. They exchanged a subtle nod. Brady let himself relax and absorb the reality of escaping Nekronok's hand and soaring through the air to...somewhere. It didn't matter where at this point, though he still didn't like the idea of going to the Eldritch. Being out of danger was what counted. It looked like the precautions Tassitus had offered to Brady weren't necessary after all.

Still, Brady only knew for certain that he could trust Chebar. Sargon and Thiago might not be as kindhearted toward the twin Topsider brothers. Until he could be sure, Brady must continue to play it cool and keep Plan B under the radar.

Tiny effervescent lights sputtered to life. Our own personal meteor shower of green and yellow specks of light flared and danced across the ceiling. The Meadow Faeries had arrived.

We got to our feet and waited for their descent. Even though I knew what to expect, there was no way to get used to the surprise and thrill of being transported from one location to another in an instant. I smiled at the sprightly flickers of light, watching them coordinate their sporadic flight patterns, listening to their lilting chimes.

My mom and sister stayed close to me, as we had been instructed on previous trips. The dazzling Faeries surrounded us, encircled us in a cyclone of glowing wings and iridescent bodies. A jingle of laughter rippled through thousands of tiny bells. As their speed increased, a brisk breeze followed in their wake and peppered us with sandy grit. I clamped my eyes and mouth shut. My damp clothes felt positively refrigerated in the whirlwind. Tendrils of hair whipped free from my soggy braid and lashed my face.

At first the Faerie noises made no sense to me, pleasant as it was. But soon their tingling, high-pitched calls fell into synchronization. "To Vituvia to save the tree! To Vituvia to save the tree!" The chant repeated, rising in pitch until it became a bee sting on my ear drum. Piercing and painful, it made my head scream for relief.

My body registered another pain. Something sharp and biting encircled my wrist. I cracked open an eye and tugged my arm instinctively, noticing nothing—but realizing my evil shadow had returned.

"*I know the keys are here somewhere,*" Ophidian hissed into my ear. "*Catching a ride to Vituvia before I force you to hand them over will make it that much easier to put them to use. And if you or yours dare to breathe a word about me, I'll have a wide selection of victims to incapacitate.*"

CHAPTER THIRTY-SIX

MY SENSES UNFOLDED. FOR THE BRIEFEST instant I felt pressed into a vacuum. Before I could acknowledge the absence of light and air and space, I became acutely aware of all three.

Torchlight illumined a familiar, stone room buzzing with activity. A menagerie of startled faces blinked and smiled and rushed to welcome us. I gasped back to coherency. The fright of Ophidian's threat simmered in the back of my mind even as I knelt to hug freckle-faced Revonika, the Gnome that reached me first.

A happy exchange of laughter, relief, and greetings ensued. Sir Noblin, General Muggleridge, and the temperamental Colonel Smarlow rushed to welcome us. My heart soared to see Lava, my favorite Dwarf, once again. He and Chief Wogsnop were in from Berganstroud. I stooped and let Lava wrap me in a hug brimming with mounds of hair and layers of animal skins. His earthiness enveloped my chilled body so that I didn't want to let go.

"So good to see ya, m'lady!" Lava pulled away, placing both hands on my shoulders and giving me a once-over. "But what a sight! Looks like ya must've slithered through a swamp to get here."

I grinned. "Something like that."

"Our Vituvian friends will get ya fixed in a jiffy. Looks like yer mum could use somethin' fer her nose. Ouch." He released me and waved a dismissive hand at the frolicking cloud of Faeries that hovered over us. "Thanks fer yer assistance yet again, dear Spriggen Fey. Back to the meadows with ya."

The Faeries swirled into a tight cluster and disappeared. Beside me, Sophie crouched and removed Lark from the sling, placing him gently on the floor. He scrambled over to Sir Noblin, and the two set to conversing with their heads tilted close.

Unsure of how to broach the subject of Prussell, I decided to wait on explaining what was on my back for the moment.

"Yer timin' couldn't be better." Lava took out his pipe and chewed the mouthpiece without lighting it. "We convened from an emergency recon assembly a few minutes ago. Lookin' forward to some vittles and ale." He winked with the last word. "Tomorrow we head to our various posts. Some may even leave tonight to scout fer yer brother."

"Looks like we picked the right time and place to pop in unannounced." I cut my eyes around, hoping to catch the subtle shift of reality that would point me to Ophidian.

"Indeed! Let me see if I can scrounge up a few more chairs." Lava headed to a long, low meeting table cluttered with maps and scrolls and books. Gnomes and Dwarves busied themselves rearranging tree stumps of varying heights around taller tables, while leaving doll-sized chairs around the low one.

My gaze fell on Great-Aunt Judith, Queen of Vituvia, being pushed by none other than Joanie, my other favorite Dwarf. I grimaced at Aunt Judith's frail appearance. It had only been five or six weeks since we last saw the spry twin to my dear Aunt Jules. The stroke had taken a swift toll on her petite frame, leaving her slumped to the left with her mouth pulled in the same direction.

"Oh, Aunt Judith!" Mom rushed to her side, kneeling so that she looked up into my aunt's face. "I'm so sorry about your stroke," Mom said. "How are you feeling?"

Joanie beamed up at us, her plump cheeks pressed the corners of her green eyes into happy crinkles. "Thank the Maker fer bringin' yer sweet family back so soon. First yer father and uncle, and now ye three ladies." She embraced us, patting our cheeks.

"Great to be back." Sophie's smile matched Joanie's enthusiasm. She turned to the queen and patted her leg. "Hello Aunt Judith."

"Yes, hello." I crouched on the side opposite Mom. "I bet Joanie is taking great care of you."

Aunt Judith appeared to be working hard to straighten, or maybe to speak. I couldn't say for sure, but her head twitched in the effort to do something, her eyes reflecting a mixture of frustration and sadness.

"Now, now, Miss Queen Bee," Joanie said, patting our aunt's shoulder. "Ya only need to sit and look pretty. Don't bother to try and converse fer now."

With an effort, Aunt Judith placed her hand on top of Mom's.

The Dwarf chortled. "She's a stubborn one. Nothin' wrong with her noggin', but she can get angry as an Ogre when her mouth won't cooperate with her brain. Mornin' is her best time fer talkin'."

"No need to say a thing." Mom squeezed the queen's fingers and then stood. "You only need to concentrate on getting well."

"Dear me." Joanie scowled at Mom. "Yer nose, love! I'm gonna get ya somethin' that'll fix ya right up."

While we visited, Dwarves retrieved three tree stump seats, adding them to the conglomeration encircling the taller tables. Servants removed the maps and other items from the rustic wood tabletop. It appeared the meeting and meal had been planned in a rush, with tables and chairs brought in to accommodate as needed.

More than food, I wanted a scalding hot shower. But, first things first. Removing the baby carrier from my back, I placed it carefully on the floor and leaned it against the chair stump. I plopped onto the seat with the grateful realization that I no longer felt chilled. But the question of the Gargoyle's whereabouts managed to send a shiver up my back anyway. I scanned the room, unable to catch a glimpse of anything that looked a little off. Feeling there was safety in numbers, I hoped he'd take the watch-and-wait approach before pressing me for more information or taking matters into his own hands.

Sir Noblin crossed to me, his wrinkled face drawn and somber. He removed his hat, torchlight splashing golden highlights through his silver hair. Steepling his fingers together, he bowed. "Princess Sadie, I've been informed by our new friend Lark that you have brought back one of our own. Vituvia is grateful that you've seen fit to deliver him to us, despite the difficulties of getting here. I did not personally know this young Gnome—er—what was his name?"

"Prussell."

"Yes, yes. Poor chap." He replaced his conical hat and smoothed the lapels of his red overcoat. "I did not know him, but I've been told of the precarious events surrounding his kidnapping and the way in which he helped you in your hour of need."

"He was our hero," I said. "I don't know what would've happened without his help. He and Lark took down Malagruel." I placed my hand on top of the blanketed body of the deceased

Gnome cocooned in Nate's carrier. "We are all grateful."

Sir Noblin's gaze dropped to the pack. "Indeed. As are we. I shall send for the Tribute Guards to come retrieve his body. Excuse me." He whispered to one of the servants, who nodded and left the room. Then he cleared his throat and clapped his hands so that everyone quieted. "I know we are pleased as pineapple to have our dear friends grace us with their presence. What they have experienced topside will serve to round out what we know thus far. Lady Amy shall report to us while we dine."

I glanced at my mom, who was sitting next to me. Her swollen nose emphasized the circles beneath her eyes. The stress of the past few weeks, combined with her recent coating of algae and sand, made her look more exhausted and broken than ever. I overheard one of the Gnomes promise to get some healing balm for her nose, but Mom looked like she could use a full spa treatment and a long nap. Come to think of it, so could I.

Sir Noblin removed his hat, his face clouding. "Unfortunately, one of our brothers has fallen while in the service of Vituvia. The Larcens have returned this brave soul for a proper burial with his kindred."

Solemn faces nodded. Dwarves and Gnomes moved to their seats around the tables, and servants entered with steaming platters mounded with food. The savory smell made me woozy with desire. How had I ignored the gnawing hunger that now growled in my gut?

"I'll let the others know that supper has arrived." Lava excused himself and headed for the elaborately carved wooden door to our left. As he stepped out, the door to our right opened. In walked Bennett, a sandy-haired soldier from Berganstroud, followed by three hulking Nephilim.

My breath caught in my throat when I saw King Aviel, his commander, Gage, and Prince Xander filing in. Their collective bulk made the room shrink. Xander's singular presence made my mouth go dry and my heart in need of a defibrillator. His eyes met mine, and he stopped mid-stride. A funny smile pulled at the corner of his mouth, and he found his way over to me. I stood up, feeling tiny next to him. My world and worries diminished as he loomed above, all deep tawny angles and shivery blue eyes.

"Hello, Princess." His long, twisted braids fell in front of his face as he stooped to one knee and kissed the knuckles that peeked from my fingerless gloves. My filthy, dirty, algae-coated knuckles.

I snatched my hand away and smothered it with my other one, as if he'd burned me with his lips. Mortification crept into my cheeks, though he probably couldn't see the crimson stain beneath the sewage-green face paint. Ugh! Why did he always see me at my absolute worst?

"Hello, Xander." I blinked, slow and deliberate, my eyelids now windshield wipers that I hoped would improve his view. "I didn't know you were here."

He stood again, all six feet ten inches of him, grinning like a mischievous boy. "I should be the one saying such a thing. You weren't in this room when I left." His gaze roamed my pitiful appearance. He shook his head. "I've never known a female with such a knack for finding adventure. I like it."

I pressed my lips together and tried not to think about the disparaging differences between us. His gladiator-meets-Superman good looks—think cape, not tights—and my groundhog-crawled-out-and-saw-his-shadow appearance seemed a laughable pairing. In fact, I did laugh—one hand covering my mouth, the other raking through my hair as if I had a shred of hope at improving my looks.

"Hey." He gently pulled my fingers away from my face, keeping them in his. "I meant that as a compliment. I love how you're not concerned with sitting about, looking pretty. It makes you more beautiful to me."

Heart in throat, I reminded myself to breathe. We hadn't been around each other two minutes and he had already dived in deep, parading his feelings for me and stirring up my own. Yet I couldn't go there right now. And not in front of this audience that, I noted with dismay, watched us with amused faces. Even my mom, who would never allow me to get serious with someone, looked like she might embrace him and call him son.

It took an awkward amount of time for me to find my voice, but he patiently watched, rubbing his thumb across the top of my knuckles. Maybe he was trying to rub off the dirt. Maybe he was rubbing in his kiss. "That's kind of you to say," I murmured. "I'm afraid I'm not the one seeking out the adventure. It seems to find me, and I can't escape. It sucks me down and spits me out after I give it a good colon cleanse."

His brows furrowed, mouth twisting with a question. I decided he didn't know what a colon cleanse might be.

"Scratch that." I held up the hand he wasn't holding. "Let's just say I'm a willing but not eager participant."

He lifted my fingers to his lips again. "Let's say I think you're beautiful. Can you accept that?"

I shrugged one shoulder. "I'll try."

"Ahem." Sir Noblin managed a loud but forced throat clearing. "Allow me to ask the blessing on our supper since we are all quite famished. Love shall have to wait its turn."

A chorus of warm chuckles enveloped us. I felt the wattage in my face flush neon red. Xander merely lifted his eyebrows up, but he dropped my hand and headed to a tall tree stump beside his father. King Aviel regarded me through his ice-blue eyes, a perfect match to Xander's. What the king thought about his son's infatuation with me, a mere Topsider, I couldn't guess.

Xander's mother, on the other hand, had made her bitter dislike of me a certainty. And, in case I had missed the hateful way she looked at me, she had told me to my face.

And so I killed her.

Okay, not really. Although I did help to bring about her demise, it wasn't because she hated me. Long story.

I sank into the chair, wishing I could crawl back inside my groundhog burrow and hibernate until spring. With my emotions fluttering about like caffeinated hummingbirds, it seemed useless to attempt any meaningful conversation.

After Sir Noblin blessed the food, everyone agreed with a hearty, "So be it," and we plunged into the meal with noisy enthusiasm. Utensils clanked and clattered. Moans of delight, especially from the Dwarves, made a homey symphony. I was glad for the distraction of eating, but before I could help myself to anything, a tug on my pants leg averted my attention.

One of the servants held up a steamy, folded cloth. "To cleanse your hands." I gratefully took it and wiped my grimy face while considering whether to remove my gloves and expose my ring. No, too risky. Odd as it looked, I opted to keep the ring hidden from the enemy in the shadows.

Joanie had brought Mom some herbal salve to use on her nose, so Mom now had a slimy-looking purple nose. Probably not the look she was going for, but hopefully it would help. Mom insisted that Joanie sit and relax while she helped Aunt Judith with her food. The motherly Dwarf scaled the tree stump beside me, using notches carved into the wood as footholds to get up.

Joanie had no sooner situated her plump body on the concave top when a mournful bugle call brought everyone to their feet. I strained to see around the Nephilim that sat at the table beside ours.

A procession of Gnomes emerged from behind their table and headed for their fallen comrade beside me. The bugler in front continued his dirge, leading four Gnomes into the hall. They carried a stretcher between the four of them. They stopped before me and placed the stretcher on the stone ground. I wasn't sure if I should help retrieve Prussell from the carrier or let them do it. Somehow, it felt right to kneel and carefully remove the brave Gnome, presenting him to the Tribute Guard myself.

Two of the Gnomes stepped forward, bowed in unison, and lifted Prussell from my outstretched arms. They laid him on the stretcher as he was, then raised the precious cargo, resting the poles on their shoulders. With straight, synchronized steps, the four marched through the room followed by the lamenting call of the bugle.

Joanie wheeled the queen to a space between tables. The guards stopped, and my regal aunt leaned forward and reached trembling fingers to the still form of Prussell, as if to give the fallen warrior her blessing. The Tribute Guards saluted and continued their march out the door.

The somber moment dampened the eating frenzy. It also managed to frighten off my internal hummingbirds and recapture my focus on why we had come. Friends were dying to keep my family alive. They were depending on us to help protect their sword, their tree, and ultimately their world.

Once the mood lightened a bit, Sir Noblin clanked his fork against his mug. "Since time is of the essence, allow me to recap for the sake of our newcomers while you finish eating, then we shall hear from Lady Amy about what has occurred topside." The elderly Gnome slid his chair back, stood on it, and clasped his hands across his belly. "King Brock is still missing. Spies have been dispatched to learn what they can. More shall pursue another destination this evening. The Tree of Life is undergoing treatment, but it is too soon to know whether the regimen is effective. In the meantime, as goes the tree, so goes the power of the sword."

"And so goes Vituvia." Smarlow pounded his fist so that his plate and utensils clattered.

"Indeed." Sir Noblin removed his hat and clasped it to his

chest. "While our blessed tree struggles for life, the flames around the sword grow weaker." He lifted his eyes to the ceiling. "And in response, the light in our crystalline sky has dimmed."

CHAPTER THIRTY-SEVEN

WHILE MOM TOLD OUR TOPSIDE TALE of woe, I mulled over the possibility of the lights going out in the Tethered World. If something didn't happen soon, if the damage to the tree could not be reversed...what might happen? A dark underground world would be an uninhabitable one. Would there be a mass exodus of the creatures retreating to life topside? Could the sword be removed without need for the key? If so, would it continue to wield any power?

A hand on my shoulder brought my thoughts back to the here and now. I turned and squealed. "Dad!" I hopped out of my chair and wrapped my arms around him. Sophie was right beside me, followed by Mom, who broke off in the middle of her story about Mystique's strange email.

"When did you girls get here?" Dad pulled back enough to look at the three of us. "Oh hon, what happened to your nose?" He leaned close to inspect her bruises.

Mom ducked behind her hand. "Don't look. Ugh! It's so ugly. And it's a long story. But I'm okay."

"You can tell me later." Dad grinned and gave her a kiss on the cheek. "I'm guessing things are under control with Mr. Delaney if you felt like you could leave. Or else things are so much worse...?"

Mom exhaled, rolling her eyes. "I'll give you the long version after dinner. I was actually in the middle of the short version for the sake of getting everyone up to speed. I should probably finish." She disentangled herself and headed back to her place at the table.

"Where's Uncle Brent?" I whispered to Dad, craning my neck to catch sight of him.

Dad squeezed my hand and released it. "He took his dinner in the Garden Dome." With a glint in his eye, he leaned in to

Sophie and me. "With Enoch."

A shuddering thrill sparked through me. "Oh goodness! I still find that hard to fathom. Have you actually met him?"

A slow, deliberate nod was his answer.

"What's he like?" Sophie bounced in place.

Dad glanced at Mom, who had resumed her explanation. He pulled us away from the others, where our conversation would be private. "He's ancient, yet somehow timeless. It's hard to explain. He doesn't say much, but when he talks you feel like you might collapse under the weight of his words. It's like everything he speaks is the most important phrase ever spoken. And your Uncle Brent is enthralled with the man. I've never seen him so focused and serious. Enoch is teaching him about many of the plants in the garden."

"And how is the tree? Has Uncle Brent been able to help?" I searched Dad's face for a flicker of hope or optimism.

He hesitated, and the creases between his brows and the frown lines that twitched alongside his mouth said it all, deflating my hopes. "Not that we can tell. The traitor that inflicted the damage butchered it something terrible. And it didn't take long for Brent to realize he knew next to nothing about botanical science compared to Enoch."

"Was there more than one traitor?" Sophie's scowl matched Dad's.

"Three have been discovered so far." He shook his head. "Might be more. I'll tell you what I know later, with Mom. Let's go eat—I'm starved."

We returned to our places at the table, and another chair was brought in to accommodate Dad. Mom finished speaking, answered a few questions, then rejoined us.

Lark stood and added his side of the story, describing how he and Prussell were captured, thanks to an ugly trick played by the Leprechauns. He gave some insight about Sargon, the Troll that had carried the two of them topside, and Mr. Delaney. "The old man and the Troll are working together." Lark jabbed a finger in the air. "But neither one trusts the other, that much was obvious. Each had his own agenda and so they argued constantly."

"They're as crooked as the banks of Brodger Creek," Smarlow said, punching his fist at the air.

Lark gave a curt nod in Smarlow's direction. "I heartily share your observation, my good Gnome." He turned to Sir Noblin. "That's all I have to add. Thank you for your time. Please don't think me rude, but I must be getting back to my family. No doubt they're beside themselves with worry."

He hopped off the table and came to say goodbye to my family. I eyed his pouch, wondering what plans he had for the key, beyond getting it far away from the one on my finger. After our farewells were said, he headed for the closest door. A sentry held it open, and Lark padded away. A flicker of light and shadow followed him out, and I knew that Ophidian had Lark in his crosshairs.

I rushed to follow, hoping I wouldn't be too late. "Mom, come with me," I whispered as I passed her. She knew about the rings, so I wouldn't be endangering her more than I already had. The guard pulled the door open as I approached, Mom on my heels. I stepped into a passageway, looking in both directions but seeing no sign of the Elf.

Mom came up beside me. "What's going on?"

"Ophidian. I saw him follow Lark out the door."

"Oh no! You go that direction and I'll go this way."

I trotted to the right, dodging a servant carrying food. The passage took a hard right turn and became narrower. Pedestals dotted the left-hand side every three or four yards. Large plants sprawled from vases on top of them. Further down the hall, wooden doors picked up where the pedestals left off.

The last pairing of pedestal and plant suddenly trembled. The column-like bottom shifted enough to rattle the vase of flowers. I took off down the hall, just as the vase was lifted by seemingly invisible hands. It crashed to the floor, but something cushioned the fall. I could tell by the sound. I knew with sickening certainty what the vase had landed on. As I approached, doll-sized shoes came into view, the buckle of one glinting in the torchlight.

"No!" I shouted at the shapeshifting beast. I couldn't pinpoint where he was but knew he was near. "Get away from him."

A mess of soil and shards of broken pottery lay heaped on top of Lark's frail body. I gaped, tears blurring the awful sight. Before I could yell for Mom or try to help Lark, scaly hands seized my throat and plowed me backward into the wall.

"Where's the key?" Ophidian's voice hissed in my ear. For a brief second his snake-like features materialized, long enough for me to see his slitted reptilian pupils staring me down. He was gone again, the space before me rippling with his chameleon-like effect, easy to see at such close proximity.

I tried to scream or breathe or something that might squeeze oxygen through my windpipe. His serpentine fingers seemed to encircle my neck multiple times. The torchlight grew dim, and a tiny corner of my brain knew my consciousness was abandoning me. I let my eyes close.

An unexpected jolt suddenly freed me of the Gargoyle's stranglehold. My eyes flew open as a dark blur sped past. I gasped like a fish out of water and stared. On the floor, Xander grappled with the slithery form that blinked in and out of view. I tottered against the wall for support. Footsteps scrambled toward us. I turned to see Gage running, sword extended, my dad at his heels. Lava and Wogsnop trailed behind with a half dozen Gnomes.

Ophidian expelled an awful, gurgling wheeze and materialized beneath Xander's grasp. The Nephilim prince was doing unto the Gargoyle as he had done to me: choking the life out of him. The creature went limp, his snub-nosed head lolling to the side. Xander huffed for breath, his braids tumbling forward as he dropped his head.

The other soldiers surrounded us, coming to a halt at the sight of the motionless Gargoyle. Dad didn't stop until he reached me, snatching me up in a hug. He pressed my head against his chest. "Thank God you're okay."

I nodded, too overwhelmed to speak.

Gage sheathed his sword and stretched his right hand to Xander, helping him to his feet. Xander turned to me and said, "You've quite proven my point, Princess." He stepped around the Gargoyle and came close. "You're always in the middle of some kind of trouble."

I grinned. "I want you to feel useful, that's all."

"What's this?" Smarlow's voice cut through the general commotion.

Xander stepped aside, and I spied Smarlow standing beside Lark. From my vantage point, the poor Elf lay twisted at an unnatural angle, and I feared the worst.

"Sadie!" Mom's voice squawked over everything else as she hurried toward us. "Oh my goodness, Sadie. Are you okay?" She stopped, hands on knees, gulping for breath.

"Yes." I nodded and gestured at Xander. "Thanks once again to my personal guardian angel." I moved through milling bodies and stepped beside Smarlow, who had hauled the largest bulk of the vase off of poor Lark with the help of Sir Noblin. I knelt and pitched broken chunks of ceramic away then gently scooped handfuls of dirt.

Sir Noblin crouched beside me, brushing at the soil with his stubby fingers. He shook his head and mumbled to himself, "Everything is coming undone. Everything."

"Oh, no!" Mom shouldered through the others who had gathered to watch, hand over her mouth. "No. Not Lark. Not him." Tears spilled over her fingers.

My own tears pooled stubbornly. They stung and blurred my vision but were so weary of fighting and death they couldn't muster up enough liquid to take the plunge. I hadn't been in the Tethered World for two hours and someone I cared for had died. Again.

I was bitterly sick of it.

The poor Elf emerged from the dirt, one handful at a time. Blood muddled with the soil as it trickled from his nose and lips. What a way to die.

"This is unforgivable." Sir Noblin buttoned Lark's jacket, brushing the stubborn earth from the lapel.

I reached for the pouch that drooped from Lark's belt. "Oh my goodness. The key!" My fingers fumbled for the familiar shape.

"No worries, m'lady." The Gnome placed a calming hand on mine. "Lark gave it to me shortly after his arrival. It is in a secure location until we can reunite it with its owner."

All at once, Lark's tiny body convulsed, his mouth opened wide, and he took a giant gulp of air. I stared, shocked and elated by the sight. The Elf was alive! Those closest to us let out a cheer and told the others. Everyone crowded around. Mom immediately crouched at Lark's feet, morphing into Amy Larcen RN, her eyes taking inventory of the situation. I watched the rapid rise and fall of his chest with disbelief and joy swelling in my own. Sir Noblin told the onlookers to give us space and called for someone to fetch the Healer.

The Elf groaned and lifted his hand to his face.

"Don't move, Lark." I placed my fingers on his arm. "We're getting help. You're going to be fine."

"Roots and fruits! What's this?" Lava's booming voice cut through the commotion. He pointed at the spot where Ophidian had fallen. Others turned to look, gasping.

Lava snatched his dagger from his belt and took a defensive stance. "The Gargoyle is gone."

CHAPTER THIRTY-EIGHT

BRADY'S CRUISING ALTITUDE ALLOWED HIM TO see recognizable landmarks. Once the griffin took to the air, Mount Thrall appeared starker and more foreboding than ever. Thankfully, the winged creatures banked away and soon hugged the tree line along the hills that stretched from Berganstroud to Vituvia.

They flew past the Dwarves' fortress, a beacon in contrast to the Dens of the Dark Dwarves. Brady picked out the half-moon shape of the walled bulwark. Soon the glistening ribbon of Brodger Creek stretched to Whitt Lake like a silver thread being pulled from a shimmering ball of yarn. The amber glow of the sky reflected in the ripples across the water's surface.

The dome radiated above him but seemed to glow with a peculiar weakness. Perhaps time spent in the dark dungeon had damaged his eyesight. Or maybe dusk happened slower depending on the seasons topside. Either way, it was like looking at the Tethered World with a pair of sunglasses that couldn't be removed.

He guessed the Trolls were headed to Vituvia, but perhaps Chebar was working under the radar with Calamus. No doubt the Nephilim would be a formidable ally for Chebar's rebellion against his father.

Nekronok. Dead. Brady swirled that concept around, liking the sound of it. He wondered how the news would be taken in Craventhrall. The chief seemed revered, but maybe that was the Trolls' cover for fear. Did Chebar and Sargon have an underground following among the locals? If they lacked support, the Nephilim army would match the Trolls in size to help establish new leadership. Maybe they were headed to Calamus after all.

By the time the griffins began their descent, Brady felt like he had mulled over the world's problems but lacked even one solution. Each visit to the Tethered World had escalated the volatile state of the realm. From the sword to the tree, and from his brother to the rest of his family, the sum total of what mattered added up to a fragile thing that Brady feared would break beyond repair. He closed his eyes and remembered the One who had remembered him the last time he felt overwhelmed in the belly of the earth.

Brady's idea about heading to Calamus had been wrong, for now at least. The griffin coasted toward Vituvia, its vast, feathered wings rarely needing to undulate as it descended. The Gnomes' city had been built into the curved arms of the Hills of Berganstroud. The three domes of the palace nestled like treasure, close to the bosom of the range, spilling down the hillside into its lap below.

A towering, thick wall encircled the town, but many Vituvians lived beyond its protection, working the pastureland for miles around. The creatures kept to a low glide across the acres of vegetation, heading to the far side of the green fields. Since this whole place existed within the earth itself, Brady found that directions like north and south didn't really apply. He only knew that he hadn't been to this part of the Vituvian countryside.

A scrubby path leading to a worn shed appeared to be the appointed landing strip. The dilapidated building teetered against the hillside, its weathered, gaping slats rested against each other at impossible angles. Brady figured the breeze caused by the Griffin's wings might put an end to the structure. Maybe they would make a bonfire from the rubble and roast hotdogs. He couldn't help fantasizing about food since he'd had so little lately.

The shed did, indeed, remain standing when they landed. The three griffs trotted to a bumpy stop, and Brady relished the thought of dismounting and stretching his legs. It sounded almost as good as eating hotdogs. He began to swing his leg over the saddle, but Chebar halted him with a raised hand. "Stay mounted."

A silvery Troll lumbered out of the shack. This had to be Grym, one of Chebar's brothers. Though his fur looked lighter in color, he was a dead ringer for Rooke. Were they twins like Brady and Brock? If so, that made Grym the next in line to rule.

Brady looked over at Brock, who met his gaze with weary eyes. Brady marveled at his brother's resolute demeanor.

Brock had never been a complainer, but certain triggers could send him into meltdown mode. Something about the Tethered World, or the Gnomes, or maybe his training, had worn Brock into a smoother, steadier version of himself. No doubt his brother was meant to be a part of this place. As much as Brady loved the adventures here, he doubted that he could ever fit in like his uniquely-fashioned brother. Although he missed his twin something fierce when they were separated, Brady knew this realm was where Brock belonged.

The silvery Troll wore the same military uniform as his brothers. He strode up to the three flying beasts, followed by three Gnomes that were dressed like Vituvian soldiers. He offered a curt bow, his gaze lingering on Brady. "How is our father?"

"Resting, as planned," Sargon replied. "I trust your meeting solidified phase two of our plan."

"Indeed." The Troll glanced at the Gnomes that stood beside one another in a rigid line, proud and stone-faced. "We should not have any problems implementing the next step."

"Excellent. Good work, Grym." Sargon's voice was loud in Brady's ear. "Mount up and let's head to the city gates."

The Gnomes relaxed their stances, and each approached one of the griffs. Grym lifted the Gnome closest to Brady and held the doll-sized soldier up to him. "Secure this warrior in front of you."

Brady complied, noting the silent humiliation that colored the Gnome's tiny face. Brock anchored another soldier, followed by Thiago taking the third on board with him.

Grym mounted behind Thiago, and the three griffs returned to the air, much to the dismay of Brady's aching backside.

There was a definite plan set in motion among these brothers. But exactly what sort of relationship did they share? Which one was ultimately in charge? Brady guessed that Chebar must be the brains behind the operation. Chebar had masterminded Queen Judith's escape as well as Brady's, all the while appearing innocent and trustworthy to his father. The big Yeti was a genius and, more importantly, a friend.

Brady had assumed that Sargon was working with Mr. Delaney, but perhaps the Troll took part in that spectacle because his father ordered him to do so. Both Sargon and Grym were too new to Brady to label as friends. The only thing they had going for them was Chebar, which counted for much to be sure.

Yet Tassitus, whom Brady should trust less than either unfamiliar Troll, had shared his concerns with such conviction that Brady could not disregard the Gargoyle's warnings.

Brady decided he would continue to watch and observe until he could be sure. He only hoped to arrive at such certainty while he still had the choice to do so.

CHAPTER THIRTY-NINE

AFTER LARK'S NEAR-DEATH EXPERIENCE AND Ophidian's disappearance, my adrenaline bottomed out. Sophie and I were ushered to our usual guest room, where we bathed and face-planted on the four-poster bed. Though I felt like I could sleep for days, Queen Judith had proclaimed that tonight was to be the first ever "Feast of Fortitude," a time to come together in faith that the Creator would make a way where there seemed to be no way. It was to be a meal that fortified both our bodies and our hope as we stood together against evil.

If there's one thing I've learned from our time spent in the Tethered World, it's that when the going gets tough, the tough prepare a banquet and strike up the band. For the Gnomes and Dwarves at least, it seems to work.

Now, I stared with dismay at the circles under my eyes and the scratches marking my cheek and chin. My hair was a wily beast with a whole set of problems of its own, thanks to sleeping with it damp. How could I possibly make myself presentable? Joanie had come by to help us get ready, but she couldn't work miracles, which is what I needed.

"Someone wants to look pretty for Prince Xander."

Sophie's singsong voice made me want to feed her to the beast attached to my head. Instead, I turned with a reasonable amount of self-control and glared her down.

"That's not true. I'm only tired of looking like a sewer rat."

"Ah now, I've seen the way the prince looks at ya." Joanie bustled about, pulling clothes out of a wardrobe and laying them across the bed. "He's as smitten as they come." She turned and wagged a finger in my direction. "And you are too, m'dear. It's nothin' short of electrifyin' to stand within ten feet of the both of ya."

My face turned seventeen shades of red. I felt every one of

them. So much blood rushed to my cheeks that my ears pulsed. My mouth opened in protest, but I didn't know what to say. I had no idea my feelings were so transparent. For starters, I had barely acknowledged them to myself.

Did Xander already know what I hadn't yet admitted?

The Feast of Fortitude was like being granted a do-over from our earlier disjointed luncheon. Not only did I feel somewhat as beautiful as Xander continuously expressed—Joanie actually *can* work cosmetic miracles, as it turns out—but everyone was there. Well, everyone who could be there, anyway. The absence of my brothers was felt by all and noted with a moment of silence.

However, as Sir Noblin pointed out once the moment passed, we had much to be thankful for, despite our trials. After all, the purpose of the feast was to bring focus and faith into the midst of chaos.

"It is most fitting to give praise to the Ancient of Days when things are not as we would prefer," Noblin said. "Who alone but the Most High sees the beginning from the end? Who alone can create beauty from our ashes? We celebrate His goodness in the midst of our pain, knowing that these troubled times have been sifted through His mighty hands before they ever found their way into our lives. His kindness has given us prophecies of old, words of truth to hang onto when our enemies seek to oppose us. The battles may be arduous, but we know Who wins the war!"

As one, we stood and applauded the passionate Gnome. He removed his pointy hat from his bristly, greying head and bowed, wiping tears from his face. I had the impression that his sermon had been spontaneous, overflowing from his heart.

We found our seats. For tonight—and only for tonight, I promised myself—I would allow Xander to make me feel special. No, that wasn't quite right. He always made me feel special. Tonight I would allow myself to enjoy it. Maybe even believe it.

Ever the gentleman, Xander helped me scoot my chair closer to the table—a feat made more difficult by my long, custom-made dress, the color of twilight and as silky to touch as water that laps against the shore. Beside me, Sophie gathered her own full skirt against her legs.

"Thank you." I pulled black satin gloves from my fingertips and laid them across my lap. "You look...nice." It was a weak compliment, but I didn't want to give him too much encouragement.

"You're so lame," Sophie whispered.

Xander flashed a dazzling, self-assured smile that set off his white shirt and black cape and trousers. The combination was very *Phantom of the Opera* minus the need to cover any part of his handsome face. "You probably say that to every prince."

His fingers brushed mine as he took his seat, and we exchanged a literal flash of electricity. I flinched, then laughed, hoping Joanie hadn't seen what happened after her earlier comment about our tangible dynamics.

"See? Sparks fly when we're together." He bent his head near my ear, and I felt the warmth of his breath on my cheek. I liked it.

My parents sat at the opposite end of the table. From the look on my father's face, I figured he'd seen the sparks all right, and he didn't much care for that kind of electricity. I smiled and waved, hoping to dispel any worries. His face relaxed, but he cocked an eyebrow, then winked.

"Who's missing from our table?" I pointed to the four empty chairs near my parents.

"I don't know who's sitting there." Xander spread his napkin on his lap and plucked a dinner roll from a nearby platter. "Perhaps they're running late."

Gage sat on the other side of Xander, and I looked forward to catching up with him over dinner. His fair, freckled skin belied his salt and pepper hair, making him seem more boyish than middle-aged. He was the strong, silent type, but I enjoyed his easy-going manner and never felt like he talked down to me.

Strong hands clamped down on my shoulders, and for a horrifying moment I remembered Ophidian. I jerked around, my emotions doing an about-face.

"Uncle Brent!" I nearly toppled my chair leaping to give him a hug. "Oh my goodness, I'm so happy to see you. And to see you *here*, in Vituvia."

He smiled and held me at arm's length. "Wow! What happened to that little girl I used to give piggyback rides to? I'm about to get my gun and fight off all the boys alongside your dad."

Xander rose from his seat and, I think, made himself more erect and imposing than usual as a way of proving a point about his status as a boy. Uncle Brent sized him up with lifted brows and a wry smile.

"This is Prince Xander. Xander, my Uncle Brent." I stepped back, feeling a bit crowded by the bravado.

"Well, well, if it isn't Sadie's guy." Brent extended a hand while I tried to cover my angst at his choice of words.

Xander gave him an enthusiastic shake. "Pleasure to meet you, sir."

My uncle winced at the strength of the Nephilim's grip, then grinned. "Guess I don't have to worry about anyone bothering my niece while you're around." He patted Xander's arm with his free hand and whistled. "Nope."

An amused smile played across Xander's face. "I promise to take very good care of her. I wouldn't want to give you any reason to become angry with me."

Brent threw his head back and laughed hard. "That's right, these muscles are my secret weapon." He flexed his arm and pointed at his bicep. "Great to finally meet you."

"And you." Xander gave a curt bow.

Brent made the rounds at our table, hugging and fussing over Sophie as well. He took a seat beside Mom, solving part of the mystery.

"So, I'm your guy, am I?" Xander's chuckle was low and tinged with pleasure. "I do like the sound of that."

I gave him an annoyed smirk. "For the record, that term has never crossed my lips. Yes, I told my uncle about how you rescued me and my father, but that's the extent of it."

He shook his head. "I think you put on proper airs and graces when I'm around, but you've thought about me every bit as much as I've thought about you. I am a prince, after all."

I swallowed and hoped against hope he couldn't tell how well his teasing hit its mark. Though I felt that confounded heat creeping up my neck, I held his gaze and said, "And I am a princess. You like to remind me of that every time I see you. A princess is not easily swayed by every prince who comes to court her, you know."

He gave me an exaggerated stare. "And with whom am I competing? How many other princes are seeking your attention?"

Sir Noblin rescued me from further interrogation by clapping his hands to say grace. I spent the prayer thanking God for the intrusion.

An ensemble of Dwarves struck up a lilting melody, and a posse of both Gnomes and Dwarves entered with the food. I had eaten my first forkful of spicy stuffed mushrooms when a servant pulled open a door on the other side of the room. Two figures shuffled into the banquet hall.

My fork clattered to the plate, and I struggled to reach the ground and scoot away from the table. "Look who's here!" I pointed at the door, and the others turned to look.

Xander, sensing my urgency, helped me maneuver the heavy chair. I sprang to the ground and ran across the room holding up my skirt, unconcerned about anything beyond the two people in my sights.

"Aunt Jules! Uncle Daniel!" I skidded to a halt in front of them and pulled my aunt into a smothering hug. "You're the best thing I've seen in weeks."

CHAPTER FORTY

A RIOTOUS COMMOTION SURROUNDED AUNT JULES and Uncle Daniel. Mom, Sophie, and I were the sole cause. We blubbered and talked and laughed over one another like we had just won the World Cup.

"Oh heavens above, what a sight fer these tired old eyes, chipmunk." Aunt Jules cupped Sophie's face in her hands and placed a noisy smooch on her temple. She used to kiss each of us on the top of our head in that manner, but even eleven-year-old Sophie had grown taller than our tiny Irish aunt.

Auntie turned to me, hands outstretched. I bent over so she could pat my cheeks. "Sweet Sadie. How is it possible that you've grown into such a lovely woman in the last month? Yer positively drippin' with beauty, pumpkin."

I felt the rush of heat to my face. "I think you're hallucinating." I gave her a peck on the cheek. "But that's nice of you to say."

"And you've had a birthday, have ya not?" She hugged me again. "Sorry to miss yer big day."

While she fawned over Mom, I shifted to Uncle Daniel. He looked disoriented by our emotional outburst. The elderly man had cleaned up nicely after being left for dead by the Gargoyles. Good food had plumped his lean features and filled out his clothes. His faithful wife helped bring color to his face and clarity to his mind. Though he wore a silken scarf around his eyes—or *eye* as it were, with one completely removed—he no longer looked like a shell of a human. He looked like a happy husband.

"Uncle Daniel," I said, "it's wonderful to see you again. You look so healthy and happy." I slipped my hand into his so he knew to shake it. His other hand rested on the brass handle of a carved cane.

He smiled in my general direction. "This must be my oldest niece, Sadie. So good to have you back in these parts, m'dear. Jules talks about you all so often I feel like I know you much better than I actually do."

I laughed. "I don't doubt that. May I help you to your seat? Dinner has already gotten underway."

"I'd be much obliged."

While I helped him get situated in his chair, the last mystery guest arrived. "Doc Keswick?" I straightened at the sight of the tall Dwarf with the close-cropped beard. "I didn't recognize you without your scrubs." I circled behind Uncle Daniel's chair and offered him my hand.

Doc looked me up and down and shook his head. "Would you look at that? No cast. No stitches. No burns. I didn't recognize you either." He laughed and pulled me into a hug. "Welcome back."

My plate of food was cold, but my hungry stomach didn't mind. And nothing could dampen the delight of seeing Aunt Jules and Uncle Daniel sitting across the table. They were here, they were healthy, and they were together. After more than forty years of separation, they'd been given a second chance at life and love.

I risked a sidelong glance at Xander and wondered if we could have anything as beautiful. Though I never allowed myself to think about the prince in such a way, the day's events left me wistful and aware that I shouldn't take anyone or anything for granted. Not a person. Not an Elf. Not even a tree.

My ring clanked against the water glass and forced my musings back to more sinister things. Had the guards found Ophidian? Was he lurking in this banquet hall, even now? I'd struggled with whether I should wear the ring or hide it in my things. Leaving it behind felt like abandonment. To protect it meant I must guard it with life and limb.

I didn't know for certain if the Gargoyle would recognize the ring on my finger as the actual key. That depended on whether or not Malagruel had shown the other one to his worm. At least Sir Noblin had taken the matching ring to a safe place, though the proximity of the two still held potential for disaster.

The band shifted to a jaunty melody, and many partygoers made their way to the dance floor. My heart hurt for Queen Judith. No one loved to dance the night away like her, but that wouldn't happen this evening.

The thought of dancing with Xander filled me with anticipation and dread. Though I wanted to feel his strong arms guiding me around the floor, it made me nervous to be so close. I ate with slow deliberation in order to put it off as long as possible.

I was dangerously close to finishing when the music warbled to a stop. Like everyone else, I looked around to see why.

"May I have your attention?" Sir Noblin's voice carried over the noise of the crowd. "Quiet, if you please. I have an important announcement."

A hush settled as everyone turned toward the sound of his voice. The Gnome stood on the stage in front of the band of Dwarves. Since the majority of the dancers were also Gnomes, I could see him well enough across the room.

"Moments ago, I was made aware that some very special guests have arrived. They have requested an audience in the Garden Dome."

Surprised murmurs and gasps peppered the room. My mind puzzled through the short list of who it might be.

"I realize this is highly unorthodox, but these are unconventional times, are they not?" Sir Noblin stabbed his finger in the air. "Due to the unique circumstance and the preeminence of these guests, I granted their request. My deepest apologies to His Highness, King Aviel and His Majesty, Prince Xander, for the deviation from this evening's festivities. As our guests, we would be honored for you to join us as we move to the Garden Dome."

He gestured to the central doors of the banquet hall, where two guards held them open. "Now if the queen and her family, our royal guests from Calamus, and the queen's cabinet would make their way out the door, we shall escort you momentarily."

Could it be my brothers? They were the only people who seemed to be missing from this who's-who gathering. But they wouldn't make such a big deal of their arrival and request special treatment. There was Enoch, of course, but he was already in the Garden Dome. I felt clueless but excited by the mysterious interruption.

As we made our way toward the exit, Xander intertwined his fingers in mine in a comfortable, familiar sort of way. No one outside of my family had ever held my hand like that, except for an awkward crush in my first-grade Sunday school class. My hand felt safe and protected, and I didn't want to let go.

King Aviel stood ahead of us and watched our approach. Disapproval settled into the lines of his weathered, wise face. I suddenly felt foolish and embarrassed, tempted to pull my hand away like a child caught raiding the cookie jar. Though the king had always been gracious enough, his stern-set face and shocking white braids reminded me of Poseidon, the Greek god of the ocean. Someone whose wrath I should avoid incurring at all costs.

Xander must have sensed my intimidation. He tightened his grip enough to let me know he wanted my hand to stay put. His father stepped to Xander's other side and whispered something I couldn't hear.

"I haven't a single guess," Xander said in response.

We stopped behind Dad, who came alongside Uncle Daniel to help Aunt Jules maneuver him among the crowd.

I felt Xander watching me. Turning, I met his gaze with my own and, for once, allowed it to linger. I hoped to communicate with my eyes what I had tried so hard to keep hidden. Would he read what I wanted to say?

If eyes were truly the window to the soul, I hoped he could see the trust and devotion that had planted themselves deep inside my heart. The trust anchored itself with penetrating roots and sturdy branches borne from a summer spent in Xander's fierce yet tender protection. The devotion now carved a series of scars in the weathered bark of this trustworthy tree. My tree. Scars that spelled his name.

CHAPTER FORTY-ONE

BRADY WENT ALONG WITH WHAT SARGON asked of him, though it seemed a little over-the-top. But he had never been one to like a fuss, not even for special occasions. It probably came from knowing how uncomfortable Brock felt in the middle of a commotion. They'd kept birthday parties low-key for that very reason, and it had rubbed off on Brady along the way.

The three Gnome warriors had escorted the company into the palace, meeting with much confusion and excitement. The Vituvians were elated to see their king and astonished that three Trolls were responsible for his safe return. Before long, Brady's old friend Reiko, head of special ops, and her right-hand warriors, Muscle and Mighty, had ushered the group into a private chamber.

When questioned, Brady and Brock had supplied details and confirmed the amazing turn of events. Of course, Reiko knew Chebar was an ally, but she cast leery glances at Sargon and Grym, sizing the Trolls up as they took turns speaking.

Brady understood her wariness because he had plenty of his own. He remembered how Sargon had played to the crowd in Pioneer Square and his smug, condescending look at Sadie when he called her to the stage. Let alone the automatic guilt-by-association for his schemes with Delaney. And Grym? It was too soon to say, but Brady would watch him as well. While the story unfolded, Thiago, the Ninja Troll, kept back—aloof but alert. Brady guessed he was now acting in a bodyguard capacity, though it wasn't really necessary in Vituvia.

Once the facts were shared, Reiko had blinked her almond eyes in bewilderment. "You could blow me over with a bumble bee sneeze. This is truly the last thing I expected."

Sargon had asked Brady to make the formal request of revealing the dramatic turn of events to the queen and her cabinet in the Garden Dome. The Troll now looked at him expectantly, and Brady stepped forward. "Reiko, since a regime change in Craventhrall is a triumph for the Tethered World, it would be fitting to present our news in the Garden Dome. Can that be arranged?"

Reiko sputtered, looking at Muscle and Mighty, then back to Brady. "As you wish, Sire. I'm afraid it remains in a rather tumultuous state with the injured tree being looked after. Our normal protocol for the sword has been scaled back to allow the Dweller and your uncle to work."

"Then we would be honored to bring a fresh sense of dignity and ceremony to the Dome with our announcement." Grym pressed his hands together and offered a bow.

Reiko had agreed and left Brock and Brady and the Trolls in the care of the three Gnomes who had brought them to the palace. While they waited for arrangements to be made, servants brought them platters of food, finally satisfying Brady's complaining stomach. He and Brock dove in, table manners ignored.

Reiko returned with the news that Sir Noblin had agreed to the request. "I assured him that I had not conjured this out of my imagination and had, indeed, spoken to Your Highness. The fact that Sir Noblin readily consented to break with tradition shows how extraordinary this situation is."

Chebar stretched his ape-like face into a grin. "Indeed. It is something we three are still trying to comprehend."

"No doubt." Reiko looked Brock and Brady up and down. "Though His Highness is not properly dressed for such a ceremony, it would spoil the surprise to have him taken to his chambers to change. However, I'm sure everyone would like to wash up. I'll have basins and fresh water brought in while you wait for preparations to be handled in the Garden Dome. Oh, and your guard—" she glanced at Thiago, "—will need to wait here. Access to the dome has only been granted to you three brothers."

"Understood." Sargon dusted off his trousers. "In the meantime, we'll do what we can to look presentable for the occasion."

Reiko paused at the door. "I hope this won't be one of our last special assemblies in the dome, but the tree appears worse with each passing day. If it dies, I'm not sure what shall become of the dome, not to mention the Flaming Sword and the

safety of our realm. I see it as divine timing to have Craventhrall on our side."

We followed Sir Noblin and Smarlow through a labyrinth of
hallways, winding down several flights of stairs. When we
turned into a nondescript, narrow corridor, I realized we were
being taken to the lower-level entrance to the Garden Dome.
The one reserved for the Guardians of the Sword.

My one and only visit to the dome, which had resulted in
my broken ankle, left me exiting through this hallway on a
stretcher. I had entered through one of four viewing platforms
that allowed visitors a bird's-eye view of the Flaming Sword
and the great, granite wall that partitioned the tree itself from
being observed.

It was Queen Estancia, Xander's mother, who had transported me from the high perch of the balustrade to the sacred
and ceremonial interior below. In an attempt to prevent her
from flying over the wall, I launched myself at her legs when
she jumped from the railing. Many bumps and bruises and
broken bones later, the queen was dead and I couldn't walk
under my own power.

I glanced at Xander, wondering if he was thinking about his
mother's last moments here. Thankfully, he wasn't around to
see the calamity unfold. I believe he would have fought alongside me to keep his traitorous mother from her greedy goals—
still, it was his mom. This visit to the garden might be difficult
for both him and his father, who also had been ignorant of
Estancia's subversive plans.

Up ahead, Dad helped Uncle Daniel safely maneuver
around the Gnomes who had stopped in front of the guarded
door. Mom and Sophie walked on either side of Aunt Jules,
following Uncle Brent as he pushed Aunt Judith.

Sir Noblin came to a stop in the middle of the crowd, not
five feet away. He cleared his throat. "If I may..." His voice
trailed off as he looked back and forth at the crowd. With a
deep sigh, he removed his conical hat and scratched at his
greying temple. "My apologies, but I'm having second
thoughts. I think I would feel less anxious if I could expound
upon protocol." The Gnome looked on the verge of a panic attack. His eyes darted about, and he shifted uncomfortably on

his feet. When no one answered, he went on. "We've only recently allowed anyone other than the guards and our monarch to enter the dome. But these are unconventional times. And in the spirit of unity, we allowed a few Nephilim and Dwarf warriors to train with us as a show of solidarity to our enemy. In the process, we also looked into our founding documents to learn that we could, indeed, allow other non-Vituvians to view the precious and holy objects within the dome."

The Gnome went on, pacing in a tight circle while he spoke. "There is but one stipulation, you see. Each visitor must reflect on the state of their standing before the Maker. If one who is unworthy enters this space, judgement may descend. At the very least, your unworthiness may be brought to light before your fellow allies." He licked his lips, apparently choosing his words with care. "It certainly has before. And although the tree and the garden itself are undergoing changes—changes that have had an effect upon our sword—that does not make the dome any less sacred. Therefore, I must urge you to consider your worthiness with sober objectivity. There is no shame in remaining outside if you have any doubts."

"My friend, there's also no shame in callin' this off." Lava tilted his head in an understanding way. "We can meet this guest in another part of the palace, can we not?"

I heard King Aviel give an impatient grunt.

"I agree." Aunt Jules shot her hand up. "No need to have ya stressin' fer our sakes."

Sir Noblin shook his head. "I believe such an occasion calls for this revered setting. Not only is it appropriate, but it was requested by someone with the right to do so. It seemed prudent, however, to counsel you all beforehand—and I have cautioned our special guests as well." He replaced his pointy hat and gestured to the door where Smarlow stood. "If you please, Smarlow, we may proceed. Anyone who wishes to remain should allow the others to pass."

The hallway had high ceilings, but we filled its width to capacity, and I was ready to escape the sardine can. In order to get through the door, I had to release Xander's hand and did so reluctantly. I noticed a few Gnomes from the queen's cabinet who remained pressed against the wall as I passed. Were they being polite or avoiding a personal calamity?

We had to pass through another series of doors and locks and guards to get into the dome itself. In the last compartment, Smarlow required everyone to remove their weapons, as the only weapons allowed inside were those belonging to the guardians. Finally, the last door opened and a bright burst of light spilled into the dim, torch-lit hall.

A hush fell over our group. We walked with sober steps into the cavernous space of the Garden Dome. I heard the soft gasps of others that entered before me. I followed behind my mom and anticipated her reaction. Sure enough, her hand flew up to her mouth to stifle a little yelp.

Stepping into the dome for a second time was as awe inspiring as the first, especially at ground level. Whether Gnomes or Nephilim, one felt like an insect under the soaring domed ceiling. It transported you into another world, as if the door at your back no longer existed because everywhere you looked was an entire, gleaming entity of its own. No doors, no windows—and none needed.

Our collective steps clattered across the expansive pearl floor, Uncle Daniel's cane adding its own peculiar thud to the mix. The floor might have been mistaken for marble, but its iridescent gleam and lack of joints or grout indicated otherwise. The solid sea of white stretched broad as a football field and curved like a crescent moon against an azure swath of water. The bright blue depths looked like a moat that protected the island on the other side. An arched bridge, which appeared to have been cut from the same enormous pearl, spanned the water and gave access to the island. At least, I assumed it was an island. I couldn't see past the massive wall, but that's how I pictured it.

Cobblestones covered the ground on the island, though they did not encompass nearly so much floor as their pearly counterpart on this side of the bridge. Rather, they came to an abrupt end at the foot of the immense granite wall that soared several stories high. Behind this protective barrier grew the Tree of Life in a garden paradise, or so we had been told. The only hint of the tree's presence was our view of the topmost branches that stretched beyond the wall toward the crystalline ceiling—an exact replica of the honey-colored geode that stretched across the sky of the Tethered World. Somehow, the sword empowered both to radiate light. Looking at the glowing dome, I felt a sense of dread. The light did appear weaker than I remembered.

Against the glossy granite wall, directly across from the bridge, a small pyramid of boulders mounded halfway up the wall's four-story surface. Embedded in the topmost boulder was the crown jewel of the realm: the Flaming Sword of Cheru-bythe. The sword's hilt glinted from the midst of blue and gold flames. Although the flames still drew me into their beauty with awe and wonder, the blaze appeared to have lost some of its fierce, consuming hunger. Did it have to do with the health of the tree?

A variety of chairs had been brought in to provide seating. Like the guests, they differed in size and had been placed in several rows on the shimmering white floor near the bridge. A center aisle divided the seats that were placed according to height, facing the aqua blue water.

Sir Noblin and Smarlow gestured for us to find a seat as we approached. Queen Judith was wheeled front and center, so that she blocked the entrance to the bridge and faced back toward the lone door. Despite her off-center tilt, she still had a serene and regal air about her. She did not wear her gold crown, but someone had fetched her scepter and laid it across her lap.

With a swish of silken fabric, I sat on a straight-backed chair between Mom and Sophie. I noted with a pang of help-lessness the absence of my brothers, but I hoped that might soon change.

In front of my family sat the queen's cabinet, though three chairs remained empty since those members had elected to stay behind after Sir Noblin's warning. Xander and his father sat across the aisle behind Lava, Trinny, Joanie, and Wogsnop.

Soldiers stationed on the viewing platforms watched us, their faces set in grim expressions beneath their metal, conical hats. Similar soldiers were stationed along the perimeter of the white floor, armed with bows and arrows and swords at their sides.

Smarlow and Sir Noblin left the dome once we were situ-ated. Silence engulfed our fidgeting fingers and tapping toes. Someone coughed. Trinny hiccupped behind her hand. I stared across the bridge. My mind replayed the drama that had unfolded in that spot, my eyes straining to see a hint of the creature that occupied the deceptively peaceful water. Not a ripple stirred. But more than once the colossal, orange-ten-tacled beast that dwelled in the water's depths had managed to haunt my dreams.

Studying the mound of rocks that ascended to the sword, I glimpsed the hacked tree roots with a stab of dismay. En-twined with the boulders, like giant fingers grasping treasure, were gnarled roots that grew from the Tree of Life on the other side of the wall. Sprouting between the rocks and roots were leafy ferns and other tropical fronds. They obscured the gouged foundation at first glance, but I could make out some of the severed, missing roots that had left the tree amputated and vulnerable.

It made me sick to see such blatant disregard and greedy vandalism—but glad the perpetrators had been caught. Clearly their evil, unworthy deeds were brought to light. To think that Mr. Delaney had something to do with the tragedy left me gritting my teeth in anger. I tore my eyes away, wondering what the evil man might be up to in our absence and hoping the damage wouldn't be as bad as what he'd already inflicted upon this tree.

Soil and loose pebbles peppered the floor around the base of the boulders and, I guessed, must be disturbed due to Uncle Brent's treatments. Oh, and Enoch! Was he here? I scanned the vast space, knowing it wouldn't be hard for a lone person to go unnoticed against a far wall.

Or a shapeshifting Gargoyle.

My pulsed double-stepped, and I sat a little straighter. I hadn't heard whether the hunt for the Gargoyle had turned up anything. Xander caught my gaze and looked at me as if to say, *Is there something I should know?*

I offered a never-mind sort of grin and assumed the Gnomes hadn't forgotten about Ophidian like I had. At the far side of the right-hand wall, I spotted a rope ladder that climbed the entire face and appeared to continue over the top. On the cobbled floor in front of the ladder sat a collection of garden tools and buckets, along with three stools. I imagined my dad and uncle sitting there with Enoch—who must look ancient—discussing the finer points of botany and the apocalypse.

At last Sir Noblin returned. The consternation in his face had been replaced with a look of happy bewilderment. What could be going on?

Smarlow entered but remained beside the door. He never looked happy, but even from this distance I thought he'd lost his usual scowl.

I leaned toward Sophie, who had been taking in our surroundings with eyes as round as golf balls. "Any idea who we might be meeting?" I whispered.

She bit her lip and shook her head, looking like she might squeal with anticipation any second. "I can only guess it's

Brock, because he's the king. But it seems like there's more to it, don't ya think?"

"Yes, I do."

Sir Noblin approached Queen Judith and bowed. "Your Majesty, shall I inform you of our plans, or would you prefer to enjoy the proceedings as they unfold?"

Aunt Judith's head gave an unsteady shake. "Sssurprise good." The right side of her face pulled into a smile.

"I heartily agree." The Gnome bowed, then walked to Trinny and whispered in her ear. The young Dwarf trotted over to the queen and shifted her wheelchair to one side of the entrance to the bridge.

Sir Noblin marched past her, up the incline, and stood on its apex facing us. He clasped his hands across his middle. "Dear friends, I am pleased at the fortuitous timing of this unexpected turn of events. Thank you for bearing with us this evening as our Feast of Fortitude makes a beneficial detour. We appreciate the flexibility of our closest allies and friends and your willingness to be a part of what will undoubtedly be an historic day in the tomes of the Tethered World."

Sir Noblin always had a knack for taking a sentence and turning it into a rambling paragraph. While he spoke, I studied the ring on my finger, aware that it was dangerously close to the Flaming Sword. And although my fight with Estancia had brought me as close to the sword as any human in recent history, or maybe in all of history, I hadn't been in a position to inspect how a ring, or two rings as it were, could be used as keys. Fighting for one's life tends to make details like keyholes of little importance. And at the time, I had no idea the key would turn out to be my Aunt Jules' wedding ring.

"And so, without further ado," the Gnome continued, "allow me to introduce our first guest. He is not a stranger to those of us gathered here this evening." He wagged a finger at us. "But he has brought with him other special guests, as well as some very fascinating news to share. Please rise and greet our friend Chebar of Craventhrall."

CHAPTER FORTY-TWO

BRADY LEANED AGAINST THE WALL, TIRED of waiting. Their entourage stood in the corridor outside the door that led into the Garden Dome, waiting to be introduced. He'd had enough training as a Guardian of the Sword to learn the layout of the palace, but he had been captured in the middle of his instruction, before he had a chance to participate in drill formations inside the dome itself.

He wondered who might be waiting to see them on the other side. Had any of his family returned to the Tethered World? Or had things gotten so crazy with Mr. Delaney that they couldn't get away? Certainly, Aunt Judith would be inside, along with a few of his Gnome friends. But beyond that, he couldn't guess. The trick would be to keep his face from showing his surprise once he surveyed the audience. He had reasons for needing to play it cool, but those same reasons made him as jittery as a jackrabbit if he let his mind dwell on them. Stealing a glance at Brock, he tried to mask his anxiety behind an imitation of Brock's almost-always calm features.

"Are you two ready to be a part of history?" Grym stepped between the brothers and placed a hand on each of their shoulders. His voice sounded so much like Rooke's that it made Brady automatically dislike him. "Remember to follow our lead and stay beside us. We need to unveil our news in our own way."

Sargon leaned against the wall, inspecting his dark fingernails. He glanced up. "Agreed. It's important that Vituvians know their future king supports our plan."

The door opened and Brady squinted in the light, unable to see who was in attendance.

Smarlow held the door. "Chebar, you're up."

I watched Chebar stride confidently across the gleaming floor of the dome. He wore a military vest and loose-fitting pants like his brother Sargon had worn in Pioneer Square. Sophie gave an excited gasp and waved as he approached. He smiled and nodded but didn't stop until he reached Queen Judith. Standing erect, he folded his right arm across his middle and bowed. Then he bent and grasped her hand—the one without the scepter—and kissed her knuckles.

The queen smiled in her lopsided way and offered an unsteady nod.

Chebar stepped onto the bridge behind her and turned to face us. "My friends, it's a privilege to stand before you this evening and share this momentous occasion with those I hold dear. Though I'm certain to surprise you with my own news, I must say that you've also surprised me tonight."

He swept his hand toward my family. "I had no idea the lovely Larcen family had returned to Vituvia. But that only makes my announcement more fitting." Chebar turned to the other side of the aisle. "Your majesties, King Aviel and Prince Alexander, what an honor to have you join in this pivotal event as well."

The king dipped his head, but his expression reflected no warmth. Xander offered a polite smile.

"And finally, it's an equally pleasant surprise to see my friends from Berganstroud in attendance as well." Chebar took a couple of steps toward us, and rested a hand on the railing of the bridge. "For some time now, as most of you know, I've been working against my father's iron-fisted rule. What you don't know is that I had enlisted the help of two of my brothers in this volatile and dangerous task. Today the three of us set out with our father, Chief Nekronok, and our eldest brother Rooke. Our goal was to personally oversee the transfer of two valuable prisoners from the Stygians' crypt to a secret dungeon in Craventhrall." He gestured to the door behind us. "Smarlow."

A ripple of hope and disbelief swirled in my stomach as I watched Smarlow pull the door open again. A grey Troll stepped out, and I recognized him right away as Rooke. Brock and Brady followed behind, single file, trailed by Sargon. Although part of me buzzed with happiness to see my brothers, I had a hard time processing the presence of two Trolls whom I knew to be brutish beasts working with Mr. Delaney.

As they crossed the expansive floor, with three Gnome soldiers bringing up the rear, I realized that the first Troll didn't quite fit what I recalled of Rooke. His fur was lighter, and his face, though similar, wasn't nearly as square. That still didn't explain the presence of Sargon.

We stood to cheer for Brock and Brady—at least that's who I was standing to applaud. A pleased smile settled on Brock's mouth, and his eyes twitched toward us as he passed. His pale blue tunic was a rumpled, filthy mess, but it looked as if he had washed his face and slicked back his hair recently. Brady's worn and wrinkled clothing was the same I'd last seen him wearing in Portland. I tried to catch his eye, but he stared straight ahead, all business.

Sargon didn't spare anyone a glance but followed the silvery Troll and my brothers over the bridge and onto the cobbled ground, heading to the pyramid of boulders. The Gnomes marched behind the Trolls and took up stations along the base of the rocky mound as the others began to climb the pyramid. Sir Noblin stood beside Chebar at the pinnacle of the bridge and fidgeted nervously, clasping his hands and looking from the queen to the Trolls, clearly unhappy with their proximity to the Sword.

Chebar, ever the diplomat, crouched and whispered something to the distraught Gnome that brought a nod and a hint of relief to his face. Sir Noblin walked to where the queen sat, her wheelchair now turned toward the bridge, and stood beside her.

Chebar gestured for us to sit. I caught Xander gazing at me yet again. He winked, and my heart did that awful, jittery dance that I hoped no one else saw but felt certain everyone did. How had I let him get to me? He stirred things up inside that reminded me an awful lot of roller coasters, and we all know how I feel about those contraptions. Maybe I shouldn't have let myself embrace the emotions of this evening. What good were these distracting feelings that I could never act on? Case in point: I was having a vigorous, internal debate about our relationship in the middle of a historic occasion.

With an effort, I turned my focus back to Chebar. He had crossed to the base of the pyramid and was gesturing up toward the pale grey Troll. "I'd like to introduce my brother Grym, the voice of reason, keeping our focus steady. You'll hear more from him shortly."

Grym gave a curt bow. Brock stood on the layer of rocks below him, hands clasped behind his back. Though I had no idea where this announcement was leading, I thought they were being rather theatrical about it. Then again, everyone in the Tethered World did things with much more pomp and circumstance than us Topsiders.

Chebar moved on to introduce Sargon, who stood with Brady in about the same place on the other side of the pyramid of rocks. "Sargon is an excellent warrior but also quite the diplomat."

Sargon gave a friendly salute. Chebar returned to the middle of the arched bridge, where Sir Noblin had been standing. "The short version of our day, as you can see for yourself, is that King Brock and his brother are not in Nekronok's dungeons tonight as my father intended. My brothers and I set a plan in motion to prevent this from happening. As you can see, we have succeeded."

A short burst of applause bubbled over from all of us assembled. Well, almost all of us. King Aviel wasn't the spontaneous applause type of guy.

Chebar went on to describe the trek through the Goblin's lair and how Grym had contacted Mudgeon, the Goblin king, and arranged for a trap to be set. As the story progressed, Chebar sauntered back across the cobblestones, scaling the mound of rocks between both sets of brothers. He spoke and climbed in an almost leisurely fashion as he described how the Goblin King, Mudgeon, had demanded that Nekronok and Rooke approach him first by crossing the rope bridge. At this point in the story, Chebar stood just below the Flaming Sword. He stopped his ascent and looked out from his perch, towering above his brothers.

"Once my father and Rooke were on the bridge, the ropes were severed from above and..." Chebar lifted his hands with slow and dramatic flair, then let them drop as he said, "*Boom!* Your enemies and mine came to an abrupt and final end."

My mind spun with the implications of such news, while I grabbed Mom's leg in triumph. We looked at each other, our faces a mirror of wide eyes and dropped jaws. Sir Noblin covered his mouth and looked at the queen and then back to the Trolls. Quiet exclamations could be heard all around, and even King Aviel looked bewildered by the news.

"I can see that my announcement is not what you were expecting. My brothers and I have discussed the implications of Nekronok's death, both personally and for the citizens of Craventhrall." Chebar dropped his head, shaking it sadly. "As his sons, we do not take his death lightly. He will be missed." He looked up, chin high and defiant. "But we also knew of his lust for power and of his newest fixation—getting his hands on the Tree of Life. And his ability to do so was getting closer than you may realize."

He effortlessly hopped down to the next level of boulders, now standing about halfway up the mound of rocks. "He had in his possession one of the two keys with the power to unleash the Flaming Sword from its stone encasement. Malagruel had located the second key and concocted what he considered a foolproof plan to get his hands on it."

"Oh heavens!" Aunt Jules covered her mouth.

I made a fist and covered the ring with my other hand. If not for Lark and Prussell, the ring may not have remained in my safekeeping.

"His plan involved bringing the first key along with him as bait for the other. Whether or not he succeeded remains to be seen." Chebar crossed his arms and shrugged. "Malagruel did not return to my father, and none of his minions know of his whereabouts. My brothers and I have discussed the real possibility of the Gargoyle double-crossing all of us, keeping the keys for his own use."

Sophie rested her hand on top of my own and leaned in to me. "Thank God that's an impossibility."

I nodded. Once this concluded, I'd have to let Chebar know about Malagruel's demise.

"Which brings us to the present." Chebar stretched his arms wide. "My father and the next in line are out of the picture. Although Malagruel remains an uncertainty, he will be dealt with in much the same way. I think you'll agree that we are on the brink of a new day in the Tethered World. The future holds great possibility."

"Hear, hear!" Lava pumped his fist in the air.

Chebar grinned. "Indeed!" He turned and looked straight at me, reaching his arm, palm up. "Princess Sadie, won't you join me up here?"

I straightened and blinked. Me? Everyone turned my way, as if maybe I hadn't heard.

Mom patted my leg. "Go on."

Standing with as much composure as I could muster while being scrutinized, I walked across the bridge with measured steps, staring at the wall that loomed so large. The wall that I had fallen from. Did he really expect me to climb a mound of rock and roots in a long dress? At least I didn't have the added awkwardness of high heels.

Chebar descended to the bottom level of rock and took my hand. I placed one foot against the soil-packed crevice between two boulders and scaled the first rock without incident. The Troll placed a hand on my shoulder and I knew he meant for me to stay there, beside him. I glanced at Brady. His eyes met mine, and he stretched one corner of his mouth in a barely-there smile. On either side, Grym and Sargon stepped to the lower level of rock so that we all stood, more or less, in a line.

"Thank you, Princess Sadie." Chebar dipped his head and released my shoulder. "Things are changing, and I believe the ramifications will be felt all the way topside. How we choose to handle these changes is our chief concern. My fellow Trolls in Craventhrall have no knowledge of the loss of their chief, and I'm not entirely sure how they will accept the news. I only know it's what was best for everyone. For Trolls, for the Tethered World at large, for our Topsider friends, and especially," he placed his hands on his chest, "*especially* for me."

CHAPTER FORTY-THREE

THE THREE GNOME SOLDIERS STANDING ON the cobblestone below, turned and faced us. They unsheathed their swords and handed them up to Chebar and his brothers. I didn't think much of it, but the next instant I was being choked.

Chebar had me in a headlock, a sword to my throat.

Gasping, I cut frantic eyes to see Brock in the same position and knew without looking that Brady was as well.

Despite it happening, it didn't feel like a serious threat. Chebar was my friend. He'd saved me before; why would he hurt me now? Why would he allow my brothers to be hurt?

All at once, a jumble of things exploded into motion. I could only gasp for air and watch the chaos. Lava and Wogsnop, Xander and his father, my parents—they all charged the bridge. Others gasped and cried out or clutched one another. I couldn't bear to see their fearful faces as they stared back at us in horror. Dozens of armed Guardians flooded in from the perimeter of the floor, bows and arrows at the ready.

"Get back!" Chebar ordered. He loosened his hold on my neck enough to let me breathe. "I will kill Sadie and order my brothers to do the same if you come any closer."

Had he lost his mind? I found myself more perplexed than afraid. This wasn't the Chebar I knew. The glint of the steely sword—only a dagger in the hands of a Troll—pressed beneath my jaw and reminded me that my predicament was serious.

Chebar was serious.

Mom buried her head against Dad's shoulder. Xander's eyes flashed and his wings unfurled. Lava reached for his sword and cursed; no one had been allowed to bring their weapons inside. I recognized the sobs of Aunt Jules, though I couldn't see her. A surreal, fragmented stillness descended. Nobody dared move, yet everyone's minds worked so frantically you could almost hear them churning.

Suddenly Chebar thrust me to the side, and I slammed into Brock. I almost toppled, but a rough hand grabbed my arm and yanked me upright. Grym now pressed his sword against my throat. Chebar had Brock.

"That's right, this is very serious. Your king's life or death is now my choice to make, and it's serious indeed." Chebar's menacing voice was almost unrecognizable. He pulled Brock upward to the next level of rocks, out of my line of sight. A muffled whimper and the desperate scuffle of his shoes stabbed me with sorrow and rage. He was too innocent and harmless to be treated like this. "I'm sorry it's come to such a dire moment. I'll admit, I've grown quite fond of many of you. Especially these Topsiders. You must know, I've tried to find other ways to accomplish this."

His voice continued to move away, and I realized he must be dragging Brock up to the Flaming Sword, like Estancia had done with me. I squeezed my eyes shut and prayed, desperately prayed, for another miracle.

"Since I'm unwilling to wait any longer to obtain both keys, I've learned of another way to release the Sword." Chebar sighed dramatically. "A very unfortunate way, if you're the ruler of Vituvia."

What could that mean? My mind searched frantically for an explanation. My mother's sobs were loud and inconsolable. It hurt to watch the pained faces that looked at us like moviegoers at a horror flick. The guardians had lowered their weapons but remained tense wads of energy flecking the curve of turquoise water. Xander stared at me, his nostrils flaring, his fists clenched and his chest heaving. King Aviel gripped Xander's shoulder, holding him back.

"Sargon, Grym," Chebar barked. "Bring Brock's siblings up here so they can watch their brother make history."

Grym and Sargon trudged up with Brady and me in tow. Our gazes fastened together long enough for me to see the sad disappointment in Brady's eyes. And something else. Something both familiar and out of place. But I didn't have time to process it as Grym dragged me like a doll toward Brock.

I grappled against the Troll's thick arm, trying to push it away and relieve the stifling choke hold that strangled me. Once I found my footing, the oxygen supply improved. Tasting salt in my gaping, gasping mouth, I realized I was crying. So many sensations were throttling me that I couldn't keep up.

Brock, dear sweet Brock, stood slightly above me on the next large rock of the lumpy pyramid. For once, his emotions were plainly written on his face. He was trembling, staring straight ahead. When he blinked, a tear slid down his cheek.

"Stop this, Chebar!" That was Lava, calling from below. "You're right. We can work together. You did a good thing by removin' yer father. Don't do somethin' stupid now. Yer better than Nekronok."

Chebar gave a grunt of impatience. "No. No, I'm not. I used to think I was different than my power-hungry father but as you can see, I am not."

My heart ached. What on earth did Chebar mean to do to my brother? Or the rest of us? How could the ruler of Vituvia release the Flaming Sword without the keys? It made no sense.

"And now, my brothers, let us make history together." Chebar yanked Brock closer to the flames that flared from the sword. Brock's hand swiped through the fire, and he pulled it away, then turned it over, looking at it with confusion.

I remembered Queen Estancia plunging her hands into the blaze to grasp the hilt of the sword. She had laughed to find the fire didn't burn. Remembering that made me feel better for Brock's sake.

"My good people of Vituvia, whether your king lives or dies shall depend upon your cooperation." Chebar's syrupy, condescending voice made me sick. "You see, the *only* other way to remove the sword is with the blood of the monarch. If you all behave yourselves and don't interfere, the boy will have nothing more than a nasty cut on his wrist, enough to fill the keyholes with his blood. But if you try to protect your precious Sword then one—or maybe all—of these Larcens shall die."

CHAPTER FORTY-FOUR

MY MIND SCREAMED WITH RAGE BECAUSE my lungs could not. Sobs choked my already constricted throat. I struggled against the hairy lump of muscle at my back and around my neck, but it was wasted energy.

Chebar yanked Brock backwards, where the granite wall met up with the top of the sloping pyramid. Braced against it, the Troll knocked Brock off his feet so that his back lay arched across the topmost boulder that held the sword. The powerful weapon protruded from the front face of the massive rock with Brock stretched across the wide granite top.

"Please, Chebar! Please stop." My mom's desperate cry felt like a jagged rip through my gut.

The savage Troll ignored her. He folded one of his legs across Brock's chest, pinning my brother with the weight of his knee and shin. The other leg reached to a lower rock, between my brother's sprawled limbs. Holding the short sword between his teeth, Chebar stretched Brock's arm straight out so that his fingers lay across the lapping flames. The keyholes, I assumed, must be somewhere near his wrist.

And what was that noise? Humming?

Chebar was *humming*.

Oh, the anger that roiled against this calculating beast. His betrayal stung deep and swelled my emotions with bitter venom.

Chebar wrapped his fingers around my brother's arm, right below the elbow. He squeezed hard, using the pressure like a tourniquet. With his other hand, he traced the purple vein that bulged, looking at it with sick fascination. Why wasn't anyone trying to stop him?

I shot a desperate look at Brady, hoping to see a shred of an idea etched in his face. He didn't meet my gaze but stared down at his helpless twin in disbelief. It crushed me to see his usual fire replaced with numb despair. Not that I couldn't relate. Impotent and outraged, I watched Chebar follow the enlarged vein with the tip of his sword.

"*No.*" I whimpered in lame protest. *Lord, please. Please help.* My prayer felt numb and impotent too.

Chebar continued to hum.

Brock lifted his head from where it lolled over the downslope of the rock. He looked at me from the space between the Troll's arms and torso. His gaze met mine with an electrified panic. I tried to communicate with my eyes, like I had with Xander. I told him to be strong. I told him that I loved him. To my surprise, his normally unreadable features seemed to say the same, though my blur of tears may have distorted my perception.

Chebar's humming grew in volume, a droning buzz of an unfamiliar tune. As the song reached its zenith, Chebar lifted the sword in dramatic exaggeration and projected it in a slow-motion plummet to my brother's wrist.

Before the blade met its mark, Brady's foot collided with it, knocking the sword from Chebar's grasp. Chebar cursed and drew his hand back, apparently in pain. Sargon wrenched Brady away even while my brother thrashed against him with a muffled, "*Nooo!*"

Chebar stood with a snarling grunt that produced a painful yelp from Brock beneath him. With swift, sure-footed motion, Chebar lunged to the rock where Brady writhed against Sargon's clutches. Grym's huge leg shot out, pinning Brock down in Chebar's absence. Despite Brady's purplish, gasping face behind Sargon's arm, he managed to land a well-placed kick to Chebar's shin.

The Troll gave a wild, angry roar as he stumbled back, then righted himself. Spittle flew from his mouth as he growled Brady's name. He cocked his arm backward to strike.

"No!" I squirmed against Grym's constricting arm.

Before Chebar could land a punch, Brady slumped against Sargon, his face nearly blue. I screamed Brady's name and heard my dad do the same. Chebar's fist trembled, taking aim.

"He's unconscious," Sargon said. He twisted his own upper body so that Brady's limp arms and legs swayed like a life-sized marionette from the headlock. "I've got it handled."

Anguished hope flared in me that Brady was only unconscious. Sargon relaxed his grip, and Brady drooped in his arms, his blue face fading to pink.

Chebar slowly lowered his fist and turned back, and with nostrils flared he scaled the rock. Grym released his foothold on Brock, and Chebar resumed his position as if nothing had happened. He pressed Brock beneath his knee, then plucked up the sword that now lay upon a fat, twisted tree root. Chebar turned and gave me a withering glare, as if daring me to try something else. I glowered back but held my tongue, not wishing to make things worse for Brock.

With swift movements and much less dramatic flair, Chebar squeezed Brock's arm between his lanky fingers once again, the tip of the blade poised on Brock's swelling vein. He resumed his morbid humming, but with a hurried, blustering tempo.

I pressed my eyes closed when I heard Brock groan. Cries from across the room perforated the Troll's disturbing anthem.

"Ah...*there.*" Chebar expelled his words like part of his melody.

Grym gave a sick chuckle in my ear. Mom shrieked, but she sounded far removed from my pounding pulse and ragged breath. The world felt very small and seemed to be populated by merely the six of us on top of the gnarled pyramid.

Against my better judgement, I opened my eyes.

"Squeeze harder," Sargon hissed, staring intently at Brock's wrist. Brady stirred, and Sargon flexed against the movement.

A crimson stain coated Chebar's fingers where they clutched Brock's wounded arm. Small rivulets of blood snaked together, flowing around the Troll's hand and dripping in sticky syncopation to the rock. He dropped the sword and strangled Brock's wrist with both hands.

"It's too slow!" Grym's voice barked, making me wince. "Cut him deeper."

"Shut up. The first hole is half full," Chebar said through clenched teeth.

I felt an impatient huff in my ear. "It's taking too long. Cut his hand off before one of these guards takes aim."

"*No!*" I elbowed my captor in the ribs, but he only flexed his bicep harder against my throat. His hairy arm felt damp and itchy against my neck—whether from his sweat or my tears, I couldn't say.

"This will never work." Dad's emotional, raw shout pulled me back into the larger reality of the Garden Dome. "I'll make it my personal mission to hunt you down if you don't stop *now.*"

Chebar glanced up. "Say another word, and I'll make it my personal mission to kill the boy. A slit jugular will make this much easier." He snatched up the weapon, then shifted off of Brock, hauling my brother to his knees.

Hysterical screams and shouts resonated through the dome, mine among them. Undeterred, the Troll raked a bloodied hand across Brock's face, grasping him by the hair. "On second thought"—Chebar stretched his arm out so that Brock's head dangled above the spattered puddle where his wrist had been—"this might be the best way to take care of it after all."

My vision filled with the set of my brother's jaw, determined to be brave. He shut his eyes, and a tear mingled with the blood smeared across his cheek.

"Do it!" Sargon stepped closer, dragging his burden. Brady had awakened, though he still looked groggy, and he struggled to keep his footing.

Chebar reached the blade around Brock's neck and thrust it beneath his jaw. I could see the tip, darkened by blood from Brock's wrist. "I don't take orders from you, Sargon. But I want this over—*oomph!*"

A rock slammed down on Chebar's head with a sickening crack. The Troll crumpled on top of Brock. Before I could process what had happened, my captor reeled sideways, his sword flinging from his grasp. We toppled onto Chebar and Brock's tangled legs. I felt warm liquid trickling down my neck, and I struggled to breathe under the weight of Grym's body. He squeezed his arms around my middle, his gurgling growl suggesting that he was badly wounded.

Footsteps tromped across the bridge, and I hoped our rescue was at hand. I twisted against Grym's arms, desperate to get up and help Brock get free from the weight of the Trolls' bodies. A painful gouge in my shoulder made me shriek. The monster was biting me! Gritting my teeth, I reared my head and butted against Grym's nose as hard as possible. He cursed and reached his huge, leathery hand around my face, covering my mouth and nose, his fingers squeezing my head like they wanted to burrow into my brain. I squirmed beneath his palm, needing to breathe even more than I wanted to scream. Desperate panic mangled my thoughts. What now? Suffocation? I was going to die. I didn't want to die!

Grym shuddered and released my face, going limp. I sucked

in a ragged, astonished breath.

"Got him!" I heard someone yell.

The big ape's arm dangled in front of me. With clumsy movements, I pushed it off my shoulder and attempted to get up. Before I could maneuver out of the jumble of legs and limbs, strong arms scooped me up and away from the carnage.

"Hello, my princess," Xander whispered into my ear. "I've got you now."

CHAPTER FORTY-FIVE

I WRAPPED MY ARMS AROUND XANDER in grateful exhaustion. Was the nightmare really over? He hovered above the chaos, cradling me like a child, his fingers stroking my hair. I allowed myself to bask in his reassuring strength.

"Thank you," I choked out.

"Shh." He buried his face against my neck. "You're safe. I thought I might lose you, but now, thank the Maker, you're safe."

I blinked my waterlogged lashes and watched his wings make graceful arcs in the air. How could terror turn to joy in a matter of seconds?

From this height, I could see behind the wall and into the garden. The massive branches of the ancient Tree of Life stretched protectively, filling most of my view. Beyond it lay a sprawling paradise, green and lush and full of vivid flowers. It beckoned to be explored. The tree was clearly suffering, however. At least half of its leaves had curled in on themselves in a yellow-brown mottle of ruin. I swallowed and looked away, then flinched at the sight of a sinewy, weathered man. He sat on top of the wall directly above the Flaming Sword.

"Is that Enoch?" I whispered.

"Must be. He was the one who threw the rock at Chebar, putting a stop to the madness."

I stared in wonder, taking in the gleam of his bald head and the length of his white beard. He looked down on the mound of rock, his face hidden at that angle. He shook his head slowly, and I gazed down with him, hoping to catch sight of my brothers. I saw Uncle Brent and Sophie standing off to the side of the pyramid; my uncle had his arms around my sister. Mom and Dad crouched near Brock and the Flaming Sword. The blaze obscured part of my view, but something looked wrong.

Very wrong.

Dwarves were dragging the three Troll brothers' bodies down from the boulders, but it looked to me like Brock hadn't moved. And...there was a tremendous amount of blood. It cascaded over and around the rocks.

"Xander, take me down there. Something's wrong."

He hesitated. "That doesn't look good. Are you sure?"

"Yes. Hurry."

In a moment, he had placed me beside my parents. My father was bent over my mother's back, and she hunched over Brock, who still lay sprawled, head first. Their anguished cries brought an immediate and knowing pierce of pain that made me recoil. Somewhere below, I recognized Sophie's hiccupping cry.

No, no, no, no, no, no!

I dropped to my knees in shock and sorrow, heaving for breath, sobs clawing their way out from deep inside my chest. How did this happen? Wasn't he saved like me, like Brady? Where was Brady?

Lifting my head, I scanned the frantic activity through the blur of tears. Gnomes and Dwarves scurried about, shouting orders. Aunt Jules was making her way across the bridge, looking bewildered. Relief flickered when I spotted King Aviel with Brady, standing on a viewing platform. The king must have lifted Brady away from danger as Xander had lifted me.

But Brock? I shifted so I could touch his leg and feel the life that flowed through him. I wanted to climb down to where I could look him in the eye, but I didn't trust myself to move. No! Anger replaced the tears. Mom and Dad were jumping to horrible conclusions. Brock had been saved. He wasn't dead. He couldn't be dead.

I swiped my face with the back of my hand, tired of the tears. Grabbing a fistful of Dad's shirt, I tugged. "Why are you crying? Brock is fine. He's fine like me and Brady. Get off of him."

"Oh baby." Dad lifted his head and wrapped an arm around my waist. "Oh, Sadie. I'm sorry. I—" He broke off in a sob but didn't let go.

All I could do was glower and shake my head. They needed to get up and give Brock space. He would be all right if they'd only move.

Mom turned her head and looked at me through swollen, red eyes, her face slick with tears and snot, like my own. She opened her mouth to say something, then buried her head in the crook of her arm.

"What? I don't understand." I yanked up a layer of my skirt to wipe my face. "Why do you think—"

Dad grasped my hand and pressed it to his lips. "I'm sorry, honey." His voice was hoarse. "Brock landed on Chebar's sword."

CHAPTER FORTY-SIX

Denial can be comforting. For a time.

I sat on one of the bottom boulders and stared at the cobblestones. My head pulsated with the pain of head butting the Troll and crying my eyes out. My shoulder throbbed viciously from Grym's animalistic bite. The physical pounding gave me something to focus on besides the agony in my soul.

Xander stepped down from the pyramid and crouched in front of me. I knew his eyes were intent on my face, but I didn't look at him. He gave my hand a feather's touch. "You want to be alone?"

I nodded. He stood, kissed the top of my head, and walked away. I continued to stare but saw nothing.

The dome resounded with hushed activity. Uncle Brent ushered Sophie to Joanie's arms, then he rejoined Uncle Daniel, who sat alone on the other side of the bridge. I watched as a sorrowful Queen Judith was wheeled away by her attendant. Joanie and my sister followed them. Vaguely, I was aware that my parents had made their way down from the boulders and had been joined by Aunt Jules.

I couldn't help but see the dead Trolls lying side by side, having been dragged far from the mound and out of the way. Their heavy bodies could not be moved easily. Dwarves would likely do something with them later. For now they looked like large, discarded rugs, and I wanted to stomp all over them with a pair of steel cleats.

Closer to me lay the three traitorous Gnomes, slain by the Guardians. Three pairs of soldiers came and carted off their remains, which now looked like pincushions for a supply of arrows.

On the far side of the dome, where its walls and the shimmering granite barrier came together, something caught my

232 | THE GENESIS TREE

eye. The rope ladder that I had noticed earlier swayed and jerked with use. Enoch descended on steady, strong legs and headed toward me. His long white beard more than made up for the hair he was missing on his head. I sniffed and swallowed and sat up straight. A pleasant smile settled on his mouth when our gazes met, but the smile didn't reach his eyes.

When he was a few yards away, I stood to greet him. His hazel eyes were sharp and bright, set in a wise, wrinkled face. Thin legs and bare feet protruded from his long tunic, his skin a natural bronze despite the absence of sunlight. He pressed his fingers together and bowed. "Greetings, young woman," he said in a voice washed by the centuries. It was a deep, scratchy whisper.

I bowed, wondering if I should have curtsied. "Hello."

"What are you called?"

"I'm Sadie."

His eyes crinkled. "Say-dee." He nodded. "Good sound. I am Enoch."

I mustered a half smile, too numb to make small talk. "It's an honor, Mr. Enoch."

"Your brother is dead. I feel responsible."

Well, he didn't beat around the bush. I took a steadying breath. "You did not intend to hurt my brother. You tried to save him."

"True enough." He cocked his head. "But my statement holds equal truthfulness."

"I suppose." I didn't intend to pick an argument with a man who had outlived death.

"For this I am deeply grieved. Please forgive me." He touched a hand to his heart and bowed again.

"Of course I will forgive you."

"Many thanks, Say-dee." He held my gaze. "I shall apologize to the other members of your family now." With silent steps he walked away.

I took several deep breaths, needing to pull myself together. My attention was drawn to a contingent of Guardians who escorted four Dwarves carrying a stretcher between them. They gaped at the Garden Dome with wonder, apparently new to the place. After tramping over the bridge, they headed to the pyramid of stone. A folded sheet lay in the middle of their stretcher. I gulped and turned away. They were here to retrieve my brother.

I pressed myself into the wall. Granite at my back, boulders to my side. Brock and my parents were around on the other side of the mound, though I could see my brother's feet at the top if I tried. Which I didn't. Where was Brady? Why hadn't he come to be with us? He'd been with King Aviel on a viewing platform at one point, but that felt like ages ago. Maybe grief had warped my sense of time.

I rubbed my tired eyes, then let my head rest against the wall at my back. Xander now stood on the balustrade where I'd seen Brady with King Aviel. The king was still there, now speaking with the prince. Though Xander's father didn't strike me as warm or welcoming, I felt he was a good man. A good king. I appreciated what he had done to help Brady get away.

Xander turned away from his father and stepped up onto the short railing. His silver wings stretched wide, allowing him to glide down to where I stood. "Hello, princess."

My heart steadied in his presence. "You called me *your* princess a while ago. I may have been distraught, but I heard you."

He stepped forward and clasped my fingertips with his own, spanning a fragile bridge between us. "Perhaps I may keep you company for now?" I nodded, and he leaned against the wall beside me. Though he twined his fingers into mine, he didn't try to talk, which I appreciated.

I could hear crying from the other side of the mound. My mother's cries. I closed my eyes as if that might close off my ability to hear. The Dwarves must be moving Brock. I hoped Dad wouldn't let her watch.

Xander tightened his grip on my hand, and I sensed his grief. *Mom has Dad. I have Xander.* That thought warmed me. Somewhere inside I reminded myself that this relationship was an impossibility, but the voice of reason was easily snuffed out. My parents didn't need to deal with my heartbreak on top of their own, and I needed someone to share the weight of my sorrow. *Xander.*

In a moment, the Dwarves came from around the other side. Xander stepped between me and my view of the bridge. "Do you think you should watch?"

"No, I don't." I blinked up at him, aware that I must look like a swollen, red-eyed mess. Seemed to be my prominent feature, lately. "Thanks for protecting me."

He squinted at my collarbone. "You have quite a gash there. You need to have that looked at."

I touched the wound and winced. "Oh yeah, the Troll sliced my neck a little, I think. I'm fine."

Xander shifted closer, and I sensed he had something he wanted to say. He searched my face. I studied his. Something was wrong. Or maybe he wanted to kiss me. Was this what guys looked like right before they kissed you? I didn't think so. And I didn't want him to be thinking of something romantic in the middle of this wreckage.

"Sadie, there's something I need to—"

A whooshing splash cut him off, and we both turned toward the sound. A spray of water blasted the cobblestones where the dead Trolls lay. Writhing orange tentacles flung themselves out of the depths and onto the bodies. Three swaying arms grappled back and forth until they gripped the closest corpse. Chebar.

The water churned as other tentacles emerged, bracing against the edge of the moat. With a forceful lurch and a mighty splash, the creature flipped Chebar into the water. Suction cups and gravity pulled the hairy body under the surface. The waters roiled and swirled, erasing any evidence of the Troll. Uneasy ripples sloshed and carried themselves across the water until they flattened out.

It happened so fast, I didn't think about preventing Xander from watching until it was too late. Chebar had met his final fate in much the same way as Xander's mother. We had witnessed a near reenactment. But the Troll had the benefit of being dead first.

I squeezed his hand. "I'm sorry you had to see that."

He furrowed his brows. "Why?" Then realization broke across his face, and he sucked in a breath. "Oh yes. It's all right."

Ugh! I wanted to kick myself. "Now I'm sorry I mentioned it."

"You needn't be." He shook his head. "Trust me, I don't harbor many nostalgic feelings for my mother."

"Then, I'm sorry she was that kind of mother."

"Me too." He stepped back against the wall.

The Dwarves had already made their exit with my brother's...body. The lone door opened, and Sir Noblin strode in, followed by Brady and Sophie. King Aviel stepped through before the door closed and followed them across the floor.

"Sadie, I need to tell you something." Xander had that strange look on his face again. "Honestly, I'm not sure how to say it." His gaze darted to the bridge where the others approached. I'd never seen him so unsure of himself, and it made

me nervous. "Sir Noblin is probably here to tell you himself."
He took my hand and pulled me gently away from the wall.
"Please come with me."

CHAPTER FORTY-SEVEN

DREAD PUMMELED THROUGH MY BODY AND landed in my feet. It took an act of will to move my legs and follow Xander. What else could go wrong? The look on Sir Noblin's face told me something had.

I studied Sophie and Brady. Their blotchy, tear-stained faces looked as haggard as mine, which told me nothing. I didn't bother trying to read the stoic King of Calamus.

We followed the four to where my parents sat on the ground, huddled against the wall and holding one another. My heart broke to see their pain. I wondered how it differed to lose a child instead of a brother. And hoped I would never find out.

Dad brushed Mom's hair back and kissed her cheek before pulling away. He held her hand and looked at us with a wary gaze, like we might have come to try and cheer them up.

"Sir Liam, Lady Amy." The Gnome bowed. "I know you are deeply grieved. Forgive my impertinence, but I'm afraid this cannot wait."

Dad stood and helped Mom to her feet. The apprehension on their faces reflected my own anxiety. I had a feeling we were the last to know this forthcoming announcement. I really, *really* didn't want to have another life-shattering shock. Judging by the look on Sir Noblin's face, I was going to get one anyway. Sophie stared at the ground and fidgeted with the ribbon around her waist, and I suspected she was afraid to reveal this horrible secret, whatever it was. Brady must have been in shock; his face looked blank. Numb.

"Friends, there's something you must know." Sir Noblin gripped and twisted his tiny hands, shifting from one foot to the other. "It's not an easy thing to say."

"Surely it can't be any worse than losing our son." Dad tossed an impatient hand in the air. "Please, just get it over with."

Sir Noblin swallowed. "That's what makes it so difficult. I—I know you're grieving for Brock, but..."

I wanted to scream for him to spit it out. My mind raced to the only news that would warrant such a difficult introduction. Another death. But whose? The queen? Aunt Jules?

"But?" Dad prompted.

Sir Noblin glanced over his shoulder at Sophie.

She stepped forward. "Dad, we didn't...I mean it wasn't..." My sister covered her face with her hands and muffled a sob.

A fresh round of tears spilled over my lashes, and I didn't even know why.

Brady moved into the gap and stood beside the Gnome. He pointed to himself. "I'm Brock."

CHAPTER FORTY-EIGHT

RELIEF DUKED IT OUT IN A bare-knuckled fight with grief. Brock, alive? The announcement felt as miraculous as a resurrection. I wanted Brock to be alive more than anything. But I didn't want Brady to be dead. No! That meant I was losing a brother all over again. Almost as if I'd lost them both.

I stood staring, sizing him up through a faucet of tears.

Dad placed his hands on my brother's shoulders. "What are you saying?"

Mom crumbled against the wall and slid to the ground. "Oh, Lord! *No.* I knew something wasn't right. I knew it. Oh God, how? Why? I can't do this again."

Sophie rushed to her side, wrapping her arms around her, crying with her. "I saw his birthmark, Mama. It's Brock."

"Son," Dad cupped Brock's face, studying him, then pressed him into a fierce hug. "Oh, Brock, thank God you're all right. But, oh...Brady! I—" Sobs smothered out whatever he wanted to say.

I couldn't move. Rooted, watching Brock give Dad a stiff hug, seeing now what should have been obvious. Admitting I had seen it and missed it. Whether from tears or their switched clothing or the drama unfolding on such a large scale—I didn't recognize the truth when it counted. When it stared me in the face.

Strong arms surrounded me. I didn't respond but didn't push him away. Xander's wall-sized chest felt solid and sure, which was more than I could say for the world around me.

Fragments of the earlier desecration thrust themselves at me. The looks I had exchanged with each of them. Brady had wanted everyone to believe he was Brock. He had been doing his best to be detached and placid, but I'd noticed cracks in his armor and dismissed them. Yet that last, desperate look while Chebar cut his arm was *him*. It was Brady looking at me. He wanted me to recognize him. And I still missed it.

And, somehow, Brock had fooled me too. He hadn't been his usual passive self. He'd fought back and tried to protect Brady. And *that* was no act. That was Brock being brave and trying to make a difference.

I don't know how long my family and I questioned and mourned and dampened the ground with our tears. Eventually we gravitated into a tight cluster, holding one another. Brock patiently endured our emotional display, hovering at the fringes of our desperate, tangled grief. Finally, spent and exhausted, we drifted apart again.

Sir Noblin and King Aviel had discreetly retreated. Xander paced the milky-white floor on the other side of the bridge, head down, hands behind his back. The chairs had been removed. A pair of Gnomes mopped the floor. They were probably waiting for us to collect ourselves before they ventured to this side of the bridge to clean up.

The single door that lead into the dome was held open by a Guardian. Two teams of Dwarves entered, taking in the magnificence of the dome with awed faces. Each team of four Dwarves carried a woven stretcher between them. I guessed they had the unhappy job of removing the remaining Trolls. Though the stretchers looked plenty big for a human, they would be less than adequate for huge Yetis. The Gnomes surely hadn't prepared for such an undertaking within the walls of Vituvia—improvising was the theme of the day.

Mom sighed and looked at me and Sophie. "I'll see you girls in a while." She leaned in and kissed our cheeks. "Dad and I need to visit with Brock for a bit."

The three of them walked away, slow and unsteady. Brock ambled with his head down, my parents on either side.

I reached for my sister. "You okay?"

"Not really." Her voice was quiet, her eyes on her feet. "What about you?"

"Same here."

With heavy steps, we worked our way around the pyramid of boulders toward the bridge. I stopped when I caught sight of a narrow trickle of water that crossed our path. I'd forgotten about the mysterious source of water that sprang from the cleft in the rock where the sword was imbedded. Somehow, both water and fire sprang from that rock. No more than a dribble, it only dampened the soil between the rocks, then collected in a narrow ribbon of liquid that inched across the cobblestones and fed into the lagoon.

I pointed to the tiny stream. "See that?"

"Is that water?" Sophie squatted down for a closer look.

"Yeah. It comes from the Sword and the rock. I remember seeing it last time."

Its curious existence drew my eyes backwards along the path it took from the pinnacle of rock up above. I only traced it halfway when the scourge of blood assaulted me. Though I should've turned away, should've shut it out, I could not. A dark stain stretched across rocks and darkened the wounds in the roots of the Tree. A staggering amount of blood blanketed a large portion of the mound like a violent bruise. A crimson-black kiss of death. A visual picture of the hole in my heart.

"Let's go." I hurried my sister across the bridge, past the Dwarves that now waited with the stretchers. She didn't protest. Maybe she had seen it too.

Xander strode over. I stopped and let him approach. He had a way of being exactly the right amount of *here* when I needed him.

His pained face attempted a polite smile. "Ladies."

I blinked, too tired to respond.

"Sir Noblin wants me to get you to the Healer, Sadie. To assess your injuries." He gestured toward the door where Gnomes continued to come and go.

Swallowing back another onrush of tears, I gave a sorrowful shrug. "I doubt she can do anything about the pain. It's much worse on the inside."

CHAPTER FORTY-NINE

ONE WEEK LATER

THE PERFUME OF THE FLOWERS NAUSEATED me. The room I shared with Sophie had been overwhelmed with vases stuffed with roses and lilies and a plethora of other scented stems. Maybe after today's funeral they would quit bringing them.

Someone tapped on the door. "You girls about ready?" It was Mom's voice.

"Yes. You can come in." I looked in the mirror, adjusting the sash at the waist of my black tunic. It was customary in Vituvia to wear plain, dark clothes to a burial ceremony, even for royalty. As Joanie had pointed out when she selected my outfit, "We come and we leave this world in a humble state. It is only fittin' to pay our respect with a humble heart, reflected in our humble attire."

Mom touched the garland of daisies that rested on my braided hair. "That's lovely." Her fingers fell to my shoulder, and she pulled me into an embrace.

"I like yours too." A wreath of pale yellow roses and baby's-breath encircled her glossy, chocolate hair. The flowers matched the vines embroidered down the sleeves of her navy tunic. Though the bruise on her nose had reached the dull yellow stage, it was faint and mostly hidden under a bit of Dwarf-made cosmetics—all very organic, I'm sure.

She looked from me to Sophie, who wore a grey version of my own plain tunic and carnations in her hair. "I know this is going to be a difficult day. One in a long string of difficult days. But I do think it will help bring a sense of closure for our family and for Vituvia. It's an important step for us all to heal."

Sophie nodded. I folded my arms and resisted scoffing at

that trite, tiresome term: closure. What was that even supposed to mean? Did people think we could somehow erase my brother's outrageous death from our memories, like shutting the door on a messy, filthy closet? As if by closing the door we could pretend all the bad stuff didn't exist.

Joanie led us to a room beside the chapel. I hadn't known that the palace even had a chapel until the other day. When we walked into the room, Dad, Brock, and Uncle Brent were talking together, hot mugs of something in their hands. We had discussed the possibility of retrieving Nicole and Nate but decided to have a small memorial service with them and Aunt Valerie later, topside.

"Those flowers are a lovely touch." Dad walked over to Mom and placed a gentle kiss on her cheek.

She glanced up at the blossoms in her hair. Or maybe she rolled her eyes. "Yes, we get to remove them and place them on his grave at some point." Her words were sour and resentful.

I noticed that we all avoided the use of Brady's name. We substituted benign pronouns to keep the pain at arm's length. *He* would want this...*His* favorite song was that. A generic dead person.

I helped myself to a plate of crackers and cheese. Eating had become something necessary to do, but I didn't taste the food much anymore.

The door opened, and Aunt Jules wheeled Aunt Judith into the room, followed by Enoch and Sylon, the Gnome chaplain who would be officiating. The redheaded minister had been a source of wisdom and encouragement as we faltered through our grief. He had a kind smile and a good sense of when to talk through our pain and when to listen. His conical hat was black, a red Celtic-type cross emblazoned on the front, and he wore a matching tunic.

"It's almost time to begin," Sylon said to no one in particular. "I will lead our procession down the aisle, and Enoch will follow behind the family. He will open our time together with a eulogy. There will be a song, a time of responsive reading, and I will close with a short homily. We will then move to the portico, mount our steeds, and proceed to the burial grounds. Do you have any questions?"

No one spoke. Mom and Dad shook their heads.

"Very well. Please follow me."

Enoch held the door open, and we fell into step behind the

Gnome. Sophie grabbed my hand. We entered the chapel side by side.

I gasped at the standing-room-only space, made all the more crowded by a lack of seats in the chapel. Their tradition was to stand, and there was hardly room to do so. The onlookers left a respectable space down the center, which allowed us to walk unimpeded. I appreciated the row of chairs they had thought to provide for our family at the front.

A dozen steps led up to a simple platform, bare except for a carved granite cross that stood as tall as me at the back of the stage. A simple wreath of flowers and ivy encircled the intersecting bars of the cross. In traditional Vituvian fashion, the deceased wasn't present for the ceremony.

We remained standing for a brief prayer from Sylon, then took our seats, if we had been given one. I noticed another row of chairs along the front of the far wall. King Aviel, Xander, Chief Wogsnop, and a few other dignitaries from Calamus and Berganstroud were given places of honor.

Xander smiled at me with his eyes. We held each other's gaze, and I drew another measure of strength from his presence. He seemed to have a bottomless well of fortitude to share, though I had been a greedy taker all week. I don't know how I would've made it through the aftermath without him. Regardless of what future we may or not have, Xander was a friend—respectful, generous, sensitive, and strong, his uncomplicated faith a source of encouragement to my own that faltered daily.

I'd seen a softer side of King Aviel, too. He still never let his royal guard down, but he had allowed it to become more transparent. I didn't doubt that the qualities I admired in Xander were due to his father's example.

Enoch stood at the center of the platform, hands clasped. His piercing eyes reflected the torchlight and flared with a fire of their own. I didn't know a person could look both assertive and unassuming at the same time. It was obvious he knew things we did not. But he didn't think more of himself for all he knew, or less of us for the knowledge we lacked. At least that's how I felt around him—like he could accept things as they were and leave them there.

"Greater love has no man than to lay down his life for his friends," Enoch began. "Brady Larcen lived that out in his life and in his death."

Many in the crowd voiced their agreement with an "Amen" or a "Hear, hear."

"Even though I have lived to see many deaths in my time—
and I am referring to the years I spent topside before Yahweh
brought me here—I have known few men willing to live and die
for the sake of others. Such a man, especially one so young, is
a gift and an example to all of us. Until recently, my life has
been spent in relative seclusion. The garden has insulated me
from the ugly and harsh realities outside of its walls. Though
I often miss the warmth of fellowship, I do not miss the pain of
living in a broken, fallen world."

Enoch paced the stage and stroked his long, braided beard.
"This week's events were a startling reminder of the battle in
which our world is yet embroiled. A sobering warning for the
complacent. The Almighty, in His providence, raised up a
young man like Brady and a young king like Brock for such a
time as this." He planted his feet and pointed to the ground.
"Though we grieve, though we have pain, we know that the
King of Kings is just. He will make all things beautiful in their
time. And although He may call some of us to make the ultimate sacrifice, we know that His asking was preceded by His
doing. He does not ask more of us than He Himself was willing
to give."

Many applauded, and the ancient man paused, nodding in
agreement. "I would like to thank the Larcen family for allowing me to take part in this solemn, grievous occasion. I hope
that I might encourage you today with a special announcement
of the far-reaching effects of Brady's sacrifice."

Curious murmurs rippled through the chapel. I clenched
my tunic, wary of further announcements. Enoch stepped off
the stage and approached my parents. He stretched a hand
toward each of them. They hesitated but finally grasped his
hands.

"Truly, my friends, if a grain of wheat dies, it brings forth
much fruit. And this week I've seen that scripture come to life
in a tangible way. Although I know it was a costly sacrifice,
and one I would have taken upon myself if I could, Brady's
blood was not only spilt to save King Brock." His gaze swept
over the room. "It also has saved our Tree."

I think everyone in the room gasped at the same time. Mom
and Dad looked at each other then back to Enoch. He released
their hands and returned to the stage. His eyes glistened, spilling over with tears.

"Brady's blood has had a miraculous, restorative effect
upon the Tree of Life." He shook his head, arms outstretched.

"I have no explanation, but I know what I have seen. Wherever his blood came into contact with the scarred, broken roots, new growth and healing has rapidly taken place. New leaf buds are forming on the tree, and I have every reason to expect a full recovery."

CHAPTER FIFTY

ENOCH'S WORDS BROUGHT THE FIRST BIT of healing to my emotional wounds. Sitting astride a tawny horse with twitchy ears, I rehearsed the amazing revelation. The knowledge of Brady's effectual sacrifice and legacy worked like a healing balm to my aching heart as well. For the first time since his death, I allowed myself to think of him by name.

The rest of his—Brady's—memorial service was meaningful and touching, but Enoch's announcement eclipsed everything that followed. Wonder and dread mingled in a mysterious kiss somewhere in my soul. God's purposes, His hand, His power...it overwhelmed and humbled me. My bitter heart had needed that shot of reality. I still had questions, still had anger, but now I found myself willing to trust. At least a little. I only needed mustard-seed-sized faith, right?

Up ahead, the burial procession began to wind out of the portico and into the streets of town. At the front of the cavalcade, the queen's militia rode on their wooly-maned, goat-faced Toboggans. A long, wooden pole threaded through the curvy horns of the first pair of creatures. From the pole between them, the royal purple Vituvian banner swayed, its tree and sword glimmering silver, telling a story that had once been a riddle to me.

Behind the Toboggans trotted a shaggy Shetland pony pulling a flatbed wagon, in which rode the queen's cabinet members, sitting on four short benches. Another flatbed followed, and Brady's simple casket lay on top. The bright, bare wood looked stark in contrast to the oiled, blackened bed of the antiquated wagon. An enormous, ebony unicorn—the first one I'd seen in these parts—pulled the old-fashioned hearse, a purple plume curling between its ears. Apparently, no driver was necessary to guide such a clever, intelligent creature.

Queen Judith's royal coach came next. In brighter circumstances, she would have ridden her Pegasus, Sonnet. Instead the lustrous, white-winged mare pulled an ornate rickshaw-type carriage which held her Royal Highness, Aunt Jules, and Uncle Daniel.

In the official order of things, Brock rode behind the queen. He wore an ordinary black tunic out of respect for his brother, but a narrow gold band circled his blond head. The rest of the family rode behind Brock, with Xander, King Aviel, and the Dwarves bringing up the rear. Enoch had retreated to his garden.

We filtered through the palace gates and onto the cobbled streets of Vituvia. One of the Gnomes that rode with the Vituvian flag kept a bugle to his lips, playing a sorrowful ballad. It called to the denizens of the town, most of whom already waited to greet us. They pressed in, lining the paths on either side, peppered with many visiting Dwarves. Flowers and loose petals rained down on Brady's passing wagon like living confetti. Tearful eyes watched us pass, some onlookers waving handkerchiefs if they weren't using them to dab at their eyes. As we approached the city wall and its enormous wooden gate, I was stunned to see a dozen or more Nephilim warriors paying their respects. Gage was front and center, a single tear glinting on his freckled cheek as I passed. His eyes met mine, and he nodded. Seeing such a battle-toughened soldier weep made me choke back my own sting of salty tears.

Outside the gates of Vituvia, we followed a curving, rutted track between the small cottages of the rural community. Hard-working Gnomes left their fields and clustered along the dirt road, waving, weeping, and bowing as Queen Judith and Brock passed.

The trek was long and dusty. Though I'd explored much of the area, I didn't recall seeing a cemetery. I glanced back at Xander, finding it hard to resist sneaking a peek at regular intervals. He pressed a hand to his chest and offered a little bow. How would any guy ever measure up to all of his character and charm? All the boys I knew were only that: boys. Xander had set the bar awfully high for my future relationships.

Is there something wrong with the present relationship?

Though I'd tamed my inner third-person over the summer, she still liked to step on my virtual toes whenever she saw an opportunity. Sometimes she could make a good point.

Past the last fertile field, we curved toward the Hills of Berganstroud. A weathered, white picket fence bordered a large section of land on three sides. A steep hummock made up the fourth boundary. Tiny granite headstones carved as crosses and trees and swords speckled the ground like an obstacle course. Gnomes were compact and didn't require much space, so it looked startlingly different, like a cemetery for children.

The parade came to a stop outside of the cemetery's arched gate. Smarlow directed those of us without wheels and brakes to tie our mounts to the fence. Although I was glad to get off the slow, plodding horse, I dreaded the finality of what we were doing. Brady was still here, near me, in a way. Putting him in the ground in Vituvia and going back to Orchards, Washington, felt unreachable and absolute. I knew I would come back now and then, but it would be a long journey to bring flowers to his gravesite.

I remained beside the horse, watching the Dwarves retrieve the casket with an angry cry of denial ready to explode from my throat. A ramp slid from beneath the flatbed and allowed them to transition to the ground, but I turned away, unable to watch without losing my composure.

Along the back corner, between the towering hill and the perpendicular fence, a section of the cemetery had been designated for the royal family and their kin. All of them Topsiders, of course. And there were only a couple dozen. My math skills might be rusty, but it seemed there should have been a lot more. Perhaps this was a newer burial ground and others existed elsewhere. I noticed a marble monument for King Clive. His prophecies were revered among the Gnomes.

A large gouge in the earth awaited us. It's dark, gaping mouth lent a terrible finality to what we were about to witness.

The casket lay parallel to the freshly dug dirt. Sir Noblin asked our family to circle around. Sylon stepped to the head of the wooden box and bowed, then faced my family and bowed again. Standing directly behind him were Xander and the king. A pair of Dwarves had unhitched Aunt Judith's cart and pulled her into the cemetery by two long poles that had been attached to the horse's sides. Aunt Jules and Uncle Daniel had slipped out of the carriage and walked gingerly to where we stood.

Sylon removed his hat and prayed. First for our family, then specifically for Brock. When he finished, he asked Brock to say a few words. My brother agreed, to my surprise. He stepped close to the casket, eyes downcast, and was silent for a full minute—probably collecting his thoughts, but those gathered around didn't seem to mind. Finally, he cleared his throat and looked up at us.

"Brady has looked out for me all my life. He was my best friend. Sometimes my only friend." His smile was melancholy. "Now I have lots of friends. But Brady was still the best. He told me I had an important job to do as king. He said his job as a guardian was to protect me, so I must do what he said. We met a nice Gargoyle who told us to switch our clothing. Brady said it was a good way to confuse the bad guys. But...I didn't know they would try to kill him in my place. What happened will always make me sad. I really miss my brother."

I caught Dad's shocked stare and gave him one of my own. Tassitus? Had he come through after all? Wow! As with much of Brock's information, it came out when you least expected it. That may have been the longest monologue I had ever heard my brother speak. And it was certainly the sweetest. But Tassitus—really?

Sylon lifted his hands like a choir director and led us in a few verses of an old Vituvian hymn that reminded me of "Amazing Grace." It made me wonder, again, how Gnomes viewed this life and the afterlife. Did they have souls? Did they have a definitive answer to that question?

While we sang and I pondered, my gaze drifted past the crowd and over the fence. Something strange was taking place about a hundred yards away in the meadow. Swirls of light eddied and swarmed like a host of fireflies.

Faeries?

I nudged Sophie and nodded my head in that direction. She stifled a gasp, grabbing my arm in a tight squeeze.

The cyclone suddenly lifted, and the rotation slowed. Beneath the cloud of Faeries stood three people. Three Topsiders. Two were total strangers.

The third looked an awful lot like Joseph Delaney.

CHAPTER FIFTY-ONE

I STARED, HOPING TO BE WRONG. Sophie breathed, "Is that...?" I gave a subtle nod, trying not to draw any attention to us. As the man drew closer, I knew I was right. What to do? Stop the music? Yell and point? I decided to just watch for the moment. I placed my hand on Sophie's shoulder and whispered in her ear, "Stay calm. Look, he's handcuffed or something."

Delaney's wrists were fixed together in front, and his wide, waddling figure seemed unsteady as he walked. Escorting him on either side were a man and woman. Long, lean, and confident, the two were clad in black, their leather coats reaching to their knees. Dark sunglasses made them look like some sort of action heroes.

Mr. Delaney bumbled along between the pair like a toddler getting pulled by two harried parents. Now I could see that his arms and legs were trapped in hand and ankle restraints. A chain between his feet kept his steps short and choppy. Another chain connected his bound wrists to his ankle shackles.

"Who are they?" Sophie whispered.

I shook my head. The way they looked around, I guessed they must be first timers in the Tethered World.

"Sadie." Mom spoke my name with that you're-being-rude sort of tone. Then she followed our line of sight. "Oh my word."

Dad turned to look, followed by Lava and Wogsnop. Within a moment, Sylon was singing solo.

The trio slowed when they were about ten feet from the fence. Dad broke away from our group and made a beeline for them. Xander and his father brushed past me and came up behind my dad, like bodyguards from the same action flick. The crowd gravitated in their direction.

"Who are you?" Dad stood with his arms crossed right above the fence pickets. "I'm going to assume you know you're in the company of a thieving, lying, murderous man, considering you have him in chains."

"Yes, sir, we are aware." The man had a European accent. He stepped forward and held out his hand to my father. He was wiry and slender and a good four inches taller than Dad. "I am Asher Malakoff. Forgive us for interrupting this solemn occasion. Please continue, and we will wait."

Dad appeared to size the man up before meeting his grasp with some hesitation. He then scrutinized Joseph Delaney, who no longer looked like a smug Cheshire cat. Rumpled, striped pajamas pulled taut against his slumped shoulders. His disheveled balding head, missing its typical hat, tattled on a weary, defeated individual. He stared at the ground.

"This man is largely responsible for the death of my son," Dad said. "I'd like to know what he's doing here."

Mr. Delaney jerked his head up. His mouth gaped open in a frown, brows pinched together. Asher glanced from his prisoner to my father. "I am very sorry, sir. My sister and I have recently learned of this nefarious man's dealings. We've taken it upon ourselves—"

"Who in the name of Beacon Rock are ya, and how'd you come to utilize the Meadow Faeries?" Lava's voice was gruff, but his words lost some of their bite from behind the fence, which stood slightly taller than he did.

The man gestured for his sister to join him. She placed her hand on Mr. Delaney's shoulder and pushed him to his knees, then she stepped beside her brother. Her blue eyes, confident but kind, roamed over the crowd that gawked at her. The man rested his hand on her shoulder. "This is my sister, Mystique. You may call her Misty."

Mom and I looked at each other with a jolt. Mom raised her hand. "Hang on—you're the one who contacted us to set up a meeting?"

The woman nodded. "Yes, and when I did not hear back from you, I tracked down your address and—"

"Don't you mean you sent a shapeshifting Gargoyle to track us down?" Mom stepped to the fence and gripped the pointed slats with trembling hands.

"No, I would never do such a thing." The woman shook her head. "Please believe me. I—we saw the ring on television and recognized it." Her gaze came to rest on my right hand. I resisted the urge to hide it behind my back. "Our father used to have one exactly like it."

Sir Noblin cleared his throat with a long, exaggerated grunt. "If you please." He lifted his hand so the visitors could find him in the crowd. "I believe I know of your father. And I see where this is leading. Though it clearly needs to be sorted out, we must return to the farewells at hand. This interruption is most unkind to the family, even if it was unintended."

"Of course, of course." Asher nodded and took two steps back, his hands raised. "Please continue, and again, our deepest apologies."

"Yes." Misty pressed her fingers together and touched her lips, head bowed. "We are terribly sorry."

My father gave Delaney a withering, pitiless glare before returning to the graveside. I found my mother and slipped an arm around her shoulder. "You okay?" The tremors in her rigid body felt like an extension of my own outrage.

"No." She gave me a sideways glance. "But I will be. We'll get through this unbelievably long and difficult day somehow." She sighed as if to calm herself. "I only wish our goodbyes hadn't been tainted by Delaney's presence, intended or not."

I nodded. My emotions were in such a flux, with so many feelings and questions jostling for attention that I felt myself going numb inside, anesthetizing myself against anything else life might throw at me. I'd reached the limit of my ability to go with the flow.

Sylon resumed the service, doing his best to bring us back into the right frame of mind, but I sensed everyone was struggling to focus as much as I was. He led us in another unfamiliar hymn, and I was happy to listen to the harmonies surrounding me while images of Brady drifted in my mind. Most of the recollections were good—truly I had few negative memories of our life together—but it took an effort to keep the image of his shattered body, bent and bleeding, pushed aside.

We bowed our heads in a final prayer. Fingertips touched the nape of my neck, and a familiar spicy, soapy scent told me it was Xander. Something about his touch crumbled the protective cocoon I'd settled inside moments before, and a fresh reservoir of tears surfaced.

I turned and buried my stinging eyes against his chest, hands gripping his shirt like a lifeline. Anger and sadness threatened to drown me. Brady was one of my best friends. Throughout our tumultuous summer in and out of the Tethered World, we had found solace and understanding in each other's company. How would I make it without him?

And what about Brock? Poor Brock! Brady's loss might undo all of the progress he'd made this summer.

I cried until my eyes felt swollen shut and my head hurt beyond recognition. Pulling away, I wiped my face with the bottom of my tunic the best I could and noticed I'd soaked Xander's shirt with my gushing facial fluids. Xander brushed a runaway strand of hair from my temple.

"Thanks." I blinked up at his patient, understanding eyes. "Sorry about your shirt."

He glanced down. "I don't care about my shirt. I care about you. I wish I could help ease your pain."

I glanced around. Sylon stood beside the queen's rickshaw. Uncle Daniel and Aunt Jules now sat with Queen Judith on the bench inside. The onlookers had retreated to allow my family to say goodbye in private. Mom and Dad and Sophie clustered near Brock and Uncle Brent, their faces streaked with tears. They seemed to be waiting for me to collect myself.

Stepping back, I grabbed Xander's hand and blinked up through wet lashes. "Your strength and encouragement have been the only thing to carry me through when I wanted to run away in my grief. Whether or not it shows, you've helped my pain more than you know."

He nodded. "Good. And I'm not going anywhere."

I let my gaze linger on his. Somehow, I felt like I could read as much or as little into that declaration as I wanted. How much did I want?

"Shall we conclude our ceremony?" Sylon's question turned me back to the others, but I kept my hand in Xander's.

While I was emotionally crashing, Brady's casket had been lowered into the ground. I blinked at the dark, dirt walls. Was this really where it ended for him? For each of us? Would his heroic life, his easygoing manner, his contagious laughter all be smothered in this dreadful patch of ground?

It seemed so futile. Except it wasn't futile. It was eternal. Brady's body might be in that box, but his life—his personality, his spirit—could not be contained. That truth hit me as stark and raw as the freshly hewn wood of the casket. Brady's vibrant life lived on, not only in my memories but also in the reality of heaven. A reality that needed to propel my life forward now. Or, at least, eventually. Surely I wouldn't feel so fragile and grief stricken forever.

Mom knelt by the grave and removed the wreath of yellow roses from her hair. She kissed it and released it onto Brady's final place of rest. Sophie and I knelt beside her and did the same with our garlands. I took a mental picture of the three floral circles, so similar to the women who had placed them there—full of promise and beauty on the outside, but empty inside. At least, for now.

Brock knelt down on the other side, holding his golden crown. He gave it a gentle toss, and it landed on top of Sophie's wreath, tilting onto the wood. I took another mental snapshot. Unlike our flowers, his crown would not decay. Brady's spirit would not decay, unlike his body. That image would burn itself into my memory in the years ahead. My choices, my goals, and my actions would lead me to one kind of crown or the other.

I stood and squared my shoulders. As much as I wanted Brady back, I knew he would do it all again for Brock, or any of us, given the opportunity. His protective nature would now live on in me. I would protect his memory by protecting my family, the ring, the Sword, and the Tree. That thought drew my spiraling emotions into a rooted calm that I hadn't felt since his death. Maybe since I first learned about this place and its uninvited intrusion in my life.

Like Brady, I knew I would choose to do it all again, despite the sorrows that had come.

CHAPTER FIFTY-TWO

THE SOUND OF A DISTANT WAIL drew me from my reverie. Someone was crying. Desperate, howling sobs snapped our collective gaze from the hole in the ground to one another. We exchanged looks of confusion, then turned toward the sound.

The source of the wretched noise was Mr. Delaney.

We made our way to the entrance of the cemetery. The funeral attendees looked on as our blubbering neighbor knelt with his face in the dirt, his ample rear swaying with the cadence of his cries. I wondered what had happened. Did our visitors sucker-punch him? I couldn't muster up any sympathy for whatever his problem might be.

Dad followed the warriors, and I tailed him. Mom and Sophie were soon trotting up beside me. Asher and Misty stood on either side of the distraught man, their arms folded. Misty was saying something and shaking her head. She looked up as we approached. Asher stepped forward, stuffing his hands in the pockets of his trench coat.

"I apologize that this outburst caused another interruption. He continues to say how sorry he is, and we cannot get him to calm down." The towering man glanced down at Mr. Delaney. "I believe his sorrow is genuine, however."

"What's he so sorry about?" Lava's meaty fists were squeezed tight at his sides.

Asher shifted his gaze from the Nephilim to Lava. "When you resumed your ceremony, the man began muttering to himself. He is lamenting his shipwrecked plans and seems to be in shock that they've resulted in a death."

"Oh really?" Mom snapped. She pushed past Lava and Wogsnop and stopped in front of Mr. Delaney. Her face had turned an angry shade of red, which made her bruised nose more noticeable. "When you shot at Sadie, you used real bullets. What did you think would happen if you hit her? It might tickle?"

Dad and Xander both turned and looked at me with stricken faces. I waved them off. "He missed." My anger bristled at the memory, and I strode over to Mom, who was glaring down at the pathetic man.

Mr. Delaney sat up straight and met the gaze of my glowering mother. "Oh, Amy—and Liam—all of you." He looked at me with pleading eyes, his face had turned a deep purplish-red, like a fat beet. "I'm so sorry. I'm so ashamed. I don't blame you for hating me. I hate myself. Seeing this," he gestured in the direction of the cemetery, "and you all, it just...it hit me. I've done horrible things that can never be undone." His fleshy face drooped to his chest as another sob escaped.

"That's an understatement." Mom's volume rose sharply, and I stepped back, certain she was about to unleash her wrath and grief all over him. "I lost my son because of you, Joseph. You hear me?"

He flinched, head still bowed. The next moment, Dad was beside him, a fistful of Delaney's stringy hair in his grasp. Dad yanked the man's head upright and hissed through his teeth, "My wife asked you a question."

Mom's enraged face had turned the same color as Delaney's. She pointed an accusing finger inches from his nose. "Because of things *you've* done, Brady gave his life for his brother. But you probably don't understand that kind of love, do you?" She drew back and walloped his cheek with a backhanded smack. "Do you know anything about love?"

Delaney cowered like a dog but didn't try to deflect her rage. Dad jerked the man's head toward himself and took aim with his fist. Sophie shrieked and grasped my hand, even as I cringed in anticipation of the blow.

Suddenly, Brock launched himself at Dad's cocked elbow, wrapping his arms around it. "Dad, stop. *Stop.*" He struggled against Dad's coursing fury, pulling back the straining, eager fist. "You need to control your emotions."

Like a splash of cold water, Brock's words visibly doused the flaring tempers of my parents. Those were Dad's words, spoken many, many times to Brock in the midst of a meltdown.

Mom pressed a quivering hand to her mouth. Dad slowly lowered his fist, though he kept his grasp on Delaney's hair.

"That's right." Brock let go of Dad's arm. "Anger will not get you what you want." More of Dad's simple wisdom spilled out, never more appropriate than at this very moment.

Dad released the cringing, blubbering man. Delaney slumped sideways, curling into the fetal position. His muffled sobs mingled with Dad's ragged, coursing breath.

"I wish Brady wasn't dead," said Brock with a quiet confidence. "Losing control cannot bring him back. But I think Mr. Delaney would bring Brady back to us, if he could."

"Yes!" Mr. Delaney cried out from his heap, head nodding against the ground. "Yes, I would. How I wish I—"

"The Vituvian court will bring him to justice." Brock cut Delaney off with his confident, kingly statement. "And the Maker will help us forgive, if we ask."

Delaney pushed himself to his elbow and reached his other hand toward my parents. "Please, I beg for your forgiveness."

Lava strode forward and batted Delaney's hand away. "I don't give a cat's whisker that you've discovered yer conscience. And though King Brock is right, I'd have liked to have seen ya get a face full o' knuckles. Now, you've disturbed these fine Topsiders enough fer today. Get on yer feet and prepare to be brought to justice in the courts of Vituvia *and* the Berganstroud tribunal."

Asher and Misty hurried over, grabbed the old man's arms, and hauled him to his feet. He looked so pitiful with his blubbering face and disheveled hair and pajamas that I almost felt bad for the guy. Almost.

Mom had gotten herself under control, though her gaze could've liquefied a glacier. Between her stony face and Dad's clenched fists, it was obvious either one might blow again, given the chance. Seeing my parents so full of rage had unnerved me, and yet, like Lava, I had wanted Delaney to get what he deserved, right then and there. Deep down I knew that Brock was right, but my emotions wanted the satisfaction of seeing the old man suffer.

Xander took my hand—something that was becoming quite natural for both of us—and placed his other on Sophie's shoulder. "Come with me," he said, leading us back to the horses and wagons. I dreaded the banquet that awaited when we returned. A pillow sounded much more tempting than food.

It took time to figure out the best mode of transport for the prisoner. General Muggleridge finally decided that they would use the ropes that had secured the casket to the flatbed wagon and tie Mr. Delaney to the same spot.

Sir Noblin argued that it was insulting to our family to place the criminal where the hero had ridden to his eternal resting place. "And far beneath the dignity of Zenith." He pointed at the unicorn.

But Zenith would, indeed, have to stoop so low because there was no getting Mr. Delaney into a saddle, and the journey would be impossibly long if he had to walk. Misty and Asher sat on the back of the wagon, legs dangling from the end.

Mounting my horse, I took one last look at the fresh mound of dirt that designated Brady's gravesite. How long until I could come back to visit, and what might happen in my tumultuous life before then?

Once we returned to the Vituvian palace, we enjoyed a short respite from the day's draining events. Revonika informed us that the evening meal would be ready in an hour, allowing us time to refresh ourselves from the journey. That news was so great I could've kissed her.

Asher and Misty Malakoff and Mr. Delaney were whisked away for an interrogation with Muggleridge, Smarlow, and Reiko. If everything checked out, the villain-hunting siblings would join us for dinner.

Dad and Mom walked with Sophie and me in silence. Their guest room was right across the marbled hallway from ours. Mom reached a hand for both Sophie and me as we were parting.

"Girls." She looked at us out of puffy, bloodshot eyes, and sighed. "I want to apologize for my outburst. It was out of line. I hope you can erase that from your memory." She gave us a weary smile. "And I hope you'll avoid following my example."

"He deserved it, Mom." Sophie jutted her chin up. "Just because he's a big crybaby all of a sudden doesn't make what he did any better."

Mom raked her fingers through Sophie's loose tendrils. "True. It doesn't make it better, but it doesn't give me an excuse to lose control like I did."

I shook my head. "It's okay, Mom. You're human, and you've lost your son. Don't apologize for feeling the injustice of it. You didn't do or say anything I hadn't thought about."

"You're right, too." Her fingers skipped lightly up and down my arm. "Thank you. I appreciate your grace."

"It's something we all need, even though we don't deserve it." I kissed her cheek. "At least that's what my mom used to tell me."

My cat nap turned into more of a snooze-and-lose event. By the time Sophie and I woke and dressed and dashed off to the banquet hall, the meal was well underway. I was glad they didn't feel the need to wait. And to no one's surprise, Xander had saved me a seat.

Sophie walked beside me as we headed to where he stood, holding out a chair for me. She giggled and whispered in my ear, "You two are so cute together."

"I don't think you could actually say we're together, but thanks."

She stopped walking and rolled her eyes. "Puh-*leese*. You two are with each other at every meal and holding hands like a real couple. What else would you call it?"

I shrugged, feeling my face flush. "I don't know. He's, you know, helping me deal with Brady's death. It's been comforting to have him here."

"Plus he's saved your life a time or two. And he's a real man." She wiggled her eyebrows up and down.

I laughed and glanced at Xander, who was probably getting impatient. "A real man? And what would you know or care about that?"

She grinned like she knew a great secret. "I've heard you complain about how immature all the boys are topside. Plus, Dad always says we should hold out for a real man who knows how to treat us like a princess and knows the meaning of hard work." She gave an exaggerated shrug. "I mean, he calls you princess all the time, and he's learning to run a kingdom and has big muscles, which probably means he works hard, right?"

"Who works hard?" Xander was suddenly beside us. "Are you girls planning to stand here chatting, or will you be joining us for supper?"

Heat washed over me. I hoped he hadn't overheard much—especially the part about his muscles. Ignoring his first question, I said, "We're heading there right now. I'm starved."

Sophie giggled again as we crossed the room to our table.

The Gnomes had roasted a pig in our honor, apple in the mouth and everything. Halfway through dinner, our Israeli guests walked in, escorted by Sir Noblin. With wide eyes, they took in the bright, torch-lit room, the banners that hung around the perimeter, and the tables laden with food. Their tailored black clothing and trench coats looked otherworldly. I could easily imagine them snatching a laser gun from their hip and making us their slaves. After everything I'd seen in this place, it wasn't such a farfetched idea.

They were offered seats at our table, which gave me an opportunity to study them. I was dying to know how they had ended up here with our nosy, nefarious neighbor. Joanie arranged to bring them slices of roast chicken instead of pork in deference to their Jewish dietary laws. Misty sat beside Aunt Jules, who kept her laughing instead of eating. The woman's blue eyes danced in response to my Irish aunt's banter. She frequently clapped her elegant hands in amusement. From her blonde curls to her shimmery nail polish that matched her eyes, she was exquisite.

And she was much closer to Xander's age than I was. With that disturbing thought in mind, I found myself glancing back and forth between the two, sizing them up as an impressive couple. I couldn't hold a candle to her blazing glory. I had all but resigned myself to being a guest at their wedding when Xander placed his hand on mine on the tabletop. Swallowing the bitter taste I'd conjured up, I blinked at his long, protective fingers that encircled my own dainty set of digits. What did he see in me? Did he have a thing for messy, weepy girls with bags under their eyes?

"You look beautiful." The warmth of his voice, so close to my cheek, sent little prickles of happiness down my arm. *Maybe he did.*

I turned my face to find his uncomfortably close. Though the view was as good as it gets, I didn't think I was ready for what I saw in his eyes. He wanted to kiss me. *Gulp.*

So much for his wedding with Misty.

I focused on our clasped hands. My first kiss was not going to be at the dinner table in front of my family, right after burying my brother. I'd always thought it terribly romantic to wait for a wedding day kiss—which of course would be in front of them and everyone else but in an altogether different context. Whether or not I kept to that notion, I knew I couldn't lean in right then and there and allow him to give me a casual smooch. Instead, I leaned back a bit.

He let out a soft, frustrated groan. "I'm sorry if I made you uneasy. My emotions have tugged me along all day. I need to whip them back to their proper place."

I squeezed his fingers, unsure of how to respond.

A clanking of metal on glass quieted everyone's low-key chatter. Sir Noblin stood on the dais in the corner holding a spoon and a chalice. "May I have your attention, please?"

Yes, you may have my attention if it means I can avoid another awkward moment with this amazing guy next to me.

The room quieted. "Thank you, friends. First, let us remember why we break bread together this evening. We're here to remember our fallen comrade, Brady Larcen, and to offer his family our condolences and our fidelity. Let us honor Brady's sacrifice now with a moment of silence."

I stared at my plate, though my mind was on my brother's mischievous smile rather than my peas and pork. A few sniffles perforated the silence.

Sir Noblin cleared his throat, ending the observance. "We will miss our newest Guardian of the Sword. Brady willingly took upon himself the job of becoming High King Brock's body double without a thought for his own life. Brady will be honored this evening with a brief ceremony in the Garden Dome."

Sophie leaned over. "Did you know about this?"

I shook my head.

How could we possibly fit one more emotionally demanding event into this day? The Tethered World had about eighteen hours of daylight before the golden dome dimmed for a six-hour dusk, or nighttime. The Gnomes knew how to make use of every last, exhausting minute.

"As I'm sure you've noticed, we have some special guests with us tonight." The Gnome nodded at the visitors. Heads turned toward Misty and Asher. I watched them exchange a glance and a grin between themselves.

"Of course, whenever the Larcen family is here, we are blessed with special guests. But tonight, we are witnessing a first for the Tethered World—and a first for Topsiders, as far as I know." He plunked the spoon inside the goblet and gestured to our table. "Our guests are Asher and Mystique Malakoff of Tel Aviv, Israel."

The room offered a polite round of applause, and Asher acknowledged it with a wave. Something glinted on Asher's

right hand, and I watched as he lowered it to the table.
He was wearing the ring that matched mine.

CHAPTER FIFTY-THREE

I RELEASED XANDER'S HAND AND CLASPED mine together beneath the table, where my ring would be out of sight. There was something freaky about the two keys being this near to each other and in such close proximity to the sword. It felt irresponsible, although I knew it couldn't be helped. Most of those surrounding us had no idea that the rings were actually the keys.

The fact that Sir Noblin had given it to Asher meant their story had checked out. I thought it was interesting that he was the one meant to become the key keeper. Who the ring was passed along to was never up for deliberation. I myself had wanted nothing to do with such a powerful piece of jewelry and had flat-out refused it. Aunt Jules had likened my inheriting the ring to inheriting my name. I had no choice in the matter. And strangest of all, the ring was one-size-fits-all. It adjusted to the key keeper when it was placed on the new keeper's finger. That part was pretty cool, I must admit.

"Tonight," Sir Noblin continued, "we have the distinct and unprecedented honor of hosting both Topsider families that have been given the solemn charge of watching over our beloved realm. Through the centuries, as you know, many families have come and gone, most having very little contact with us in the Land of Legend—outside of our monarch. Circumstances dictate necessity, however, and our circumstances of late have been unlike any in the history of our great land. The Maker has seen fit to bring each of these families to our banquet tables tonight. I hope each of you will take time to greet our new friends and make them feel welcome."

"Hear, hear!" Lava stood and held his mug toward the Malakoffs.

"Hear, hear!" The crowd echoed. As one, we rose to our feet and clapped.

Misty and Asher stood, waved, and bobbed their heads. Asher's face flushed a little, which both surprised and disappointed me. I had hoped that my propensity to blush could be outgrown. Evidently not.

The shuffle of so many bodies took time. I decided to use it getting to know my key keeping counterpart and his sister. With Xander by my side—and ignoring my trivial insecurities—I made my way over to them. They noticed my purposeful approach and waited for me.

"Hello." I stuck my hand out. "I'm Sadie. And this is Prince Xander of Calamus."

We shook hands, and Asher wore the wow-you're-impressively-huge expression I had noticed earlier. Gazing up at Xander, Misty's face morphed from awestruck to coy, and I couldn't help but dislike her. *God, help me to be nice!* I prayed under my breath.

"This is the most amazing day," she said, her smile broad and blinding. "I know it is not a happy day for your family, so please don't misunderstand. But the things we've seen and experienced are beyond comprehension."

I couldn't help but notice how her exotic accent matched her exotic name. Hopefully my envious feelings were masked behind a polite exterior. Where was this petty jealousy coming from? I chided myself for being shallow and unfair. "It's natural to be overwhelmed." I smiled, even though I wasn't feeling it.

My parents came over to where we stood, and Dad extended his hand. "We didn't properly meet you over dinner. I'm Liam Larcen. My wife, Amy."

More handshaking, then Misty gave my mother a warm hug.

"I'm sorry I didn't answer your email," Mom told Misty. "Things went really crazy right after I received it, and I didn't know who to believe about anything."

"No apology is necessary. Sir Noblin and some of the others briefed us on the events of the past week. Tragic, to say the least. We are so sorry for your loss and, once again, express our regrets for the way we interrupted your memorial today."

"Nonsense." Mom smoothed her burgundy dress. "Though I regret my unbecoming behavior this afternoon, I've decided that Joseph Delaney being taken into custody on the day of Brady's memorial is a just ending to an unjust situation."

Dad's arm encircled her waist, and he gave her a squeeze. "Well stated, honey."

"You didn't do anything I wouldn't have done in your posi-tion." Misty touched my mom's arm. "I was happy you were letting him feel your pain."

"Excuse me." Revonika waved to draw our attention. "Would you like to make your way to the Garden Dome? The ceremony will begin soon."

We strolled in the direction of the dome, and I had a chance to ask my burning question. "How did you guys end up with Mr. Delaney in your custody?"

Asher jerked his thumb toward his sister. "Misty is quite the sleuth. After we noticed the ring on television, we wanted to locate your family to discuss it. Misty found it easier to fol-low the trail to your neighbor across the street."

"I don't know how much of his story you followed before you returned here," Misty said, "but Joseph Marshall, or Joseph Delaney as you know him to be, fell out of favor with the press within a few days of his big media splash in Portland. Televi-sion stations were contacting him to interview the Yeti or get a better look at the creatures he captured. But his creatures had mysteriously disappeared. Social media and the press labeled him a hoax. His little experiments with the tree roots backfired as well when the botanist claimed there was nothing special about the saplings."

"The media dismissed the story as fast as they had em-braced it." Asher raked his fingers through his hair. "By the time we showed up on his doorstep, armed with what we sus-pected to be the truth about where he was getting his prisoners and who he must be working with, he confessed. He was dis-traught that his plans had come to swift and utter ruin and cost him his marriage."

"Wow." Mom stopped walking, which meant we all pulled up short. "Here I had planned to stay topside in order to put out fires and downplay the media frenzy, and God had it han-dled. Hah! Isn't that typical. Right when we think we're indis-pensable and doing Him some big favor..." She walked on, shaking her head.

Colonel Smarlow stood beside a soldier at the first of the many doors that led to the Garden Dome. There was no miss-ing the scowl on his face. The soldier pulled the door open, and Smarlow stepped over the threshold. "We are waiting to begin." He jabbed his arm into the dim passage.

"Sorry, my small friend." Xander gestured for me to go first, and I gave him a scolding look. Ever since my last visit, there had been a good deal of tension between the two after Smarlow accused the Nephilim of working with the Gargoyles.

Smarlow mumbled under his breath as I passed.

At the last door, Smarlow asked us to remove any weapons we were carrying. Xander removed his sword and placed it against the wall. The Malakoffs pulled daggers from their belts and inside their boots and laid them aside. Then they stunned us all when they withdrew pistols from holsters hidden beneath their trench coats.

Smarlow looked like a land mine ready to detonate. "Bringing firearms to the Tethered World is strictly forbidden. I'm going to have to confiscate those immediately."

Asher raised an eyebrow and held his gun out of reach. "That would not be wise, Colonel. These have been issued to us by the Mossad. They are property of the Israeli secret service, and if we don't return with them in our possession, I cannot be responsible for what the Mossad might do in order to recover their property. You don't want large, firearm-sniffing dogs converging on the palace, do you?"

Well, that explains the action hero vibe.

Smarlow scowled harder than I thought possible, causing me to stifle a snicker. "Very well then, but next time you leave your weapons topside. Got it?"

Misty ejected the magazine and dropped to her knee. "Yes, sir. We were unaware of such a restriction." She placed the gun on the floor and pocketed the bullets. "Better to keep the ammo separate in case someone gets curious while the guns are lying here."

Asher did the same with his, and soon we were blinking at the pearly brightness of the Garden Dome. Rows of chairs were set up on the near side of the bridge. The granite wall loomed large, and the Flaming Sword burned on. It looked exactly as it had the week before.

I buried my face against Xander and cried.

CHAPTER FIFTY-FOUR

WHEN I FINALLY PEELED MY DAMP face from Xander's shirt, I found Mom and Dad in a similar state. Whose idea was this? We shouldn't be here. Not yet. Not this soon. I took a deep breath and wiped my eyes.

Xander cupped my cheek in his hand. "You are not required to attend this ceremony, Sadie. You should not feel obligated."

I sighed. "Maybe not. And, for the record, it's lousy timing. But I think Brady would do it for me. This is about him, not us."

"True. But no one will look down on you if you decide to leave."

Sophie and Uncle Brent were already seated on the row designated for our family, at the front. Xander walked me to my seat and retreated to the other side, where his father and Gage sat. A larger crowd had been admitted for this ceremony to honor and remember Brady. The marveling eyes and pointing fingers meant it was the first time in the Garden Dome for many.

A hand patted my shoulder from behind. "How ya doin', ladybug?"

I grabbed the fragile fingers of Aunt Jules and turned in my chair. "I'm ready for this day to be over. How about you?"

She gave an understanding nod and smile. "Fer certain, love. And I understand yer tears and shed a few of me own. Not quite ready to be back in this place so soon."

"Yeah. Exactly." I patted her hand and released it, turning away.

The pressure of her fingertips stopped me, and I looked back.

"I think that Prince Xander is a very handsome boy." She winked. "You two are the talk of Vituvia."

My eyes widened. I morphed from laughing at her labeling the seven-foot warrior a boy to pink-faced mortification. To think that we—that *I*—was the topic of Vituvia's social gossip. Ugh!

"I believe we're ready to begin." Sir Noblin and his impeccable timing saved me from another awkward moment. "Thank you all for being part of a day set aside to remember and honor Brady Larcen. His brave forethought and steadfast follow-through has ensured the safety of the next in line to the Vituvian throne. Brady Larcen was a son, a brother, a grandson, and a nephew. He was also in training as a Guardian of the Sword. And as an identical twin, he was uniquely suited to pose as our high king in training, Brock."

Revonika and her assistant Izzy stood on the row of boulders below the Flaming Sword. A black cloth covered the boulder between them. Sir Noblin gestured to where they stood. "I do not wish to revisit the fateful event that took place on our sacred hill. Tonight we celebrate a life well lived in the service of others and the Almighty. But I would be remiss if I failed to mention that Brady's sacrificial death brought the gift of healing to our precious Tree of Life. In commemoration of all these things, it is with great pride that I present to Brady's family a memorial carved into the stone—the place where their beloved son paid the ultimate price."

Izzy and Revonika lifted the cloth with a flourish and descended the boulders. A weary sigh escaped my lips. This was a kind gesture, but did I really want to stare at the place where my brother breathed his last?

The turquoise depths of the lagoon lay in placid perfection not ten feet away. I stared, remembering the sea monster that lived in its depths. Aunt Judith had told me his name was Levi, short for Leviathan. His terrifying tentacles had made short work of Queen Estancia and then of Chebar. Too bad the octopus couldn't as easily consume all the negative stuff from my life and leave me with similar deep, transfixing peace.

I glanced at the menagerie of friends I had made this summer, from knee-height Gnomes to Jolly-Green-Giant-sized Nephilim. I would never trade a safe-and-sound existence for their friendship.

Sir Noblin beckoned our family to make the pilgrimage across the bridge to view the monument. My reluctant feet fell into step beside Sophie. I placed my arm around her shoulder and followed Mom and Dad and Brock to the other side. Revonika stood at the base of the pyramid and smiled as we approached. Izzy stood beside her, holding a basket of folded handkerchiefs.

Revonika gestured to a knobby rock that offered a couple of options for a foothold. "If you wish to view the memorial up close, this is the easiest route up."

Brock climbed up with the ease of a mountain goat. My parents took a handkerchief and hiked up behind him. Sophie and I followed, handkerchiefs and all. Even though I told myself to gloss over the scene before me, I found myself inspecting the roots and rocks. Indeed, the roots had begun to grow together where they had been severed. Like a scar that heals from the inside out, the new growth was not as thick as the old root but spanned the gap nevertheless.

I couldn't help but inspect the boulders, too. They looked as if they'd been scoured clean, I noticed the dark stains that streaked the wood of the great gnarled roots. No doubt the Vituvians hoped to allow the tree to continue healing by letting his balm of blood remain.

My fingers reached for a nearby root that bore the black-red scar. Touching it would be like touching a bit of my brother's life that lingered behind. A shock of electricity sparked around my ring, and I drew my hand back, my heart thudding. I blinked and inspected my fingers. Everything looked and felt normal, but I knew it was more than an extraordinary coincidence. What it meant I couldn't guess. I kept my hand close to my body and pretended it hadn't happened.

Sophie and I reached the etched stone and joined hands with our parents. Brock was not a fan of hand holding. I smiled to myself as I read:

Rock of Remembrance:
Brady Larcen
Guardian of the Sword
Beloved brother to High King Brock
Restorer of the Tree of Life
Upon this rock he gave all to save all.
"Greater love has no man than
to lay down his life for his friends."
John 15:13

I sniffed back a few tears but found myself smiling despite

the pain. The tribute was perfect and strangely therapeutic. Facing down this mountain of heartache so soon was like getting back on a horse that tossed me from its back. I had to show this mountain who was boss. In the process, I realized it was only a small mound of rock and not nearly as overwhelming and threatening as I believed.

My family stood together, lost in thought. I finally glanced up to see that a line had formed across the bridge. "Hey, looks like they're waiting on us." I bobbed my head to the bridge.

My parents flicked their eyes in that direction. Dad nodded. "You ready, babe?"

Mom kissed her fingertips, then pressed them against Brady's name. "I am now."

Dad climbed ahead and offered us his hand as we hopped off the bottom rock. My leather sandals had just smacked the cobblestones when a reverberating gong rang out. I grasped Dad's arm and looked around. Where had it come from? Another resonating note was struck. It thrummed through my chest, deep and ominous.

Guardians swarmed from the outer perimeter. Sir Noblin called for everyone to stay calm and move toward the door.

Before we could cross, soldiers tramped across the bridge, dodging those who attempted to make it back. The first four encircled our family while the rest split off and headed for the far side of the wall.

"Your Highness, we need to move you and your family to safety," said one of the guards. "There's trouble in the garden."

"What does that mean?" Dad asked. "No one is in there except Enoch."

"Yes sir, that's his signal to us that there is a problem—an urgent one." The soldier moved ahead of our group and waved us over. "If you please, we must get the king to safety."

We followed the Gnome but took turns craning our neck toward the action. What kind of trouble could a lone gardener come up against? Maybe he was ill, or maybe the tree had taken a turn for the worse. I tried not to think about that possibility.

We reached the other side of the bridge, where Xander waited for me. "What's going on, do you know?" he asked.

I shook my head. "Some sort of alert."

"Sadie, let's go." Mom turned and gave me an impatient stare. "I'd like to stay with Brock if there's danger."

I nodded and took Xander's hand with a final glance back

at the commotion. Someone flung a rope ladder over the top of the wall. Xander saw it too, and we both stopped again. Enoch's bald head slowly emerged above the top. He grasped the far edge of the wall with one hand and struggled to lift something with the other.

"Get ready!" he shouted to the soldiers below. "I have something to hand over to you."

"*Sadie.*" Mom said my name with an impatient bite.

"Hang on." I turned and held up a finger. "I want to see what he's got."

Enoch now had one leg on each side of the wall, straddling it. With his hand freed up, he reached behind the wall and pulled with both arms and a loud grunt. A sleek, black thing hung limp from his arms. He heaved it on top of the wall in front of him, its head and arms slumped over the side.

Ophidian had been found.

CHAPTER FIFTY-FIVE

I SMACKED A HAND OVER MY mouth. Wow! No wonder they hadn't found the Gargoyle. With all the activity surrounding Brady's death, I had stopped wondering about the creep. I'd figured they would let us know if he was caught—then, to be honest, I'd forgotten about him.

"The creature is not dead," Enoch announced. "I knocked him unconscious with a rock."

The old guy was pretty handy with those rocks.

My parents and Sophie stood beside Xander and me while we looked on, fascinated. Or at least curious. I spotted Lava and Wogsnop standing near the water directly across from the ladder and pointed at them. "Let's move over there."

Dad made a beeline, and we followed.

"Would ya look at that?" Lava put his hands on his hips. "Sneaky little demon must've slunk over the wall when the ladder was down fer repairs. Guess it's a blessin' in disguise that tree is sufferin' and has lost its fruit."

Chief Wogsnop shifted to a wide stance and crossed his arms, shaking his head. "No telling what kind of havoc he wreaked inside the garden. Never thought I'd live to see the day."

"He's moving!" Sophie squeezed my arm.

Enoch had maneuvered so that both feet stood on the third rung from the top, on the outside of the wall. He kept one hand pressed against the Gargoyle's ribs. I saw Ophidian lift his head and zero in on the ancient man with his snake-slit eyes.

"Beware, Dweller! He awakens," a guardian yelled up to Enoch.

The Gargoyle's writhing, snake-like fingers reached for his captor. Enoch shoved the creature away by the ribcage, which catapulted him down to the ground. Ophidian somersaulted and landed butt-first, head whipping back, with a loud thud that sent the nearest soldiers scattering.

"You think he's dead?" Sophie whispered.

"I'm gonna find out fer myself." Lava headed for the bridge.

"Can I?" Sophie pleaded.

"No." Dad shook his head. "Stay over here, out of the way."

The soldiers crowded around the body, blocking it from view. Enoch made it down the ladder about the same time Lava arrived behind the soldiers. I marveled at the ancient patriarch's strength and agility. *Must be nice to reach a limit on aging and deterioration.* He stepped around the guards and appeared to straddle the creature with wide legs.

A low, snarling groan emanated from Ophidian. The soldiers spread out, keeping their distance and providing us a glimpse of the prone beast.

"Leave me be." The Gargoyle's words came out with effort, slow and slurred. Dark blood trickled from his mouth.

Enoch looked down and shook his head. "You had no right to be in the garden and no business in Vituvia."

Ophidian wiped his mouth with the back of his hand and looked at the blood. He cursed, then turned his head and spat. "Who's to say, old man? I don't answer to you. I don't even answer to God."

"You're desecrating a sacred place with your foul language and blaspheming." Enoch stepped to the far side of the Gargoyle and crouched down. He pointed his finger at the beast's bleeding face, his sinewy arms trembling with anger. "You are cursed! Instead of mercy, you seek your own way. By the hand of the Almighty, you shall reap the same consequence as your ancient father."

"You don't—*oomph!*" Ophidian curled onto his side, writhing and gurgling. Blood bubbled from his scaly mouth. Enoch stood, fisted hands at his side, watching. The Gargoyle flopped from side to side like a fish out of water. With a yowl he stiffened, rigid as a board. His arms pressed against his sides and his legs drew together. He let out a harrowing gasp, then suddenly shriveled like a slug doused with salt. He twisted and squirmed and, somehow, decompressed until his limbs melded into his body. Whatever the creature had become squirmed from side to side until finally it thrashed onto to its belly, its metamorphosis complete.

Ophidian had transformed into a sleek, black snake that still bore Ophidian's head wound. Everyone except for Enoch scattered at the sight. The snake slithered out of its crumpled, black trousers, away from the ancient man, and neared the water's edge. Its forked tongue poked at the air, then the creature slinked off the cobblestones and slipped silently into the water.

I hurried to the water's edge, peering through the clear, cerulean depths. I could make out the snake's dark body, but I gasped at how deep the water appeared to be.

A wave rippled the surface from the direction of the bridge. Like a great, orange shadow, something glided beneath the arched structure. Something with tentacles and an appetite.

I grabbed Xander's arm with both hands, my brain buzzing in a perpetual state of wonder. The enormous octopus dove deeper but drifted directly below where I stood. A swirl of color flashed in the depths. Bubbles drifted up with syncopated *pops*. The water churned and roiled and then...nothing. No movement, no bubbles, and no more Ophidian.

The immense orange submarine continued on its way until we could see it no more.

CHAPTER FIFTY-SIX

THREE MONTHS LATER

BROCK STOOD BEFORE THE ORNATE MIRROR in his new, fit-for-a-king quarters. He'd dismissed his staff and asked to be left alone. Peggelton, his personal valet, had flipped one of the smaller hourglasses onto its empty head.

"We can only spare half an hour, Sire," he said before leaving.

Brock didn't need an hourglass to keep track of time, but the Gnomes were still learning to trust his inner clock. But he liked the hourglass anyway. Sometimes he would use his entire time in seclusion watching the tiny grains of sand slip into the bubble of glass. But not today. Today he wanted to be alone with his brother. Even though Brady had been gone for three months, Brock had a tremendous amount of detailed memories he could call on when he missed him.

Today was one of those times. He wore a pair of his brother's jeans, the ones with a giant hole in the knee from a failed skateboarding stunt. Studying his reflection, Brock touched the skin of his knee through the ripped fabric, remembering how Brady had shrugged off his bleeding, gravel-speckled wound.

Brock straightened and turned to look at the back of Brady's favorite T-shirt. It used to belong to their dad when he was a teenager. Brady had adopted it as his own because he loved the band emblazoned on it. The thing was so old that it no longer looked white. Three bearded men in psychedelic colors looked out from beneath the words Bee Gees World Tour, and the back listed all the cities the Bee Gees had visited in 1981. Brock had never understood why Brady liked a group of boys that sang like girls, but he'd never told his brother that.

He'd never told his brother a lot of things, mostly because he hadn't thought to do so. A long time ago, he didn't understand how to form the right words. But even after he'd figured that out, he never needed to say much with Brady around, because Brady often knew what Brock wished to express. He could read Brock's mannerisms and body language with fluency.

Living in Vituvia and training to be king, Brock needed to speak more than he preferred, but that was getting easier. The Gnomes made him feel respected and smart, unlike most humans. If they made him talk too much, he looked forward to retreating to the silence of his room. In the past few weeks, he had found comfort in removing his Vituvian clothes and donning some of Brady's favorites. His parents had brought him a large box of his brother's clothing when they came to visit six weeks and four days earlier.

He loved that they smelled like Brady, which made Brock feel like they were together again. What would his brother say to him today? What sort of casual advice would Brady give for Brock's coronation? Brock couldn't guess. It was hard enough to come up with his own words, so he couldn't begin to decipher what someone else's words might be.

Brock sat on his bed and picked up the framed photo of the two of them together. He traced his finger across Brady's smile. As much as they looked alike, others could always pinpoint Brady in a photo by the size of his smile.

He stretched out on his four-poster bed and laid the picture face down on his chest. He would lie still for a while and think about the time Brady took him down to the creek to catch tadpoles and they came across a homeless man who needed food.

He had seventeen minutes left in the hourglass.

CHAPTER FIFTY-SEVEN

I PRACTICED WALKING ACROSS THE ROOM in front of Sophie and Nicole. High heels and long, flowing skirts seemed like a dumb and dangerous combination, but I soldiered on. Joanie's amazing handiwork demanded that I wear the right pair of shoes. In fact, I had picked out the shoes before I found the champagne-colored fabric I brought to her on one of our visits.

My family had returned to Vituvia twice since...since we said goodbye to Brady. With Queen Judith's frail health, Brock's coronation was moved up to Christmas. Literally, Christmas Day.

There were tons of preparations that required us to pop down for a visit. It meant I did a lot of cramming for school when I was topside so I could be free to visit and help when we came below. I can't tell you how wonderful it felt to come down without someone I knew running for their life. In fact, our lives were now so invested down below that my parents had decided to call Vituvia home—as soon as we could sell the house and Dad's cosmetology business. I think I might be as excited as Sophie.

Now, in my gilded finery, I struck a pose for my sisters, hands on my hips.

"Awesome!" Nicole clapped her gloved hands. She'd taken the news of our ulterior life in stride, thrilled to be treated like a princess. I think she was convinced we were all playing dress-up with her.

"Xander is gonna flip." Sophie mimed a pair of binoculars with her hands. "Wowsers!"

"I mean, am I graceful in these heels? I feel like I'm going to snag them on my skirt and rip my dress or fall on my face."

"You don't look too weird I guess." She shrugged and turned back to admire herself in the mirror.

I rolled my eyes. "Gee, thanks."

Tap-tap-tap. "Are the young princesses quite ready?" Joanie's voice carried through the door.

"Yes, ma'am!" Sophie bolted for the door and then realized she wasn't dressed for sprints and slowed down. "Come on in." She pulled it open.

Joanie bustled inside, looking lovely in a new frock, as she called her dresses. Mom and I had brought her loads of colorful fabric, and she'd had a heyday sewing.

She inspected the three of us, her green eyes twinkling in approval. "My, my—Trinny did a fabulous job on yer hair. She's truly got the touch, I'd say."

"Definitely." Sophie ran a hand over her braided up-do.

"Yer mum and pop are waitin' near the Great Hall. Lady Amy wanted to peek in on yer brother before the ceremony."

We followed her through the passageways, though by now we knew our way around. We were never alone in the palace, except in our own rooms—and even that bit of privacy wasn't guaranteed.

Nicole held my hand and skipped beside me in her frosty pink gown. She had squealed with delight when Trinny presented her with a delicate tiara to wear. She reached her hand up to touch it about every ten yards.

"You're going to lose your tiara and mess your pretty hair if you keep skipping." I tugged on her arm to slow her down.

She backed off and touched her tiara again. "How come your crown is so much smaller than mine?"

"Well, tiaras aren't truly crowns. They're like a fancy decoration for your hair. And I like simple decorations, so I chose a smallish one." I ran my finger across the gold band that dipped onto my forehead. It was actually a lot more like the crowns I'd seen Brock and Aunt Judith wear, but I wasn't much for sparkles and bling. Shimmers were more my style.

We rounded the final corner and came to the small crowd of friends and family who had been invited to the private ceremony. They milled around the wide marble passageway outside of the Great Hall, talking and laughing. Nicole spied Uncle Brent and ran in his direction. I felt bad that Aunt Val and the kids had stayed home. Aunt Val still feared Vituvia and had persuaded Uncle Brent to spare the girls. She didn't want them to be burdened with the secret of this place. Can't say I blamed her, but I was thrilled with Brent's newfound devotion to the Land of Legend. My mom was over the moon about it.

"Hello, princess." Xander's hand touched the small of my back, and I turned. "What's this—you've grown taller?" He looked genuinely perplexed at my extra three inches. I laughed and flicked one heel to the side, lifting my long skirt to show him. "Temporarily."

His eyes widened, and he leaned over to inspect the heels while I used his arm for balance. I guess it wasn't so surprising that he'd never seen a pair of high heels. What would a seven or eight-foot-tall woman want with them?

"That is the strangest footwear I've ever seen." His brows knit together as if he was concerned for my safety. "Why would you strap your feet into something like that?"

I laughed. "My seven-foot boyfriend, for starters. Don't you like having me a little closer to you?"

"Well, when you put it like that." He grinned in a lopsided way that made me melt. "But really, Sadie, you're still way down below eye level. Don't torture your feet on my account."

He had a point. But I still felt more like a young woman and less like a child when I wore heels rather than flats. They felt right today, on this occasion.

Mom and Dad rounded the corner, Nate toddling between them and holding their hands. His miniature striped suit and navy bow tie made me melt a little more.

"Sadieee!" He ran to me, chocolate-colored curls dancing on his head.

"Nateyyy!" I scooped him up and placed him carefully on my lace-and-chiffon-adorned hip. "You look so handsome in your suit."

"Got a bow tie like Daddy." He grabbed the tie in his plump fingers and tried to look down and see it.

"Hey, Nate the Great." Xander had picked up on his nickname and liked to use it. "I like that bow tie. We don't have those where I come from."

Nate gave Xander a dimpled smile and reached his hands to get snatched high up, as he called it. Xander whisked him from my arms and set him on one side of his broad shoulders, holding onto the little guy with one large hand.

Nate clapped and hollered, "High up! It's my favorite."

My parents had stopped to chat with Revonika and Muscle, who were now engaged. I was terribly excited to attend a Gnome wedding and thought they were a good match. Plus they just looked absolutely adorable together.

Dad excused himself and joined us.

"Sir Liam." Xander extended his hand. "Are you ready for this milestone?"

Dad's hand disappeared into Xander's, but he still gave the Nephilim an enthusiastic shake. "Ready as I can be. I'm not entirely sure what to expect, to be honest."

The two had become quite friendly over the past three months. What was mind-blowing, to me, was how easily my parents had accepted our relationship. When we'd returned home, I'd fully expected a lecture about holding hands with a young man seven years older than myself. Of course, my parents are also seven years apart in age, so that may have deflated any initial problems they had. Still, *I* was the one who had asked *them* how they felt about Xander and me.

They'd looked at each other and then at me, and Dad had said something like, "Well, yeah. We think he's great. He treats you with respect. And we know he helped you get through your grief when we were emotionally checked out. We like him a lot."

It was weird to say the least—in a good way. It's just not the way I expected it to be handled because of the way my parents had raised me. But then again, this whole summer wasn't something I had expected. I was seventeen years old on paper, but I felt like I had lived a lifetime and could barely relate to friends my age any longer. Making plans for senior prom and college was all right, but fighting epic battles against evil was ever so much better. Maybe my parents understood that a new approach to how we did life was inevitable.

The heavy wooden doors opened, and Gnomes and Dwarves filtered inside. Xander plucked Nate from his shoulder and zoomed him into my mother's arms.

Nate giggled and thrust his fists in the air. "High up!"

Xander leaned in and kissed my forehead—a feat made easier by my high heels, I might add. "I shall see you when it is over. I've heard there's to be dancing." He raised one eyebrow in his teasing way.

The doors closed leaving my Dad, Mom, Nate, and me standing in the hall. The guard instructed us to wait until we were announced.

"Where's the girls?" I looked around for Sophie and Nicole.

"Oh, I bet they went inside." Mom walked to the door and peeked in. "Psst. Sophie! You girls need to wait out here with us."

In a moment they emerged and we all fidgeted nervously in the hall. I didn't relish the idea of walking into a silent room under the watchful eyes of our fifty closest friends. In three-inch heels.

"I wish Brady was here with us." Nicole verbalized exactly what I was thinking. "Brock is his twin. He should see this."

Mom hugged her close. "I know, baby." She stroked Nicole's hair and looked thoughtful. "Brady would be so proud of his brother. I guess we'll have to be proud enough for him, too. Try to think about him when you're in there—remember his smile or his eyes or his laughter. If we can think about Brady a little every day, then it's like we get to be with him a little every day."

Nicole nodded. "I want to do that."

"Me too." Sophie smoothed her coral dress and looked older than her twelve years—she'd had a birthday in November. "Sometimes I leave a chair open for him and pretend he's running late."

A trumpet blasted, and the Gnome guard pulled the door open. "Sir Liam, you may lead your family to the gilded seats on the front row. To the right."

Dad held Nate on his hip and walked with stately, deliberate steps, as we'd been instructed. I managed a respectable glide down the center aisle to my seat. Uncle Brent, Aunt Jules, and Uncle Daniel were seated with us. I was so nervous I didn't notice where Xander was sitting.

The Christmas season had kissed the Great Hall with branches of evergreen and holly cascading off tables and woven with ribbon into graceful garlands. Bowls of acorns and pinecones cozied up to clusters of candles whose flames danced in celebration of the day. We had enjoyed a private Christmas Eve celebration the night before as a family, since today would be filled with the coronation and feasting.

Sir Kittrick, chancellor of the court, signaled for us to rise. The queen's cabinet, along with Sylon, came in through a side door and took their seats on the platform. I didn't bother to watch for Enoch; in the months since Brady's passing, the Dweller had retreated to his garden.

The trumpet player lowered his instrument. In a loud, clear voice he called, "Her Majesty, Queen Judith of Vituvia."

Applause and cheers swelled throughout the room. It hit me then that she wouldn't be the ruling monarch after today. The Gnomes would host a retirement ceremony on another occasion.

Joanie wheeled Aunt Judith up a ramp and helped her to switch from the wheelchair to the gleaming, golden throne. Her mobility had improved with therapy, and she occasionally walked with a cane if she felt up to it. She looked splendid in her emerald green gown and cape with gold trim—like a Christmas queen. Her scepter lay across her lap and her crown rested on her head, still a bit lopsided with her upper body tilt. Behind her hung the purple and silver banner of Vituvia. To one side, an empty throne waited for my brother.

Sylon opened with a prayer, then Sir Kittrick requested that the audience turn toward the double doors. Attendants pulled the doors open, and Brock entered, his hands clasped in front. Two Gnomes trailed behind him, holding up the train of his cloak. I studied his pensive face as he passed us, and tried to read the emotions hiding in his stoic face, his walk, his posture. Tried and failed.

His white tunic and pants with their purple stitching made him look as royal and handsome as any fairytale prince. A purple sash encircled one shoulder and crossed to the opposite hip. The purple cloak around his shoulders was attached with golden ropes and tassels. He knelt in front of Sir Kittrick, chancellor of the court, bowing his head.

The chancellor signaled for us to find our seats, then he crossed the platform to Queen Judith and bowed. She handed him her scepter. Returning to Brock, who waited on one knee, Sir Kittrick held the scepter in both hands across his chest.

"We are here before these witnesses on this most solemn occasion to declare the will of the Lord. Brock Larcen, do you understand the charge presented to you as a son of Adam, a citizen of upper earth, and an adopted citizen of Vituvia?"

"With God as my witness, I understand the charge given to me," Brock replied.

"Do you, Brock Larcen, understand that you must forsake your upper earth citizenry and leave the comforts of home and family to serve where God has called you in the Tethered World, within the Land of Legend, and in the realm of Vituvia?"

"I understand."

"Do you, Brock Larcen, swear allegiance to the Vituvian crown and promise to serve the Vituvian citizens, the Land of Legend, the Tethered World, and, above all, the God of the Universe with all your might and loyalty?"

"With God as my witness, I swear allegiance."

Sir Kittrick stretched the scepter toward Brock and tapped him on each shoulder. "Rise."

Brock stood then, and I was struck by how regal and digni-
fied he looked. Kingly indeed!

"You may approach her majesty, Queen Judith, for a blessing." Sir Kittrick offered a stiff bow.

My brother walked to the queen and lowered himself to both
knees. With trembling hands, she grasped Brock on both sides
of his head and pulled him closer. She leaned in and whispered
things I could not hear. I marveled that Brock would let her
hold his head in such a way without pulling free.

When she released him, Sylon stepped onto a stool behind
an ornately carved wooden table. "Brock Larcen, show your
submission to the crown and to the King of Kings by lying pros-
trate for the Holy Declaration."

Brock complied, lying face down with his arms outstretched.

Sylon lifted a twisted, gold crown from a purple cushion
that sat on the table. "Hear the word of the Lord from 1st Sam-
uel 2. May these words be spoken as a blessing for the High
King of Vituvia, Brock Larcen:

'He raises the poor from the dust
and lifts the needy from the ash heap;
he seats them with princes
and has them inherit a throne of honor.
For the foundations of the earth are the Lord's;
on them he has set the world.
He will guard the feet of his faithful servants,
but the wicked will be silenced in the place of darkness.
It is not by strength that one prevails;
those who oppose the Lord will be broken.
The Most High will thunder from heaven;
the Lord will judge the ends of the earth.
He will give strength to his king
and exalt the horn of his anointed.'"

Sylon stepped off the stool and walked to where Brock lay.
"You may rise." Brock rose to his knees and lowered his head,
and I guessed that Brock and Sylon must have rehearsed this
entire ceremony. Sylon kissed the crown, then placed it on
Brock's blond hair. "In the name of the Father, Son, and Holy
Spirit, I crown you, Brock Larcen, High King of Vituvia."

Everyone stood, and the crowd erupted in cheers that made
my brother wince. The entire Larcen clan clapped and shouted

with great enthusiasm. Our Brock was officially royalty!

Sir Kittrick knelt before Brock and presented him with the scepter, then indicated that he should take his place on the empty throne.

I regretted more than ever that we couldn't bring a camera to the Tethered World. Like firearms, they were forbidden. But Brock—King Brock—looked so regal and at home that I wanted to cherish this moment forever.

Remembering what Mom had said in the hallway, I made a conscious decision to think about Brady. I imagined his broad smile and heartfelt cheers. Beside me sat an empty chair.

In my mind, it was Brady's seat.

He must be running late.

CHAPTER FIFTY-EIGHT

ON THE PALACE LAWN A CELEBRATION was underway. The partygoers had no qualms about jumping into the revelry before the king arrived. And I wouldn't have expected anything different. Evergreen boughs and berries surrounded golden candlesticks ablaze with hundreds of flickering lights. A rustic carved Nativity scene, with Gnome-size figurines, sat prominently beside the arched entryway. I smelled balsam and cinnamon and cloves and hoped they might have hot cider mulling, though the temperature was as mild and comfortable as always. It felt in every way like an extraordinary, elaborate Christmas party from times past.

The sky at dusk fashioned a lovely, soft glow—and had made a full recovery in connection to the sword and tree, I might add. Meadow Faeries added to the ambiance with their glints of lemon-drop brilliance. Minstrel Dwarves were in full swing on the platform of a gazebo, plucking and thumping on their unique instruments with their toes tapping to the beat.

I spied Asher and Misty across the grass, looking much more like average earthlings in a suit and a floral dress. They hadn't known whether they could get off from work to be here, so I was glad to see them. We had gotten better acquainted in emails and a few phone conversations—enough to learn that the ring had been their father's and had been stolen from his safety deposit box before he could pass it on to Asher.

I headed over, wondering what had happened to Xander. He had told me he'd be right back at least twenty minutes ago.

The Malakoffs saw me coming and met me halfway, which was good because my stupid heels kept sinking into the grass. I reached down and removed them, tossing them toward a nearby statue to find later.

"Glad to see you guys made it." I hugged Misty, trying not

to compare myself to her stark beauty.

"We begged and bartered in order to be here." Asher shook my hand and our rings clinked together, releasing a spark. I flinched and pulled back. "What happened?" he asked as he looked at his hand, turning it over.

I wiggled my fingers and pointed to the ring. "These little gold bands have a certain kind of attraction or reaction. I'm not sure what it means, but it freaks me out to have the keys so close together."

He lifted his eyebrows and gave a low whistle. "Perhaps there's a reason our families have remained anonymous to one another." He switched his ring to his left hand. "There, at least we can shake hands."

"Nothing personal, but we should probably keep our contact limited and out of necessity." I grinned, hoping to soften my straightforward approach. "And my brother's coronation party is definitely a necessity."

They asked about Brock's ceremony and made small talk about the banquet and the band. Finally, Misty dropped her voice and said, "So, what happened to your terrible neighbor, Mr. Delaney?"

I spread my arms in a shrug. "Where do I start? The Gnomes threw him in the dungeon—they don't really have jails in Vituvia. Dungeons are a more appropriate description. His cell was next to this Troll who had come here with Chebar and his brothers. The Troll came down with some weird respiratory virus and apparently shared it with our old neighbor. Mr. Delaney became seriously ill while awaiting trial, and everyone thought he was going to die. He called my whole family to his bedside and begged our forgiveness."

"And did you give it to him?" Asher asked.

"Yes. I mean, we aren't excusing his behavior, but we could see that he regretted his actions and wanted to do the right thing. That's the best-case scenario for a perpetrator, in my opinion. Not that it makes what he's done any better. He also told us where to find his wife. He pleaded with us to tell her how sorry he was and that she could have the house."

"That must have come as a shock to her," Misty said. "I hope it was a good one."

I nodded. "She was certainly shocked, but also very happy. She had left with only the clothes on her back, so she was thrilled to regain everything she thought she'd lost. And the best part? She let us pour a truck full of concrete down the tunnel hole in her backyard. Then my uncle welded the lid closed." I made a slicing motion in the air. "So long, easy access."

Misty looked relieved. "We're glad to hear that. Ever since you told us about its existence, we've feared hearing some crazy report on the nightly news coming from your neighborhood."

"Is Delaney still sick?" Asher stuck a finger behind his knotted tie and pulled, loosening it. "Or back in the dungeon?"

"He recovered enough to go to court. But there wasn't much of a trial because he pled guilty."

"So...?" Misty tilted her head.

"He's sort of under house arrest. If he went back to the dungeon, the conditions might do him in—and for a while that didn't matter to me, honestly." A Faerie landed on Misty's shoulder and waved at me. I wiggled my fingers in greeting. "Sometimes I still think, you know, an eye for an eye. And if he violates the conditions of his palace imprisonment, he'll be sent back. They've assigned him to kitchen duty for now. Most days he peels potatoes, fetches water, whatever. I hear he's doing a good job and is well liked. Crazy, isn't it?"

"I would say so." Misty made a sour face. "It seems he didn't get a punishment that suited his crime."

"Yeah, I *really* wanted him to pay for all the trouble he caused us." I raised my fist and shook it. "And pay out the nose. But his complete change of attitude and demeanor, the way he's accepted the blame and the punishment—I don't know, it's sort of miraculous. I think it's a good thing for all of us. Forgiveness costs a great deal, but it has its own rewards. Bitterness keeps taking from your loss until you're hollow and empty."

Asher nodded. "Well stated. But difficult, I'm sure."

"Excuse me," a burly Dwarf said, approaching Misty with his hat in his hand. "May I have this dance?"

Her smile was dazzling. "Of course!" She followed him out to the dance floor.

"Shall we?" Asher offered me his hand.

"I'd love to." I followed him into the crowd, wondering again where Xander was. How could a seven-foot-tall angel-man be so hard to spot?

Asher and I did our best to keep up with the jaunty tune. It sounded like a polka, which meant we skipped and trotted in circles, orbiting the dance floor with sideways steps. I was amazed to make it through without my bare toes getting smashed or stepped on. Between twirls and laughter he asked about the fall out in Craventhrall since the death of Nekronok.

"A big mess from what I hear." I tripped over his foot and he righted me. "They're so busy battling the Gargoyles—who are no longer their ally—they haven't caused anyone else trouble for now. Spies are keeping their eyes on them of course. Probably only a matter of time."

"No doubt," Asher agreed.

When the song wound down, I finally spied Xander walking beside an unfamiliar, dark-haired young man. I blinked, thinking my eyes were deceiving me. A Topsider?

With a breathless thank you to Asher, I excused myself and hurried toward them. The young man nodded at me as I approached, as if he knew me.

"Here you are. Exactly who I came to find." He pressed his lips to my knuckles. "I'd like you to meet a new friend."

I stepped closer and stretched out my hand to the stranger. "Hello, I'm Sadie." Normally I would curtsy like a proper princess, but that felt haughty in the presence of another Topsider.

The young man gripped my hand in a very deliberate way. "Pleasure to meet you." The smile that crinkled his hazel eyes made me think he knew something I didn't.

Maybe I *had* met him before. There was something in his square face that struck me as familiar. He wasn't much taller than me, or much older. I probably stared harder than would be considered polite. "And you are?"

"A friend who's happy to meet you." He smacked Xander on the arm. "This guy talks about you constantly."

Xander cocked a half smile that hinted at mischief.

"Okay, what are you two hiding? Spit it out."

"Spit what out?" Xander ran his tongue along his teeth and eyed me suspiciously. "Is that one of those strange Topsider expressions or do you really expect me to spit?"

I crossed my arms and didn't take the bait.

They looked at each other and cracked up. The nameless guy clapped his hands together.

"Xander..." I cocked my head and gave him my best intimidating stare.

He lifted his hands in surrender. "Very well then, Princess Sadie, allow me to introduce my new personal assistant. He's been with me about three weeks now, and it's working out well. Wouldn't you agree?"

The guy nodded. "Yes. Quite well, thank you."

I was no longer amused. They were acting like some sort of stand-up comedy team.

Xander chuckled. "Sadie, I would like you to meet Tassitus."

"What?" My jaw dropped, and I took a step back. "No way. Oh my goodness, are you serious?"

The guy—Tassitus, if that really was his name—pressed his fist against his chest and bowed. "I believe I had the pleasure of meeting you in Pioneer Square this summer. Much has happened since we met."

I shook my head and pointed my finger at him, wagging it up and down. "No, no, no. You need to explain. This is crazy and—and impossible."

His face grew serious. I had to admit that his square features fit what I remembered of the Gargoyle with the knobby forehead. But that Tassitus had been precisely that: a Gargoyle. This Tassitus was definitely not.

"I want you to know how sorry I am about your brother Brady." His eyes glistened like he might cry. He stuffed his hands into his trouser pockets. "I never meant for him to be locked up with Brock, and I did what I could to find an alternative plan. I wanted to help them escape from the crypt, but—"

"The crypt? What are you talking about?"

Xander put his arm around my shoulder. "We can go over the long version later. Just hear him out."

I motioned for Tassitus to continue.

"I wanted to get them out of the Stygians' dungeons. At the Eldritch I learned of a plan to sacrifice Brock in order to use his blood to release the sword. Although I couldn't set your brothers free in time, I hoped Brady might see the wisdom in posing as the king. I realize that you would have lost a brother either way, but I had hoped to prevent bigger repercussions when I made the suggestion. It seemed more dangerous for Brock's blood to be spilt, on many levels. Of course, Brady didn't have to go along with my idea, either. He had no reason to believe what a Gargoyle told him. But I'm thankful he did."

The information made me dizzy. "Yeah, I agree," I said, after absorbing what he explained. "I've thought about what happened, imagining both outcomes. It seems like Brady's loss is the lesser of two evils. Fewer ramifications anyway. Of course...I wish I didn't have to consider either option whatsoever."

Tassitus withdrew his hand from his pocket and pressed a folded piece of paper into my palm. Instinctively, I grasped it, even as I scrutinized the stricken look that suddenly shadowed his features.

"Brady wanted me to give you this." His voice was unsteady but he held my gaze even as he continued to clasp my hand. "He made me promise to get this to his family if"—he dropped his eyes—"if anything should happen to him."

I didn't dare move. Breathing felt dangerous. Like it might whisk away his words and I'd find that I misunderstood his insinuation.

When I didn't answer, Tassitus went on. "Your brother hoped I'd never need to deliver it, and so did I. But he wrote it...just in case."

My fingers curled around the square piece of paper, and I pulled my hand away from his. I trembled, head to toe, feeling the familiar sting of tears. Xander's hand slid to my waist as if to steady my syphoning strength.

A letter? Brady had written a letter? I fumbled to open the note, my blurred eyes eager to recognize my brother's writing and confirm the miracle that I held.

Yes, yes, yes! Brady's upright scrawl greeted my disbelieving gaze. My brother was reaching out from heaven and giving me one last hug on this small but heavy piece of paper. I read with ravenous eyes that dripped with astonished tears.

Dear family (the greatest family in the history of ever),

If you're reading this note, I guess I didn't make it through the worst-case-scenario that no one thinks will actually happen to them. Which stinks. It means that I'm, well, dead, and that you guys are pretty upset. But hopefully it also means that Brock is alive, that he can become the awesome king he's destined to be, and that the sword and tree are safe. Those are the things that count.

I'm a Guardian of the Sword, sworn to protect my king, right? And more importantly, I'm Brock's brother, his defender, his biggest believer. Please know that I understood the risks of our deception and gladly took them on. (Weird to be talking in past tense, but Mom should be proud of my grammar, ha ha).

Seriously, I want you guys to know that I did this understanding what it might cost—yet hoping I'd never need for this note to be delivered. But if it has reached you now, then the deed is done. And it was totally worth it for Brock's sake.

Know that I love you all more than this sheet of paper has space for me to write. You guys are the best, and I thank God that I was born into such a great family. Mom and Dad, I'm super sorry about breaking your hearts. I can only hope I've spared you from a different sort of heartbreak— that of losing Brock. Fifteen years isn't a long life, but it's been an amazing one thanks to parents like you. Sadie, Brock, Sophie, Nicole, and Nate...I wish I had room to say how much I love each of you and how great I think you are. Hope most of your memories of me are good ones.

Guess I'll sign off now and pray that I'll be throwing this letter away one day in the future. No matter if I see you again here or in heaven, at least I know I'll see you again. And as long as you guys understand how much I love you, and how proud I am to be Brock's brother, I can go forward in peace.

All my love, forever and ever,

Brady

I read it and reread it, letting his words nourish the parts of me that were starving for any connection to this brother that I adored. His sense of humor shined, even in this serious con- text. Slowly, I became aware of Xander's fingers tracing circles on my arm. He and Tassitus were patiently waiting for me to process the gift I had been given.

Pressing the note to my chest, I sniffed back the last of my tears and smiled from one to the other, seeing the shared joy reflected in their faces.

Xander brushed a lock of hair from my cheek. "Are you well?"

I nodded. "Better than I've been in a long time." I stepped toward Tassitus and placed a hand on his arm. "Thank you for being true to your word and bringing this letter. Actually, thank you for having the foresight to get Brady paper and pencil so he could write it in the first place. It's priceless to me."

Tassitus dipped his head. "The least I could do."

"So..." I trailed off then gestured at the former Gargoyle. "How do we get from this part of the story to the part where you're standing here looking absolutely human? I'm at a loss."

He shrugged and slipped his hands back into his pockets. "I'm not a human, really—not like a Topsider."

"Well, you're not a Gargoyle."

"He's a Nephilim." Xander placed a hand on the shoulder of the shortest, scrawniest Nephilim I'd ever seen. "Remember how Gage's arm began to turn black like Gargoyle skin—before it was amputated? Well, Tassitus had the opposite experience. It seems our distant, shared origins allow for a transformation one way or the other." He playfully elbowed Tassitus in the ribs. "So this guy is the newest member of the Nephilim family."

Tassitus gave a sheepish grin. "Technically that's true, though I don't look it." He scuffed his foot in the grass. "Still feels strange to say so, although, according to Xander, Nephilim are but humans with particularly unique DNA."

"Slight understatement." I winked at Xander.

"Anyway, I believe Brady gained more trust in me after I shared with him how I'd been reading a copy of the ancient scriptures that I found in Malagruel's library—of all places. Reading those scriptures changed me. Profoundly."

He kept staring at the ground and shifting his weight like he was searching for the right words.

"Tell her," Xander said.

"Prince Xander told me how Brady's sacrifice, his blood, somehow saved the tree." He looked up and pierced me with an emotional gaze. "Well, the same thing happened to me—and my disabled sister too, because I shared what I was learning with her. I...I've been changed by the blood sacrifice of the Lamb of God."

CHAPTER FIFTY-NINE

I STOOD WITH MY FAMILY AT the massive banquet table. Moments
before we had shared in the wonder of Brady's miraculous letter. Tears and delight had engulfed us as we traced his words
with our fingertips and passed the note around in astonishment. But now it was time to honor Brock, the new High King,
and everyone held their goblets high.

"Long live King Brock!" the crowd shouted at the conclusion
of Sir Noblin's flowery toast. Whistles and cheers zinged between the partygoers and pressed Brock's lips into a smile. His
eyes roved the celebration as if memorizing the scene. A vine-
like, twisted crown glowed like a halo around his head, and he
did indeed look noble.

The Dwarves' boisterous voices rose in a chant. "Long live
the king! Long live the king! Long live the king!"

Xander clinked his glass to mine. "And long live our love."

My heart leapt to my throat, and I looked at him, willing
myself to hold his drowning blue gaze while I brought the goblet to my lips. I swallowed the tart cherry wine, hoping it would
relocate my heart to its proper place.

The implication of his words filled my head with sweetness
and maybe a little fear. Yes, I recognized the love that had nestled into my soul as soft and contented as a purring kitten.
But was I ready to admit it to him? I shifted my gaze to the
overflowing food arranged on silver platters down the center of
the table. Today had been filled with so much joy and wonder,
I didn't want to spoil it with fumbling words or awkward moments. I would let his statement sit there for now, something
to replay and contemplate later.

Maybe Xander sensed my happy anxiety. He could read me
better than my parents these days. Instead of drawing me into
a speculative conversation, he laced his fingers in mine and

gave them a gentle squeeze. I marveled at his tenderness. He helped me into my seat right as Sylon was stepping forward to ask the blessing.

Hats were removed and heads bowed.

"Our great God and Father, Maker of Heaven and Earth, with humble souls and joyful hearts we lift our thanks to You. Your mysterious ways are beyond contemplation. Even so, You draw near in Your word and Your hand moves on our behalf. We know that if we are silent, even the rocks will cry out that You are God and You are good. You work all things to Your glory and choose to involve both Adam's kin and lowly creatures in the working of Your will. For this we stand in amazement.

"Thank you for ordaining our new ruler, High King Brock. May he rule with wisdom of mind and purity of heart. If we are faced with further troublesome times, we pray for guidance for all creatures great and small. From the light of the Faeries to the might of the Nephilim, let us strive for peace but stand against evil. We now request Your blessing upon this food. As we break bread together, unite our purpose and vision for the days to come. And let us not forget Sir Brady Larcen, who gave his life in service of the king. Continue to comfort his grieving family and spring hope upon hope from their grief.

"In the name of the Father, Son, and Holy Spirit, we ask these things. So be it."

"So be it!" Another round of cheers exploded.

My heart felt full of the beauty of his words. They summarized truth and encapsulated our place in the world with breathtaking accuracy. I marveled at how the events of summer had not only changed me—changed all of us—but also had eternal value with implications beyond anything we could have imagined. The ripple-effects were profound.

Between bites of beef tips in mushroom gravy and a layered, huckleberry cake, my gaze traveled the length of the table, taking inventory of the characters who had played a part in my transformation from fretful bookworm to fearless princess.

From Aunt Jules' visit, during which she had explained our family's shocking history, to our first meeting with Tassitus, the Gargoyle-turned-Nephilim, there were many tales to be told in the lives before me. The Tethered World itself played a role in my drama. Not to mention the Flaming Sword, the Tree of Life, and the Garden Dweller who had never tasted death. All were threads in my tapestry, selected and woven by the intricate hand of God. The truth and wonder of it simply crushed my capacity to comprehend it.

"May I have this dance?" Xander's whisper interrupted my musings.

"Yes, please." I dabbed at my lips and set my napkin next to my plate. Xander pulled out my chair and led me to the dance floor. My feet were still bare, and the cool grass felt like a thick, luxurious carpet.

Brock was there, pushing Aunt Judith in her wheelchair in time to the music. His simple crown reminded me that he was no longer my autistic little brother; he was now my gentle and wise king. Uncle Daniel held his bride of thirty-eight years, letting the feisty redhead take the lead. Mom and Dad weaved through the crowd to claim a spot of their own. They danced beside Uncle Brent, who swayed with little Nicole, her leather slippers planted on top of his shoes. With awkward grace, Gage and Joanie spun into view, laughing, no doubt, at the disparaging height between them.

Xander placed one hand at my waist and clasped my fingers with his other. A summer full of banquets and dancing created a fluent comfort between us. I trusted his lead and understood the little nuances of pressure that safely guided my feet. We worked our way around the grassy dance floor and found ourselves near the banquet table as the song wound down. I spied Sophie sitting with Nate on her lap. She laughed at something Lava said from two chairs away.

An empty chair sat between them, silverware untouched. Plates unused. I smiled to myself, knowing why.

The melody ended, and I looked up at Xander. His silver-blue eyes pulled my gaze to his like a tide responds to the beckoning moon. The look we shared conveyed words we weren't quite ready to speak—at least that's what I tried to tell myself.

Maybe I'm wrong.

He released my hand and slipped his fingers into my hair, caressing the nape of my neck. Anticipation tumbled through my senses making me sway against him. Xander grinned at the obvious effect he'd generated and rested his forehead against mine as if to steady me. Closing my eyes, I inhaled the nearness of his spicy-clean scent.

Gentle hands suddenly cupped my face and drew me closer. "Long live our love, my princess." His lips danced across my own as he whispered each sweet word like silken wings fluttering against my mouth. "Long live our love."

And we sealed that love with such a tender kiss, I knew I never wanted to be anywhere else but here.

Author's Notes

Although my 'topside' home is now in Texas, I was blessed to be born and raised in the beautiful Pacific Northwest, covering the miles between Seattle, Washington and Salem, Oregon. Though we frequently moved, we remained in the vicinity of Vancouver (Orchards) Washington from second grade until high school. With mountains, rivers, Beacon Rock, and the ocean so close, the Portland/Vancouver area was the perfect setting for the Larcen family. Local Bigfoot folklore provided an excellent impetus for sending the Larcens off on an adventure that would encompass three novels. For me, *The Genesis Tree* became a bit of a love letter to my childhood home by including more of the things I loved about the Northwest than my previous two books.

The Columbia River did, indeed, teach me my directions, long before I learned to drive my mom's stick shift Pinto station wagon around town. I spent many summers swimming and tanning at Wintler Park back in the 80s on the north bank of the river. Both Pioneer Courthouse Square and Nordstrom department store were favorite haunts as a teenager. And *yes*, my bookish friends, Powell's City of Books is a real bookstore—a labyrinth of shelves on color-coded floors that meander across a full city block! Something for your book-loving bucket list for sure. My last visit to Portland in the summer of 2015 left me determined to put the legendary bookstore into The Tethered World Chronicles.

Another intriguing place, the clandestine Shanghai Tunnels, is not a destination that I've visited—although I plan to. This underground city is fascinating to read about even though it's a sad, dark stain on the history of the city I love. Kidnapping, bootlegging, slavery, and all manner of illegal activity lurked beneath the streets of Portland in the mid-1800s until the 1940s. Trapdoors (*yes—trapdoors!*) in the streets would deposit unsuspecting young men into holding cells where "shanghaiirs" forced them onto ships that came to port on the Willamette River. They would be whisked out to sea, enslaved to work without pay. In the same way, young women were captured by "white slavers" and sold into prostitution. Through a network of tunnels, the basements of buildings were connected underground, allowing an entire city to flourish in the shadows beneath the streets of Stumptown (so called because of the scalped trees left by the loggers). During prohibition, saloons simply moved their business to the "Forbidden City" below. This chrysalis of debauchery was simply too evocative not to include in the setting of my story.

From Burgerville, the fast food restaurant in *The Tethered World* where the Larcen parents were kidnapped, to Cannon Beach Oregon, where Aunt Jules' home was ransacked in *The Flaming Sword*, there's a lot of my childhood in the pages of these novels. The ease in which one could slip from the mountains to the rivers to the beach was something I took for granted until I moved to Texas. Let's just say there's "none of the above" available to me now, and I truly miss it.

One last little fact you might enjoy knowing: *The Tethered World* was originally titled *Grand Larceny*. As you know, larceny is a fancy word for theft. The kidnapping of Sadie's parents was the "theft" implied and the spelling of the family name *Larcen* came about with that title in mind. Conversely, I chose the Tethered World as the name of the secret land introduced by Aunt Jules on a temporary basis—or so I thought—until I could come up with a better name for the place. As you can see, I was wrong on both counts. Stories, to some degree, insist to be told in their own way. Characters often hijack a writer's brain and commandeer their fingertips so that, for me at least, there's an element of surprise in writing the tale, just as much in reading it!

Acknowledgments

How is it that we've arrived at the end and also *The End*? It seems unfathomable that the contract I signed with Mountain Brook Ink a little over two years ago is officially fulfilled. Done. Complete. I mean, two years ago I was polishing up *The Tethered World* and had only a smidgen of *The Flaming Sword* written—with only the faintest idea about what would happen in *The Genesis Tree* (whose title at that point was "book three").

As the world's-worst plotter, and, quite possibly the world's-biggest pantster (defined as one who writes by the seat of their pants), it's been a wild, faith testing, almost-walking-on water-but-not-quite-that-impressive kind of ride. Without the pressure of deadlines set by the ever-professional Miralee Ferrell (publisher extraordinaire), I might still be floundering around in the middle of book two, wondering how to get Sadie and Brady reunited with their family.

But in God's providence, He brought me to Mountain Brook Ink and placed the pressure of fast-paced deadlines in my creative path. Since He made me, He knew precisely what I needed to produce these adventures. He knew that I worked much, much better under such pressure. And in the midst of panicked prayers He was faithful to fly with my fingers through two more books in under a year and a half. I look back with wonder at the process. It fills me with thanksgiving to see how He graciously gave me the story of the Larcen family.

You see, I'm not that clever. I mean, I'm ridiculously right brained and disorganized and drink way too much coffee. And I'm blonde. The Lord gets all the credit for how these chronicles were, well...chronicled. *The Genesis Tree* in particular posed a huge creative challenge. How to tie up the loose ends? How to revisit different characters and resolve important situations? How would the sword and the tree make it through an attack...and what if some of the characters didn't? These were difficult ideas. Vague notions that stirred my subconscious as the story unfolded. It needed to be right. Believable.

Painful? Maybe. Life is painful, right? But with Christ there's purpose in the pain, beauty for the ashes, so I didn't want to neglect being honest about that aspect too. The Lord managed to take my threadbare plot, like a simple piece of paper, and fold it and crease it and bend it just so until it became a many-layered story that resembled a complex piece of origami artwork. The end of which looked nothing like what I had imagined when *The Tethered World* was conceived.

But, of course, He also surrounded me with all the right people to make the story come to life and have an opportunity to shine. First and foremost, God gave me the man of my dreams, to help me fulfill my artistic dream of becoming an author. Without my supportive and loving husband Billy, I wouldn't be venturing out into the vast publishing world with nearly so much confidence. It doesn't hurt that he's incredibly easy on the eyes after a long night staring at my computer either :) We're kinda sweet on each other after twenty-seven years and I want this writing gig to work out as much for him as for myself. He's the hardest working man I know!

And my kids—grown now and all independent-like—have been there to cook and clean and do laundry as my deadlines loomed large and I grew weary. Thanks to Delaney and Olivia for doing all that and more! To Garrett, whose growing independence has inspired the growth of the character Brock. And to McKenzie for plowing through the first draft when I had questions about certain, major plot twists that left me insecure! You were a life saver. And an added thanks to my dear, speed reading friend Misty who plowed through a rugged and unfinished version early on, giving me valuable feedback with a forty-eight-hour turnaround—or was it twenty-four?

With each of my stories, I've had the pleasure of working with a different editor. I've learned new things from each one and, once again, owe a huge thanks to Miralee for sending Jenny Mertes my way to make *The Genesis Tree* grow and flourish. It was smooth sailing, easy communication, and a great experience to work with Jenny on this project. I feel truly blessed to have worked with her.

A final thank-you to Lynnette Bonner who put together yet another stellar cover for *The Genesis Tree*. It's a thrill to look at the triplets—books one, two, and three—sidled up together, giving off their intriguing, mysterious vibe and whispering, *"read me..."* to anyone who might give them a passing glance. I've had quite a few people comment that *The Genesis Tree* might be one of their favorite book covers ever!

I'd like to give a shout out to my prereaders that were willing to suffer through a not-quite-finished copy of my books in order to furnish a review on launch day! Thanks for looking past the flaws and seeing the pearl inside the oyster. And to my "fire-ignitors" (aka my street team) that are faithful to spread the word about The Tethered World Chronicles and help me brainstorm ways to market and all those awkward introvert-challenging things...I can't tell you how much I appreciate a slice of your valuable time being spent on my books. It's such a blessing and a privilege to know each of you (even through cyberspace), and I hope I can return the favor in some way in the future.

Finally, to you my dear, treasured reader...THANK YOU. I don't take it for granted that you've spent both time and money to read one or more of my novels. I pray that they have taken you to amazing places, satisfied you with adventure, and made you see the *bigness* of God and the importance of *you* in the course of history. Like Sadie, we may fear or dislike the things that the Lord allows to come our way; but I hope each of us—myself included—might look at this broken world and believe He wants us to get involved with its restoration and not settle for being a spectator.

Book Club Questions

1. We have watched Sadie evolve from a reluctant participant in her role with the Tethered World, to a heroine who embraces her place in the family. What do you think helped her escape her fears? What drives her now? Have you ever been in a place you had to work through your fears and what helped you get through?

2. In *The Genesis Tree* we come across characters that seem evil but are really good, and others that seem good but are actually evil. Have you misjudged someone based on appearance? Have you watched someone's character undergo a change from one extreme to another due to circumstances? Explain.

3. Lots of people look for their "15 minutes of fame". Some stumble into it because they perform an unplanned, heroic act. While others, like Mr Delaney, seek it out at the expense of others. What do you think motivates people to want the spotlight? Do you think it's wrong to seek attention or approval from others?

4. We often don't expect much from people who are quite different from ourselves. Maybe they have a disability, or perhaps they are much younger or older, or maybe they even look like a Gargoyle! *The Genesis Tree* shatters those preconceived notions. Have you underestimated someone in this way—or maybe even yourself? What steps can you take to change your mindset and give people the benefit of the doubt?

5. Selflessness is one of the highest forms of love—laying down your own rights, demands, wants...and sometimes even your life. Jesus is the ultimate example of this. *Romans 5:6-8 tells us, "For at just the right time, while we

were still powerless, Christ died for the ungodly. It is rare indeed for anyone to die for a righteous man, though for a good man someone might possibly dare to die. But God proves His love for us in this: While we were still sinners, Christ died for us." History bears out a few of these heroic acts of sacrifice. Can you name other examples of those that have lain down their life for a friend, their country, or even those that persecuted them? What makes such courage and self-denial possible in humanity? Are we naturally capable of such a deed?

6. Have you ever been placed in a position that forced you to choose between two roads? The first would benefit many. The second would only benefit yourself? What did you choose? Would you change your decision in hindsight? Is it wrong to make decisions that will benefit yourself over others?

7. We won't always make the right choices. Sometimes it's because we don't have all the information we need to make the best choice. Can such a scenario still turn out well in the long run? What character do you think had to change their choices based on new information?

8. Who was your favorite character in The Genesis Tree? What about the series? Was there one character that you loved to hate?

*Berean Study Bible version

More Ways to Connect with Heather and The Tethered World

Learn more about the characters
and creatures of The Tethered World at
www.heatherllfitzgerald.com

When you visit, sign up for Heather's newsletter
and receive *The Asylum*, a free eBook!

"Like" Heather's Author Page on Facebook at
https://www.facebook.com/thetetheredworld

For more interaction and the latest news,
join Heather's Facebook author group at
https://www.facebook.com/groups/1731996177017368/

Follow The Tethered World on
Instagram @tetheredworld

Tag your quirky and mysterious photos with
#tetheredworld hashtag too!

Follow Heather on Twitter @HeatherLLFitz

Follow Heather on Pinterest at
https://www.pinterest.com/HeatherLLFitz/

OR follow Sadie Larcen at
https://www.pinterest.com/sadielarcen/

Follow Amy Larcen's Bigfoot Blog at
https://landoflegend.net/

Heather will be grateful to hear from
you however you'd like to stay connected!

Cast of Characters

FAMILY, FRIENDS, FOES

Sadie Larcen: bookish, seventeen-year old girl. Although she once preferred reading about adventures over experiencing them firsthand, she now accepts her role in the Tethered World and is willing to fight for those she loves both above and below ground; resides with her family in Orchards, Washington

Amy Larcen: Sadie's mother; leading expert on Bigfoot; blogs about all things myth and legend; Kidnapped by Trolls, tortured by Ogres in *The Tethered World*. Visit her blog at https://landoflegend.net/

Liam Larcen: Sadie's father; cosmetologist; previously kidnapped with his wife, Amy

Brady Larcen: age fifteen; protective twin to Brock; easygoing and bighearted; Sadie's right-hand man in the Tethered World

Brock Larcen: autistic twin to Brady; High King of Vituvia in training; excellent memory and fighting skills

Sophie Larcen: clever and adventurous eleven-year-old sister; pretends to live in the medieval times; desirous of moving to the Tethered World; brave beyond her years

Nicole Larcen: sweet, seven-year-old sister; a big help with her baby brother, Nate; loves to twirl around the house and wear the color pink

Nate Larcen (aka Nate the Great): adorable baby brother adopted from Ethiopia; almost three years old

Uncle Brent McGriffin: Amy Larcen's brother; willfully walked away from his family's connection with the Tethered World; pharmacist; botanist

Great-aunt Julie McGriffin (aka Aunt Jules): Fun-loving Irish aunt and twin sister to Judith, Queen of Vituvia; Sculpts garden gnomes; key keeper and family historian; remained in the Tethered World with husband Daniel after a thirty-eight-year separation

Daniel McGriffin: Blinded and left for dead by the Gargoyles in *The Flaming Sword*; recovering his health in the Tethered World after years in captivity

Queen Judith of Vituvia: twin sister to Julie McGriffin; training Brock Larcen as her predecessor so she can retire; suffering from the effects of a stroke; savant

Joseph Marshall: nosy neighbor that lives across the street from the Larcens; smokes like a locomotive; working with the Trolls and Gargoyles to unite the Tethered World with those topside

CREATURES

Gnomes: Approximately eighteen inches tall; stout bodies; pointy hat adds another eight inches; small but deadly; will protect the Flaming Sword of Cherubythe at all cost; reside in Vituvia
- Reiko: head of Special Forces, officially known as Stealth Gnomish Warfare and Clandestine Operations (SGWCO); answers to Colonel Smarlow
- Mighty and Muscle: sibling soldiers in the SGWCO; answer to Reiko
- Sir Noblin: Premier Advisor to the Queen Judith
- Revonika: Sir Noblin's assistant; in charge of public relations
- General Muggleridge: military advisor to Queen Judith

- Colonel Smarlow: Chief of Covert Reconnaissance; answers to General Muggleridge

Gargoyles: the physical counterparts to the stone gargoyles perched on medieval castles and cathedrals; shape-shifters; working with the Trolls to gain control of The Flaming Sword of Cherubythe
- Prince Malagruel: leader of the Gargoyles; rival to Nekronok; deceives Sadie; winged with the tail of a serpent
- Ophidian: One of Malagruel's "worms" who serves without question; flightless; able to become nearly invisible with the chameleon-like ability to blend in with surroundings
- Tassitus: Another of Malagruel's "worms" with same characteristics

Nephilim: half angelic, half human; Average height eight feet; well proportioned; wings a recessive trait, mostly seen in the royal family; see Genesis 6:4; reside in Calamus
- Prince Alexander (aka Xander): first-born son of the royal family; commands the Nephilim army; infatuated with Sadie
- King Aviel and the late Queen Estancia: monarchs of Calamus
- Gage: seasoned soldier and Xander's right-hand man; lost part of his left arm in battle with Malagruel

Trolls (aka Bigfoot, Yeti, Sasquatch): hairy, broad-shouldered creatures; ape-like faces; XXL feet; reside in Craventhrall at the foot of Mount Thrall
- Nekronok: chief Troll; prefers to be addressed as "Worshipful Master"; wants control of the Flaming Sword of Cherubythe and the Tree of Life; self-proclaimed leader of The United Dynasty of Thrall whose goal it is to join forces with powers topside
- Rooke: first born son of Nekronok; next in line for the throne

- Chebar: sixth son of Chief Nekronok; loyal to Queen Judith; a mole living in the Eldritch, working against his father
- Grym and Sargon: two more of Chief Nekronok's sons who desire to rule in their father's place

Dwarves: half as tall and twice as wide as the average Topsider; fond of facial hair and pipes; Reside in the Berganstroud Mountains
- Chief Wogsnop: leader of the Dwarves of Berganstroud; head of the Berganstroud army
- Glavashian (aka Lava): soldier in the Berganstroud army; has a special connection to Sadie
- Joanie: motherly nurse/housekeeper
- Doc Keswick: Berganstroud's one and only physician; terrible bedside manners
- Trinny: Lava's daughter; assistant to Joanie and Doc Keswick

Leprechauns: stand approximately two feet tall; well-proportioned bodies; male leprechauns born with a beard; affinity for moss, mushrooms, and gold; reside in the Hallows of Nimmickdell
- Fig: accompanies Sargon topside

Elves of Willowmist: slender, petite creatures with pointy noses and ears; shy but playful; can turn invisible; reside in the Woods of Willowmist
- Lark: captured by Sargon; helps the Larcens

Dark Dwarves (aka Stygians): same build as Dwarves; pale, grayish skin; patchy hair and beard; allied with the Trolls and Gargoyles; reside in the Dens of the Dark Dwarves beyond Berganstroud
- Glump: guides Tassitus through the tunnels of the Dens of the Dark Dwarves
- Oradini: Chieftain of the Dark Dwarves

Goblins: approximately one foot tall with knobby limbs and a protruding belly; dwell in the deep recesses of the Berganstroud mountains; vicious creatures with a penchant for attaching themselves to intruders and gnawing on body parts
- Mudgeon: self-proclaimed Goblin god; a five-foot-tall version of the of the potbellied Goblins that serve him

Clovenboars (aka Toboggans): curvy horns, fangs, and dreadlocks; about the size of a panther; the Gnomes' transportation; able to see invisible Leprechauns; native to the wilds of the Tethered World and also kept in the paddocks of Berganstroud and Vituvia

Hippogriff: winged creatures with the head, breast, and talons of an eagle and the back legs and rump of a horse; offspring of a mare and a Griffin; easier to tame than their legendary counterpart; utilized for travel and war by the Trolls; reside in the wild and in Cravaenthrall

Griffin: winged creature with the fore-body of an eagle and the back legs and rump of a lion; less popular than Hippogriffs, but still utilized by the Trolls

Meadow Faeries: resemble butterflies with tiny arms and legs, carried by gossamer wings; transported the Larcens to Vituvia in their faery cyclone in previous adventures; reside on plant stems in the meadow between the Woods of Willowmist and Vituvia

Ogres: sweaty, large, and thick-bodied; average seven to eight feet tall; tortured the Larcen parents; reside on the Isle of Skellerwad in the Sulfur Sea

50143119R00196

Made in the USA
San Bernardino, CA
14 June 2017